Flee to the Mountains

Book One of the Sanctuary Ranch Series

Donna J. Benson

Where God Guides, God Provides!

CROSSBOOKS

CrossBooks™
A Division of LifeWay
1663 Liberty Drive
Bloomington, IN 47403
www.crossbooks.com
Phone: 1-866-879-0502

© 2012 Donna J. Benson. All rights reserved.

Scripture taken from the HOLY BIBLE, NEW INTERNATIONAL VERSION®. Copyright © 1973, 1978, 1984 Biblica. Used by permission of Zondervan. All rights reserved.

This is a work of fiction. Names, characters, places and incidents either are the product of the author's imagination or are used fictitiously. Any resemblance to actual persons, living or dead, events, or locales is entirely coincidental. Any resemblance to any other books is entirely coincidental.

No part of this book may be reproduced, stored in a retrieval system, or transmitted by any means without the written permission of the author.

First published by CrossBooks 11/16/2012

ISBN: 978-1-4627-2146-7 (sc)
ISBN: 978-1-4627-2147-4 (e)
ISBN: 978-1-4627-2148-1 (hc)

Library of Congress Control Number: 2012916856

Printed in the United States of America

This book is printed on acid-free paper.

Any people depicted in stock imagery provided by Thinkstock are models, and such images are being used for illustrative purposes only.

Certain stock imagery © Thinkstock.

Because of the dynamic nature of the Internet, any web addresses or links contained in this book may have changed since publication and may no longer be valid. The views expressed in this work are solely those of the author and do not necessarily reflect the views of the publisher, and the publisher hereby disclaims any responsibility for them.

DEDICATION

THE SANCTUARY RANCH TESTIFIES to my love and faith in my Lord and Savior Jesus Christ. He is the center of my life and the source of my joy and happiness. He is the source of all my hopes, dreams and visions for the future. I know He will always be with me, in good times and bad; He will never leave nor forsake me. I know He has my future in His hand, and I can rest in Him.

I also want to acknowledge my partner in life and love, my husband, Bob, who helped me with the writing of the book, by reading and rereading it several times and giving me ideas and suggestions. He spent many hours researching wind, solar, methane and hydro power, which we hope to use in our own sanctuary. His encouragement and unending support were greatly appreciated, and these gifts from him have increased my love for him all the more.

It is our hope that our children, Joanna, David, Shawna, James, Rachel and also our grandchildren, Corban and Peyton, glean information from this endeavor that will help them with their own preparations. It is our sincere hope that you will walk humbly with our God and Lord Jesus all the days of your life and that you will listen carefully to His voice. We have shared our concern for our nation and our world for several years now, and we can see your increasing understanding of that concern. Now is the time for preparations for each and every one of us to prepare.

ACKNOWLEDGEMENTS

I WISH TO GIVE my sincere thanks to Gladys, who is a second mom and sister in the Lord, for her strong support and encouragement. Even when I doubted that I could write this message of both warning and hope, she was there urging me on.

Finally, I want to give my sincere appreciate to Rose for the long hours in editing this book. I cannot thank her enough for her careful attention to detail and desire for excellence. More importantly, we have reestablished our friendship and sisterhood in the Lord which is a great blessing to me.

A Cold Night Encounter

CHAPTER 1

"OH, HOLY NIGHT THE stars are brightly shining; it is the night of the dear Savior's birth . . . " The voice from the radio rang out the familiar old Christmas carol, as Franklin Hampton drove his 18-wheeler down the dark interstate. It was late, much later than he usually drove. Christmas was this weekend, and he needed to get home. The kids were coming home this year. He smiled as he sang along in his clear tenor voice. He loved Christmas; he just did not like the weather that came with it; though tonight unveiled a beautiful, starlit sky, creating an evening that was very stunning, it was also very cold. The temperature hovered around two degrees. Franklin was thankful for his heater. *"I am really grateful, Father, that I live in this day and age. I really appreciate this heater. I am sure the teamsters of old endured some really cold nights."*

He came around the next bend in the road and saw a car on the shoulder of the road with flashing lights that were barely blinking. What a cold night to have car trouble, he thought, as he slowed his rig, watching for signs of movement in the car. After all, he could not, in good conscience, leave a stranded traveler in the cold. At first, he did not see anyone in the car, but just as he passed, he noticed movement in the back seat. He immediately pulled to the side of the road and stopped. Pulling on his heavy coat and grabbing a blanket off the bed in the sleeper, he climbed down from the truck and walked back to the car.

Janie Weber stirred when she heard the air brakes engage on the truck. She was cold, colder than she had ever been. This was an awful time for her car to conk out. The tow truck was supposed to be here any time. She hoped this was it. Earlier, she had crawled into the back seat, wrapped up in her coat and put some of the clothes from her suitcase on top of herself so she could stay warm. As she sat up, she realized it was a semi-truck she had heard drive up and not her tow truck. She did not want to roll down her window and let even more cold air inside, but she could not be rude.

She spied the blanket the older man was carrying. She smiled, as she rolled down the window.

"Hello, missy, car trouble?"

"Yes, I think it's the alternator. The lights went dim, and then it just conked out. I called the auto club, and the tow truck is supposed to be here anytime." *"I don't know how I am going to pay for it, but maybe it won't be too much,"* she thought.

"Well, wrap this around you and come get warm in my truck till it gets here. It's too cold for you to stay here with no heat. And don't you worry about me; I have a grand-daughter about your age and great grandkids to boot."

Janie hesitated but realized she was getting dangerously cold. Soon, she would begin to get hypothermia. "All right, I am really cold." She climbed out of her car awkwardly, as her limbs began to work again. *"I hope this man is the nice old man he seems to be."*

"My name is Franklin Hampton," the older man said, as he wrapped the blanket around the small woman. He guessed her to be in her mid-twenties. He reached out to steady her, as he saw her falter when she got to her feet and they began to make their way to his truck. Janie had some difficulty climbing into the cab, but Franklin knew he could not help her. He stood behind her, though, in case she fell. She made it into the warm cab and sighed with relief, as she sat in the passenger seat. Immediately, she began to shiver, while pinpricks of pain knifed into her hands and feet. *"I must be colder than I thought."*

Franklin saw her shiver, "Why don't you get back in the sleeper and climb under the covers on the bed. I know, I know that would make you uncomfortable, but you need to get warm, as soon as possible. I will stay up here and keep a look out for that tow truck."

Again, Janie hesitated. She was so cold. She could be with a rapist for all she knew, but she was so cold that she was beyond caring. However, Franklin looked just like he said; he was a grandfather and a nice one at that. Nodding, she rose painfully and climbed into the bed, clothes and all, burrowing under two blankets, while still wrapped in the blanket he had brought to her car. She fell asleep as soon as her head hit the pillow.

Franklin knew Janie was asleep, so he did not wake her when the tow truck arrived nearly an hour later. Franklin gave the driver directions to have the car towed to his brother- in-law's shop, nearly an hour away. The tow truck driver grumbled about the distance, but he finally agreed, after Franklin offered to pay him for the extra miles. Franklin knew Henry's shop would get the car fixed as soon as possible, and Janie would be able to get on her way. It was nearly midnight, but the truck-stop shop was open twenty-four hours.

Janie did not wake as the semi-truck moved out to follow the tow truck that was towing Janie's car. Two hours later she woke, a bit disoriented, but she immediately remembered her car. She sat up quickly and looked out the window. She was at a truck stop. She could see her car in the shop with the hood up, and a technician was working on the engine. She also could see Franklin standing to the side, talking with the mechanic. She looked around for her purse and remembered she had left it in the car. She must have really been out of it. She tidied herself as much as possible, climbed down from the semi, and made her way to the shop. She felt better. She was not cold any longer, and though she was tired, she felt better.

"Well, hello there," Franklin said, watching as Janie entered the shop. "Henry here will have your rig ready in about three hours. You've got the best here, the owner. His tech got sick so he is filling in tonight. Luckily, his brother owns the local auto parts store, so he was able to get you a new alternator and belt. He has keys to the store; he just let himself in and left a note telling them what he took. He'll settle with them later. Why don't you and I go inside and get some coffee?" He gestured toward the coffee shop across the parking lot.

"Ah, sure," Janie said, hesitantly. As she walked away, Henry said, "I'll call you when I'm finished," never looking up from his work. Janie turned back to her car, retrieved her purse from the floor in the back seat, and followed Franklin inside the truck stop.

They sat in a booth facing one another. "I cannot thank you enough. I think I might have frozen if you had not come along when you did. I did not mean to fall asleep and leave you to handle things," she said, a little sheepishly. Franklin ordered coffee, and Janie requested tea when the waitress came to ask what they would like.

Turning back to their conversation, Franklin said, "Don't think anything of it. I was glad I was there to help. Others have helped me in the past and now it's my turn."

"You are different than I thought truckers were. I always thought they were dirty, foul-mouthed, fat men." Janie put her hand over her mouth, as she realized how that sounded. "I am so sorry, here you help me, and I insult you."

Franklin, unoffended, laughed, "Oh, there are lots of those kinds of drivers, always have been and always will be. Actually, I used to be one of those foul-mouthed drivers, but not anymore. As for other drivers, more and more family men are driving these days, as well, and husband and wife teams. There are even a few single women out here. They are clean, normal people, who are just trying to make a living. Anyway, Jesus found me out there on the road, and I have never been the same. Actually, there are many believers out here, living for Jesus and ministering to those they meet along the way, people like you. Are you a Christian?"

"I guess so. I mean, I went to church as a child, but I haven't attended much in the last several years." She was not sure she wanted to talk with some Jesus freak, but he had helped her so she would listen. Besides she always thought of herself as a Christian. She believed in God; she just was not one that talked about her beliefs. "What made the difference? What changed you?" She asked, curious about the answer.

"Well, my wife was going to leave me. She called one Saturday night and said she was tired of being alone. I was gone most of the time. The kids were grown, and she was lonely. I was devastated. I had just dropped my load in Pomona, California, so I went to the truck stop in Ontario. I was depressed. It was Sunday morning and as I walked toward the restaurant, I heard music coming from the chapel. It drew me, so I slipped inside and into the back row of chairs. Chaplains Ron and Gladys were singing. It soothed my soul. I don't even remember what Ron spoke about, but I realized half way through the service that I wanted a change in my life."

"Anyway, after the service they invited everyone for a barbeque lunch. Ron barbequed hamburgers and hot dogs, and Gladys made homemade chili; it was quite a spread. I couldn't remember the last time I felt more welcomed among strangers. In the midst of my pain, God brought me to a place I could find some peace. I enjoyed the talk around the table. There were ten or eleven drivers talking about life on the road, their families, and their faith in Jesus. I was touched in a way I had never been touched before." He took a deep breath and then continued.

"Later that afternoon, I had the opportunity to talk with Ron and Gladys by myself. They loved me, even though they didn't know me. I could feel their love and concern. I poured out my heart; I couldn't seem to stop the words from pouring out. They wouldn't allow me to make excuses for my mistakes, or blame my wife or family. My decisions affected my family, and I had to take ownership of them. Later, I could not believe I actually told them everything going on in my life, but I am glad I did. They gave me good counsel. On my way home, I realized I wanted what Ron and Gladys had. I wasn't sure what it was, but I wanted it." Franklin chuckled to himself, "Oh, I know that doesn't make much sense, but that's what I felt."

Janie nodded. She did know that feeling. She could see a spark, a life inside Franklin, and there was a longing inside her that wanted what he had. As he spoke, she could feel the desire for that same spark growing within her.

"I went home, convinced my wife I loved her and asked her to consider getting her commercial driver's license, so we could work together. She didn't even hesitate; she said, 'Yes'." He paused, smiling at the memory. "Sarah saw a change in me, and after I explained about meeting Ron and Gladys, she wanted to meet them. After she finished driving school, she became my co-driver and we went back to Ontario. Ron and Gladys led both of us in the sinner's prayer. My wife and I gave our lives to Jesus, and we have been growing in Him ever since. We shared our new faith with our kids, and even though it took several years, each one has come to a new life in Jesus." His smile was bright and full of warmth.

"We went to see Ron and Gladys and worshipped with them every time we went to Southern California, until they retired a few years ago. Special people they surely are. Now, we visit with them at their new home in Pennsylvania, or on the phone frequently. Sarah and I drove together and ministered to others on the road until two months ago. We have been on the road for fifteen years, but Sarah wants to retire. She wants to spend more time with our family, especially our grandchildren. But our company is small, and they needed me until the Christmas delivery season was over. They have been very good to us through the years, so I continued. I just finished my last run."

Curious, yet skeptical, Janie asked, "Just accepting Jesus made the difference?"

"No; there are many Christians that believe in Jesus, but they never allow him to completely change their lives. Their life is pretty much like it always was. The only difference is they pray some and attend church here and there, but you can only see minor changes in their lives. Ron showed us there are many references in the Bible about Jesus Christ living in each believer. He called Him the Holy Spirit. Every believer has the Holy Spirit, but some allow Him to completely change who they are, how they think, and what they do; others do not. Those who do allow the change find their new identity and esteem in Jesus Christ. What I mean is when you accept Jesus as your Savior; you are reborn. God removes the old sinful nature and replaces it with a new, righteous and holy nature. Then the Holy Spirit comes and lives inside you, guiding and directing you. Some people allow the Holy Spirit to change them completely, others only allow some change, and others very little change. The choice is yours. Sarah and I wanted a complete change, a complete transformation by the Holy Spirit. I don't want people to be able to tell the difference between Jesus and me. We can have the same spirit, the same love for others, and the same devotion to God the Father. But even after fifteen years I have not arrived to that place in my life where only Jesus exists, and I am just His vessel, but I am closer every day. As long as I continue on that path, I believe I can finish my life happy."

They sat quietly for several minutes, each lost in their own thoughts. Janie wanted what Franklin had. Never had she felt so much care and consideration. His words touched her more than any she had ever heard before. Was it that easy to accept Jesus? Would it make a difference in her life? Would having Jesus give her peace and a renewed heart for others? Something had died within her, after her best friend died of cancer. Since then, her life was such a struggle— school, boyfriends, her family. They all seemed to take something from her, until she felt empty. Something needed to change in her life.

Franklin's cell phone rang, startling Janie out of her thoughts. She heard him say, "Okay, you know what to do. We'll be right out." He turned off the phone and said to her, "Your car is done. You have a new alternator, regulator and belt. George charged your battery, cleaned the posts and now you're good to go."

"It's done already?" Time seemed to have flown by. She glanced at her watch and realized that two and a half hours had passed in a flash.

"Yep, it's done." Franklin waved toward the waitress to bring their bill.

Janie smiled, but she cringed inwardly. She hoped she had enough on her debit card to cover the bill. "Great," she said with a slight grimace. Franklin noticed the expression, but just smiled as he left bills on the table to cover their drinks and a good tip. He always tipped better during the holidays. He appreciated anyone who worked during the holidays, while others did not.

They both rose and headed out to the garage. When they reached her car, Henry stood, smiling, as he handed her the keys. "Here you go little lady. I checked things out; you shouldn't have any more problems any time soon. I changed the oil and filter. I even checked out your tire pressure. You're in real good shape now." He smiled broadly and turned to walk away. He turned suddenly and added, "Oh, and Merry Christmas and a blessed New Year to you," before turning toward the office again.

"What do I owe you?" she asked, as she hurried to catch up with him.

He turned, smiled and winked at her. "Oh, that's all taken care of. You be safe now, ya' hear?" Janie felt her mouth drop open, as she stared incredulously after the man.

She turned questioning eyes to Franklin. "Did you do this?"

"Well, not entirely. Henry did the labor for free, his brother will give us the parts at cost, and I did the rest."

"Why?" she asked, with feelings of surprise and thankfulness filling her heart.

"You needed help, and the Holy Spirit asked me to do it. So, I shared that need with Henry; we each did our part."

She was so overcome she walked to her car, opened her door and sat down; with her feet hanging out, she put her face in her hands and cried. Franklin knelt in front of her, patted her shoulder, and prayed for the vulnerable young woman God had brought into his life. *Father, I do not* know what is going on in the life of this pretty young woman, but You do. Comfort her heart and help her come to You."

She raised a tear-streaked face to her new friend. "I don't know how to thank you. I did not know how I was going to pay for the repairs. I could barely afford the gas to get me home for Christmas, but I haven't been home for Christmas in a long time."

"When you have walked with Jesus as long I have, He tells you when you need to reach out and help another. *He* did this for you; I was just the person He used. So, save the thanks for Him."

In that moment, Janie knew she needed Jesus in her life. She wanted to be like Franklin, someone God used to help others. She wanted Jesus to be real and alive in her life. "I want to accept Jesus into my life, like you have. Would you help me? What do I say?"

Franklin's smile was radiant. "Well, of course little lady, it would be my honor." During the next few minutes, a new member was reborn into God's family. Janie's heart swelled with love, hope, and the beginning of a great faith. Then in the course of a few minutes, they exchanged phone numbers, a quick hug, and went their separate ways. Both hearts were light and filled with thanksgiving.

Janie drove away, knowing her life would never be the same. She would become like Franklin, allowing Jesus to live within her. She wanted to grow in her understanding, knowledge and faith in Jesus. She would never forget this man that Jesus lived within and that Jesus had changed her life through him. She knew she would stay in contact with Franklin for as long as he lived. "Maybe being a Jesus freak would not be so bad," she thought, smiling to herself, while offering a simple prayer:

"Father, Jesus, I am really new to this, but I know that You hear me. Thank You for loving me. Thank You for saving me. I ask that You be with me each and every day, directing me. Help me to learn about You and what You want me to do. Thank You for fixing my car. Thank You for sending Franklin into my life to share Your love for me, and thank You for his willingness to show me the way to You. Amen." She fingered the Bible setting on the seat beside her. Franklin had run to his truck and had given it to her right before she left. She knew it would help shape her life from here on.

Franklin climbed into his 18-wheeler, smiling and rejoicing over a new life coming to Christ. He was humbled and grateful that Jesus had allowed him to be the one to minister to Janie. No Christmas gift he would receive would equal the gift God had given to him, the gift of allowing him to lead someone to Jesus. No gift, except the gift of his personal salvation, would ever be as sweet.

"Thank You, Father! It always humbles me to be allowed to help someone come to You! I thank You and praise You today and always!" As he drove toward home, he sang a rousing Christmas carol, "Joy to the world, the Lord has come, let earth receive her King . . ."

Hope Foundation

CHAPTER 2

Nervous butterflies bounced around in Janie's stomach, as she looked at the home office of Hope Foundation. She had scheduled an interview and arrived early for her appointment. She wanted this job, and she thought God wanted it for her too, but if she did not get this one, she knew God had a better job waiting for her somewhere else. As Janie waited, her thoughts reflected back to the events of the recent past.

Oh, how her life had changed since that night four years ago, when her car broke down on that wintry night and she had given her life to Jesus Christ; certainly, her life had taken a dramatic turn. She smiled as she thought about Franklin and Sarah. They had given her a grand farewell two days ago. After coming to Christ, she had moved to Boise, and they had become her spiritual parents. Though she loved her own family, they had not known Jesus. Thankfully, both of her parents and her brother had come to Jesus in the last few years; however, in the beginning of her new life, she had needed the love and support of strong, longstanding, and well-founded believers.

After meeting Franklin and accepting Jesus as her Lord and Savior, Janie read her Bible, went to church, and had such a hunger for the Word that she decided to attend Bible College. After much discussion, Franklin and Sarah invited her to stay with them while she attended school. She learned a great deal about the Bible; however, it was Franklin and Sarah that taught her the most about the Lord and the believer's day-to-day walk with Jesus. She even had the opportunity to meet Ron and Gladys, during their driving vacation that took them through Boise to visit their children. The light of Jesus burned brightly in their lives, and it was a great joy to finally meet them.

Now, in this new chapter of her life, she was excited at the prospect of working for Hope Foundation, a non-profit, non-denominational Christian company that provided help to missionaries, churches, and other organizations that helped and supported Christians here in the states and around the world. Though she personally felt that more effort needed to be put into saving the lost in the United States, she understood that many would rather minister for Christ in another country. It was difficult to reach people who believed they had little or no need for God, or who already believed they were saved. In addition, Janie knew the United States had two kinds of people, those who believe people should take care of themselves while the others wanted the government to take care of everything; those who looked to God to take care of them and those who looked to the government to take care of them. With the exception of September 11th, or an occasional natural disaster, the United States, as a whole, felt almost invincible in these modern times, and even though many claim to be Christians, most do not attend church or pray regularly. It grieved Janie greatly that there were so few who were living a righteous, God- fearing life, a life totally committed to Jesus Christ. Janie knew that American society, at large, believed in a God, but sadly, few lived a life reflecting that belief.

Quickly turning her thoughts back to the forthcoming job interview, she headed toward the two-story building across the street. *"Okay, Lord, here we go. If this is what You want for me, let things go well."* She took a deep breath, squared her shoulders, and marched to the front entry, confidently entering the main door. At the reception desk, she was directed to the second floor. New butterflies slammed around in her stomach as the elevator climbed. When the door opened, she took a deep breath and stepped through.

The elevator opened into a large reception area with a large picture of Jesus carrying a lamb over His shoulder; He was using a shepherd's rod to knock on a door. Janie smiled and relaxed, seeing this as a sign that Jesus was reminding her that He was with her. This same picture had hung in her bedroom for the last four years. It had always had a special significance to her. She knew Jesus had knocked on the door of her heart, and she had answered. Now, her life was full, complete, and filled with joy. As she stepped forward, the woman behind the desk looked up and smiled. "You must be Janie Weber." She reached out to shake Janie's hand.

Janie returned the handshake. "Yes, I am."

"I am Sherry Barton. Please come this way." She led the way to the end of a corridor. Knocking on the door, she opened it without waiting for an answer.

A gentleman, looking to be in his late fifties or early sixties, came around the conference table to greet Janie. He had a friendly, open face, graying hair and a warm smile. "Miss Weber, it is very nice to meet you. I am George Hamilton. Please come in and have a seat." He indicated the only empty seat on the right side of the conference table. Janie took her time seating herself, so that she could collect her thoughts and adjust to the idea of a different sort of interview than she expected. She had been expecting only Mr. Hamilton would be interviewing her.

Returning to his own seat, he introduced the rest of the people at the table. "You have already met my sister, Sherry; the man to her left is her husband, Martin Barton, and beside him is their daughter-in law, Jill, and their son, Curt. Next, my daughter, Mary, and her husband, Jake Woodard; the empty chair is where my son Paul usually sits. He was called away on an emergency. Last, but not least, is my lovely wife, Elizabeth." Janie, a little overwhelmed by the large group in attendance, nodded to each one as they were introduced.

"I know you were expecting a different sort of interview, but we already know you are hired. We have gone over your resume, the answers to your paper interview questions, and we have discussed your telephone interviews with Sherry and me. We have all prayed over each applicant, and you were overwhelmingly agreed upon. This meeting is simply a welcome to Hope Foundation meeting." He smiled. "The packet in front of you is the new hire package. Your duties, salary and benefits are all outlined in there. If you have any questions, Sherry or Elizabeth can answer them later." They all looked at her expectantly.

"I do not know what to say, except thank you. I will try my best to be an asset to the foundation." She was overwhelmed, but very pleased. "*Thank You, Jesus!*"

"We all believe that dear, which is why you were hired." Elizabeth Hamilton said kindly. "We had nearly a hundred applicants for this position. We do not advertise the fact that we are a Christian-based organization, but because we are, we must be very careful who we hire. Many who applied did not share our beliefs; because of government regulations, we have to screen very carefully. We do not accept any government money, which allows us some leeway; however, we do not want to open ourselves to any kind of problems. At any rate, we are all impressed with you. The references you provided were the deciding factor though. We are acquainted with Ron and Gladys Duncan. They said they had met you, and they had very nice things to say about you."

"Oh," Janie hesitated, "It really is a very small world." There were nods and smiles around the table. "I really felt God led me here, even with a mild case of butterflies." Everyone laughed, and Janie relaxed. "But I know God paved the way, didn't He? I do not know why I am constantly amazed at what He does and how He works in our lives. At any rate, again, I will do the best I can for the foundation; thank you for your faith in me."

"Your job will be to coordinate overlapping ministries, making sure money is not being wasted in those overlaps. We expect you to make changes that will make things flow more smoothly. After you have that in hand, we will expand your responsibilities to helping sort through the requests for funding that we receive. You will check them out and make recommendations to us for the ones you feel we might want to pursue. There is another large project we have on the back burner; you will be helping with that also when the time comes," Elizabeth added.

"What we are going to do now is give you a closer look at what our foundation does. We work in teams here, mostly husband and wife teams. Each team has different areas of interests and ministries. We all realize that God is the ultimate authority, but He gives us the vision, and we try to be His hands and feet," George explained. "My wife and I oversee the food banks, food kitchens, and the boys and girls homes that we fund. We try to purchase truck loads to keep the cost down and stretch our dollars. We have a semi-truck, trailer, and husband and wife team on the payroll.

They pick up our supplies all over the country and bring them here. We have a warehouse and distribute from there to the regional food banks and kitchens we sponsor." He signaled to Curt.

"First, we would like to welcome you to Hope," nodding to the woman on his right, Curt continued. "Jill and I head the ministry that provides generators, electrical supplies, and power of all kinds to missions. We also help churches after natural disasters. We determine what is needed, deliver and set up whatever that need is. We have six others that work with us; four are electricians, and two are assistants. In addition, we help with any building project Paul is working on."

Jake spoke next, "Mary and I work with the orphanages. We directly sponsor three; one in Kenya, another in eastern Washington, and one in Tennessee. My cousin, Cherie, and her husband, Brian, work at the orphanage in Kenya. That is their passion, and we support it because she is there. There are several others that we help financially, but we do not actually have any hands-on work there. Children and children's ministry are our focus. In addition, I do family counseling, locally."

"My wife and I work in the medical area of ministry. I am a doctor's assistant, and Sherry is a registered nurse. We travel with a medical team," Martin said. "We also help here, on and off."

"George and I travel wherever the others need help, but mostly we stay here. We also do a great deal of fund-raising. Though we have money devoted to Hope Foundation, all of this can be rather expensive, so we try to keep the coffers full. Jesus has never let us down. Actually we have a three-fold mission statement. Number one is 'Be a witness for Jesus, everywhere you go, and use words, only when you have to.' Number two is 'Love God, Love People and Serve Both,' and finally, 'Where God guides, God provides," Elizabeth Hamilton added.

Janie smiled, "That pretty much says it all, doesn't it?" Everyone around the table smiled their agreement.

"Paul heads our building department; he is gone the most. He is a lay pastor and counselor, but his passion is building. He helps missionaries, if they have spiritual or personal problems, as well as building whatever is needed. He also handles any troubleshooting. Sometimes, there are problems with supply shipments, government paperwork and the like. He takes care of all that in the field."

"There are a couple other irons in the fire, but, as of now, we have not moved on them," George added. "We try hard to prayerfully consider every move before we make it. All the money belongs to God; we are just the stewards, who supervise how it is spent, so it is very important that we move carefully. Well, there you have it in a nutshell; do you have any questions?"

Janie looked around the table at the expectant faces. "I cannot think of any right now, but I am sure I will have many, as we go along. I am grateful for this opportunity."

Now, the meeting was over. Before leaving, Janie met with each person, thanking them for their confidence in her. As she got to the door, Jill and Mary locked elbows with her, one on each side. "We would like you to join us for lunch. Please, say you will come," Mary said.

Janie looked at the slim brunette. She was a pretty young woman in her mid-twenties, and she had a warm smile. The other woman was about the same age, but taller, and could have been a model, even in her pregnant state. Both wore friendly and expectant looks on their faces.

Hesitating only seconds, Janie accepted. "I would be pleased to join you." She did not know if this was a continuation of the previous meeting, or a get-acquainted lunch.

The question was settled seconds later as Mary said, "We were fascinated by your answers to the questionnaire, especially about how you came to know Jesus, but wait until we get to the restaurant before telling us. We don't want to miss anything."

CHAPTER 3

THE RESTAURANT THEY CHOSE was around the corner from the office, and it only took a few minutes before the three were settled in a back corner booth. Mary and Jill sat across from Janie listening avidly as she told of that night four years earlier, when Jesus came to live within her heart and life. She spoke at length about Franklin and Sarah and the great love they had demonstrated to her.

"Franklin and Sarah spent hours discipling me, along with many more hours that we spent in Bible study. They are the truest kind of spiritual parents," Janie said sincerely.

For more than an hour, Mary and Jill asked questions, and Janie answered. Surprisingly, though to many it could seem like an interrogation, it was not. They laughed together, when Janie told of funny stories the children in her Sunday school classes related. They shared her sorrow, when she told them of her cousin's death, someone who did not know the Lord.

Jill and Mary began to share their own experiences, as Janie ran out of things to say. "I do not remember when I accepted Jesus into my life. I don't remember Him not being there. I was baptized when I was ten on Easter Sunday. Jake was baptized the same day," Mary shared. "I met Jake when we were in Sunday school; we were both six years old. I loved him then and love him even more now. I even think I proposed, when we were twelve or thirteen." She smiled at the memory. "We married very young; we were both eighteen. Our parents were not excited about our marrying so young; they wanted us to wait until he graduated from college. We explained that we did not want to sin, and if we did not marry soon, it would become a big problem. So they relented." Her eyes twinkled, and her smile broadened in the memory. "We decided that children could wait, but we are thinking about having one very soon, like in seven months, or so."

"Oh Mary, that is so great!" Jill squealed with delight. "I am going to be an auntie. What a hoot! We will both have little ones to grow up together. Does the rest of the family know yet?"

"Jake and I told Mom and Dad last night—and now you. We will tell everyone else at dinner on Sunday; I'm sure everyone will already know by then. You know how well secrets are kept in this family."

"Yes, how well I know," Jill said, turning to look at Janie. "When Curt and I got engaged we wanted to wait and announce it on Christmas, but we never made it to Christmas. It was Thanksgiving when everyone found out."

"Jack—that's another brother, found out, and he let the cat out of the bag Thanksgiving Day," Mary added.

"Yes, but he did it in a nice way. He had Aunt Myrtle make his favorite cake, and then he made it into an engagement cake. I think he was afraid no one would make cake, since pie is the dessert that's usual for Thanksgiving. Men love their desserts.'" They all laughed together.

"Congratulations; children are one of the greatest blessings from God," Janie added.

"I totally agree with that. I have always wanted a big family; waiting was really hard for me," Mary continued. "Anyway, Jake went to the university and just finished his PhD in psychology. He wanted to be able to counsel abused kids and troubled families. His cousin was abused by a neighbor and then tried to commit suicide. Thank God he was not successful. Jake felt helpless at the time. Now he can do what he can for other kids and their families. I have a business degree, so when Mom and

Dad started Hope, we decided to jump aboard. They helped Jake start a Christian counseling center; it is on the first floor of the Hope building."

"You seem like a great couple. In fact, all of you at the meeting seem very comfortable as couples and in the larger family setting, even though you work together," Janie observed.

"Oh, yes! We love working together." Jill said. "It is very much a family operation. You will see that more and more, as time goes on. Curt's sister, Shelly, helps out, here and there, but she decided not to be an active part in the day-to-day operations. And Mary has another brother, Jack, who is at the university. He is finishing up his studies to become a doctor's assistant, like my Dad. He plans to join the medical division, when he completes his studies next spring. Then there is Curt's Uncle Stu, who is a builder. Paul worked with him through high school. Uncle Stu takes a crew to different building projects, when he is needed; otherwise, he runs a successful business, building office complexes and houses. You already heard about Paul, Mary's older brother. Mary is the baby, and now she is having a baby." She smiled as she teased Mary.

"As for me, I did not accept Jesus until I was in high school," Jill began. "Mary and I had been classmates, since my family moved here when I was in sixth grade, but we didn't get close until we were freshmen in high school. She kept asking me to attend church with her, so finally I did. My parents are not believers." A look of sadness crossed her face, momentarily, and then cleared. "I saw Mary was different from others, the first time I met her. But later, when we became close, it was really clear. She was happy, and comfortable with who she was, and she had a peace I certainly did not have. I wanted what she had. No one was as friendly, accepting, and caring as Mary. In fact, her whole family was different than mine. So, I set out to find out what made her different. She told me many times why she was different. It took awhile for it to sink in, but in our junior year, I finally understood what it was . . . Jesus was her Lord and Savior; He made the difference. It wasn't long after that I asked Jesus into my heart. It was not an overnight change, but slowly, Jesus changed my heart. My family was not happy with me; they believed that religion is a crutch, a myth. Sadly, they still do. Things are much better now, and I am still hopeful that they will come to Christ someday." There was a thoughtful silence.

"It took a couple of years for my family to accept the changes Jesus made in my life and come to accept Him. I think it was seeing the changes in me that made the difference. Also, I prayed for them every day and finally my prayers were answered. So, keep praying, and I will pray for them also," Janie commented.

"They have remarked on changes in me, but they don't see that as proof of the existence of Jesus. But I know prayer works, so thank you for adding them to your prayers," she smiled sadly.

"Anyway," happiness filled her face as she spoke, "I had a crush on Curt for a long time. Being Mary's cousin, I saw him at church and occasionally at her house. It took me several years to get his attention. Only after I left for college and returned for Christmas my freshmen year did he finally see me in a new light. We had a long distance relationship for the next year. After he proposed, I moved back and finished my education here. Curt is a master electrician. I do all the scheduling, travel plans, ordering, and miscellaneous other odd jobs for him. We have a little boy, Peter. He is twenty-six months old, and we have another one on the way in January," Jill said, as she placed a loving hand on her stomach. "I am just as excited about this one. I used to travel with Curt, when he went out of the country, but I am happy working from home now, and he stays home more also."

"My brother, Bill, is married and has a couple of kids, Corban and Peyton. I really enjoy being auntie to them. Someday . . . " Janie trailed off. Being married and having children was a hope and dream she held close to her heart. She was waiting for God to bring the right man into her life. "Someday, I hope to marry and have children."

Jill and Mary exchanged a look that Janie missed, as she checked the display of her cell phone when it rang. She ignored the caller and looked back at her companions. "Well, this has been really nice," Jill said, as she gathered her purse and coat. "But my elderly neighbor is watching Peter. He will be up from his nap soon. If I know Peter, now Mrs. Johnson will need a nap, if she hasn't napped while he napped, which is what I have been doing lately." Standing, they exchanged hugs and promises to meet again for lunch soon.

"I will see you Monday at nine. Dad asked me to show you around and get you settled," Mary said.

"Great! I will see you Monday." Janie turned toward her car, as Mary and Jill headed back to the office, where Jill's car was parked.

"She is perfect! I love her already!" Mary said excitedly.

"Yes, I agree." Jill gave Mary a pained look. "I know we promised Paul we wouldn't play matchmaker after he and Diana broke their engagement, but Janie and Paul would make a great couple. They are both smart, friendly, and they share the same faith in Jesus, unlike him and Diana, I might add."

"I really did try to like Diana, for Paul's sake, but it was difficult. She said she was a Christian, but I certainly couldn't see Jesus in the way she acted. Anyway, I know it broke his heart when she left, but I was secretly relieved. Anyway, we will just have to make it a matter of prayer. God knows best, but I agree; I would sure like to see Janie as a member of the family. Funny how you like some people immediately, and others you can never warm up to. She is easy to talk to. You can see Jesus in her. There are so many Christians, or so-called Christians, like Diane; you can't tell the difference between them and unbelievers. With Janie, you can see the love of Jesus; she is like a mirror reflecting His love. Funny how we are match making and we haven't even known her three hours yet."

"It was that same light that drew me to you all those years ago, and Jesus still shines brightly through you." Jill reached over and put her arm around her sister-in-law, giving her a side hug. "And as for not knowing her long, we met her through her application and introduction questions a few weeks ago."

"Yes, I guess you are right. And you know you have that light now, too." Mary hugged her back, as they made their way to the office.

Janie could not stop smiling. She was excited about this job. *"Oh, thank You, thank You Jesus! I think this will be a wonderful job. I really like Jill and Mary. I think they will be great friends and co-workers. I can't wait to tell Franklin, Sarah and my family. I know they all were a little concerned about my moving. But I know You are in this. Help me to be a witness of Your love, not only in my words, but in my actions."*

CHAPTER 4

A**FTER LUNCH, J**ANIE WENT back to her car and immediately began her search for an apartment. She didn't need much. She found the perfect one after visiting five complexes; it was one mile from the foundation building—a one-bedroom unit with a small kitchen, dining room and living room. There was a washer and dryer in a closet in the bathroom, a real plus. Janie was given the keys and was able to move in immediately after paying her deposit and first month's rent. Having no furniture, Janie went to a store to purchase a mattress, box spring, dresser, small kitchen table, two chairs, and a futon that she could use as a sofa, or as a guest bed. Having prepared well in advance, she was able to pay cash for all her purchases and still had some remaining savings. Her new things would not be delivered until around six p.m., so she still had four hours before her furniture arrived. Looking around, she saw a linen outlet and headed that way.

A short time later, Janie had purchased bedding, including sheets, pillows, two blankets and a comforter, as well as extra bedding for the futon. After depositing her purchases in the trunk of her car, she made her way to the kitchen shop. She had received dishes and a few pots and pans as going-away gifts, so she filled out her kitchen needs. Practical in nature, she purchased only those things she knew she would use on a regular basis. Last on her list were a couple of paintings, or pictures, for her walls. For those, she returned to her car and drove to a Christian Bookstore she had seen on her way to the outlet mall.

In the bookstore, Janie found *three* pictures she really liked and had difficulty choosing. The first was a picture of a ship caught in a storm. Jesus was looking down, bringing calm in the midst of the storm. The next was a picture of a chapel, surrounded by a beautiful garden, and a stream was flowing next to it. The final picture was of Jesus kneeling in the garden of Gethsemane, praying. Though her practical nature balked, she bought all three pictures, two fictional books, and a new devotional book. Satisfied with her purchases, she headed home to her apartment. Her apartment; that sounded nice to Janie; she had never lived on her own before. She had lived first with her family, and then her cousin, while she had attended a business school and worked her first job; finally, she had stayed with Franklin and Sarah, while she attended a Christian college. Her own apartment would be nice for a while.

After carrying her purchases into her empty apartment, she put everything away that she could. She opened the bedding and put the sheets and pillowcases in the washing machine and turned it on. She did not have any detergent, yet, but at least they would get rinsed out before she slept on them. Glancing at her watch, she still had one hour before the delivery people got there. Figuring she had time, she went to her hotel, and gathered her suitcases and checked out. It cost her an extra day because it was after check-out time, but Janie wanted to spend tonight in her own apartment.

Janie arrived back at her apartment, just as the delivery truck bearing the name of the outlet store arrived. She hurried to her first-floor apartment and unlocked the door. She was thankful that someone had cancelled their delivery today, allowing her things to be moved in today, instead of two days from now. It took less than two hours and her empty apartment looked homey. In fact, everything looked wonderful. The bright bedspread covering the queen-sized bed was blue and ivory, with small flowers of lavender and pink. All of her clothes were put away either, in the dresser or hanging neatly in the closet. Walking into the living room, Janie noted that a couple of throw pillows would look nice and dress up the futon. Turning, she decided that she needed to purchase two more chairs. She realized she would not be able to have more than one friend to dinner with only two chairs. A centerpiece for the table, along with some place mats were added to her list of additional improvements. All in all, Janie went to bed satisfied with her day and grateful to God.

"*Thank You, Lord, for all Your blessings today; it has been a very good day. I appreciate Your being with me and guiding me though the day. You are worthy of praise and glory, and I love You. Thank You for loving me. Good night.*"

Janie woke suddenly, her dream still vivid in her mind. Was this a dream from God? Was this something important to her and to others? Letting her mind settle, she went over the dream in her mind. The dream was about a sanctuary, a place away from cities, a place of protection and rest for believers who were working hard to survive in the end times—or the hard times; she was not sure which. Janie believed that the end times were rapidly approaching, so, could this be a directive from God to prepare for the difficult times ahead? Janie puzzled over this for some time.

"*I am not worthy of such a vision, Lord. I still struggle with old habits, bad thoughts, bad decisions, and much more. I do not consult You as I should, when I make decisions. I do not pray enough; I do not understand all I should. Who am I that You would give me such a vision? And, more importantly, what am I supposed to do with it? I do not have the money to purchase the land and materials to build such a place . . . ?*"

"**You are a child of the Most High God! You have been washed with My blood. You are Mine. You have been adopted into My family. You are worthy because I am worthy. You are righteous and holy because I am righteous and holy. Where I guide, I will provide.**"

Humbled and willing to be used, Janie continued her prayer. "*Thank You, Lord Jesus for reminding me that You are in control. I will write this all down and leave the rest to You.*"

Janie rose and went to the bathroom, where she took care of the morning needs and then took a shower. After dressing in only her underwear and a robe, she went to the computer and opened a new file, which she entitled The Sanctuary. Without deliberate thought, she began writing down all that she remembered from her dream. She began with the setting, a valley surrounded by mountains on three sides. She described a small, old-fashioned church, the buildings, main lodge, and several small houses (or rather cabins), a large meeting hall with dining room and kitchen, a very large barn, a bunkhouse, pig pens, a chicken house, goat pens and a paddock with several horses and another with milk cows. A huge garden, ringed with fruit trees, was surrounded by a high fence. At first, she wondered why the fence was so tall, before remembering that deer and other animals could destroy a garden. Deer were known to jump over short fences without difficulty.

Further, she envisioned a wheat field, an alfalfa field, and a field where cattle grazed. The church sat halfway up the hill, overlooking the valley, with two wind turbines above it near the top of the mountain. There was a medium-sized lake off to one side, fed by a stream or creek. She then drew a diagram, showing where everything was and the size of each building, compared to the others around it.

Finally, feeling hungry, Janie looked over at the clock. Surprised and shocked, she realized she had spent nine hours working at the computer. She was surprised at the minute details of her dream, including the floor plans of each building and the wood stacked outside each house or building that needed heat. She rose slowly, stretching the cramped muscles in her back and legs. Making her way to her small kitchen, she realized that in all her shopping, she had not gone to the grocery store.

Tired and hungry, she prepared to go out, surprised again to see she was still in her robe. Dressing quickly, Janie was putting on her shoes when there was a knock at the door. Wondering who it could be, as she had not given anyone her new address yet, she went to the door and opened it.

A pretty young woman with brown hair and tawny eyes, accompanied by a small boy about two years old mirroring similar features, was standing at the door, holding a covered dish and smiling at her. "Hello," she said. "I am your neighbor, Bonnie Morgan, and this is my son, Harold. We live in the apartment two doors down. We saw you move in yesterday. We noticed the delivery of your furniture and saw you bring in some suitcases, but we never saw any grocery bags, so I made this for you."

"Oh, how wonderful of you!" Janie exclaimed, smiling at Bonnie. "In all my shopping yesterday, I simply forgot groceries. In fact, I was just getting ready to go the store. Please come in." Janie gestured them inside. "Have a seat. I am Janie Weber, by the way."

"I hope you don't think we are nosey or anything," Bonnie said uncertainly. "Most of the people in this building are much older, and

I was overjoyed to see someone close to my age move in. My husband, Nathan, is a fireman and is gone several nights a week. On his off days, he works part time at a mechanics' shop. It makes for some lonely days and evenings. My mother always told me, to have a friend you must first be a friend. So, here I am."

Janie smiled warmly. "I can always use a friend. I am new in Spokane. I start a new job at Hope Foundation on Monday."

"I have heard great things about them," Bonnie observed. Harold was getting a little tired of sitting still, and he began to wiggle and look around. "Well, I shouldn't keep you if you are headed out."

"Oh, no, please stay. Have you eaten? We could share this; it smells wonderful." Janie peeked under the foil that was covering the dish. "Spaghetti is one of my favorites."

"Well, Harold would need his bib and high chair . . . " she trailed off, thinking.

"Then it is all settled. You run over and get the things you need, and I will set the table. It is always more fun when you do not eat alone. Is water okay for a beverage?"

"Water is fine. I will be just a few minutes. Harold, let's go get your things, so we can eat with Janie."

Janie hurried around the small kitchen, gathering dishes and silverware. She didn't have anything to go with the spaghetti, but she was going to have her first dinner in her own apartment, and that was wonderful. *"Another new friend; thank You, Father. No one can have enough friends. I do hope she knows You, but if she doesn't, I will simply have to introduce her to You."*

There was a knock at the door again, "It is open, come on in." Janie called from the dining room. Bonnie appeared, holding Harold's hand and pushing the high chair. "Here, let me help you." Janie crossed the room and took the chair, rolling it across to the table.

"I brought some French bread and green beans," Bonnie said, as she lifted a covered dish and a foil-covered loaf of bread from the seat. She handed them to Janie, who took them and set them on the table, as Bonnie lifted Harold and put him in his seat. After tying his bib around his neck, she took a seat next to him.

"This is so great; thank you so much. Would you join me in the blessing?"

"Sure." Bonnie said hesitantly. She did not have many praying friends.

"*Father, we want to thank You for this food and ask that You bless the hands that made it. Thank You for this wonderful new friend, Bonnie, and her son; they are a great blessing. Be with us this evening in our time together. Thank You, Jesus, for everything You do for us, each and every day. Amen.*" Without losing a beat, Janie turned to Bonnie, "So, tell me all about yourself, Harold and your husband."

"Nathan and I have been married a year next month." She paused, thinking, "*I might as well get that out in the open immediately; having a baby before a wedding turned most Christians off right away. If this one won't accept me, I might as well find out, here and now,*" Bonnie thought. When Janie said nothing, and there was no change in her expression, Bonnie shrugged inwardly and continued. "Nathan and I met six years ago. There was a fire at my parents' house. He was one of the firemen that responded. I watched him work with his partner, as they tried to save the house. Unfortunately, the fire was too far along before they were called. The house burned to the ground. He came over to me and said he was sorry before they left. Two days later, I made cookies and took them to the station. I wanted them to know that my family and I appreciated their hard work. He asked me out, and we moved in together two months later." Still, Janie had no comment, and Bonnie relaxed.

The next hour flew by in a blur of conversation and laughter. Bonnie relaxed more and more, as time went on. At first, after the blessing at dinner, she was afraid that Janie was one of those religious fanatics. The only Christians she had ever been around had been pushy, overzealous, and condemning . . . all fire and brimstone. She liked Janie very much and did not feel the least bit uncomfortable with her. She found herself liking her more and more each minute. Janie was friendly, and happy, and had a joy that shone like a beacon, unlike anyone Bonnie had ever known.

"Let's move to the living room. Harold can play on the floor that way," Janie offered.

"Sure. He gets fussy, if he has to sit for long periods of time. Otherwise, he is a really good little boy." Bonnie lifted Harold out of the chair, after wiping him down with the wash cloth Janie offered her. Janie hurriedly cleaned off the table and put up the leftovers, while Bonnie attended to Harold.

"I will do the dishes later," Janie said, as Bonnie put Harold down. While they talked, he was content to play on the floor with a couple of cars Bonnie had brought with her.

"Tell me about yourself," Bonnie said, as she settled down on the futon.

"Nothing really interesting; I am the second of two children; I have an older brother. My parents live in Arizona. They got tired of the cold weather and moved a few years ago. We lived outside Portland, Oregon, while I was growing up. My brother is still there. I went to Denver, studied business, and then took a job there. During Christmas several years ago, I was on my way home for a visit, when my car broke down. A truck driver stopped to check on me. He was wonderful. Though he was a total stranger, he stopped and gave me a blanket, and then, because it was so cold, he asked me to come back to his truck." At Bonnie's horrified look, Janie quickly added, "He was neat and clean, and I just felt it was safe, so I went. I was colder than I thought and couldn't stop shivering, so he told me to get under the blanket on the bed, and he would wait for the tow truck. I fell asleep. When I woke up, we were already at a truck stop, and my car was in the shop. I was alone so I went inside. Franklin, that's his name, asked me to join him in the coffee shop, while we waited. He told me how Jesus had saved him, and now his life was different. I thought he was a Jesus freak, you know, the ones who are friendly to your face, then beat you up with the Bible. But he was so different from any of the Christians I had ever met. After visiting for a while, my car was fixed. Franklin and his family paid for everything. I was so overwhelmed that all I could do was cry. But I saw something in Franklin that I wanted. So, I asked what it was. He said it was Jesus; I accepted Jesus right then and there, and my life hasn't been the same since. I went on to Portland for Christmas, but I talked with Franklin and Sarah several times during the holidays. On my way home to Denver, I stopped at Boise to see Franklin and meet Sarah. I was so excited about my new life in Christ that I decided I wanted to go to Christian college. It was during that visit that they invited me to live with them, while I attended school. I was with them for four years. They were wonderful mentors in the faith. Just after I graduated, this job came open, and now I am here."

While they were talking, Harold had crawled into Bonnie's lap and had fallen asleep. After a time, she looked down at her sleeping son, "I really should take him home to bed. This has been a wonderful evening.

I have really enjoyed it." Holding Harold close to her, she rose and started toward the door; though she really had enjoyed their time together, Bonnie was not ready to talk further about religion.

"I have enjoyed it, as well. I hope we can do it again soon. Here, let me help you with his chair." Janie rolled Harold's chair to Bonnie's apartment and then said, "Good night."

CHAPTER 5

THE NEXT MORNING BRIGHT and early, Janie made her way to a mid-sized church, a mile or so from her apartment. She enjoyed the worship, but the message seemed a bit off. The pastor used too much of his opinion, instead of the Word to make his points. She understood that many used their own interpretation of the Bible, when they presented the message to their congregation, but Janie was used to pastors backing everything up with the Bible and taking great care not to take undue liberty by adding their opinions. She knew she had been spoiled by the pastor at Franklin's and Sarah's church, Pastor Mark. He was a wonderful man and an anointed speaker. Janie wanted to find a church where she would be challenged to grow and expand her knowledge and understanding of the Bible. She also wanted a church in which she could take an active part and not be just a Sunday seat warmer. There were other churches in this area; she would look, until she found the one that was right for her. God would let her know when she was where He meant for her to be.

Janie went to a super grocery store on the way home from church. She cringed a little at the register total but knew that many of the staples she bought would last a long time. She had found the throw pillows and place mats she wanted; then she returned to the outlet mall and purchased two more matching chairs. The salesman helped her get them into her car, which was a struggle, but they finally were able to close the door. She was glad it was a short drive home because she had to move her car seat forward, and it was uncomfortable driving.

After arriving home and putting away her purchases, she returned to the computer. She wanted to go over her file on the Sanctuary. Janie went over her notes three times, adding this and that, before deciding she had remembered everything she needed to. She connected her printer to her computer and asked it to print. Nothing happened. Checking all the connections, she could not see what could be wrong. The printer was much older than her computer, and she figured it must have finally died. Her computer and printer were some of the only things she had transported when she moved. It was just like the crazy thing to quit working *after* she moved instead of *before*. She decided that she would buy a new one, after she received her first pay check. In the meantime, she placed a disk into the computer and backed up the Sanctuary information, intending to print it at the office during a break.

She rose and tidied her apartment, looking around she was satisfied at what she saw. It was small, but it was hers, and she liked the quiet. It was comfortable and cozy.

"Father, I know You have a plan for me. You know my heart and my desire to have a husband and family of my own. I do not want to be impatient, so help me each day to wait on You. Thank You so much for all Your many blessings! Jesus, thank You for saving me, loving me, and providing Your guidance and direction each day; help me to hear You, when You talk to me, and then please help me to do what You ask. I do not understand everything about the Sanctuary, but I know it is important. So, direct me where it is concerned. I love You so much."

Janie found it interesting, frustrating, and challenging, working with the people in each department. The problem was each acted independently, using very different filing systems, paperwork, and organization. It caused her more work because of all the differences. After six weeks of struggles, she plopped down at her desk, face in her hands, nearly ready to cry.

She had used Curt's forms for Jake's project, which he complained about, loudly; she answered Mr. Hamilton's phone under the wrong department name, causing the customer to get angry; and finally, she gave the expenses for one department to another, causing even additional confusion. Janie wondered how they got anything accomplished.

Elizabeth was passing by Janie's office and peaked in to see Janie's face buried in her hands. "Janie, is something wrong?" Elizabeth asked, concerned.

Janie looked up, dejected. "Is anything wrong? Everything is wrong! I have never seen such confusion and disorder. There are different forms for every department, when one would get the job done with only minor changes. There is no coding for expenses, so you cannot tell what department each expense goes to. And on and on it goes. I am supposed to make things flow more smoothly, but everyone is stuck on having things their own way. When I make suggestions, I am met with, 'Thank you for your suggestion, but this has worked since we started, and it will do just fine.' Maybe it is fine for them, but not for anyone else who needs to work in more than one department. For a Christian organization, I have never met so many people in one place who have to be the boss. The idea of servanthood—working for the good of all, has been lost here. Here, it is a my-way-or-the-highway mentality." With misery in her eyes, she said with a small voice, "I do not think I can work this way."

Elizabeth looked at the beautiful, efficient, young woman. *"Finally! I was beginning to think she had the patience of a saint. I was afraid she would never get tired of the confusion, and we would be stuck with it forever."* She knew Janie's job was going to be difficult. She knew how headstrong each person in her family was. This was the reason Janie had been hired. Elizabeth and George had tried to get each department to coordinate with each other, with little or no success. Finally, they had decided to look outside the family for help and had found that help in Janie. *"Father, forgive me for not explaining in more detail, so she could have avoided feeling like this. Help me know the ways to make it right."*

Pulling a chair over to Janie and sitting down, Elizabeth lightly rubbed Janie's back, as she spoke. "I am so sorry this has been difficult for you. When we decided to hire someone to coordinate between departments, we thought it would be an easy task for someone outside the family. We should have warned you what you were up against. We have some very stubborn members of our family." She stopped, taking a deep breath, then plunging ahead. "This is what I want you to do. First, make a list of all the changes you would like to see made. Second, give me specific changes, like what would the form look like that all the departments should use." She looked at her watch. "But now, what I want you to do is to go home and enjoy the rest of the day off, and I don't want you thinking about this at all this weekend. On Monday, I want you to do nothing but work on the list of changes and recommendations. Please look closely at every department, including mine. When you have done this, bring the list to me, and we will go over everything. After we are done, we will have a meeting, and you can tell—that's right *tell* everyone—how things are going to be done from here on out. It will not be left up for discussion. George and I will let everyone know that they are to do as you request. Does that sound like a good plan?"

"Yes, Mrs. Hamilton, and thank you." Janie replied meekly.

"Elizabeth, please. Call me Elizabeth. Mrs. Hamilton was my mother-in-law," she said smiling. "Now, gather your things and get out of here. And don't think about that list all weekend. Enjoy yourself; have some fun."

"Thank you, Elizabeth."

Elizabeth watched Janie gather her coat and purse and head to the elevators. Then she turned toward her husband's office. Knocking lightly, she entered, without waiting for a reply, however, seeing that he was talking on the phone, she sat across from him and waited until he finished. "Hello, dear."

"Hi, Hon; you have that serious look on your face. What's up?"

"Janie. I found her with her face in her hands, and though she didn't cry, I could tell she was really close."

"Is she alright?"

"I think she will be. She finally got the courage to say the things that we have known for some time. She thinks we are a disordered bunch of people and are also somewhat difficult to work with." She chuckled, "I believe she thinks we are a self-centered lot, who all want things their own way— too many chiefs and not enough braves."

George smiled back and said, "What did you say to her?"

"I asked her to make a list of changes and present them to me."

"Well, well. It's about time. I was afraid we misjudged her, and she wouldn't have the back-bone to call a spade a spade. You and I knew we needed to make some changes; I am glad she finally said something. It restores my own faith in my judgment of character and the discernment I felt was coming from God. I thought all along that she was just who we needed to get things organized and to make the changes needed to run things more smoothly. I hope everyone will receive well those proposed changes."

"Oh, I think they will. Everyone likes Janie very much. She has already made several changes in filing and in ordering supplies, just nothing major. I would like you to tell them we support the changes and are going to require everyone to use them. But now that Janie knows she has our blessing to make the necessary changes, I think she will do fine. She has a way about her that gets people to do what she wants them to. She just didn't want to make waves. Unfortunately, we need a few waves around here. She is right about not working together as a group. Each department thinks theirs is the most important and deserves the most attention. That is not good for the foundation, as a whole. We are a team and should be working like one, a team with a common goal, serving the Lord with our talents."

Smiling, George looked affectionately at his wife, "Well, this should be interesting. That is why we hired her . . . to coordinate things. By the way, that was Paul on the phone. He will be delayed another week."

Janie entered her apartment with a feeling of relief. It had been a difficult six weeks, with problem after problem and squabble after squabble. She had been around everyone long enough to know they all loved the Lord Jesus, but they certainly had not learned to serve one another, and Elizabeth was right when she said they were stubborn.

"Father, Elizabeth sent me home and told me not to think about the Hope Foundation, so calm my heart, help me to relax, as I give all this to You. I know You have a plan for Hope, and I am a part of it, so help me accept the things I cannot change and work to change those things that I can change. Open people's hearts, and make them willing to listen, and help implement the changes needed to make Hope a really effective tool of Your love and ministry to the world. Thank You for allowing me to be part of this wonderful ministry; thank You for loving me and giving me the ideas needed to fix the problems, and thank You for just being You. Help me to be a reflection of Your love in everything that I do, and help me to be a servant to all at Hope Foundation. Amen."

CHAPTER 6

THE MORNING DAWNED BRIGHT, crisp and cold the next day. Janie had nothing planned, so she wanted to continue to expand her thoughts about the Sanctuary. She had dreamed about it again last night. She had been so busy at work that she had not printed anything out, yet. So, she decided she would go over everything she had written before and add anything from her dream last night that was different. After a small breakfast of cereal and hot tea, Janie moved to the small desk she had set up in the corner of the living room.

After checking her e-mail, Janie opened her file on the Sanctuary. She reread the entire file, making notes and adding thoughts, here and there. She closed her eyes and tried to picture the entire complex.

The Sanctuary was in a protected valley, nestled between high mountains with tall evergreen trees of fir, balsam and pine, mixed with aspen, larch, and shrubs of all kinds. Ferns and wild- flowers grew in the patches, here and there, where the sun broke through to the forest floor.

The center of the valley was a large meadow, not entirely clear of trees, but nearly so. The grassy floor was covered with wildflowers of blue and white, with a few yellow and red blossoms, here and there. A small creek wound down from the mountains, filling a small lake on the south end of the meadow and then continuing on out of the valley. In her mind, she watched an eagle flying majestically over the valley, like a protecting angel. This was a haven, a place of retreat, a respite, providing refuge, safety and rest from the stormy times to come in a violent and sinful world, and she knew its location would be a tightly held secret.

A single track, dirt road wound around the valley going from pasture to barn, bunkhouses, individual cabins, lodge, and a large dining hall, with a connecting meeting area with classrooms upstairs and storage in the basement. The chapel was at the north end of the valley, surrounded with flowering trees and shrubs. There had to be a chapel because all of this was ordained by God, she thought. They would need a place to worship. The chapel looked like a church of old, with a steeple with a bell tower, large side windows, and large double doors at the entrance. A beautiful flower garden surrounded the church and a bench set under some trees in the corner of the garden. Most importantly, it was a place that reflected all the love, gratitude, and thankfulness of the people for their Lord, Savior, and God—Jesus Christ.

The doorbell rang, startling Janie. She had been so lost in the vision of the Sanctuary that it took her a few seconds to orient herself. The Sanctuary seemed so real that it felt strange to leave that place in her mind. She wanted to return. It was a place of extreme love, comfort, and safety; it felt as though Jesus was already there and waiting for her to join Him. Just thinking about it brought a longing to her soul, making her feel bereft. The doorbell rang again. Janie forced herself to leave the computer and go to the door.

Opening the door, Janie found a very upset Bonnie and Harold. "Bonnie, please come in. What is wrong?"

"I am sorry to bother you, but Nathan was caught in a fire this morning and is in the hospital. Do you think you can watch Harold, until my Mother gets here from Coeur d'Alene?"

"Of course. How is Nathan?"

"He was burned, though I do not know how badly yet. The building fell in and several firemen were caught. All I know right now is that it doesn't look good. I need to be with him."

"Sure. I can watch Harold. I can do anything that will help. Why don't I watch Harold at your apartment; he will be more comfortable in his own surroundings."

"Yes, that would be good," she said, distracted and worried.

"Let me get my sweater and keys. Go back to your apartment and I will be right there."

"Thanks. I can't thank you enough."

"No thanks are needed. This is what friends are for."

Janie hurried to save her file and shut down her computer, grabbed her keys and locked up on her way out. Bonnie's door was open a crack, so Janie knocked and entered. Bonnie was busy getting ready to leave and was writing on a sheet of paper.

"This is Harold's schedule. He eats at twelve. There are leftovers in the fridge. He goes down for a nap at one and will sleep for two or two and a half hours, and then he'll want a snack. There are graham crackers in the cupboard. Mom should be here before dinner time. She is at work and has to wait until her replacement can get there."

"Don't worry about a thing. Harold and I will be just fine." Janie hesitated, "Bonnie, would you feel comfortable praying with me before you go?"

"I think I would like that," Bonnie said, with tears in her eyes.

Lord Jesus, You are the great Healer. You told us in Your word that by Your stripes we are healed. Jesus, I am claiming that healing for Nathan. Help Nathan and Bonnie look to You in this time of trial. Help them see You working in their lives. Comfort Bonnie and give her Your peace. I ask this in the name of Jesus. Amen.

"Amen," Bonnie added, really looking at Janie for the first time that day. "Thank you. I have been reading the Bible you gave me. Sometimes, I don't know if I believe, but at times like this, I really wish I did."

"God is not the author of the bad things in our lives, but He can turn them around into something wonderful. Reach out and accept that tiny seed of faith, and Jesus will water it with His love, strength, and comfort, as it grows—until it is large enough for you to claim it as your own."

Bonnie nodded, kissed Harold and left. Janie prayed, off and on, for Nathan and Bonnie all afternoon. Janie played with Harold and followed the schedule Bonnie had left. She was glad she had spent time with Bonnie and Harold in the last two weeks, so that Harold felt comfortable with her.

Bonnie's mother arrived at four o'clock. "Hello, I am Bonnie's mother Noelene. Have you heard anything from Bonnie?"

"No, I could watch Harold for a while longer, if you want to go to the hospital," Janie told her, as the other woman took off her coat.

"No, Bonnie asked me to relieve you, so I will wait, until I hear from her. Besides, I would like to be here when Harold wakes up."

"Alright. He should be up anytime. I think I will head over to the hospital then. I will stop by and give you an update, when I get back."

"Thank you. I would be grateful for any news you can pass along."

Janie went back to her apartment, picked up her purse, and immediately went to the hospital. After parking, she went inside and asked about Nathan and Bonnie. She was directed to a small waiting room down the hall. It was filled with people. Janie looked around and spotted Bonnie sitting with an elderly woman, talking quietly. She made her way to them, passing by several groups of people. She caught snatches of conversation about the fire and the four men who were caught when the roof fell in. Bonnie saw Janie heading her way and quickly excused herself.

"Mom must have arrived," she said, matter of factly, when she reached Janie. She hugged herself; Janie knew it was a sign that Bonnie was trying to hold herself together.

"Yes, I offered to let her come here first, but she wanted to be there when Harold woke up. How is Nathan?"

"Thankfully, the burns were minor, but he is still unconscious. They are still doing tests trying to find out why."

"How are the other firemen?"

"Two are fine and have been released. They had minor burns. John was severely burned. That is his wife over there in the purple blouse." Janie looked toward the woman Bonnie pointed out. Janie saw a woman who was around forty, with brown hair, and then she turned her attention back to Bonnie.

"John is Nathan's partner?"

"Yes, but Nancy has never been very friendly. In fact, before we got married she would not come to our house because we were 'living in sin,' as she put it. They are Christians, too, but her husband is more like you; he accepted us, whether he agreed with us or not. He didn't automatically judge us, like she did. I guess her attitude is one of the reasons it is hard for me to accept Jesus. I heard her say at a party one time that Christians are all supposed to become like Jesus, but I thought, if Jesus is like her, I didn't want to be anything like Him. But I remember in one of our conversations that you explained that Jesus accepts us right where we are, and afterward, He slowly changes us into the person He wants us to be; I guess Nancy just has a really long way to go because I have learned from you that Jesus is not like she is," she said seriously.

"Yes, well," Janie smiled ruefully, "unfortunately, many accept Jesus, but He has a hard time breaking down the old habits and patterns they learned in the world, or they just don't see the sin in their own lives. I think the difference really takes place when Jesus really gets into your heart. When that happens, there is no way you can stay the same. His love becomes so great that it pushes out all the self-centeredness and bad attitudes. There's just no room for those things anymore. He replaces all that with His love, acceptance, mercy and grace; when we finally accept that truth, we can see our moral brokenness more, our sin. Then we can see our need for the forgiveness that Jesus gives us, and that helps us ask for forgiveness and then to accept His forgiveness. But that's only the beginning. The love Jesus brings to our hearts continues to grow, until it takes over and flows out of us and into the lives of those around us. That is when we can love others and accept them right where they are and love them into the family of God. None of us will ever be perfect; I still get angry at times. However, we can grow in love, acceptance of others, mercy and grace, and when we do, then each day we become more like Jesus."

Bonnie sat thoughtfully, before speaking. "I have watched you these past few weeks. There is a big difference between you and me. I have found myself envying you, trying to be more like you."

"You don't want to be like me," Janie said matter-of-factly. "It is Jesus you see in me. Jesus has made all the difference. You can have the same thing, anytime you are ready to say 'yes' to Jesus."

"I do know that, and I must say that I am getting closer all the time. Even Nathan has noticed a difference in me, even though I haven't asked Jesus into my life, yet. You must have rubbed off on me." She smiled weakly.

"Jesus will not stop calling you, until you say 'yes.' Isn't it wonderful that He loves us so much that He never gives up on us? Well, I should not say 'never'; if a person totally rejects Him, He will let them have their way. They have free will to choose to reject Him, and He will allow them to choose hell. However, it must grieve Him terribly."

"Nathan was raised in church. His uncle was a minister. He said he just stopped going when he left home. He told me last week that he still believes in Jesus, but he knows Jesus isn't happy with some of his decisions."

"We all make bad decisions sometimes. But there is nothing Jesus will not forgive, if we simply ask and then repent."

"Repent must be a catchword, but what does it really mean to Christians?" Bonnie asked.

"Repent just means to change directions and to do things God's way, instead of doing them man's way. You see, our ways are not God's way. In everything, He keeps in mind how it will affect others. For example, He hates adultery because of the harm it does to everyone involved— the husband or wife, the other person, their family, the children . . . Besides, breaking the marriage promise, itself, adultery never involves just the two people who commit the sin. The same thing happens with most sins. They rarely affect just the person sinning.

Take stealing; again, it is not just harmful to the person who loses their property. It hurts the family of the person who gets caught. I could go on and on, but you get the picture. God always takes into consideration how our actions affect those around us. It is like throwing a rock into a lake. The ripples the rock causes continue, on and on, ripple after ripple. Sin is like the rock; the ripples from that sin go on and on."

They sat quietly for a while, each lost in their own thoughts. Janie prayed and would have been pleasantly surprised to know that Bonnie did also.

"Bonnie?" Both women looked up, surprised by the soft, hesitant voice.

"Hello, Nancy, how is John?" Bonnie replied. Janie noticed she was a tall woman, several inches taller than her own five-foot-four inches. She was a little overweight and had a friendly face.

"He is better than they thought at first. He only has second-degree burns, thanks to Nathan. They let me see him for a few minutes. He said that when the building started coming down, Nathan saw it and pushed John away from the worst of it. It saved them both. They were trapped for a short time, but it was in a corner that was free of fire. It was on the way out that Nathan got hit in the head with a falling beam, and John was burned. It didn't knock Nathan out, and the beam rolled off of him, but he staggered badly. It was the falling sheetrock that got John. They helped each other out. It was after they got out that Nathan collapsed."

"Thank you for telling me, and I am glad that John is going to be alright," Bonnie said sincerely.

"Have you heard anything about Nathan yet?"

"Not really; they did a MRI and some other tests. Now, we are waiting for the results."

"Well, I will pray for him."

"Thank you. I appreciate that." Nancy gave Bonnie a quizzical look, before returning to her family.

It was nearly eight o'clock when the nurse approached and told Bonnie that Nathan was awake and asking for her. "You can go in for a few minutes."

Bonnie jumped up, smiled, and then hugged Janie. "He's awake!"

"I will wait until you return, so I can take word to your mother."

"Okay." Bonnie hurried away, following the nurse.

"Thank You, Father for your protection of Nathan and the other firefighters during that fire; it could have been so much worse. I know You are working in Bonnie's heart. It is so wonderful to see. Help her take the final step and accept Jesus as her Lord and Savior."

Janie was reading a magazine when Bonnie returned. The doctor came with the results of Nathan's tests, just as Bonnie arrived.

"Your husband has a slight concussion, but that is all. The burns are minor. We want to watch him overnight, but he will probably be released in the morning. He will have a headache, but that will fade in a few days. He was a very lucky man. When he first came in, I was sure I would find bleeding in his brain. But I didn't find a thing to worry about. Go on home and come back in the morning. After we check him out, if all is still good, you can take him home."

"Thank you, Doctor, but he wasn't lucky; he was blessed, protected, and healed by God!" Bonnie said in an awed voice. As the doctor turned to go, Bonnie fell heavily into her chair, and put her face in her hands and wept. After a few minutes, Bonnie controlled herself and turned to Janie. "Jesus healed him, I just know it. When I first saw him, I thought he would die. The whole left side of his face was a mass of red and purple. It was so swollen that I hardly recognized him. Yet, when I saw him a few minutes ago, the swelling was down, and it was not nearly so bad. I did not know what to think; the change was so dramatic. Now, the doctor says all the test results look good. It was your prayers; I know it was your prayers. Jesus healed my Nathan." She had a look of awe and gratitude on her face.

Janie just smiled. She knew Jesus healed. This was not the first time she had seen it happen.

"Janie, I am ready. While I was waiting here earlier, I told Jesus that if He would heal Nathan, I would know He was real—and He *did*. Would you help me ask Jesus to save me?"

"Nothing could make me happier," Janie said simply. "All you need to do is to tell Jesus that you believe that He is the son of God and that you accept the sacrifice He made for you on the cross. Tell Him you understand you can never do enough to save yourself, and that you cannot earn your way into heaven, and that you know He took all of your sins and paid for those sins with His blood, His sacrifice, and His life. And you believe that He died in your place, and He rose again and now lives in Heaven with His Father. Tell Him that you are sorry for your sins and that you will turn from all of your sins, and you will walk in His righteous and holiness. Then thank Him and keep thanking Him every day for the rest of your life." Janie held Bonnie's hand, as she made Jesus her Lord and Savior and became Janie's sister in Christ Jesus.

CHAPTER 7

JANIE SPENT ALL WEEK gathering information. First, she sent questionnaires to each department head. Then she went through all the procedures and listed the ones she felt could be used by everyone. Afterward, she collected the questionnaires, meeting with each person to go over each one, so that she understood what they thought; she was not relying only on their written answers. Finally, she put together a plan. On Thursday she met with Elizabeth to go over her findings and implement her changes. Now, it was Friday, and the meeting to present and explain her changes was scheduled to begin in forty-five minutes. She had spent last night going over everything one last time. As she left for work that morning, she saw her computer disk for the Sanctuary and picked it up, and brought it with her; she thought that she might as well print it out, while she printed everything else out for the meeting. She had finished working on the Sanctuary file last weekend and kept forgetting to bring it to the office, so she could print it. She really needed to take the time to get a home printer, she thought.

Grabbing her file folders, she hurried out of her office and down the hall. Turning the corner, she ran into a tall blur of a man. Her files tumbled from her arms, as she sprawled on the floor, the air knocked from her lungs. "Ugh." She drew in a breath and tried to reclaim her dignity. *Thank You, Lord, that I wore pants today.*

"I am so sorry! Here, let me help you," a deep voice said from beside her.

"Let me catch my breath first," Janie said. She took stock of her condition. She gingerly moved her legs, straightening them in front of her. Her files littered the floor around her. Still sitting, she began gathering them.

"You must be Janie. I have heard nothing but nice things about you. I am Paul," he said, as he began helping. When he came to a file marked *The Sanctuary*, he paused, looking at the file, and then at the young woman.

"*The Sanctuary.* I am surprised that Dad mentioned it to you. Well, I'll just take it with me and read it over. I didn't know anything had been written down, concerning our plans." He reached out a hand to help her stand.

"Nice to meet you, and thank you for helping me gather things together. But that file is . . ." Janie trailed off, as he handed her files back, minus the one on *The Sanctuary*, and he rounded the corner out of sight. What did he mean about his Dad 'mentioning it'? Had God shared the Sanctuary with him, also? Had *he* had a dream? Janie pondered, as she entered the conference room. She knew she could not limit God. If He shared the Sanctuary with her, He could with others, also. Forcing *The Sanctuary* file from her mind, Janie turned her attention to the meeting ahead.

Elizabeth was the only one in the room, when Janie entered and cheerily announced, "Hello."

"Hi. Are you ready for your presentation?" Elizabeth looked up from the papers she was reading. "Are you okay? You look a bit disheveled." Usually a very tidy young woman, Janie looked like she had been through a wind storm.

"Oh, I'm fine. I had a little accident with the files just now, so I will need to organize them. I think I will tidy up first," Janie said, putting down her files and turning toward the door. "I will be back in a minute."

"That's fine; I need to finish readying this new proposal anyway. I wasn't expecting it to arrive this morning, and, unfortunately, we will have to move on it immediately."

Janie hurried to the ladies' room and combed her hair, straightened her clothes, and returned to the conference room. It took her fifteen minutes to re-organize her files and separate her handouts; she then rounded the table, leaving a folder at each place. Sighing in relief, she sat down to wait. She was pleased that she would be ready when everyone arrived.

Paul opened the file on the Sanctuary and began to read. It was more detailed than he expected, right down to the description of the trees and flowers. The placement of buildings, gardens, and pastures was surprising in its detail. It was almost like the person writing the report had actually been there and had seen the entire complex, but that was impossible because it was not built yet. The land had been purchased six months ago. They began bouncing ideas around, however, no decisions had been made before Paul left on his last trip. He did not realize plans had proceeded so quickly. He felt somewhat disappointed that so much work had been done without his input.

Details of each building, describing the approximate size, number of rooms and what each was used for, were clearly outlined. The main lodge was a large house. It had nine bedrooms and six bathrooms, a large kitchen, and a very large dining room. The living room had a huge stone fireplace at one end and room for several sofas and chairs. The next building was a large meeting hall that had a commercial kitchen on the first floor and numerous sleeping rooms, men's and women's showers and bathrooms on the second floor. There was a small clinic with two adjoining apartments. A bunkhouse was down by the barn. The barn was a huge building, large enough for hay storage, eight horse stalls, a milking area, tack room, and parking area for a tractor, backhoe, and snow removal equipment. Adjoining the barn were pens, and several corrals already were labeled "pigs," "horses," "cows," and "goats." There was even a large chicken house. An additional building was labeled "warehouse." The garden and two greenhouses covered a large area. Rows were lined out to show the vegetables and fruits grown there. Fruit trees surrounded the garden area, and the entire area was fenced. There were two water wells, one for the buildings and another for the fields. Paul was astounded, as he studied the final page, a map of the valley. All the roads, buildings, pastures, gardens, greenhouse, stream, lake, and even mountains, where two wind generators were located, were drawn in great detail. The stream showed a generator and another backup hydrogen generator next to the main meeting hall. There was a note about a methane gas system, next to the septic system. That was something he had never thought about before.

Paul sat contemplating the report. Why hadn't Dad said anything? When they had had dinner last night, nothing was said about the Sanctuary. Yet, major work had been done on the project. Again, Paul was a little disappointed they had proceeded without him. This was a family project; sure, God had given his Mom and Dad the task of putting everything together, but they had said it would be a family project. However, here in his hands was a complete set of plans. Picking up the phone, he dialed his Dad.

"Hello," the familiar and loved voice answered.

"Hi, Dad."

"How is the first day back at work?" George asked.

"Oh, so I have been on vacation, huh?" he chuckled. It had been far from a vacation. They had built a small city complex for a missionary group in a tiny African town. "Fine, except I ran down your new coordinator."

"Oh, how's that?"

"We collided coming around the corner; she went down, and files went everywhere."

"Janie wasn't hurt, was she?"

"No, though it took a couple of minutes for her to catch her breath. The reason I called is that she had the file on the Sanctuary. I was really surprised you had done so much work on it and even more surprised to see her with it."

There was a short silence. "That I know of, nothing has ever been said to Janie about the Sanctuary. You say she had a file about it?"

"Yes. It looks like a final draft."

"Are you busy right now?"

"No."

"I will be right down."

Moments later, George entered his son's office and took the seat across from him. "So, let's see the file."

Paul handed the file to his father and watched his face, as he carefully read through the pages. After studying the map, he closed the file and looked up with both a surprised and a perplexed look on his face. "I can guarantee you that she did not get this from anyone in this office."

"So, where do you think she got it?"

"I would say the same place we did. We do not have a corner on God. If the times ahead are going to be as bad as we believe they will be, ours will not be the only sanctuary God directs to be built. The question is, how many will listen and obey? God told me to buy property, away from cities and people. He wants us to build a sanctuary, a haven for Christians during the hard and violent days to come. My vision was vague in its content, whereas your Mom got a bit more concrete information—and He even provided the money to build it. But I know it does sound crazy to the carnal mind."

"It is not a coincidence that Janie came to work here, is it?"

"After reading this, I would say a definite 'no.' "

"Well, I am anxious to talk to her about it." Paul began to pick up the phone.

"She isn't in her office. We have a conference," looking at his watch, "in five minutes. We can ask to speak with her after the meeting."

"Okay, it will be very interesting to hear what she has to say," Paul sat thinking. "I am sure that is our valley. I recognize the creek and lake and their placement in the valley. It will be interesting to see what she has to say about that."

"Oh, I am sure it will not surprise her that much; she is a very committed believer. She is a wonderful person, too. You couldn't do much better, if you ask me," a twinkle in his eye.

"You are not playing matchmaker are you, Dad? I don't even know her yet."

"Maybe. In the last several weeks, Janie has proven to be a practical, knowledgeable, devoted employee; add that to being a very friendly, giving, forgiving, and loving young lady, and you have a powerful combination. The icing on the cake is that she is a believer."

"Well, I am afraid I was a bit rude after I ran her down, I was so distracted by the file on the Sanctuary. I walked off in a hurry, wanting to read the file," he said ruefully.

George chuckled, "Well, that's one way to meet someone; run them over then walk off. I can tell you, if I was twenty years younger, and I didn't have your mother, I would certainly look twice in her direction. I really like her."

Paul gave his Dad a surprised look, and then he shrugged. "I guess I will have to give your wonder girl another look."

CHAPTER 8

THE MEETING BEGAN PRECISELY on time. Janie got over her nervousness quickly and got right down to explaining the changes she wanted and why. Though there was a little grumbling about the form changes, everything else was well received. She answered a few questions, and then the meeting was over.

"Thank you, Janie; that went very well. I am pleased with the changes. I think they will help a great deal," George said. "By the way, I want you to meet our son, Paul."

"Nice to meet you—again." Turning, she shook the outstretched hand and smiled at the younger version of her boss. He was tall, over six feet, and had the same brown hair and eyes as his father. Addressing George, she continued to smile and said, "We ran into each other earlier. . . literally." Paul caught her quick wit and smiled also.

"Yes, he told me, but I thought a more formal introduction would be nice," George smiled, "You are alright?" his smile changing to concern.

"Yes, of course. I think I will be more careful at that corner in the future," she said smiling.

"Well, I am glad you are alright. Do you have some time? We would like to speak with you about *The Sanctuary* file."

"Ah, sure. I do not have anything pressing, if you would like to talk about it now."

"Yes, that would be good; let's do it here. I want Elizabeth to be here, also. Let me catch her before she leaves." Janie watched, as he crossed the room to speak with his wife. She wondered why he would want to talk with her about the Sanctuary, and then she remembered that Paul had made comments about a sanctuary earlier. She understood that God worked in mysterious ways and knew George might have had a similar vision.

"How do you like working at Hope?" The voice interrupted her musings.

"I like it very much," Janie said, as she turned her attention to him.

"I like the changes you have implemented. There have been times I wanted to pull my hair out, working under the old system; Sherry and Martin want things one way, Mary another, Curt another, and so forth. It made things hard at times. What I am surprised about is that they took the changes so well."

"Oh, I went to each person, told them what I was doing and asked for suggestions. Then I took all the suggestions and made them into something that would work for everyone. It did take a little longer than I had hoped, but I am satisfied that it will work. Besides, I think your Dad told everyone to go along with me."

"I am sure he did, but it was smart to involve them in the changes the way you did." Paul was impressed with this small, pretty, young lady.

George and Elizabeth returned, as well as everyone else. Surprised, Janie turned a questioning look at George, as everyone returned to their seats, and he motioned her back to hers.

"Janie, Paul said he took this file from you this morning, after he ran you over." Janie saw the name, *The Sanctuary*, on the front, as he picked it up and turned it toward her. She nodded. "We would like to know where you got the ideas and the details in this file."

Janie hesitated. Would they believe that she had had a dream? She might as well tell them. She knew they were all believers. "Well, I had a dream, several actually. I felt I was supposed to write them down. It was strange really. While I was writing, it was like I was there, walking around as I wrote. Nearly a month later, I had another dream, so I went back and expanded on my original writings. I finished, but my printer was broken, so I made a disk. I finally remembered to bring it with me, so I could print it out. This morning, after I printed the packets I handed out earlier, I printed that one also. I must have picked it up by mistake, when I was gathering my papers for the meeting this morning."

"Janie, the Sanctuary is a real place. We purchased the valley you describe six months ago. There are no buildings, roads, or anything else, yet. We have talked about what we need to do. . . what we would like to do, but we haven't done anything else. So, you can understand why we are a little surprised because it's all right here in this file."

"Oh, my!"

"Oh, my is an understatement. You see, six years ago, Elizabeth and I had a vision, a dream, whatever. At first, we didn't tell each other about it, but being married as long as we have, we began talking to each other about what we saw. We were working at different jobs at the time, and we knew we could never afford the cost of such a place. The land, buildings, and other necessary items would be in the millions."

"The complex will hold approximately two hundred people. More if there are children. I can see where it would cost a great deal," Janie said, a bit overwhelmed.

George exchanged looks with several around the table and then continued. "We have prayed about this throughout the last several years. Finally, God told me we would win the lottery. The money would be used to build the haven, or Sanctuary, as we later named it. We did not generally buy lottery tickets, in fact, we hadn't purchased one in ten years, or more. But where God guides, He provides. So I figured He would tell me when to buy tickets, and then I did. The first time I bought tickets, nothing happened. Elizabeth bought a few tickets, here and there, too. In fact, several times during the next few years we purchased a ticket. I began to think that maybe I misheard God. Maybe I just imagined the whole thing. But when I was urged again to purchase a ticket, we did, and we won. We won over one hundred million dollars."

"Wow!" Janie was stunned.

"Of course, we had to pay taxes, so we didn't end up with that much, but it was a large sum, just the same. We took the money and established this foundation. Then we began looking for the land we were told to purchase. It was interesting that, as we traveled around for the foundation and began looking at land, we met others who God had told to do the same thing. Some actually did as God told them to do, but more just talked about it. We felt it was confirmation that we needed to get ready. Ready for what, we are not sure. It could be war, or it could be natural disaster, or it could be the end times that the Bible talks about. We still are not sure, but we are more than sure God is behind this, and we are trying to be obedient to His leadings. So, now we have the land, and I believe these are the plans."

Janie sat, stunned. *"You were giving me the plans for their sanctuary, Lord? Wow!"* "Well, you are welcome to them. I thought I was kind of crazy myself, as I was working on them. But now I know God was using me to help you. Wow!"

George turned his attention to the room at large. "My feeling is that time is getting short, and we are supposed to start work on this—immediately. What do the rest of you think?" George asked. There were several nods around the table.

"Can we see the file?" Curt asked.

"Elizabeth, please take the file and make copies for everyone," George said, as he handed the file to her. Elizabeth nodded and headed out of the conference room. Speaking to those around the table, George continued, after the door closed. "The plans are very detailed. I am sure we can make minor changes, but if this is from God, I would think we should follow them closely." The others nodded. "As soon as Elizabeth is back, I would like everyone to read through the file and make note of any questions you have. But let's not bombard Janie with questions, until everyone has read the file."

Janie barely heard George; her mind was in a whirl. Her dreams and visions were the basis they would use for a haven? Wow. That word again; couldn't she think of any other word, rather than 'wow'? There were others: fantastic, surprising, amazing—and there had to be more. What a silly thought. Her mind jumped from topic to topic; she could not focus on anything. There was whispering around the table, as they waited for Elizabeth to return. Minutes later, though it seemed more like an hour, she came in with a stack of papers. She walked around the table, handing out the copies to each person, including Janie.

Janie read her file. As happened before, when she read, it was like she was in the valley and walking around. It was the same for the others, too, as they read the file. This place was so beautiful in their minds. For

Janie, the season was late summer, or early fall, and the garden was in full production, the fruit trees were ready to harvest, a light breeze moved the turbines of the wind generators at a slow speed, and the creek flowed into a large five-acre lake and out the other side; a couple of boys were fishing off a small pier. She could see people working by the barns, butchering pigs; others cutting and stacking firewood, preparing for winter. Someone was working on a tractor, while others were talking, as they looked at a large generator. Children chased the dogs, while chickens ran helter-skelter, to get out of the way, and the small chapel was surrounded by a riot of brightly colored flowers.

"Janie! Are you alright?" Janie was startled back to the present. George instantly knew she was seeing the valley again, just as he had.

"Yes," she said, distracted. "When I think about the Sanctuary, it's like it appears in my mind, and I am there. It is so peaceful and normal. It is hard to believe a war is going on. There is turmoil in our country."

"A war?"

"Yes, I believe it is a war, but I could be wrong. There was a prophet, sometime around the end of the 1800's that said there was going to be three wars. He was correct to the date about World War I and II. He said there would be a third. I believe he thought it would start around 2012, give or take a few years. I guess I assumed it was a war that caused all the trouble. Anyway, I believe God wants us to prepare. We need to have a store of supplies and be ready for a long and difficult time. Groups of believers, or families, must band together and create havens, or sanctuaries, around the world, especially here. People in the United States have had it easy for so long; they will not know how to survive in a war or hard times. I believe many will starve. Others will be murdered for their food. And the children . . . many children will be abandoned." Janie collected her thoughts and then continued.

"People depend on grocery stores, but they only have a week or two worth of food. If trucking is reduced, due to war, or if the supply lines are cut off, there will be shortages everywhere. People need to find places away from city centers, places where they can go back to the basics and provide mostly for themselves. These need to be places they can defend, as well because if things get bad in the cities, marauders will try to steal, or even kill, for food. It will need to be large enough to provide for lots of children. I think I read somewhere that during the Great Depression, lots of children were left behind to fend for themselves, when their parents couldn't or wouldn't care for them anymore. I am afraid that it will be even worse now because today people are so self-centered. At any rate, even if there is not war, times are going to get very difficult." There were thoughtful nods of agreement around the table.

"Janie, we have decided to go to the Sanctuary land tomorrow morning. I would like you to come with us. I would like you to see it. Would you consider coming with us?"

"I would like that very much. I need to see this place for myself."

By unspoken agreement, they decided not to question Janie further. "We will pick you up at seven o'clock in the morning; will that be alright?"

"Sure." Janie was still overwhelmed by the last few minutes. "Is there anything else?"

"No, take the rest of the day off. You have been putting in a lot of hours and need some time for yourself, as we are going to take up your weekend. You will need to bring a change of clothes and whatever else you need for an overnight stay. We won't be home till late Sunday afternoon, or evening," George said kindly. He knew she was having a little trouble putting all the amazing facts of the last hour together.

After Janie left, the room broke out in excited conversations. Everyone had read the file and all were going through the same amazement that George and Paul had earlier. George sat back and listened to the exclamations.

"I can't believe it—a full set of plans for the Sanctuary. Isn't that amazing? God is so amazing."

"At first, I was a little insulted that God didn't tell one of us, but then I realized that it is not about us. It is about God and His providing a place of safety for His people."

"Can we all go to the land this weekend?"

"Yes, anyone that wants to go can go. Let Elizabeth know, so we can reserve the rooms we will need. Fifty miles, or so, from our land, there is a little town that has a small motel. We can stay there overnight on our way back," George said. Most of them remained in the conference room for nearly an hour, going over the plans and making notes, before they drifted out.

CHAPTER 9

Paul slipped out right after Janie. He wanted to talk with her privately. He could tell she was overwhelmed. He understood that feeling. When his parents told him about their visions and dreams, at first he thought they were crazy, at least until Dad won the lottery. He proceeded to pay off all their personal bills, including their houses, and then they established the Hope Foundation. The balance was put in safe, easy to access accounts they could use, when the time came to build the Sanctuary. They never spent a penny on anything frivolous. As far as his parents were concerned, the money belonged to God and must be used for His purposes. He respected his parents even more for their honesty, integrity, and devotion to God.

Paul found Janie in her office, staring out the window, completely still. If he knew her better, he would have known this was unusual for her. She was a constant whir of motion, while she was at work. He knocked on her open door to get her attention, "Hello."

"Oh, hi. I guess I am still in shock . . . dreams, visions, lotteries . . . not usual things in my life. Since I came to the Lord and really began to understand things, I knew that, as the end times get closer, the Bible tells us there will be more of this sort of thing, but to live it is another thing altogether."

"I know what you mean." Making a quick decision and looking at his watch he said, "It's lunch time; how about joining me?"

Janie gave him a rueful look. "The matchmakers in the company will have us married before the end of the day. Are you willing to take the chance?"

"Oh, you heard about that, have you? Well, we'll just have to give them something to talk about. Besides, my father told me that if he was twenty years younger and didn't have Mom, he would be interested in you. He admitted he was not beyond matchmaking himself. He really likes you."

"Oh," a little stunned, Janie didn't know what else to say.

"Well, Jill and Mary have been singing your praises ever since the first day, so I think they have the same idea. I guess I would like to see if you are the saint they make you out to be. As far as the rest, we will just have to wait and see what God has in mind."

Paul laughed and stuck out his arm as she picked up her purse. When she reached him, she gave him a bright smile and linked arms with him. They made their way out of the building, with whispers following them down the hall, into the elevator, and out the front door. By the time they reached the restaurant, word had reached the conference room, where smiles and high fives interrupted their conversation. "They aren't married yet," Elizabeth said.

"Yes, my dear, but you couldn't resist me, and she will not be able to resist our son! All we have to do is give them time and throw them together, as much as possible," George said confidently.

Paul led Janie around the corner and down to Fourth Street, where they turned right and then entered a small restaurant. Paul liked this young lady. She was short, only about five feet four inches. Her brown hair was long and held back with a ribbon of bright blue. There was nothing exceptional about her appearance, but her smile and the light of Jesus was shining brightly in her life. It was that light that drew all around her to the warmth that radiated from her. It reached out and tugged at a person.

When she smiled, her whole body smiled and made you feel good and at ease in her presence.

A waitress met them at the door and led them to a back corner table. The restaurant was not full yet; however, Paul knew it would be standing room only within a short time. He was glad they were away from the front entrance and away from the noise of entering customers. After giving them menus and taking their beverage orders of unsweetened iced tea, the waitress left, and they perused the menus in silence for a few moments.

"The French dip sandwich is very good here. Or, if you like chicken, I would suggest their special. It is a barbeque sandwich, with all the trimmings. Either is great. They have delicious soups, also. That is what I come here for in the winter."

"The barbeque sandwich sounds good to me. Barbeque *anything* is a favorite of mine."

"I will remember that."

Janie put her menu down and looked around the restaurant. It was a pleasant place, filled with antiques. For example, there were showcases with dolls of all sizes and styles, while others held plates, cups, and saucers. There was even one filled with small railroad cars.

"This is a wonderful place," stated Janie. "It reminds me of my favorite restaurant, while I was growing up—The Old Hoosier Inn. It was very similar to this. My favorite foods were chicken fried steak or garlic steak. They always served both soup and salad with their meals. I remember that because it was unusual to get both."

"I found this place right after we moved here. I was trying to get a feel for the place. I took long walks at lunch time; my family called it 'my walkabout time.' I always get to work by seven a.m. and leave about six p.m., so that I can have long lunches. I get antsy when I sit too long. Walking helps burn off the restless energy that office work creates in me. I would much rather be in the field working than sitting in the office."

"I guess I really don't know what you do, besides working in the building department."

He nodded. "Dad and I decide where and what we are going to build, and I do it. We get requests from all over the world. Sometimes, it is difficult to decide which projects to take. I also trouble shoot. If there is a problem on a project, or if someone has an emergency situation, I go and help out. This last project was building a hospital, church, orphanage, and cottage for missionaries; their entire compound was burned out by terrorists last year. We had to wait until the government cleared them out, before we could go back and re-establish the outpost."

"So, you are a carpenter?"

"Yes, a carpenter and a jack-of-all-trades; I do whatever needs to be done. I can even do the electrical, but I usually leave that for Curt. Through the years, I have done just about everything that has to do with building. I have even had a hand at making furniture; of course, it's very simple furniture, but it is serviceable."

"Mary said you had pastoral training. I take it you don't use it much."

"Yes and no; I minister to those at the missionary posts I visit, counseling or preaching, if they ask me to. I am glad that I went to school and learned what I did, but I really think building is my calling for now. Maybe God will change that later, but I really like what I do."

"I suppose you will be working at the Sanctuary." It was a statement, not a question.

"Yes, actually, I will head the building part of the project. We originally planned to start in two years, but after hearing you this morning and seeing the plans, I believe we will begin very soon."

"I think that would be wise; I am not sure why I feel that way, but I do," Janie said thoughtfully.

"I did not bring you here to pump you for information about the Sanctuary. That will come soon enough. Please tell me about yourself." Paul wanted to get to know this interesting, young woman that his family thought the world of.

"My life is very normal. I grew up outside of Portland, Oregon. I moved to Denver, where I received a business degree. On my way back to Portland, just before Christmas four years ago, I met Franklin. He was a truck driver, who rescued me and led me to Christ. Several weeks later, I moved in with Franklin and his wife, Sarah, while I attended Bible college. After school, I worked at a small non-profit, until God led me here. That's it."

Paul laughed, "Rescued by Franklin, I think that because you have told this story so many times recently, I got the short version."

"Guilty. I consider my life pretty boring."

"Well, to those who are really interested, it is not boring at all."

"Thank you, but you are just being kind."

"Alright, so what's this about being rescued by Franklin?" They spent nearly three hours talking. Janie shared her conversion story, and Paul told her about his teen years spent working for his uncle after school, weekends, and summers. He shared about his Bible college years, when he received a pastoral and counseling degree. However, he missed the outdoor work, so when the foundation was formed, he took on the trouble shooting and building areas. They talked at length about Jesus and their core beliefs.

"I have really enjoyed myself, but I really need to go," Janie said apologetically. "I am babysitting for my neighbors this evening. They are attending a new believer's class at their church."

"I enjoyed this also; I will walk you back to your car." Paul was smitten; if he wasn't in love with her already, he knew it would only be a matter of time. His father was right. Janie was a beautiful, young lady both, inside and out. Paul intended to snatch her up before someone else could.

On her way home, Janie didn't want to examine her feelings too closely. She liked Paul very much, but when love tried to push into her thoughts, she deliberately pushed it aside. She wanted a husband and children, but she had just met Paul. She was attracted to him. He loved the Lord, and she could see the gentleness and kindness in his smile and manner, but she would wait on the Lord to confirm if Paul was the one for her. In addition, she knew hard times were coming, whether it was the end times, war, or just a period of hardship and struggles. As fear now tried to enter her heart, she firmly said out loud, "*I am saved by the blood of Jesus. He is my strength, my fortress and high tower. In Him I will not fear. I have victory in Jesus. In Him alone will I entrust my life; it is in His hands. And as for Paul, I will wait on You, Lord, to guide and direct me.*"

CHAPTER 10

THE EVENING WAS PLEASANT, as Janie played with Harold. Thoughts of Paul sprang to her mind again and again. Following those thought were thoughts of a child, like Harold, only one that was hers. It was a dream that she could not let go. After putting Harold down for the night, Janie spent time praying. *"Father, please give me patience. If Paul is the one, You will let me know without a doubt. I have only known him one day. That does not seem like a suitable period of time to be thinking about spending the rest of my life with him. Love at first sight seems like a worldly idea. Yet, after being with Franklin for only a short time and seeing the difference You made in his life . . . I fell in love with You, so maybe it is not so worldly after all. You know the present and future; I will wait on You, alone, to lead me in the right direction."*

Bonnie and Nathan returned shortly after nine. "Thank you for babysitting; I know we could have taken Harold to the nursery, but he gets cranky when he stays up late. With Nathan still home recovering, it is much nicer when Harold is in a good mood."

"I enjoyed it. How was the class?"

"We are learning so much. I heard all of this as a child, but now I am really beginning to understand. It is truly incredible what Jesus did for us, isn't it? I mean, He left the splendors of heaven to come to a fallen world for the express purpose of bringing us back to God. Understanding that disobedience caused all the problems in the world, bringing sin and causing the entire world to fall, is sometimes overwhelming, especially, knowing that I have added to that sin. I figure Jesus knew He would have to take our punishment to save us from God's eternal punishment and restore us to right standing before a holy and righteous God, way back before the garden of Eden. It is still mind-boggling," Nathan said.

"Yes, and remember, He did so willingly. Jesus had free will to say 'no.' He is God's Son; He knew the past, present and future, so He knew what would happen, and He knew there was no other way. If there had been another way, I am sure they would have come up with it. The Old Testament tells us that the blood of the animals that were sacrificed under the Law covered the sins of the Israelites. It foreshadowed what had to happen for men to be totally reconciled to God. It explains that this was planned from before the beginning of the world. Jesus knew His blood would be required to cover the sins of the world; He knew He would suffer a horrible death at the hands of the same men He was dying for. Yet, His love for us was so great that He suffered for us anyway."

"Adam and Eve really messed it up for all of us," Bonnie commented.

"I used to think that too, and it is true, but put yourself in their shoes. How many times have you known you shouldn't do something, but you did it anyway?" Janie asked gently.

"More times than I care to count," Bonnie said ashamed.

"Me, too," Nathan said.

"Me three. So, even if they had not fallen, we would have; Jesus would still have come to save the three of us. That is what is mind-boggling for me."

"I never thought of that."

"Jesus is love, and that love is beyond anything we can imagine. It is unselfish, in a way we can only obtain in a small measure, as we grow more and more like Jesus every day, as we walk with Him."

"Janie, why are there so many Christians that accept Jesus and then go on living just like they always did? Remember what I shared with you about Nancy? Why is she like that?"

"Ah, the million-dollar question. I have several ideas, but I am sure there are many reasons. I think many never really make their relationship with Jesus personal. What I mean is this: they learn about Him, they talk about Him, but they never allow Him to take complete control of their lives through the Holy Spirit. They continue to sin and do not make an effort to change, even though that is what Christianity is all about . . . life-giving change. Change from the ways of the world to the ways of God. Change from doing it our way to doing it God's way. Change from selfish ambition to servanthood. Change from taking to giving. The list goes on and on, but you get the idea."

"I see what you mean. Pastor Frank said repentance means turning the other direction; the same thing you said at the hospital that night. Sometimes, I am so used to doing something that displeases God that I do it before I think about it, even when I know it's a sin. It is a *struggle* at times to do what is right in God's eyes," Bonnie said thoughtfully.

"It will get better with time. I remember when I first came to Jesus. I was overjoyed with the love I felt, and then, because we are living in the real world, things would come to try and steal my joy. Situations would arise, and I would behave very poorly. I sometimes thought I would never grow up in Jesus and leave my old habits and behaviors behind. Then there were my old friends, who couldn't understand the changes they saw in me. Some of them even stopped being my friends; it was hard. But slowly, things changed. I didn't get so angry, when things didn't go my way. I didn't automatically think the bad about someone; I gave them the benefit of the doubt. I am still growing and figure I will be till I go to be with Jesus. But you know, I wouldn't have it any other way. I am happy, joyful and thankful. I love Jesus, and I enjoy living my life pleasing Him, not just pleasing myself."

"Yeah, I know what you mean about the joy, especially when Nathan rededicated his life to the Lord, too." She reached over and squeezed his hand. "It is so much easier having us walk together in this. We can hold each other accountable and talk about our successes and failures together. But it makes me sad that there are so many that attend church and say they believe, but you can't see Jesus in them at all."

"I know, but we all have free will. If they choose to still do things their own way, instead of looking to Jesus to guide them, it is their loss. Also, there is some really bad teaching out there. You have to be careful that everything a pastor, or teacher, says can be backed up in the Bible. Even then, you need to read the passages that surround the ones they are using because some teachers take things out of context and twist their meanings to match what they want the Bible to say, rather than what God meant for it to say."

"Yeah, Pastor Frank told us the same thing. I am so glad I met you. If I hadn't, I would never have seen the difference between you and other so-called Christians. I would never have decided Jesus can really make a difference in a person's life."

"It's Jesus in me, not me. I was crucified on the cross with Jesus. Now, it is Jesus that lives in me and not I. I know that sounds confusing, but think about it. Jesus gave His life for me; He took my punishment; because I believe that, I accept, and acknowledge Jesus as my Savior. I accept that I died on the cross with Him. I died to myself. When my old self died, all the sin, shame and guilt died, too. Afterward, Jesus gave me a new life in Him. I have a new nature, one born of God, instead of the old life that was born to the fallen nature of this world. That's what we call being 'born again.' When we finally really believe this, we realize we are completely free from being enslaved to sin any longer because we are dead to it; we can live without intentional sin in our lives, and if we are tempted to sin, we have Jesus, who will stand with us against that sin and give us the strength not to sin. See, we are no longer living our lives alone; Jesus, through the Holy Spirit, is always with us, and if we do not have the strength to do something, we can tap into the strength of the Holy Spirit, and He has more power than we can imagine. Unfortunately, even when we fully understand this, it's still difficult to always live and walk in this truth because we still live in a fallen world. Occasionally, we ignore the Holy Spirit and sin, but even when that happens, when we simply go to Jesus, and ask for forgiveness, and then work harder to listen to the Holy Spirit, with His help we can fight the sin in that area of our life."

Janie could see that Bonnie was holding back tears. "I didn't mean to upset you, Bonnie." She reached over to lay a hand on her arm.

"Oh, no, you didn't. What you said finally sunk in. I am free in Jesus. I don't have to feel guilty for living with Nathan and having a baby before we were married. That was in the old life, and that life is dead."

Janie smiled brightly, "How right you are! You are completely, one hundred percent forgiven, and you are free! All your sins are on the cross. Do not let anyone ever make you feel sinful or guilty over that again. All of your sins—past, present, and future, are gone. That does not give us a license to sin, but rather freedom not to sin. We may still have regrets, but we walk in a new life."

Bonnie gave Janie a hug. "I am so glad you came into my life."

Janie hugged her back. "You are a blessing to me, also."

Nathan looked on, as his wife and Janie hugged. He was thankful, too. He had accepted Jesus and been baptized when he was fourteen, but he had turned his back on Jesus, when he left for college. So many at college told him faith, especially Christianity, was a dead religion. After his injury and after Bonnie told him about Janie's prayer, he knew God was drawing him back. He and John had talked about Jesus many times, but the feelings of guilt kept him away from God. He knew his injuries had been healed. He knew things had been much worse than the doctors found, and he firmly believed Jesus had healed him, to give him a chance to turn his life around. He meant to make a difference now, as a believing husband and father.

"I am going out of town tomorrow morning; I will be gone until Sunday night. I will call you when I get back. Don't get up. I can let myself out. Good night," Janie said, as she opened the front door.

"Have a good time; see you next week," Bonnie replied.

Janie gave a wave as she closed the door. *"Lord Jesus, You are so good. Bonnie and Nathan are wonderful friends and family members. Thank You so much for their friendship; they encourage me when I get lonely. Bless them with Your Word and Spirit."*

Bonnie rose and went down the hall to peek in on Harold, before kicking off her shoes and settling on the sofa. Nathan moved to sit next to his wife. "That's why you have been down lately, isn't it? You felt guilty about our living together and having Harold, before we were married," he asked gently.

Bonnie cast her eyes down and stared at her hands, as she softly spoke. "Yes. Even before I was a believer, my parents taught me it was wrong to sleep with someone before I was married, but they weren't around, so I just pushed the thoughts away and did it anyway. But it has been eating at me for a long time. It got better after we married, but . . . " She was crying now, and Nathan reached over and got her a tissue from the box on the end table. She looked up, as she wiped her eyes, "I didn't want to feel bad because I loved you so much and still do."

"I was a believer. I knew it was wrong, too, but I bought into that whole idea that marriage is just a piece of paper, and it didn't really mean anything. I loved you, and you loved me, so I kept telling myself it didn't matter. The only reason I finally asked you to marry me was because John kept reminding me I was sinning against you by living with you, without marrying you. He fell just short of calling me a fornicator. He knew I was raised as a Christian, and I guess God was using him to help draw me back. I was hesitating because you seemed so closed to the idea of Christianity."

"I saw he was different, but not Nancy. She can be one of the rudest people I know, and, unfortunately, there are more Nancys in the world than Johns and Janies."

Nathan took her hands, "I am sorry that I caused you pain and caused us to sin. I love you; please forgive me."

"We both sinned, so I will forgive you, if you will forgive me," Bonnie replied, with a watery smile.

"Deal." He hugged her close. He drew back and dropped down to kneel before Bonnie. Then he asked seriously, "Bonnie, will you marry me?" Seeing her surprised look, he put a finger on her lips to stop her from speaking. "I would like us to renew our wedding vows. Only this time, let's do it before God and our close friends, the way we should have done it the first time." He removed his finger from her lips and waited for her answer.

"Yes," she said, with a radiant smile. "I would really like that. I know our anniversary is in three weeks, but I would like a new date, a new anniversary, to celebrate our new life together in Christ Jesus."

"I will call Pastor Frank in the morning and see when he has a free hour." He stood and reached out to pull her up beside him. "Come on, it's time for bed," he said with a wolfish smile.

"Aren't we supposed to wait until the wedding?" she replied with a saucy grin.

CHAPTER 11

THE TRIP TO THE Sanctuary was uneventful, yet with each mile Janie grew anxious to see the valley. She watched as the scenery flew by, and she was struck by the majestic mountains towering high above them. There were three vehicles traveling to the land George and Elizabeth had purchased for the Sanctuary. She and Paul rode with Elizabeth and George. The men sat in front, leaving Janie to visit with Elizabeth as they traveled.

Elizabeth was a wonderful Christian lady, one that Janie was growing to love more and more each day. She was sound as a rock in her faith and encouraged everyone around her in their faith walk, also. They spoke about the mission trips and Christian outreaches the foundation had helped with over the last year. "I call them Faith Adventures," Elizabeth said. "They are the times we step out in faith and go somewhere, or do something, that goes totally against the understanding of the world. Yet, we believe in God and look to Him to guide and direct us, wherever and whenever."

"Your faith seems so strong. I hope I am like you, as I grow older."

"We all go through our ups and downs. The spiritual people call them trials and testings, but to me they are just ups and downs. The Bible tells us that we will be tested; it doesn't say 'if,' it says 'when.' So, I figure it's just another bump in the road, God tests and corrects us, to guide us where He wants us to go, both physically and spiritually. Story after story in the Bible tells us of God's testing and correction. It is comforting to me to know that God loves me enough to consider me one of His own, one of His children. "

"You and George are a great example to me. I have watched you since I came to Spokane; you are a great Christian couple. How did you meet?"

"Thank you, dear, we try to walk out our faith. Words are empty, unless they are joined by action. We truly try to be like Jesus, and though we are not always successful, the old adage, "You may be the only Jesus some people will ever see," is very true. We try really hard to reflect His light, His love to everyone around us."

"As to how we met . . . Well, the story really begins when I was young, long before I met George, I prayed for him. I asked God to send someone into my life that would love me, like Jesus loved me. I think I was about eight or nine. When I was sixteen, George and I met at a youth convention, and I think I loved him at first sight. He noticed me, only because I sang a solo at the convention. He was with his girlfriend," she said, giving Janie a crooked smile. "We attended churches in neighboring cities, so I did not see him often. Several weeks after the conference, a gathering was planned for the area churches, and I finally saw him again. This time I caught his eye; he did not have a girlfriend anymore. From that time on, we saw each other often. We were young, but those who God brings together stay together, especially if they give their heart to God first. We got married right after we graduated from high school." She smiled at the memory.

"We have been truly blessed through the years. It has not always been easy, but we determined right from the start that divorce was not an option, so we worked through the rough times. Besides, George spoils me, and I try doing the same for him; he and Jesus are my best friends."

"How long have you been married?" Janie asked.

"Nearly thirty-five years. Paul was born five years after we were married, then Mary two and a half years later. Jack was our surprise; he was born a year and a half after Mary. They are wonderful children, and I couldn't be more proud of them. But grandchildren, now that's the real joy in life; we are very excited about Mary's little one, and I claimed Peter as one, too, even though he is actually our grand-nephew. We are hopeful that Paul and Jack will marry soon and provide us with even more." The last comment was said with a twinkle in her eye and a hopeful look at Janie.

Not knowing what to say, Janie let the comment pass. She knew they all were rooting for a relationship to develop between her and Paul, but it was too soon to speculate what the future would hold. There were uncertain times ahead, and the need for the Sanctuary proved that. However, she really liked Paul and knew her feelings could grow quickly, if she allowed them to.

"George said you both received the vision from God," Janie said, changing the subject.

"Yes, though we didn't know it right away. We both spent a lot of hours thinking and praying, before we shared with one another. We had a lot of doubt, but God brought people to confirm the vision and encourage us. There were things we needed to learn, too." She stopped, thinking, and then continued. "We needed to learn to communicate better. You see, even though we have been married for a long time, we assume we know what the other one is thinking sometimes. That got us into trouble. We had a decision to make, and after talking about it, we came away really not understanding the other's point of view. The decision was made, and afterward, we realized each of us was trying to please the other and had not listened to God. George was trying to please me, I was trying to let him make the final decision, and we missed God. We knew that had to change. We agreed to share completely every thought, feeling, and understanding of what we thought the other was thinking and not assume we understood, already. In addition, we agreed to share what we thought God was saying, and we agreed never to do something, when we felt God was saying 'no,' or even 'maybe.' It has made all the difference."

"Thank you for sharing that with me. I hope someday to have a relationship like you and George."

"You will dear, I am sure you will," Elizabeth said smiling.

Janie turned her attention back out the window. She was looking to see if anything looked familiar. Suddenly, they turned off the main road and down a one-lane, dirt road. It looked as though it had been graded recently. There were piles of trees stacked on the side of the road every one or two hundred yards that had been taken down to make way for the road. They drove over a small rise, and Janie caught her breath; there was the valley, directly ahead of her. The mountains surrounding the valley were just as she saw them in her dreams, even down to the sheer cliff wall in the mountain to the east.

"This is it," Janie said in wonder. "Just up ahead is the creek, and the lake is around the next bend." When they reached the lake, they stopped the cars and got out. Janie was awestruck. "Over there is where the barn was, with a bunkhouse a few hundred yards to the north." Turning to the north, she said, "All the rest of the housing is in the north end of the valley." Janie began walking through the meadow toward the area she indicated. "Over there is the hydro generator in the creek; up on the mountainside are the two wind generators." Everyone followed, watched, and listened, as she pointed and talked as she looked around. "The chicken coop is there, not far from the barn and paddocks." Excitement filled her voice, and those who walked silently behind felt her excitement and shared it. As the valley came alive in her mind, the others could see it in their minds, also, as she painted the picture with words. In those shared moments, all the doubts that they were doing as God directed died in the flame of excitement and awe. Many times in the previous months they had occasionally had doubts, as to whether God was directing them. All the doubts and fears of ridicule faded, as the reality of the Sanctuary grew in their minds and hearts.

They spent the entire day walking around the valley, becoming familiarized with the lay of the land. Each carried the original file notes Janie had shared with them, and they made their own notes, adding things, here and there, that would make life easier in a mountain retreat. Hours from any main city, they would have to be self-reliant. They realized that running to the store for the things they needed would not be an easy trip, nor a trip that would be made often. They understood that when the times of despair and violence came, they needed to keep this place a secret. All work done by outsiders, which included concrete, well drilling, and excavating, would be done in the first few months. After those things were completed, all work would be done only by those who would live at the Sanctuary, or by those who could be completely trusted to keep the place a secret.

Several hours later, Paul found Janie, sitting under a tree next to the lake. She held a paper plate with the remnants of a late picnic lunch. "Is it everything you remembered from your dreams?"

"Oh, yes and more. Can you feel it? The presence of the Lord, I mean?"

Paul sat quietly for a few moments. "Actually, I can. It's peacefulness, a calm reassuring peacefulness." He looked at her with a wondering smile. "I have known Jesus for a long time, and this is the first time I can say, without a doubt, I can feel His presence. I mean, I have felt Him in church, or in a great worship service, but it is almost like He would be sitting right next to me, if I turned around."

"Yes, it is wonderful, isn't it?" They were quiet for a long while, just looking around, listening to the quiet of the valley. Once in a while, they would hear the soft murmurings of the others visiting and walking around the valley, otherwise it was like they were alone in the world. The birds fluttered here and there, singing to one another, the soft music of the trees drifted on the wind, chipmunks chattered at one another, and honey bees buzzed from plant to plant, collecting their nectar.

Paul happened to look toward Janie, as a look of deep sadness crossed her face, "What is wrong?"

Janie turned toward him. "I was just thinking about the reason for this sanctuary and all the lost and dying people in the world. It makes me sad that God is preparing this place for His children, a place of safety, while so many will die in their sins."

"There will be other sanctuaries, you know. Dad has met others who God has directed to do the same thing."

"What about all the rest, those who do not know the Lord? I know God is probably leading others to establish sanctuaries, havens and the like, but the lost will remain lost, with no one to minister to them and lead them to Christ."

"God can speak to people any time and any place; they only have to listen. And I believe there will be those God asks to remain behind. They will stay and minister, until the end, and we can support them with food and prayer from here."

"But how many will listen? So many Christians go to church, and claim to have accepted the Lord, but they do not listen when He talks to them. Though, I do understand that it is difficult to always know when God is speaking to *me*. I sometimes wonder when my thoughts are just my wishful thinking—or Satan trying to deceive me. Until you told me about the Sanctuary God directed your parents to build, I thought I might have had a loose screw, or something like that. Sometimes, I just wish God would speak in an audible voice. I know the Israelites were afraid when they heard God speak, but I like to think I would treasure hearing Him. At least I would know it was from Him and not just me."

"I understand entirely." Paul noticed that the others were heading for the vehicles. "We have to have faith that those God calls will respond. As for the lost, all we can do is share what we know, for as long as we can. Then we have to leave the rest to God. I think the others are getting ready to go."

"I really do not want to leave. I feel like I will be leaving Jesus behind, yet I know in my head, He is always with me."

"I know what you mean," Paul said, as he stood and reached a hand out to help her up. Janie took the offered hand and rose. Instead of dropping her hand, Paul joined elbows and intertwined fingers with her. Janie looked down at their joined hands, and smiled into his smiling face and said nothing more. They walked in silence, drinking in the beauty of the valley, while making their way back to the cars.

As they drove out of the valley, Janie felt a deep overwhelming sadness. It was like leaving a part of her behind. There was silence in the car on the way back; each was lost in his or her own thoughts and prayers. Others were struggling with the same sense of leaving a beloved home, just like Janie and Paul.

The sun was setting when they reached the hotel, nearly fifty miles from the Sanctuary land. They had rooms reserved, and everyone headed to their rooms, immediately. Janie had a room by herself, for which she was grateful. She needed time to deal with her thoughts and feeling about the Sanctuary. Janie knew that she would be moving to the Sanctuary with the others, so she kept reminding herself that it would be her permanent home soon, and peace filled her heart.

"Lord Jesus, it is a beautiful valley. It will make a wonderful place to live. I know it will be hard work, harder than I have ever worked before. But I know working side by side with other believers will be fulfilling. I have appreciated being born in this time in history because I like my creature comforts. I like washers, dryers, microwaves and all the other modern appliances. But I know we will have to make do with less. We will not be able to go to the store and pick up canned goods and fast foods. I know we will have to raise our own meat—or hunt. Then we will have to butcher and package the meat. We will have to grow, harvest, and can, or dry, our fruits and vegetables. We will have to make our own bread and so many other things we take for granite. It will be a different kind of life than we are used to. But, somehow, I am okay with

that. I know we will be living off grid, but at least we will have electricity. I know we might have to limit what we do, and I am sure we will have to get used to drying our clothes on a line outside, but that's okay too. Life will be harder in some ways, but it will be simpler, too.

One of the good changes I see is the bonds between people. We will be bound, not only by our ties to You, but we will be relying on each other to work together for the good of all. Lord, be with us, as we develop the plans to make everything come together for the Sanctuary. Guide and direct us every step of the way; thank You, Jesus, for Your love and care, each and every day."

The next day, after a light breakfast, they all went to the local church for worship. Their group nearly doubled the small gathering of believers that were worshiping in the small, country church. The worship was not like the modern, fast-paced worship choruses that they usually worshiped with, but the old-time hymns. It was a nice change from the repetitive phrases of today's music. The piano was out of tune, and the leader had a beat of his own, yet you could feel the presence of God, and it was wonderful!

The sermon, given by a pastor of undetermined age, spoke of the end times and the difficulties that people will face. It was almost as if he knew why they were visiting there that Sunday. He spoke of the great falling away of believers, deceived by the great deceiver, Satan. He also shared that, in his opinion, those who would fall away were those who felt God abandoned them when times become hard. He felt they would be those who looked for the goodness of God without any trial, tribulation or persecution—people from 'feel good churches.' He spoke of preparing for difficulties and banding together to help one another.

"As believers, we must give a helping hand to other believers. Sure, we should help unbelievers and try to share the gospel with them, but our brothers and sisters in the Lord need to be our first priority. We must reach out, share, and protect one another, when the time of the evil one comes. Many will be deceived, many will be lost, and we cannot help everyone. Use caution when dealing with people you do not know, even those you do know. Keep your eyes on Jesus, listen to His voice in the wilderness, and walk by faith—not by sight."

The members of their group exchanged glances throughout the service, amazed and awed that God would use this man to speak confirmation to them. If there were any remaining doubts about the Sanctuary, none remained now. After the service, the group was invited to a pot-luck dinner. "We are very pleased you were able to join us this morning. We hope you enjoyed the service. We have plenty of food and would like you to join us downstairs in the fellowship hall," the pastor said, after the closing hymn.

The pastor approached George after the service and introduced himself. "I am Phillip Samuels. I am glad your group was able to join us today. We really would like you to join us for our pot-luck," he repeated with a broad smile. "Our women put on quite a feed; we always plan on extra people. Mabel, my wife, said she was sure we would have extras today and sure enough, here you are. We'd be mighty blessed if you would all stay." George liked this pleasant pastor and wanted to get to know him better, so he decided for the group. He had seen several nods, as he looked at them right after the announcement. So, they would stay for the pot-luck, understanding their hosts would be disappointed, if they did not stay for lunch. Besides, he felt in his spirit that God was leading him to this brother in the Lord.

"Thank you, Pastor. We would be pleased to stay."

After going downstairs, listening to the blessing, and filling their plates, they all enjoyed the lively conversations of the local people. "That was a good message you gave this morning Pastor. It was confirmation for a project we are working on," George said, as he finished his lunch.

"The good Lord has been telling me to get ready for a long time. In fact, several years ago God gave Mabel a vision—a dream. In the dream, she saw us helping people who were fleeing persecution in northern areas. We were to take them to a place of safety. God shared with me later that He would send to us those He was giving the responsibility of developing the safe haven. I believe it is you and your group." He smiled a knowing look. George said nothing but smiled and gave him a quick nod.

"Anyway, shortly after that dream, we were led here to pastor this church. After we arrived, Mabel has seen us freeing other believers, those who have been put in concentration or detention camps. We believe there will come a time when Christians are blamed for all kinds of things around the country; whether it is true or not will not matter. There will be no trials; if you refuse to deny Jesus, they will cart you away. I have been expecting the end times my whole life, but since her visions or dreams, we are certain we will see them, or at least some very difficult times. My flock here is a simple people; they either grew up here, or they came here to get peace and quiet. But none of us are going to have it easy, as times grow more and more difficult. I would be derelict in my duties, if I did not warn them to get ready—both in spirit and in reality."

"Share with him; he is one of My beloved children. You will be working closely with him in the days ahead," George heard clearly in his spirit.

"That is very interesting; you are right. We have been given the vision of a sanctuary. We are currently making plans for the ranch, or retreat, whatever you might want to call it. We plan to be very careful who we allow to come. There has been a lot of discussion about who will be invited and who will not. Some want just believers, others want to include unbelieving spouses, but whatever is decided, it is important there be harmony at the Sanctuary. We will be completely off grid, self-sufficient, and secret. Only a select few will know the location; all others will be led in, blindfolded."

"That would be wise. I trust we will be working together a lot in the days ahead, brother," Pastor Phil said solemnly.

There was no surprise, just a quiet acceptance. Each in the Kingdom of God had their responsibilities. All those listening to the conversation knew they would be working with these believers. They understood they had a role, and Pastor Phil had his role. All would have to work together, if they were going to survive the long and difficult days ahead.

CHAPTER 12

Monday morning found a very fervent group meeting in the conference room of Hope Foundation. The initial awe was replaced by an excited energy. Everyone was ready to get started. The room was alive with conversations of twos and threes around the room. When George entered several minutes later, the group quieted immediately and took their seats, looking toward him expectantly.

"Let's start this meeting in prayer, shall we?" George said to the group.

"*Our Heavenly Father, holy is Your name. Thy kingdom come, Thy will be done on earth, in our country and in our lives, as it is in heaven. Give us this day Your knowledge and wisdom that we need to do Your work ahead. We ask You to forgive us, as we forgive others. Lead us in the direction You would have us go and deliver us from all evil, for You are our power, our strength, and our life, forever and ever.*"

We come to You in excited expectation of doing Your will. You are worthy of our love and devotion in that You loved us first and called us to be Your children. Guide us and direct us, quicken our understanding and help us each to do the tasks necessary to complete this project in a timely fashion. We are Your willing and devoted servants. We are honored and privileged to do Your will. We love You. Thank You, Jesus, for Your saving grace; we work for Your honor and glory. Amen." A chorus of amens followed, and with that, they went to work.

"Alright people, this is a big project, and everyone will have a lot to do in the next twelve months. Our target date to move to the ranch is September 1st. So, we have one year to build the roads, the buildings, and get the power going. We will be breaking up into groups to work on each area. Curt, you will be in charge of anything electrical, of course. Wind, hydro, solar, and hydrogen are the sources we will pursue. Jake, I need you to take on the job of excavating and septic systems. We want to explore the idea of capturing the methane gas from the septic system, so you will need to research that, also. I know you do not know a lot about any of that but work with Paul to get a general idea, and then run with it. We need the road widened and the building sites cleared. I want an additional pond for the animals on the south end of the valley. When you are finished with that, you will be helping Paul.

"Paul will be in charge of building. The first to go up is the main lodge, and then we will focus on the meeting hall, warehouse, workshop and barn. After that, several small cabins and living quarters will be built. However, in phase one, I want all the concrete poured for all buildings, while we are pouring the foundation for the lodge because, once those people are gone, they will not be coming back. If we need to pour any more concrete, we will be doing it ourselves. We do not want everyone and their brother knowing about our location and what we are doing. As far as anyone knows, we are building a retreat for the foundation. That's basically what it is, only people will be staying for a while, so it will not be dishonest to tell people that. I want first drafts of the building plans within one month. Is that doable?" At Paul's nod, George continued. "Sherry and Martin, I want a complete medical room, equipped with everything you will need for caring for any injury or illness. You know what you need. Be sure to check with Jack, since he will be working with you.

"Jill, Mary, and Janie, I want several lists from you: one list for perishable foods that we will need seeds, or nursery stock for, and one list for imperishable food we will need for a stay of seven years or more. I don't know if this is the end times, but we know there will be hard times. I want to be prepared for whatever comes our way. Also, list all non-food items that we will need, like toothpaste, toilet paper and the like. Any other things you think are important add to the list. I want that list in ninety days, complete with manufacturers and shipping information. Everything will then be shipped to our current warehouse and later sent to the Sanctuary.

"Elizabeth and I will work on the red tape, making sure all the permits are applied for and maintained. If you think of something we have forgotten, we will be meeting together monthly, until April, and then we will be meeting weekly from then on. We do not want to overlook anything. Anyone have questions or comments?" He looked around the room at those present; he had faith in each and every one, and he knew they would do their best. When no one spoke up, he continued. "Remember this is God's project; be sure to enlist His help. We do not want to leave Him out of His own project. We will be meeting often for prayer, in fact, Wednesday mornings, whoever can meet for prayer can come here at eight thirty in the morning. We need God more now than ever; let's not forget that.

"Oh, and by the way, I have been in touch with Brian and Cherie. They have decided to return to the United States. They are bringing several of the Kenyan children with them. They will be working with our team in Tennessee to establish a ranch there. That will give us a place for the children at the home as well."

"I am so glad, Dad. I was a bit concerned about them and the children back east. I am glad you thought of it." Mary said smiling and relieved.

Jake asked, "We will be using the original plans Janie gave us, right?"

"Yes, though we can make some changes, if we find it necessary. Nothing is in stone at this point. Ok, family let's build a sanctuary ranch." Everyone began gathering their things and headed for the door, when George remembered something, "Oh, Janie, didn't you say your parents owned a greenhouse?"

Janie turned back to George, "Yes, sir; they are retired now, but they operated a greenhouse for several years."

"Please contact them and get names of greenhouse manufacturers. I would like two complete greenhouses to grow starter plants for spring plantings, since our winters are so short. We can also grow vegetables into the fall, until it takes too much to heat the greenhouses, and we can restart them in the early spring."

"Yes, sir."

"What's with this 'sir' stuff?" George asked with a smile.

"I don't know. Maybe because you're my boss, but more importantly, you are the spiritual leader for the Sanctuary. That puts you in a special place, like Moses, or something."

"I am no Moses, but I understand what you mean. Please, go back to calling me George."

"Okay, George," Janie said with a smile. George patted her arm and returned her smile.

"I think we should each make a list, and then we can compare notes," Jill said, speaking over lunch later with Janie and Mary. "That way we can make sure we aren't missing anything."

"That makes sense, but let's divide it up into divisions and subdivisions, like household things with subdivisions, like cleaning supplies, paper goods and the like. Others would be spare pots and pans, plates, silverware . . . things like that. Then we can go to personal items, like shampoo, toothpaste, and shaving cream. Should we forego the makeup?"

"NO!" Janie and Mary chorused together, then laughed together with Jill.

"Okay, then we will streamline them, so we will not have too many choices, but that should be okay."

"That's fine, but I think I will stock up on my own, too. In fact, I think I am going to stock up on *all* my favorites— clothes, makeup, face cream, hand lotion, and anything else that would be hard to get," Janie said. The others nodded in full agreement. "Alright" she quipped, taking a sip of her hot tea, as she went over her notes. "You know, it would be so much easier if we owned a store, then it wouldn't look so strange for us to order so much stuff."

Jill and Mary exchanged looks. "That's a great idea. I will talk with Dad about it this afternoon. I think it would be good, if it was closer to the Sanctuary, maybe in that little town we stayed in on our way home," Mary said.

"They already had a small general store and gas station. We wouldn't want to hurt their business, since we really aren't interested in making money," Janie said thoughtfully.

"Well, I will talk with Dad and let him decide whether it's a good idea and where it should be—if he thinks it would be good."

They continued to talk for another half hour, as they finished their lunches. As they were preparing to leave, the conversation turned to Janie and Paul, a topic Janie was not ready to talk about, yet.

"We noticed that you and Paul were kind of cozy this weekend. Anything we should know about?" Jill asked smiling.

"Jill, you know we have only known each other a few days, but I really like Paul. We will just wait and see." She hesitated and then added, "Promise me, no more matchmaking?"

"Okay," Jill said reluctantly.

"That didn't sound too sincere; please promise."

"I promise I will not try to do any more matchmaking between you and Paul." Jill crossed her heart with an "x."

"And you?" Janie turned to Mary, "Do you promise, also?"

"I was hoping you would forget to ask me; alright, I promise."

"Thank you. I know you both love Paul, but . . . "

Mary interrupted her, "And we love you. We think you would make a perfect couple. We just want you both to find what we have." Mary glanced at Jill.

"I love you both, too," Janie reached over and, taking each of their hands, gave them a squeeze, "but we need time to get to know each other, and there is so much going on. Let's just let things develop at their own speed." Janie rose and began putting on her coat. "I still have normal duties at the foundation and have a meeting this afternoon, so I need to get moving. Can we meet for lunch on Friday? Does that give you time to get your lists together?"

"That will work for me," Jill said. "I really need to get as much done in the next few months as possible because I will not have much time, after this baby comes. My Mom wants to take Peter home Thursday and bring him back Saturday morning, so it will work for me."

"I have a doctor's appointment at ten, but I should be done by, say, one o'clock," Mary added.

"Okay, it's a date. We will meet here? At one o'clock," Janie replied.

"That will work."

"Great. See you guys later," Janie said, as she turned and walked toward the door. She waved as she walked out.

"No matchmaking, and she made us promise. Bummer!" Jill pouted.

"Yes, but my Dad would really like to see them together," Mary said, smiling gleefully. "I don't think he will pass up any opportunities to throw them together during the next few months. That's why I didn't hesitate when I promised. We don't have to matchmake; Dad will do it for us." They each exchanged a conspiratorial smile.

CHAPTER 13

MARY KNOCKED ON THE door to her father's office and poked her head in. Seeing her father was on the phone, she started to leave, when he said, "Hang on Jim. Come on in Mary; I will be right with you."

Quietly entering, Mary sat across from her Dad. She watched him, as he continued his conversation. She remembered sitting on his lap as a little girl. He would wrap his arms around her and hold her tight. She always knew he loved her; her Mom did too. They always had time for her, talked with her, and listened to her childish dreams. Love swelled in her heart, as she watched him. He and her mother had taught her about Jesus as a little girl. They had not always gone to church, something she knew they regretted later, but she had seen Jesus in them from an early age. It wasn't until she went to college that she understood that Jesus made the difference in their lives.

Mary had been at college for only a week, when she realized how protected she had been as a child. College had been a nightmare, at first. She had a few close friends, but most people were unfriendly, selfish and self-focused. For many students, learning was secondary to partying. Then there were the teachers and professors, who tried to fill her head with their ideas on religion. Most believed Christianity was a myth—or a crutch that weak people used to get through life. They tried to convince her that the personal rights of an individual were not as important as those of society at large.

Many of her professors believed that, if everyone is equal, they should have all their basic needs taken care of, as if they were rights. Therefore, the government should provide for everyone, equally. They taught it was the responsibility of the society, or of the government, to create a level playing field, taking from those who had—those who worked hard—and giving to those who did not have. It sounded so good to the carnal mind: spread the wealth and give to the poor and unfortunate. However, the idea that we can eradicate poverty, by spreading the wealth, is a lie. It sounds good, but, the reality is, many who are poor are poor because they spend their money unwisely. There are others who are only willing to work the bare minimum, and there are those who are lazy and unwilling to work at all. Others spend their money on every get-rich-quick scheme that comes along, only to find that these schemes do not pan out, or the only one getting rich is the one promoting the scheme.

Mary understood it is important to help the sick, or injured, until they can take care of themselves, but, for her, this did not include those who fried their brains on drugs voluntarily. The Bible teaches that the poor will always be with us. We are to help the widows and orphans, but all other able-bodied people need to work, in order to eat. She believed that people got satisfaction and worth from a job well done. Mary felt that when people get continuous handouts they become ungrateful and sometimes demanding, wanting more and more, at the expense of others. She knew many would call her heartless, but she knew, as well, that there are consequences in this life for our actions and choices.

Mary knew most of her college professors did not acknowledge the authority of the Bible, so it was no wonder they had it all wrong. In fact, most of them believed that if you believe the Bible you are ignorant, simpleminded, or weak. However, she believed the Bible, and she knew that true wisdom, knowledge and understanding comes from God alone. She believed that those who do not believe in God look to their own wisdom, or to worldly wisdom, both products of man's twisted and perverted view of the world. She knew the world's view is simply man doing things his own way, deciding what is right or wrong, while looking for what is really important in life, and ultimately finding it everywhere *but* in God. It was true rebellion against God, Jesus, and the Holy Spirit. This was sad and unfortunate but very true.

Now several years later, Mary realized that all the propaganda many taught in school was garbage. The education she received in college was only man trying to teach man what to think and believe. It was their way of circumventing God, so that they could justify their choice not to believe in God and Jesus. It was a way to help them feel good about their decision. However, it was wrong to force their beliefs on others, or to belittle those who disagreed with them. She chuckled to herself. Some of her professors said Christians were intolerant. But she had found them to be the intolerant ones. It was they who did not want to listen to another view and wanted to force their view on others. They accused Christians of trying to shove their faith down other people's throats, but Mary knew true believers accepted that each person has free will to choose, and each person can choose to not believe in Jesus. In fact, a person could choose to go to hell because Jesus will not force anyone to accept him as Savior. It was as simple, or as complex, as that.

Sadly, her professors did everything they could to change her thinking, or prove her wrong. She remembered one who gave her a very poor grade because she refused to change her beliefs to match his. Talk about intolerant. She had to remind herself that there were some good professors, the ones she believed were closet Christians. They hid their faith to avoid ridicule. And there were those like Mr. Addison, who allowed her to share her opinions and listened to her careful defense of her faith, yet made it clear he would not change his opinion that there was no God. He had even given her an A in his class. These teachers were the exceptions—not the rule.

She knew she should have chosen a Christian university, but she knew fighting for her faith had made her stronger and given her the skills to defend her beliefs. Sadness filled her, as she thought about several friends who had turned away from their faith, as a result of listening to these false teachers. There were many casualties among her classmates, those who believed the lies and were now just as intolerant as their teachers and professors. Unfortunately, now they were lost in their sins in an uncaring, lost world.

"Sorry that took so long sweetie," George said, bringing Mary back from her musings.

"That's okay, Dad; did you get everything settled down?" The call had been from a missionary in South American, who was having problems with a shipment of supplies.

"Yes, Jim was just a bit impatient; anyway, what's up?"

"I had lunch with Jill and Janie. We decided how to approach our part of the project. Anyway, Janie said it would be nice if we had a store in the area, then we could bring in supplies without it drawing attention. What do you think?"

"Hmmm . . . It might be a possibility, but for now, let's just figure on bringing everything here to our warehouse, and then we can move it with our own truck and trailer to the Sanctuary. I will run it by some of the others and see what they think. But my gut feeling is that we don't want to build a store, or buy one, only to abandon it later."

"Yes, we thought of that, too. Anyway, I think we have a good start." She stood. "Well, I know you are busy, so I will let you get back to it. Bye, Dad." Mary rose and headed for the door.

"Boy that was quite a wait for such a short conversation," George said chuckling. "Bye, honey."

"I know, but I have some thoughts I want to write down before I forget. See you later."

George watched his daughter walk out the door. He was grateful that all his children were on board with the project. He knew it was God's grace in his life that allowed them all to believe in Jesus and live the Christian life.

"Thank You, Father. My children are one of the greatest blessings in my life. I thank You that all three accept, know, and love You." The sudden knock on the door caused George to look up.

"I have the plans you asked for," Paul said, standing in the open doorway to his father's office.

"Already?" George looked up at his son. "Everyone's right on top of things. Mary just left, and the girls have a good start, too."

"I started working on them right after I first read the files. Janie shared her thoughts last weekend, and I filled in the blanks. Then I contacted Lucas, and we brainstormed for a while. We added an underground cellar to the fellowship hall kitchen. We need a place to store the vegetables we grow, where they will not spoil, something like an old root cellar. In addition, we need a place of safety, should marauders come around." Paul handed the rolled plans to his father and took a seat across from him.

"Good idea." George unrolled the papers and began a careful perusal of them. "I see you show the pig pens, chicken coop and horse paddocks. Do they need to be that big?"

"I believe it is better a little too big, with room to grow, than too small and unable to accommodate our needs. As for the other buildings, we can always build another rooming house, or more cabins, and use the same plans again. I plan to check out the cost of a portable mill to cut our own logs. And I think we can buy a used concrete mixer, too."

"You don't plan on cutting all our own two by fours do you?"

"No, the original buildings will all be done with lumber from the lumber yard Pastor Phil told me about. But a portable mill is not too expensive, and I think it will come in handy later on, if we need to expand further."

"Sounds like a reasonable plan." Turning pages, George remarked, "You decided to put the workshop and warehouse in the same building?"

"We could separate them, but I think this will work out. With our winters, we wouldn't have to go out into the weather to get what we need, when we are working on something. Besides, it will be easier figuring the heating system. I do not show it on the plans, but I want to put a full basement under the warehouse. I think it would be a good place to store guns, reloaders, and whatever else we need along those lines. I believe a tunnel from the meeting hall to the basement might be a good idea, too. What do you think?"

"The basement is an excellent idea; I think it would be a good idea to have a fireproof safe to house guns and money, come to think of it. As for tunnels, why not have an underground tunnel to the barn, also. That way, we would not have to fight the winter weather to check on and feed the livestock."

"Good idea, also. We could have a tunnel system from several of the buildings. It can also serve as an escape route, if we ever need it," Paul added, thinking about the possible uses of a tunnel system. "The only problem would be if the buildings are too far apart."

They went through the plans, going over each one and making notes on changes or additions. "I like them," George said, when they were finished. "I think I will send them to your cousin in Canada and have her draw them up, professionally. But please, have your mother look at them first. I know she mentioned a couple things she wanted. I always remember what my father told me, 'Happy wife, happy life.'" He smiled broadly at his son, who then returned his smile.

"Okay, I will have Mom take a look, and then make the changes and have them ready to send next week. Have you talked with Lori?"

"Yes, I called her early this morning; she is on board. I think she and Corey will be coming, but I'm not sure. His mother is elderly, and Lori's not sure if she will come with them. If she won't, she doesn't know if Corey will leave her." Lori had married a Christian man she met at a Christian conference, and they had moved to Canada several years before. They lived on a ranch, raising cattle and wheat. "Corey would be a great asset to the Sanctuary Ranch; his experience with ranching would really help us."

"I hope they work things out. I really would like to see them both come. How is everyone else coming along?"

"Great. The girls came up with the idea of buying a store, so that we will not draw attention to ourselves by all the merchandise we will be purchasing. What do you think of the idea?"

"I don't think it makes much sense to buy something, only to sell it in a few months, do you?"

"That was my thought, too, but I can see where it would have merit, if times were different. I think it will be best to have everything warehoused here and moved later, when the Sanctuary warehouse is finished. I would like to make sure it is done and the goods moved, long before the snow flies next fall."

"I think that is doable."

"Have you and Janie spent any time together this week?"

"No, she had Bible studies Tuesday, and she babysits for her neighbor on Wednesday, so they can attend a new believer's class. Tonight was the first available night, but I decided to ask her out for our first date this Saturday evening. She accepted, and I plan to take her to dinner and a movie."

"Good. You already know your mother and I like that young lady. We sure would like to welcome her as a member of the family." At Paul's look of patient amusement, he changed the subject. "Jack is coming home for Christmas this year."

"Excellent. I haven't seen him since spring. It will be good to see him."

"He is bringing a young lady."

"Really. He didn't say anything about anyone special, when I spoke with him last week."

"Her name is Rose; he met her a few weeks ago, when the computers crashed at the hospital. She came to fix them; Jack is smitten with her."

"Smitten; Dad, that really shows your age," Paul said with a chuckle. "Although, I used that word when I was thinking about Janie, didn't I?" he thought smiling.

"Maybe it does, but that about sizes it up. They went out that night, and the way it sounds, they are pretty serious. As busy as he is, he is making time to see Rose."

"I hope she is a believer. I would hate for Jack to fall like I did, when I was in school, only to find out she isn't a believer."

"She is. In fact, she invited him to her church on the first day they met. That was their first date, the way he tells it. They went to an evening service, then out to dinner afterwards. He liked her church, and you know how picky he can be. He wants a church that has great worship, an interesting, yet Biblically sound, pastor, and activities, so you can be involved."

"Even though he doesn't have much time for being involved," Paul said smiling.

"Yes, well, he makes time for the things he feels are important, and church is important to him. I think Rose is becoming very important to him, too. Maybe we can have two weddings before we move to the Sanctuary."

"Dad, don't rush us. I want to make sure Janie is the right one, the one God has for me. Jack needs to be sure, too."

"I know, but I can hope, can't I?"

"Yes, I guess you can, Dad." Paul smiled, as he left the room. As Paul left the room, George turned back to God.

"Heavenly Father, be with my boys. You know their hearts and their love for You. You also know the right young woman for each of them. The times ahead are going to be difficult, but sharing difficulties with another, sharing the burden, can make things more bearable. I love Janie. Elizabeth and I believe she is perfect for Paul. You know best though, so I look to You. Thank You for Your many blessings!" George finished praying and turned his attention back to the tasks at hand.

CHAPTER 14

JANIE HURRIED TO NEW Life Covenant Church to attend Bonnie and Nathan's renewal of their marriage vows. When they had invited her last week, she had been thrilled for them. She understood their desire to start fresh in a marriage before the Lord. She had seen the joy blossom between them and was happy for them. The changes she had seen in Bonnie were amazing. It was like a cloud that had been covering her had been lifted. Now, she radiated love, happiness, and completion. Janie knew it was the reflection of Jesus, shining through Bonnie to the world, and it was wonderful to see.

Entering, Janie heard voices and laughter in the room to her left, so she headed that way. Knocking on the door, she waited for the "come in" before entering. Janie found Bonnie looking radiant in her wedding gown. "Bonnie, you are beautiful."

Smiling, Bonnie came over and took Janie's hands. "I feel beautiful. When I was first married, I wore this dress, but I always had a nagging thought that, since I wasn't a virgin, I shouldn't be wearing white at all. But this time, I am clean, free from all sin, all doubt, and all reservations."

"Yes, you are. You are lovely; Nathan is a blessed man."

"Janie, I want you to meet Shelly, our pastor's wife. Shelly, this is the sister I told you about."

Janie smiled. "It is so nice to meet you at last. Bonnie has talked about you often."

"Bonnie has talked about you, too; I am so pleased to meet you, as well." A knock, then a voice, came, informing them it was time.

Janie took her seat in the front of the church. The wedding march began. Bonnie walked alone toward Nathan, who was standing at the front of the church. She had shared with Janie earlier in the week that, in her heart, Jesus was going to escort her down the aisle. There were only eight people in attendance, and Janie was somewhat surprised to see John and Nancy. The service was short, only the bride and groom exchanging their vows before God and loved ones. As the bride and groom turned to face those present, their joy, happiness, and contentment were shining brightly for all to see.

They made their way to the reception hall, where a small cake and punch were waiting. After Bonnie and Nathan cut the cake, the small group took seats around a decorated table. Janie started to take a seat across from the couple, when Bonnie drew her attention, motioning her to sit beside her.

Conversation was light and happy. Within a short time, people started to give their congratulations and then exited, leaving only Bonnie, Nathan, the pastor, his wife and Janie.

Nathan and the pastor and his wife were in a conversation about an upcoming work day, as Bonnie turned to Janie. "I guess you were surprised to see John and Nancy here," Bonnie commented.

"Not really because I know how close he and Nathan are."

"John and Nancy came over Sunday night. I was kind of surprised when John called. I knew Nathan spends a lot of time with John at the fire station, but they have never come over before. Anyway, I knew Nathan told him we were renewing our vows and why. I guess they have had several long talks, and one night Nathan shared with him everything that I had said about Nancy. I was really embarrassed when he told me that." She blushed slightly. "Anyway, I guess he went home and talked with Nancy, telling her everything Nathan said. I guess it didn't go over very well.

Nancy got mad. But several days later, she went to John and told him she wanted to come and see us. He didn't know what she wanted to say, but he agreed to bring her.

"I admit that I was not stoked to hear they were coming over. Anyway, when they got there, I could tell Nancy was upset. Luckily, she came right to the point; she asked us to forgive her. She said she had been a Christian for a really long time, and she did not realize how judgmental she had become. She shared that she didn't realize that her attitude was causing unbelievers to turn away from Christ. She admitted that, when John first told her, she got mad, but then the Holy Spirit started convicting her. She said she started really looking at herself and her attitudes. She didn't like what she saw. She said it took several days of praying, before she was ready to come and apologize and to ask our forgiveness."

Janie smiled. "Now, you have seen the Holy Spirit in action. This is what He does all the time. I have been taken to the woodshed by Him many times. It is not fun, but sometimes it is very necessary. The sign of a maturing Christian is their ability to hear the Holy Spirit and follow His direction, to accept His correction. In Nancy's case, she made a big step forward in her walk with the Lord. She accepted His correction, came to you to ask forgiveness, and now she will work to change. You and I should make a point of praying for her."

Bonnie nodded, thoughtfully. "I will; I guess I really should have apologized to her for thinking she was a religious snob."

"Well, next time you see her, if the Holy Spirit leads you in that direction, you can do that. But I wouldn't worry about it too much. Sad to say, it sounds like she really was a religious snob. Now, let's change the subject. You said Shelly and Pastor Frank were going to babysit for a couple of days. Where are you going?"

"Nathan won't tell me." Bonnie pouted, then she smiled, "But I don't really care."

"Well, have a wonderful time; I will see you next week." Janie hugged Bonnie and said her good-byes to the others. On her way out, she prayed for Bonnie and Nathan, then added Nancy and John to her prayer, too.

CHAPTER 15

Weeks passed in a blur of activity. Planning for the Sanctuary Ranch, as well as conducting the normal day-to-day running of Hope Foundation, filled the days for everyone. Janie and Paul had lunch several times a week and dinner on Fridays, or Saturdays. They shared their likes and dislikes, their hopes and dreams. Thanksgiving Day was spent at George and Elizabeth's home, along with the large, noisy family. Filled with laughter and love, Janie enjoyed herself, immensely. Now, Christmas was only a week away.

Winter had finally arrived in a blizzard of white. More snow fell than Spokane had seen in twenty years, nearly crippling the city. Janie had purchased some new snow boots in an effort to keep her feet warm. Now, she was seriously considering a new coat; hers seemed too short, when the winter wind blew against her legs. She wanted a coat that would reach her new boots. She hurried to the conference room, where the ladies would be working today.

Janie was looking over her paperwork, when Mary broke into her thoughts, as she came into the room, lightly rubbing her slightly rounded stomach, while announcing, "Christmas is one of my favorite times of the year. I am sorry you are going to miss meeting Jack and Rose."

"I am too, but I really need to spend Christmas with my family. They are looking forward to seeing me, and I am anxious to see them too. My parents are flying in from Phoenix. We are all looking forward to being together at my brother's house," Janie said. "It will be the first Christmas in four years that we have all been together. Paul asked me to stay until after the foundation Christmas party, so I will be here until then."

"Any special reason why?" Mary asked innocently. She had gone with Paul to look at engagement rings and wanted to know if Janie knew, or suspected, what he had planned. He had even shared the thought of letting Janie pick out her own ring, but she wasn't sure what he decided.

"Not that I know of. I think he just wanted me to be at the party. I will only be gone a week and a half. I want to see Franklin and Sarah while I am gone. I plan to fly back by way of Boise and spend two days with them."

"You are wearing the dress you bought, aren't you?"

"Yes; it is a lovely green, perfect for a Christmas dress," Janie answered.

"It is a beautiful dress. I am glad I talked you into going shopping with me. It was fun, and I simply didn't have a dress that would fit. Now, I do—and so do you," Mary added, as she patted her stomach again, smiling brightly. "You know I love being pregnant. I can be fat, and I have an excuse."

"You are not fat; you are a radiant mother-to-be," Janie corrected, laughing.

"Thank you. Jake thinks so, too," she said smiling. "I guess Jill is running late. While we are waiting, let's go over what we have, and she can catch up when she gets here. I fine-tuned the list of food items. Did you get the household items finished?"

"Yes." Janie exchanged lists with Mary, and they began going over them. They had decided to add some canned goods, such as tomato sauce, to the list enough to supplement the tomato sauce, vegetables, and fruits they would have after the first season's harvest and canning. Green beans, peas, corn, applesauce, peaches, pears and various kinds of soups were also on the list. "Since we are moving at the end of growing season, we need to cover the entire first winter and spring. We can't count on anything coming from the garden, until early summer. Fruit will be the hardest because it will take several years before the trees produce enough to harvest. Then there are the things that we will not be able to grow, or make ourselves. I think we can buy a lot of those things and use them, until they run out or they spoil. Oh, and I found some dried foods from a survival store that have a thirty-year shelf life. I put some of that on the list. Remember, we have to order enough canning jars and seals, too. I found some seals and rings that can be reused. Do you have a figure, yet, on what you think we will need?"

"Not yet but I think we need to plan on five to ten years anyway."

"Five to ten years. Isn't that a long time?"

"Not really. Think about it. If there is war, it could take a long time for the fighting to stop. If anything else happens, it might not take as long to normalize things, but the supply chains will take time to be reestablished. Any way you look at it, it will not be fixed overnight."

"I guess you are right. Okay, what are some of the other things you have on the order list?"

"They had corn, beans, peas, potatoes, fruits, tomato sauce, onions, celery, flour, and a bunch more. I figure we can order a few of everything and try their products over the next few months. The things we like, we will order more of. It can't hurt to get some things for when we have a crop failure."

"Good idea."

"So, back to the seals and rings. Did you come up with how many you think we should order?"

"Not yet. You know, I was thinking; why not buy some vegetables and fruits this fall and can them? It would give us a chance to practice and give us a better idea of the canning supplies we will need. That will help us come up with a more practical figure."

"That's a great idea. What do you have in mind?"

"Some of everything we plan to can or preserve in the future. We can purchase the vegetables and fruits we need at a farmers market."

"I think it is a good plan. Megan does some canning, and I know she makes strawberry jam. I will ask her to help with the project."

"I am sure she will; that's right up her alley. She finally agreed to move to the Ranch. I am so glad she is coming. She is like one of the family, and her kids are the best."

The door opened, and a very pregnant Jill entered. "Sorry, I am late. I don't waddle as fast as I used to." They all shared a smile, as Jill took off her coat and hung it on the coat tree in the corner. "Peter didn't want to take his nap. Mom was having a bit of trouble getting him to go down, so I stayed to help." She sat down with a sigh. "Except for the ride over here, this is the first time I have sat down all day."

"I think you are going to have that baby on the run," Janie observed.

"Could be. So, where are we?" They continued going over the lists each of them had worked on. They had nearly finished and were going to order everything after the New Year. They had paper towels, toilet paper, cleaning supplies of all kinds, including window cleaners, disinfectants, floor cleaners, mops with refills, brooms, bagless vacuums. Laundry detergent and fabric softeners were next on the list. They had stain removers and bleach, too. Rags for dusting and other cleaning items finished the list.

Moving on they had dishes, pots, pans, silverware, serving and stirring spoons, knives of all sizes and types, as well as measuring cups, bowls and other kitchen items listed in detail, including the number of each. They knew they would have all of the dishes that each of them had brought with them, but they didn't think it would be enough, as the Ranch residents grew in number. They went through each room in the main lodge, listing everything they needed, from sheets in various sizes to pillows and blankets. Once they moved to the Sanctuary, they knew they may not venture out for a long time, and they wanted to be prepared for any and every possible need. They remembered that during the forty years in the desert the Israelites clothes did not wear out, so they hoped God would help them in like manner. However, they did have bolts of cloth and thread on the list, also.

"How are you coming on the greenhouse information?" Jill asked Janie.

"Good. I have the name of two different kinds of houses and the cost. My Dad is looking into heating with wood stoves and will make a recommendation soon. Now, I am working on the seeds. I was going to ask you what you thought about the kinds of vegetables and varieties of each that we need. Do you have any favorites?"

"Well, Mom used to plant Roma tomatoes and some kind of cherry tomatoes. Aunt Sherry mentioned she liked Early Girls. Then we had summer squash, zucchini, pumpkins, carrots, lettuce . . . three different varieties, if I recall. There were red potatoes, both red and yellow onions, corn, beans, peas, and beets on the list. By the way, I really hate beets, so don't expect me to eat them." She smiled before continuing, "Cucumbers. Aren't there several different kinds?"

"I'll check, and I agree—beets are *not* on my list of edible vegetables, either. Anyway, I'll ask Mom which cucumbers are the most popular. Okay, I have the rest of those. Can you think of anything else?" Janie asked.

"Herbs. There are several herbs we will need. Chives, thyme, oregano, to name a few, but there are several others we will want. Most are perennials up here, so that is good. We only have to plant them once, and they come back, year after year."

"Gees, I use herbs all the time. Why did I forget them?" Janie asked of no one in particular.

"Because you have too much on your mind, that's why. Don't worry about it though; that's why we are working together. What you forget, we remember, and what we forget, you remember. Ask Megan what herbs she likes to cook with. Now, what about the fruit trees? What kinds do we need?" Jill asked.

"I have yellow and red apples, pears, peaches, plums, cherries, and walnut trees. Next, I have blackberries, boysenberries and strawberries, along with rhubarb. I wish we were going to keep the greenhouses going in the winter; I would get a few orange trees and put them in there. Mary and I were talking about them earlier. The only problem with the fruit trees is that it will take a few years before they are really producing. We decided that it would be a good idea to purchase fruits and vegetables and have a dry run next fall. That will give us a jump start on learning what to do. We can also purchase canned goods to fill out our needs," Janie told Jill. "How long do canned goods last, anyway?"

"I read somewhere that the cooler and darker the storage room the longer they last, but I'm not sure. I will take some time and look it up on the internet. Apricots . . . don't forget a few apricot trees. Oh, and I almost forgot. We don't want to order any seeds except heirloom seeds. We can harvest seeds from our crops each year and replant them the next. Hybrid seeds are sterile, so we do not want those at all."

"Right. Apricots and heirloom seeds only," Janie jotted these down and went over the lists several more times. "Light bulbs . . . We almost forgot light bulbs. They need to be LED lights but it wouldn't hurt to have a few others also. Oh, and batteries; they have to be the rechargeable kind," Janie exclaimed.

"What else is in a house that we may have overlooked?"

"Matches, disposable lighters . . . those kinds of things, and candles—though we can buy them, we should also find out how to make them," Jill said. "I think I will look that up on the internet. What about toilet paper, I don't want to have to use leaves; didn't they used to use corn cobs in the old days?" They grimaced at the thought.

"No corn cobs or leaves for me, either, thank you," Janie said seriously. "Speaking of the old days, I do not want to use rags that time of the month, so we must remember to order female supplies, also."

"I think I have brain freeze," Mary said, after they had been working for more than four hours. "Time for lunch. I can't think anymore, until I have food." Agreeing, the girls gathered their coats and purses and started toward the door. Seeing Elizabeth and Sherry visiting by the reception desk, Mary waved and called out, "We are going to lunch. You want to join us? We can get a table for five."

Elizabeth looked toward Sherry, who nodded her assent. "Sure, honey. Go ahead and get a table. We will be there in a few minutes. You're going to Charlie's, aren't you?"

"Yes, we will see you in a few minutes." The girls headed to the elevator.

"Honey, that's something we could use. I'll check into getting some honey bees," Mary said, thinking about bees, honey and whatever else they would need.

"That's a good idea. Let's not forget to write it down. We wouldn't want brain freeze to cheat us out of sweets," Jill commented. They shared a smile at the thought.

As they walked together toward the restaurant, Janie watched the cars and trucks that had stopped behind a stalled car that had its hood up. "You know something? We forgot parts for our cars, trucks, and tractors. We will need air filters, oil filters, fan belts and other things that I do not even begin to know. I think I will talk with my neighbor, Nathan. He knows a lot about cars and would know what we might need."

"Curt would know, too. He used to work on cars in high school. In fact, he almost went to school to become a mechanic. I will ask him, too," Jill said, as they came to the restaurant and entered. They found a table in the corner and claimed it by sitting down and making themselves comfortable. Elizabeth and Sherry arrived just as the waitress was taking their drink order.

Lunch was a spirited event, with laughter and friendly conversation. They stayed longer than usual; everyone was putting in long hours and needed the time for relaxation and diversion.

"I am looking forward to the party tomorrow," Mary said. "Megan planned everything this year. She is a whiz at putting together parties. When Jill had her first baby, Megan helped me with the baby shower, rather, she did most of the work, and I got the credit," she explained to Janie, who hadn't been around at that time. "No one had time to help her this Christmas, but she was in her element. She is a whiz in the kitchen and has volunteered to manage the kitchen at the Sanctuary. Dad already gave her his blessing; she is a wonderful cook."

"Then we need to ask her about herbs and anything else we might have forgotten," Janie reminded them.

"Right," Mary said, taking a sip of decaf coffee. "Oh, I didn't see coffee on any of the lists; please don't let us forget coffee and tea. Anyway, I will call her after the party and ask her to go over our lists with us. Why don't we ask her to join us after New Year's, at our first meeting in January?"

"That will work." Janie ran down her mental list, "No coffee. I am sorry. I guess, because I don't drink it, I left it off because tea *is* there; that's my drink of choice. Anyway, I am glad George didn't want me to head up the kitchen. I can cook, but it is not my favorite job," Janie commented. "I have been thinking about what I would like to do when we get there, but I haven't decided yet. The gardening and greenhouse work is something I know about, so that will probably be the ticket for me, but my parents are thinking about joining us, so that might be their job. Still, I need to get some books on seed collection. I also want to have some flowers. I think we can squeeze some flower seeds in the greenhouse, to liven things up, don't you think?"

"I think that would be a great idea," Elizabeth said. "I love spring and summer flowers, and I would miss them, if there weren't any. In fact, I think a few rose bushes and other flowering bushes and trees need to be added to the nursery list."

"Don't forget the maple trees for shade next to the buildings. We aren't going to have air conditioning because it takes too much electricity. The shade trees will be appreciated on hot days in the future. Besides, they are beautiful, both in the summer and fall," Sherry said.

"I agree; the Ranch is already a beautiful place, but flowers just add that special touch of something nice to an already wonderful setting," Mary added. The others all agreed, and the matter was settled.

"Funny how some people call the Sanctuary a ranch and others call it a sanctuary; I even heard someone call it a haven." Sherry observed.

"Well, all are right. It doesn't really matter what we call it; it's going to be home," Elizabeth said matter of fact. They all nodded. "You know, you girls need to spend some time picking Sue's brain about all of this. She and Jerry lived on a station in the Australian outback. I was visiting with her last time she and Jerry were here. They lived a very interesting life over there, and much of what they did would help us."

"They are the truck driver team, right?" Janie asked.

"Yes; they are wonderful people, and we are fortunate to have them working for us."

Janie grabbed her planner from her purse and wrote a note to herself to contact Sue. She had met her once, when they were making a delivery to the warehouse. She liked her very much.

"I hate to call an end to this wonderful visit, but I have a meeting this afternoon," Sherry said. "We are meeting with a medical supply rep in an hour or so."

"How is it going?" Jill asked.

"Great! We have set up so many clinics in the past year and a half that we know what we need, and Jack supplied us with his medical list two weeks ago. We already knew most of it, but Martin has his favorites and figured Jack would, too. This is our final meeting; everything will be ordered today." Everyone began to get up. "You gals don't need to leave just because I have to." Sherry paused. "I do have a question for you," she said, settling back into her seat and focusing on Mary and Jill. "What about birth control?"

"I guess we hadn't thought about that," Mary said, as she looked at Jill. "No, I guess we didn't. Can we get some birth control pills for the clinic? The more important question is, if we can get them for the clinic, how much will they let us have, and how long are they good for?"

"Well, there's always abstinence," Jill said. They all laughed, knowing the men in their family. Janie just smiled, not entirely understanding but getting the drift. She blushed slightly, but no one remarked on it.

"That's not realistic, though," Mary said thoughtfully. "God made sex to be a beautiful part of marriage. I enjoy being with my husband that way, so we will have to consider our options. I think I will do some study on natural methods, like the ones they used in the old days—before pills."

"Well, it is something we must look at. I will talk with Martin and Jack about our options," Sherry said matter of fact. "I really must go."

"I need to run, too," said Janie. "I still have foundation work I need to finish. The Sanctuary planning has taken most of my time, and I promised Robin that by tomorrow I would have a report she needs."

"I will see you tomorrow at the party then," Sherry said, as she left. They all left shortly thereafter, each going their own way.

CHAPTER 16

JANIE SAT, LOUNGING AGAINST one end of the sofa, and Paul sat at the other end, watching the ending credits of a movie a few hours later. "I heard you gals had lunch together today."

"Yes, your Mom and Aunt joined us. We had a grand time. It is so surprising that we all get along so well. I really think Jesus makes all the difference. We all know we are working toward a goal He has set before us, and so it makes it easier to give up on an idea, if others don't like it. Besides, usually they explain why they don't like it, and that is all it takes to see their reasoning. Only once have I thought that it was a decision I would not have made."

"What was it?"

"Actually, it had to do with building a separate building for the medical clinic. I think it should be close but not connected with the chapel. Martin thinks that they should be connected because, if someone is ill, people can go next door to the chapel to pray. I think that it would be nice to have a small, old-fashioned church with a bell tower. Everyone needs a place to go off by themselves, and I can see a garden in full color, surrounding a wonderful little chapel, down by the creek."

"Maybe we can have both."

"Really?" Janie turned to face him, "That would be wonderful. I have always thought . . . " she stopped abruptly and quickly turned back to the television.

Paul moved over next to her and whispered in her ear, "You have always thought what?"

"Oh, nothing really. This is such a silly movie. The airlines never let children fly without a parent checking them in and another picking them up." They had been watching *Sleepless in Seattle*.

Paul gently turned Janie's face, with soft pressure on her chin, to face him again. "You have always thought what?"

Sighing, she said, "I always thought it would be nice to be married in a small, old-fashioned chapel, like the one in that picture, with flowers everywhere." She pointed to the picture on the wall. It was a picture of a small, country chapel with a riot of flowers and shrubs surrounding it.

Paul smiled. "Sounds beautiful to me, so why don't I build it, and we can be married there the end of August? I love you Janie, and I would be honored, if you would be my wife."

Janie caught her breath. "I love you, too," She whispered. "But is it too soon? I mean, we haven't known each other very long."

"Honey, I am very sure. I have been praying for you long before I even met you. God knew you were the special person He has for me. If things do get as bad as we expect, I want you by my side. Besides, by the time the wedding rolls around, we will have known each other for a year."

"I have been praying, too; I would be honored to be your wife. A wedding at the Sanctuary Ranch chapel sounds wonderful to me." He kissed her tenderly, to seal their engagement.

"Is it alright to announce our engagement tomorrow at the party?" Paul asked.

"I would like to call my family first, and you can tell your parents. I would like to have their blessings first. Okay?"

"You're right. You are still under your father's spiritual authority, until you are my wife. It is only right that I ask him for his blessing. Would you like to call them now?"

Janie looked at her clock; it was already nine thirty. "They retire early, so they are probably in bed. We can call them tomorrow. I would like tonight just for us, okay?" He nodded and kissed her nose. "Can we meet for lunch and call them then?"

"That will work. I have a meeting with Dad at nine. I can ask Mom to join us for a few minutes. Can you meet me there, and we can talk to them together?"

"Okay." She reached over and pinched herself.

"Why did you do that?"

"Because I wanted to make sure I wasn't dreaming. I was attracted to you the first time your family spoke about you. There was a picture of you on the wall; I liked what I saw, but I was lost when you ran me over." She smiled, "I just needed time to really know you."

"I liked what I heard about you, also, but after I ran you over, I was too distracted by the file on the Sanctuary to think about you." He looked pained at the admission. "But later, at the meeting I was smitten."

She laughed. "Smitten was it? You mean it was not love at first sight for you?"

"No. Maybe second sight. Would that work?"

"I guess it will have to." She looked at the clock again. "I hate to scoot you out, but I have a phone meeting with a sales rep at seven, and I have to get to bed."

"Why so early?"

"He is leaving on vacation and will be gone for six weeks. I want to get the greenhouses and supplies ordered, before he leaves. He is very knowledgeable, and I have been working with him for over a month. I hate to start with someone new at this point."

"I would like us to pray together before I leave. Okay? It is something I want us to make a habit of doing together every day." Janie nodded, and Paul reached over and took her hand.

"Father, Janie and I come before You with thanksgiving and love. We are greatly blessed and for that we are truly grateful. We ask that You be with us each day for the rest of our lives. Bless our union as only You can. Help us to seek You in all decisions we make now and in the future. Give each of us a servant's heart so that we might put the other's needs, wants and desires before our own. Just as Jesus died for His bride, the church, allow each of us to die to our selfishness and pride. Help us to walk humbly before You in all things."

As Paul finished, he squeezed her hands to signal that she could continue if she wished.

"Lord, we are grateful and thankful that You brought us together. Bless Paul, as the spiritual leader in our union, with Your wisdom and grace. Help me to be a wife worth more than rubies. As we work as co-laborers in our marriage, help me to give my opinions and then allow Paul to make the final decision. Help him to use Your wisdom in making decisions. We want to serve You and others in whatever You bring before us. We give You praise and glory!" Janie squeezed Paul's hands, to let him know she was finished.

"Lord we praise You and give You our lives and our love! Thank You for Your many blessings. Amen." Paul hugged her and gave her a passionate kiss, before moving to the door.

"Okay, I will see you at nine in the morning," Janie said, following Paul to the door; after one last good-night kiss, he left. Janie leaned against the door again and pinched herself again. Yes, she was awake, and this was real.

"Father, You have far exceeded my dreams of a man who would love me. Thank You so very much! I love him and his family already. Help me to be the wife You want me to be. You are so wonderful! Thank You so much!"

"Good-morning! You look like the cat that caught the canary," George said, as his son came into his office, followed by Elizabeth. He gave her a quizzical look, and she shrugged her shoulders, answering his unspoken question: "Did we have a meeting I forgot this morning?" They took their seats, just as there was a knock on the door. "Come in," George called out, now even more confused.

Janie peeked in, and when she saw Paul, she opened the door the rest of the way and entered. Paul rose and went over to take her hand, and they stood together, facing his parents. "Mom, Dad, we want you to be the first to know—we have decided to get married. We would like your blessing."

George and Elizabeth jumped to their feet and immediately went to them, throwing their arms around the couple. "We couldn't be more pleased! Of course you have our blessing!"

"Janie, welcome to the family," Elizabeth proclaimed, turning to hug Janie, individually. "I have prayed for this day."

"When is the happy day?" George inquired, still standing with his arm over the shoulders of his son.

"We would like to get married at the Sanctuary, around the end of August. Janie would like to be married in the small church we are going to build there."

"Oh, Paul we are so happy for you both," Elizabeth said, wiping a tear from her eye. "Can we announce it tonight at the party?"

"Only if we can get hold of Janie's parents first; we would like to get their blessing also, before we tell everyone else."

"Yes, yes of course," George said. "When do you plan on telling them?"

"We are calling them at lunch today," Janie replied. "I don't think they will be surprised. I call them frequently, and I talk about Paul a lot." She smiled.

They spoke for a few more minutes, before Janie and Elizabeth left the men, who had other business to discuss. In the hall Elizabeth spoke quietly, "I hope you can get hold of your family soon; I am going to bust at the seams trying to contain the news until they hear."

Janie laughed, "I am sure it will only be a short time. I will let you know, as soon as we get in touch with them."

"Be sure that you do!" As they parted, Elizabeth kissed Janie on the cheek, and they both went back to work.

Janie was having a hard time keeping her mind on business. The meeting earlier with the greenhouse rep had gone well, even though Janie had been somewhat distracted. She smiled, and she refused to pinch herself again; it was real and it was finally sinking in. She was going to be Paul Hamilton's wife, and she would be the best wife she could possibly be.

Shortly before noon, Paul joined Janie, and they called Janie's parents. Paul officially asked her father's permission to marry his daughter. Pleased to be asked, instead of just informed, he said "yes" and both of Janie's parents gave them their blessing. They told them they would be traveling to Spokane, come summer, to help plan the wedding. "It will be a small wedding, Mom," Janie said. "It will be at the Sanctuary."

"I can't wait to see this place you have talked about so much," her mom said. "We will plan on coming mid-July and stay until after the wedding. Will that be okay? We will bring our motor home. We are still thinking of coming to live at the Ranch, but we are still praying about it. Your dad is not taking to retirement very well. I think helping in the greenhouses there would be good for him."

"I hope that you will stay, Mom, and I trust God will lead you to the right decision."

"We know that dear. We are really happy for you both."

"Thanks, Mom. I will see you day after tomorrow in Portland." They said their good-byes and hung up.

"Well, it is official; we are engaged," Paul said smiling.

"Yes, it is." Janie smiled back. "You better let your Mom know. She told me she was going to bust out her seams, holding the news until she could say something."

"She can wait until we have our celebration lunch. Come along. I have something special planned," Paul said. He led her to the restaurant where they had their first lunch together. He had called ahead and had everything arranged. When they arrived, they were taken to a small back room that could be reserved for small dinner parties. One table was setting in the center of the room. It was set for two, with candles and flowers. Soft music was playing in the background. The windows looked out over a small garden. Its plants were bare because winter was in full swing, but Christmas decorations created a festive atmosphere.

"Oh, Paul how lovely," Janie said looking around. Paul helped her out of her coat and hung it on the coat tree in the corner, then pulled out her seat and she sat down. Taking the seat on her right, he sat down too.

"I wanted this to be something you would remember and tell our grandchildren about fifty years from now." Seeing her look of "We may not have fifty years," he said, "I know, we do not know for sure how long we have; only God knows. But today, we have fifty-plus years." Janie resumed her cheery smile and nodded.

Paul reached into his pocket and pulled out a small ring box. Janie looked expectantly at the box. "I looked at a lot of rings and almost decided to let you pick out the ring you wanted for yourself. But as I talked with my Dad this morning, I decided I wanted it to be special, something I chose for you. So I went to the jewelers; I hope that's alright?"

"Well, let's see, and I will let you know," Janie said mischievously. Paul opened the box, and Janie looked at the beautiful rings inside and caught her breath. "Oh, my!" Janie loved it. "They are beautiful. I couldn't have done better myself." There were two bands; Janie's was thinner than Paul's, but otherwise they matched. They were single bands with sapphires and diamonds.

"I know there isn't an engagement ring, but I liked these better than any of the others I saw. I have been looking for a couple of weeks. I always came back to these."

"They are just right. I will be honored to wear it on our wedding day and every day for the rest of our lives."

Reaching into his pocket, Paul took out another long slim jewelry box. "Here. This is something you can wear now."

Janie took the box and opened it. Inside were a chain and a beautiful cross. "It's lovely," she said, as she took the delicate jewelry out of the box and held it up.

"I thought you could take the cross off and put it up for now and put our wedding rings on the chain until the wedding. Then you can put the cross back on the chain and wear it."

"What a wonderful idea." She unclasped the chain and removed the cross, gently setting it back inside the box, and then she took the wedding rings, as Paul handed them to her, and put them on the chain. Holding the two sides of the chain out to Paul, he took them as she turned, so he could clasp it for her. Turning back to look at him, then down at the rings hanging around her neck, she threw her arms around him and hugged him tight. "This is perfect, absolutely perfect," she whispered in his ear. Pulling back to face him, she placed both hands on his cheeks and tenderly kissed him.

Lunch was wonderful and filled with laughter. They talked about children and their desire to have several. They shared more stories about their childhoods, but they avoided the Sanctuary and the reasons for building it. They avoided anything that would put a damper on their joy and their dreams for their future. They were young and had held dreams, hopes, and desires for living in a land of prosperity, safety and freedom to serve God.

The land of freedom their families had enjoyed for more than two hundred years was changing, however. The land their forefathers had fought for, died for, and worked so hard to preserve for their children and grandchildren was rapidly fading away. Freedoms were being taken, and the nation was being weighed down by laws, regulations, and national debt. The land of prosperity was being taken from the ones who worked hard and sacrificed to achieve that prosperity, and it was given to others, those who had not worked or sweated for it but felt entitled to it, nonetheless.

God had once been the center of the country but no more; now, God was being removed from every facet of government—and from society at large. The citizens did not look to God for their moral compass anymore; now, people at large did whatever seemed right in their own eyes.

The reality was the Sanctuary and the reason for building it changed the future for everyone. The plans that each of them had once had for the future did not include living in a secluded place, living a life of a pioneer, and helping refugees who had to escape from a world gone crazy.

CHAPTER 17

JANIE WAS RUNNING LATE, something she hated. She heard a pastor say once that being late was a very selfish habit. It showed others they were not as important as whatever caused you to be late. He said it was simply poor planning, lack of organization, or simply not caring about the people who might be waiting for you; since hearing that, she always made a point of being on time. She wanted others to feel she placed great importance on them and her time with them. Checking her watch, she realized she only had five minutes to spare. She had planned on arriving at the banquet hall thirty minutes ago. The last-minute return call from Franklin and Sarah had delayed her in leaving the Hope Foundation building.

Janie was pleased to hear from them. She had tried several times throughout the day to reach them, finally leaving a message. She shared her engagement, and they talked about the Sanctuary. She had told them in previous calls about her dreams and the visit to the land. They had shared that God had given a similar vision to several in their church. They were currently working on their own plans. This greatly relieved Janie's mind. She now knew two of the most important people in her life would also be safe.

Janie slipped into the ladies' room to check her appearance. She thought of the lovely green dress that had been a temptation she had given into. Now, it hung in her closet at home, waiting for another occasion to wear it. Tonight, the simple red blouse and long black skirt would have to do. She simply had not had time to go home to change. She tidied her hair and makeup and then smiled into the mirror. It was time to join the party.

Janie entered the side door of the banquet room and glanced around the room. She saw many who worked at the foundation, as well as many she did not know. The Christmas party was attended by supporters, workers, and many others in the community. She did not see Paul, so she made her way to the kitchen. She wanted to speak with Megan about the cake she had asked her to order. Mary's birthday was next week and she had wanted to have an early cake and celebration because she was going to be gone.

The kitchen was empty when Janie arrived. She was looking in the refrigerator, when suddenly she heard voices of three women enter the kitchen.

"With all the money they have, I can't believe they have such simple fare."

"And no liquor; the least they could do was supply champagne."

"Who cares about all that?! Paul is here tonight. I would sure like to get my hands on him. He looks like a million dollars tonight."

"You're only saying that because his parents have millions, and you would like to get your hands on a few by cozying up to Paul."

"That might be true, but he is a nice package, as well."

Janie closed the door, already having seen the cake, and turned to the newcomers. "Hello." She did not want to hear more of what they had to say.

"Oh, we didn't see you. The punch is almost gone, and the veggie trays are empty. We do not eat meat. Could you be a dear and fill them up for us?"

"Sure, I'll see what I can find." Janie turned back to the refrigerator.

Patricia looked over at the young woman and clearly dismissed her. She was plainly dressed in an unflattering red blouse and long black skirt. Why didn't she have an apron on? In addition, white is usually the color serving girls wore, yet she wore red. "*If she is a guest, clearly she is not fashion* conscious, and if she is one of the help, she should have worn more appropriate clothing," Patricia thought uncharitably.

"Hello, ladies," Paul said looking around the room for Janie.

Janie found another vegetable tray and the punch, as she heard the beloved voice behind her. Pulling them out, one by one, she placed them on the counter, before turning to give Paul a bright smile. She watched as the blond walked casually over and linked her arm suggestively through Paul's. "Paul, it is so good to see you; it has been ages since I've seen you." Patricia purred. "Why didn't you call when you got back to town?"

Paul carefully disengaged himself from the pretty woman. "Patricia, I have been very busy with the foundation and other projects." Patricia frowned, as she clearly understood the rejection. Paul moved across the room to help Janie. Reaching her side, he clearly kissed her cheek, before taking the punch bowl. "Hello. Let me help you with this."

"Hello, yourself. I came to find the cake for Mary; these nice young ladies said some of the supplies are running out, so I thought I should help."

"I'm sorry, I thought you knew them. Janie Weber, this is Rochelle Hansen, Robin Fuller, and Patricia Owen."

Rochelle and Robin made their polite hellos with great curiosity, while Patricia was reserved and somewhat hostile, yet tried to conceal the fact. "It is nice to meet you, Janie. You aren't the caterer?"

"Oh, no. I work for the foundation. Besides, we didn't have a caterer; Megan put all this together. Just wait until you see the meal she has planned. She did a wonderful job, don't you think?"

"Uh . . . sure." It was clear Patricia didn't think Megan did a good job at all. *Are they serving spaghetti and meatballs, or something else equally loathsome? Ugh,"* Patricia thought unkindly.

"Well, it was nice to see you all again," Paul said, carrying the punch bowl toward the door.

"It was nice to meet you," Janie added, as she followed him out, carrying the vegetable tray. She could hear surprised voices behind them.

"Well, Patricia, you better find a new boyfriend. Did you see the look he gave her? I wish Joe would look at me that way. He really loves her," Rochelle observed. Their voices drifted away, as the door closed behind them.

"Wow! I didn't know I was hooking up with a ladies' man," Janie whispered, laughing after they were nearly to the food table.

"I am no ladies' man. Patricia has been trying to get her claws into me since she heard my folks won the lottery," he replied with disgust. "She attends a sister church in Post Falls, so we see her from time to time. For a while, I couldn't go anywhere that she didn't show up. I never dated her or showed any interest, but that didn't slow her down. The others are friendly, and Jack dated Robin for a while, when he was in high school. I really like her. Speaking of Jack, he and Rose flew in early to meet you. Come on let's go find them." They placed the bowl and tray on the food table, before Paul took her hand and, after looking over the heads of people taller than Janie, he headed to the far corner.

Janie spied a tall man with the same height and a slightly heavier build, standing with the rest of Paul's family. He stood with his arm around a stunningly beautiful woman, about five feet five inches and a perfect figure. She wore a bright smile and had that inner glow that tagged her as a believer. Janie knew instantly that she would like Jack's Rose.

The next several minutes were taken up with introductions, hugs, and whispered congratulations. Jack and Rose were engaged, also, and their announcement would also be made this evening. After a few minutes of visiting, George and Elizabeth moved to the front of the room to make their formal welcome and announcements.

George and Elizabeth were a handsome couple, dressed in simple, but elegant, clothing. George wore a three-piece suit he bought off the rack at a men's store, and Elizabeth wore a festive gown of dark green velvet. Neither of them spent great amounts of money on their clothing, but rather, they tried to be frugal and practical. Though they had millions at their disposal, they rarely used it for personal expenditures. Both thought of the money as "God's money," and though they lived comfortably, they still lived in the house they had lived in for fifteen years, still drove older cars, and lived off their modest salaries from the foundation.

"My husband and I would like to welcome all of you to our annual Christmas party for Hope Foundation. We have had a very successful year, due to the help of all of you. There is a complete accounting for all our missionary projects on the table. Please pick up a copy of the report and feel free to ask any questions you have. This is God's ministry, and we want to be good stewards of His money; that means we are accountable to God and to you to make sure we are doing the right things and spending the money in appropriate ways," Elizabeth told the assembled crowd. "This is a party to celebrate the birth of our wonderful Lord and Savior, Jesus.

They have just finished filling the buffet table. I would like to thank Megan for all her hard work in putting everything together for us." She stopped speaking and clapped in honor of Megan. The room erupted in applause. As it died down, Elizabeth continued. "Dining is informal so feel free to fill your plates from the buffet whenever you desire. We hope that you will have a good time this evening. Our band is setting up, and dancing will begin at nine. Please enjoy."

The crowd started to turn as George's booming voice rang out. "Ladies and gentlemen, if I might have your attention, before you go back to enjoying yourselves." He waited as the group turned their attention back to him. "My lovely wife and I have two very important announcements to make. This next year will bless us with the birth of our first grandchild in April and a new grandniece the end of next month." George waited as the applause once again rose and died down. "The new year will also bring two new members into our family. We would like to formally announce the engagements of our sons. Jack and Rose will be wed in May on her parents' wedding anniversary, and Paul and Janie will wed the end of August, or early September." The applause again rang through the hall. George reached his hand out toward the two couples, beckoning them to come forward. "Janie, Rose . . . welcome to the family." Janie and Rose went to George and Elizabeth, receiving hugs and kisses from both of them, before being joined by their future grooms. The next hour was filled with warm wishes and congratulations for the Hamilton family.

"Bonnie, Nathan . . . I am so glad you decided to come," Janie called out, as she grabbed Paul's hand and pulled him toward the couple getting ready to leave. They hurried past clusters of people, to get to the couple who had turned toward her voice.

"Hi," they said together, somewhat shyly.

"I want to introduce you to Paul Hamilton, my fiancé. Paul, these are my neighbors that I told you about, Bonnie and Nathan Morgan." They exchanged pleasantries. "You are not leaving already, are you?"

"Well," Bonnie hesitated. "we don't really know anyone but you and . . ." she trailed off lamely.

Janie grasped the problem immediately. "I am so sorry! Here I invite you and then neglect my duties." She raised her hand when she knew Bonnie was going to let her off the hook. "No! I really wanted you to come. Please, come with us; I want to introduce you to Paul's family and a few of my friends at the foundation." Janie and Paul stayed with the couple, until they saw them drawn into a conversation with Jill and Curt. They knew Jill and Curt would keep them entertained, as no one was as friendly and talkative. Later, when Janie looked for them, she saw them laughing at something Curt was saying, and she smiled to herself. She loved this couple and wanted to include them in her happiness. She was also hopeful they would be joining them at the Sanctuary; they would be a great asset to the Ranch.

Later, Janie and Jill nabbed Rose to help them surprise Mary with the birthday cake, just before ten. They could see her getting tired and wanted to catch her before she left for the night. Mary was delighted to cut her birthday cake, and she made a big production of it. Jake, Curt, Jack and Paul had stood to the side, watching, as their women laughed and joked, as they entertained the crowds with their antics. As Mary cut the cake and placed the pieces on plates, the three handed the pieces out with a bow, curtsy or some other form of giving each person their cake in a special way. Everyone enjoyed the little show, including the men. The only person who seemed out of joint was Patricia, who left in a huff when Robin and Rochelle moved, smiling toward the cake table.

The party was winding down when Bonnie waved to catch Janie's attention. Janie gratefully excused herself from the older woman, who introduced herself as Mrs. Horace Farley. She seemed like a very nice lady, but Janie could tell she was lonely. She had been patiently listening for nearly fifteen minutes.

"Please, excuse me, Mrs. Farley; I will call you as soon as I return from my Christmas holiday. I will see when I can arrange for one of our team members to visit you. They will arrange for the repairs you need to your house. Right now, my friends are leaving, and I need to say good night."

"Thank you for listening to an old lady, dear. My phone number is on the card I gave you. It would be very nice to have someone come visit me."

"I have enjoyed our visit very much."

Turning to Bonnie, Janie reached over to take her hand. "Thank you so much for coming. I hope you had a good time."

"Oh, yes! We both really liked Jill and Curt. Curt worked as a mechanic, while he was in high school, and he was a volunteer fireman while he was in college. The guys enjoyed talking about their experiences and shared interests. Jill, well, she is wonderful. Her little boy Peter and Harold are nearly the same age; it was fun visiting about our kids. I think they introduced us to everyone in the room. I shook more hands than I have ever shaken before. We plan to get together after the holidays." She laughed delighted.

"They are wonderful. I think I can say the same about the hand shaking." Janie joined her laughter and pulled her into a hug. "You have a great Christmas and I will see you, as soon as I get back from visiting my parents."

"Have a wonderful time. Merry Christmas! Oh, and congratulations on your engagement; Paul seems like a very nice man," Bonnie said, hugging her back.

"Thank you. I think he is wonderful. We will all have to get together when I get back. Merry Christmas to you, too," Janie said, as she stepped back.

Janie watched Bonnie turn to go through the crowd, where Nathan was still talking with Curt. She turned to find Paul; he had expressed a wish to dance with her, and the night was drawing to a close. They had been separated by all the people who had wanted to wish them well and to talk about this and that. "I believe this is my dance," Paul said, bowing slightly and holding out his hand.

"Yes, my dear sir, I believe it is," Janie said, smiling and giving a little curtsy.

Having never danced together, they enjoyed the brief closeness it brought. Yet, they both knew this kind of intimacy would need to be carefully monitored. They wanted to come into their marriage righteous, so they had already put into practice strict rules that governed their time together. They spent only small amounts of time alone, meeting, instead, in public places with others to hold them accountable for their sexual purity. In society, privacy for engaged couples was accepted, yet this could lead to the problem of premarital sex, if they were not careful. Paul and Janie had decided they wanted to do things God's way and wait until they were wed to complete their physical joining and cement their marriage covenant.

"How are you enjoying your engagement party?" Paul spoke just loud enough for Janie to hear.

"It is wonderful. I met your grade school teacher. I believe she was warning me that you were a handful as a child, and it could mean you will be a bigger handful as a husband." Janie had a smile in her eyes and a hint of teasing in her voice.

"Ah, yes. I spoke with Mrs. Shipley. Note the gray hair; I think she got her first one when I was in her class. I admit I was a bit of a handful."

"I figured you were. My favorite story was when she sent you to the hall for misbehaving, and when she came out, you had made "people" out of all the coats, hanging them just so, then placing boots under them. She said it was very meticulous."

"I remember that. She had to stop sending me to the hall because I had too much fun out there. I visited with everyone that went by."

"I am sure you did." Janie yawned.

"Tired?"

"Yes, but I am not ready for the night to end." The music stopped. "I should see if I can help clean anything up," Janie said, looking around. The crowd had thinned out even further.

"They have a handle on it. Dad paid the hotel for cleanup, and the extra food is being sent over to the local food kitchen. There really isn't anything for you to do." Just then, the final dance was being announced. "Come on, this is the last dance, and I want my sweetheart to finish the night in my arms." Janie smiled and they joined the other dancers.

The Christmas party had been wonderful. Janie laid her head against the head rest in the car, as Paul drove her home, reliving her memories of the night. She had truly enjoyed herself. She regretted that she had so little time to get to know Rose. She was looking forward to spending time getting to know her future sister-in-law. She was glad they would be going to visit before the wedding. Mary and Janie would be joining Elizabeth for a long weekend next month. It would give the females of the family a chance to get to know one another better. Jill was disappointed that she could not go, but the baby was due soon, and flying was out of the question.

Janie was not looking forward to getting on the plane and leaving Paul behind; however, she was leaving in the morning. Filled with a slight depression, Janie tried to put an upbeat smile on her face, as Paul walked her to her door. "I had wonderful time tonight."

"I did, also," Paul replied. "I have several things on my plate for the next few days, but how would you feel about my coming on Thursday afternoon to join you, and then we can fly back together. I would like to meet your parents, Franklin and Sarah."

"Oh, yes! I would like that very much. I was dreading the separation." Janie said excitedly.

Smiling, Paul took her hands, "Between now and August, we are going to have many times of separation that cannot be avoided. I am going to be spending a great deal of time at the Ranch and you will have foundation work here. I am all for as much separation as we can avoid." He kissed her good-night. "I will pick you up at ten in the morning." Janie started to protest. "I want to take you to the airport."

"Alright, I will see you in the morning." Janie smiled and turned to unlock her apartment door. Turning back, she said, "Good night."

"Good night," Paul turned and walked down the sidewalk, as Janie went inside. It had been fun tonight, she thought. No one had been surprised by the announcement of their engagement, except Patricia, she thought. She felt sad for the pretty woman. She was overwhelmed with the love and acceptance she felt from everyone she met and spoke with. She smiled as she remembered George and Elizabeth's excitement when announcing their engagement. They would be wonderful in-laws. Janie loved them already. Janie felt blessed that, after having no sisters, she now had several: Mary, Jill, Bonnie, and now Rose.

"Father God, thank You for this wonderful day. You have expanded my family, and each one is truly wonderful. Help me to be the wife, daughter-in-law, sister-in-law and friend You would have me be. I give You my love, praise and thanksgiving for everything You do. You are awesome!"

CHAPTER 18

Usually, winters crept by and seemed to go on forever, but the days went by in a rapid blur of activity. Winter, with its mono color, disappeared into a spring awash in color. Trees budded and flowered; shrubs, perennials, and flowers appeared in full and deep hues. The conference room was a buzz of activity, in preparation for the final meeting before the Sanctuary work started in earnest.

It was the middle of April. February first brought the birth of Sari Marie; mother, Jill, and daughter were doing well. Now, Mary was days away from another little one joining the family. Making her way to the conference table, Mary stopped to lift her niece into her arms.

"Sari is so beautiful. I hope we have a little girl, so Sari will have a playmate."

"I still do not understand why you didn't let them tell you what you are going to have."

"I wanted to be surprised. Besides, if we have any more while we are at the Ranch, a sonogram will not be an option."

"I know, but I will cross that bridge, if and when I come to it." Jill yawned, and then she quickly covered her mouth. "I am so tired."

"I offered to watch the kids, so you could rest," Mary replied, as she sat to rock the baby in the rocking chair, which had been placed in the corner of the conference room for Jill.

"I know, and I am going to take you up on it, before that little one is born and you become as tired as I am," Jill said, yawning again.

"How about I follow you home after the meeting today?"

"You know, I think I will take you up on that."

"Great! I can have some auntie time with this little one."

"Hello, everyone. Please take your seats. We have a lot to cover today," George called out, as he took his seat at the head of the conference table. Everyone did as he asked and turned their attention toward George. Without hesitation, George began, "Let's get started with prayer."

"Heavenly Father, we come before You today in thanksgiving for Your love and guidance. Jesus, we thank You for saving us and making us part of God's family; we are humbled by Your faith in us to do Your will. As we begin the actual building of Your sanctuary, guide our hands. Give us Your favor, as we work with outside workers. Help us to be witnesses to Your love, to any who do not know You. We are in Your service; help us to be Your hands and feet. We give You our praise and worship in all things; in Jesus precious name we pray. Amen."

"Amen," came the chorus around the room.

"Today, the final plans will be approved, and a schedule will be drawn up for everything concerning the Sanctuary Ranch. I want us to go over everything, step by step, so we make sure we are not forgetting anything. Please listen carefully to each report and make notes of anything that you feel has been forgotten. We will take those notes up later. For now, let's start with each phase, as it comes on the building schedule. Ok, people, turn to the layout for the roads. Jake, let's start with you."

"Good morning. As you can see from your handouts, I have the layout for all the roads and buildings that will require excavation. We purchased a bobcat with several attachments, including a backhoe. In addition, we have leased a grader; we have the option to buy it, if we think we might need it later on. We have two experienced men who will operate the machinery and teach me how to operate the bobcat, so we can use it to maintain the garbage dump later on. Down the road, we plan to use the methane gas from the garbage, so we have to do things correctly from the start. We plan to burn everything possible that will not help with the creation of the methane gas.

"We will begin working on the roads next week. All of the roads will be graveled; they will have a base of larger rocks, with final crushed gravel on top. We hope to have the roads bladed and building pads completed in four to six weeks. Next, we will blade all the building pads that are scheduled to be built later this summer. After that, we will dig an additional pond that we can use for watering the cattle and horses in the southern pasture. We will complete some additional roads to pastures, after all the other building sites are done. We plan to have those finished by the end of the summer." He paused, as he consulted his notes and flipped the page of his report. "We have three water wells that will be drilled, as soon as the roads are in. Two of the wells—the one for the main lodge and small cabins and the one for the meeting hall, chapel, and bunkhouse—will be smaller. The third will be a field well. We will use it to water the garden, greenhouses, and fields. We plan to interconnect the three, in case one goes down. Curt will be in charge of those, as well as the generators and wind turbines. He was called out on an emergency this morning, but he said everything is in place to begin, as soon as the main road is in. The only thing left is the septic system. We are waiting on the engineer to finish the plans for that. We would have had to have it designed anyway, but our plan now to collect methane gas from that is requiring more time for drawing up those additional plans. The engineer should be done sometime in May, or early June, though. Anyone have any questions or comments?"

Everyone shook their head negatively, and George went on, "Thank you, Jake. Next on the list are the buildings. Paul, that is your department; you're up."

Paul stood and winked at Janie before beginning his presentation. "If you will flip through your reports, look for the picture of the log building. These are the floor plans for the barn, paddocks, animal pens, chicken coop, warehouse, chapel, meeting hall, main lodge, bunkhouse, and several small cabins. Each of you has gone over them, at one time or another, so you are familiar with them, already. We plan to begin pouring concrete around the first of May, weather permitting. As we have said before, it is our plan to pour, at one time, all the concrete needed for the entire complex. This way, we will not have any outside people on the property after the concrete is completed. Please note that the plans for the recreation area are not complete. We have a horseshoe area and playground for the kids in your packet, but we decided to add a basketball court and tennis court. We are considering an enclosed swimming pool, also. They are marked on the site plans, but we are still considering our options; so, if you have any ideas let me know, as soon as possible. We also will have two metal Quonset buildings constructed; one will be the warehouse and the other a repair shop. Henry Foster will be putting those up for us. There are going to be four three-man building crews working. Lester will be overseeing the meeting hall and chapel. Harvey will head the crew working on the barn and bunkhouse, along with all the out buildings, paddocks and fences. I will oversee the main lodge, small houses and clinic." Paul flipped through his notes, "That's all I have for now."

"Sherry, you're up," George said, looking at his sister.

"Good morning, everyone. Jack, Martin and I have put together a small clinic. We will be able to care for any everyday medical and dental problems that might arise. We believe that prayer is an important part of healing, and we stand firm in our belief that we can and will be healed through our faith in Jesus. Yet, we will have the ability to care for people, if the need arises. All supplies, medical furniture and medicine will be delivered in August; by September first, we should be operational." Sherry sat down.

"Janie, I understand you are speaking for your group," George said, moving on.

Janie stood and took a deep breath. She wasn't nervous, but there was a lot to go over. "Please, pull out the blue folder; first, I want you all to know this was the combined efforts of Mary, Jill, and me. We believe everything has been addressed in this report; however, please go over it carefully, and if you find we missed anything, please let us know. This is the master plan for the supplies and operational needs of the complex. Please, go to the first tab. This is the list of outside needs. It is separated into different areas: tools, animals, feed, and supplies, including medical supplies for the animals. There are detailed lists under each topic. For example, under tools, we have shovels, rakes, tillers, tractor, spare parts and so forth. Please note, we will have a wood splitter, but we will have axes, also. We have sharpeners listed, to keep the cutting edges sharp. We have both horse-drawn equipment and motorized. Take a look at the next page." There was a shuffling of paper, as everyone flipped pages. "We have a list of animal stock. We have cows, both for meat and milk; goats for milk, and pigs, and chickens enough for egg production and eating. We have planned for several riding and draft horses. The number in the first column is the number we plan to purchase. The number in the next column, printed in red, represents the female and the number in blue indicates the male. We hope to breed the animals and increase our stock, as we go along. We also have twenty beehives coming. Lester volunteered to be our beekeeper. He used to help his parents care for their hives, so he knows what to do. He said, as long as we have the proper equipment, including several bee suits, a spinner used in harvesting the honey, and extra hives, he would be happy to take on that job.

"Flip to the next tab, and you will see the greenhouses. We have planned on having three. Originally, we thought two would be enough, but we figured better safe than sorry and added the third. We will also have a spare one that we do not plan to put up now, and that can be held in reserve, if we need it. We will operate one of them year round. It will have vegetables, like tomatoes. We are going to plant a couple of orange trees inside, also, as they would not survive outside in our climate. We visited a greenhouse that had a twelve-year-old tree inside, so we figured we could do it also.

"Okay, next is a list of vegetables we plan to grow. Most will be started in the greenhouses and transplanted into the garden, when the weather warms in the spring. As you can see, we have Early Girl, Roma, and cherry tomatoes, and bell, cayenne and red peppers, as well as red and yellow potatoes, and onions, pumpkins, several varieties of squash, corm, and herbs, like oregano, chives, dill, basil, tarragon, to name a few. But please, go over the list. If you see anything missing, let us know.

"The next tab is the fruit tree list. As you can see, we have several varieties of each fruit. Some of them require a pollinator, while others do not. We took great care to order the right kinds for cross pollination. We have chosen Cameo, Fuji, and Haralson apples, and also Reliant peaches, Bartlett pears, Stella and Rainer cherries, Moorpark apricots, Santa Rosa plums, and Black walnut trees. We also have blackberries, boysenberries, strawberries, and rhubarb. There are two kinds of strawberries because one is everbearing, and the other will provide only one harvest. At the bottom is the list of the canning jars and supplies we think we will need. We found some resealing lids. That will allow us to reuse them, year after year. But we decided to order lots of extras, as well as some paraffin wax we can use, if need be. We also have a lot of pectin coming for our jams and jellies. The last page is a list of shade trees, nursery stock, and perennials we plan to plant around the Ranch. Those include lilac, spirea, potentilla, and several other flowering shrubs. Then we have a couple of varieties of maple, ash, and flowering crab trees. We all agreed that we need color, especially flowers in the spring and summer, so we will be seeding annuals, when we seed the vegetables." She smiled at Elizabeth, who smiled back at the comment.

Janie reached over and took a sip of water, before going on. "Next tab is the other food. Since we will be going through the first winter before we grow and harvest next summer, we need canned goods and other supplies. This is the list we came up with. As you can see, there are fruits of all kinds and vegetables, like corn, green beans, and peas, as well as cereals, flour, rice, sugar, cooking oil, yeast, and seasonings. We have also included fresh fruits and vegetables that will be stored in the root cellar, things like apples, pears, potatoes, carrots, and onions."

"We realize that there are some staples we will need that we cannot easily produce ourselves; we have planned large amounts of those, like rice and flour, that will be stored in a special airtight room in the warehouse. We may be able to grow wheat, but those fields are not cleared yet, so we wanted to be prepared, if it takes a while to prepare that land," Mary added.

"Yes," Janie acknowledged. "The next page lists all those items. Most are seasonings we like but would have a hard time producing, like chili powder, for example. We believe we will have enough of these items to last at least several years."

"The kitchen tab is next. After doing an online search, we found we have overlooked a great many things that would make our storage and processing of food easier. On this list you will find meat grinders, dehydrators, grain mills, and blenders. We feel that dehydrating will be a great way to store and preserve our fruits and vegetables. The meat grinder will make it easier to process our hamburger and sausage. We also have added a bread machine, along with mixers, coffee makers, and other small kitchen appliances. We plan to have four stoves in our main kitchen. Two will be electric stoves with ovens, the other two will be wood-burning stoves, just in case something happens to our power.

"Going on, the next tab is household supplies. You will find cleaners, soaps of several kinds, like laundry, hand—both bar and liquid, as well as dishwasher soap, disinfectants, bleach and window cleaners. We will also have a large supply of lye, so we can make our own. We have ordered these items in cases, so we think they will last for quite some time. Next, we have light bulbs, rechargeable batteries and chargers in all sizes, toilet paper, paper towels, rags, towels, sheets, pillowcases, bolts of cloth, plates, bowls, silverware, glasses, pots, pans, skillets, cooking utensils, knives, tablecloths, napkins, candles of all kinds and sizes and wax to make more, and oil and lamps. Brooms and mops are also listed. Personal items, like makeup, razor blades, and personal hygiene products, follow on the next page; most of us are stocking up on our individual favorites, also.

"The next tab represents the furniture needs. Each family is bringing their own furniture to furnish their own cabin, or room, but we need additional tables, chairs, beds, and dressers, for example, for the meeting hall and the sleeping rooms above. Since we do not know who God will lead to us, we need to be ready with extra of everything.

"The next tab lists the mechanical parts. This is one area we were not sure about. We would appreciate some help with this one. I am sure we are missing items we will need, so please let us know what to add. We have the basics, like spare fan belts, hoses, headlights, and other lights, oil filters, air filters, alternators, starters, grease, tires, brakes, and extra engines and transmissions. In addition, we need the tools to work on vehicles and equipment. For much of this, we have no clue what we will need, so we really will appreciate your input."

Janie smiled, "The final tab is our miscellaneous tab; everything we thought of that did not fit on another list is here, like a couple of barbeque grills, flower pots, and gardening tools that will not be mixed with the other tools. We have four sewing machines on the list, 2-way radios, a couple of water filtration systems, and the like. You can read the list.

"We also will need recreation things, like tennis rackets, balls of different kinds, horseshoes, and bats. We will even have a couple of canoes for the lake. Repair kits of all kinds, extra hats, sunglasses, shoes, jeans, and the like. There is a piano for the chapel and one for the recreation room. Most of us are stocking up on personal reading books, but we are adding some "how to" books to the list, any we can find, in fact. We are encouraging everyone to bring as many books as possible. Paul and Pastor Phil have a list of Bible studies, commentaries, and Bibles in several translations that they feel would be helpful in our studies. We have several cases of Bibles in the event that those who come do not have a personal Bible, or in case Pastor Phil needs them when he travels."

Janie flipped through the pages and checked her notes. "I believe that is everything I have. Please, let us know if you have any favorites in any of the listed items, so we can be sure to include them." Finished with her report, Janie sat down.

Curt spoke up, "I met with Nathan, Janie's neighbor, yesterday, to go over a list of what we will need, as far as mechanical things are concerned. He suggested that we choose one type of truck, car, and van to take to the Ranch. That way all the parts will be interchangeable, and we will not need a parts store to keep them in good repair. It would also streamline the tools needed. He also suggested we purchase a lift, so it will be easier to work on the vehicles. His final suggestion was for us to get a fuel tanker. That way we can store ethanol in it, and it can be moved easily. I think an old wrecker would be a good idea, too. It can be used as a snowplow, as well as a repair truck. We will need some storage tanks for the methane gas, also."

"Good ideas. Curt, check those out, will you? Okay, let's take a break and get back to it in fifteen minutes. Good job everyone!" George said, before he turned toward Elizabeth, Martin, and Sherry.

Mary, Jill, and Janie exchanged smiles. "You really did do a great job," Sherry said over her shoulder.

"You bet your socks we did!" Mary said with a grin.

Paul came over and put his arm around Janie's shoulders and kissed her on the cheek, to the whoops from Mary and Jill. He smiled at the others and whispered into Janie's ear, "You were great!" Janie blushed as she returned his smile.

After their break, Martin spoke about having all the shipments delivered to the foundation warehouse, then transferred to the Ranch warehouse, as soon as possible. "We will begin receiving shipments in late June. Sue and Jerry Warner, our team semi-drivers, will be transporting as much as they can themselves. Whatever freight we cannot coordinate getting on one of their runs, we will hire outside trucking companies to do. I do not want to use the same one very often though. It is better that we spread the freight around and use several companies so that no one company knows what or how much we are bringing in.

"Trevor, one of the carpenters, and his wife, Shirley, are moving into the mobile home that is being set up, even as we speak. It will be located on the main road, next to our main entrance. They will be our caretakers, until we move to the Ranch. After that they will decide if they want to stay in the mobile home, or move into a room above the meeting hall."

"Speaking of Sue and Jerry," Jill said, "they have been a treasure trove of information. I have spent quite a lot of time on the phone with her. Her information has been a great help. Anyway, she told me she would be happy to help with the dehydrator, when we get ready to work with the fruits and vegetables. She also has a lot of experience cooking with dehydrated foods. They plan to join us at the Ranch with their son and grandson in September. They think they will have all the transportation done by then. I am so glad they are coming. I was afraid they would find a sanctuary in a warmer climate. Sue confided that she hates the cold weather."

The meeting continued over lunch, though the conversation changed some. "Everyone gets along so well," Janie observed. "And everyone accepts the idea of the Sanctuary. I mean, there are no reservations."

"I don't think any of us accepted it when my parents first told us about it. We thought they were totally losing it and were ready for the nut house," Paul said, smiling at his parents. "We all know history, and we have been well schooled in the Bible. In addition, we have also studied Revelation and know what it says about the end times, but it wasn't supposed to happen in our lifetime, though we still do not know if we are in the end times or whether God is just warning us about some bad times ahead. We had our lives all planned out. I know we didn't really ask God about it like we should, but that didn't matter. We figured life would always be as we have always known it to be. So, we all had feelings of fear, anger, and disbelief all mingled together. But the overwhelming feeling was that it was not fair. We already had our plans for life, plans we thought God would approve of, and those plans did not include a sanctuary."

"That is an understatement," Curt added. "George was so serious, all I could think was that we are young and have plans for the future. I mean, we were all taught that we live in the world, but we are reborn of God through Jesus. That meant we had a different standard of living, a different moral code, living by the Bible, instead of the world's wisdom, but it still meant we worked, had a family, and enjoyed relative safety. We live in the best country in the world, after all, a place where things like persecution aren't supposed to happen. We had hopes and dreams of a promising future. None of our plans included a sanctuary away from the world, or the thought we would even need a place like the Sanctuary. I really had a hard time accepting that our government would run amuck, or that there was a possibility that there could be a World War III, much less the end times in our lifetime—not even close. It's not that we don't want Jesus to return, but, unfortunately, our wants and desires were the focus of our lives. I am sad to say that the Lord's agenda took second place in my plans for my life."

"I cried," Mary admitted. "The Bible says that the end times will be difficult for pregnant or nursing mothers. I wanted children, and the idea that I might not be able to have them, or that the times would place them in danger, scared me. It still scares me. But I finally realized that life goes on, and God is bigger than all of this. He will take care of things."

"At any rate, all of this has been a big wake-up call," Curt began. "I think we all realized after a while that we were putting our wants, needs, and desires for our lives ahead of the Lord. It really shook me up for a while. I had to ask forgiveness for my attitude and lack of commitment. Uncle George kept saying that this might not be the end times, but these are going to be really hard times, and if we are wrong, we will have a really nice ranch to live on. He went on to say that it would be a great place for our children and grandchildren, if the end times arrive in their life time instead of ours. The Sanctuary Ranch is in a family trust that will be passed from generation to generation."

"We all had a hard time accepting this, at least until my parents won the lottery," Mary confessed. "Every time the Sanctuary would come up in the conversation, Dad or Mom would say 'Where God guides, God provides.' The lottery was the final piece of the puzzle that fell into place. When that happened, whether we wanted to believe it or not, we knew God was confirming everything Mom and Dad had been telling us. After the awe, surprise, and excitement wore off, life changed for all of us."

"The reality brought a new fear. Would we do everything God wanted us to? But, as time went on and Hope Foundation was established, we all came to a place of peace. We came to understand God opens doors when we are headed in the right direction, and He closes them when He wants us to change direction," Paul said.

"Janie, George and I had our own doubts, too," Elizabeth said sincerely. "But faith is believing, even when you cannot see, and walking on, even when you don't know where He is leading, just as we believe in God,

His son Jesus, and the Holy Spirit, though we have never seen Them. When we thought we were crazy and filled with doubts, Jesus would bring someone to encourage us, to help us stay the course. When we realized the country we love will have to change greatly even for there to be a need *for* a sanctuary, we really did not want to believe it could happen. Then again, Jesus would send someone to encourage us; He never let us down. I know He understood our doubts, and that is why He would send someone to encourage us. Back then, things seemed to be just fine, but now it is sad to say that all you have to do is look around, and you can see the deterioration of our beloved country." Elizabeth smiled sadly.

"I must admit that George did not have the struggles I have had. He was my support when I would waver. But when God won the lottery—that's how we see it, God's lottery, God's money, we felt a sense of relief because we realized that God was leading, and we were following. We didn't try to second-guess ourselves anymore. We knew God was guiding, God was providing. Even the property we purchased was God directed. We were looking in a different area of the country, but God kept closing doors. Finally, we got the hint, and God led us to a wonderful, perfect place."

"I am excited that God has included me in the great and wonderful plan," Janie replied. "I am so thankful and grateful for all His blessings."

"We are in total agreement with you on that," George said, smiling warmly at the young woman who would be his daughter-in-law. "This has been a great start on the planning. Let's get finished because tomorrow the real work begins." With that, everyone got back to work.

CHAPTER 19

EXCITEMENT FILLED JANIE, AS she drove the final mile to the Sanctuary. She had not been back since the early spring. There had been great progress made in the past several months. She made the turn just past a mailbox with a rainbow on the side. She noted the road was now graveled. After traveling five hundred yards, the road turned out of view from the main road, and the gravel changed to asphalt; it surprised her because she thought everything would be graveled.

She traveled slowly, looking for any new changes, not wanting to miss anything. Around the next curve was the barn; it was a large, two-story building with a hayloft. She knew it also had a tack room, store room, stalls for eight horses, a milking area and a work area. Newly built corrals and pens could be seen attached to the back and side of the barn. Next, the chicken coop, with a fenced area surrounding it, came into view. The bunk house was a one-story building. Janie knew it would house six to eight single men. She knew the next building she would see would be the meeting hall, with its full commercial kitchen, dining hall and storage closet downstairs, and the guest rooms with bathrooms would be upstairs. Following the road around three more curves, Janie drew in a breath at the beautiful log home situated at the far end of the valley. It was just as she had dreamed. The chapel stood between the meeting hall and log home. Also, a log building, the chapel stood proud and lovely in a course of aspen and pine trees. There were only a few shrubs surrounding the chapel, but Janie could imagine both the riot of flowers that would be blooming and the little native creek, gurgling along behind them. It was wonderful.

She stopped the car in front of the chapel and made her way inside, overwhelmed with all she saw. All she could think of was how great God is and that her dream was becoming a reality. Stepping into the chapel, Janie enjoyed the smell of fresh-cut wood, stain and sealant. The chapel was beautiful. Kneeling at the altar, Janie poured out her love, thankfulness, and praise to God.

"You are so good to us Father! This is a wonderful place to worship You. I love You, and I thank You for all Your blessings!"

Paul had been watching for Janie's car all morning. He had expected her two hours earlier and had to fight becoming anxious. But she was here now; relief and love surged through him. He watched her drive up to the chapel and then enter it. When he walked in, he found her kneeling at the altar, and he waited, taking a seat behind her. He looked around, enjoying the simple beauty of the place. Large windows on each side of the chapel had been set within chinked, log walls. The altar was a simple log table, with a large cross that was stained a deeper brown on the wall above the altar. There were fifteen rows of half-log benches, with another half log attached, providing backs. All these handmade seats were lined up on each side of a center aisle. Paul was pleased with the overall simplicity of the chapel. It reflected the love they all had for God, yet the focus was on Jesus and not the building.

Janie rose, filled with awe. She had never described her vision of the chapel. She had simply told them where it was. This exceeded all her hopes for the chapel. It was perfect. It would be lovely to be married here, she thought, scanning the room. Suddenly, she realized she was not alone. "Paul!"

Paul looked up, realizing he had been thanking God for His direction and guidance the last few months, months that had been filled with long days and short nights. Building was physical work, yet proved very satisfying. There was a unity in the workers that he had never encountered before. Everyone worked hard and to the best of their ability, knowing they were working for God and not for the foundation or Ranch. He stood and reached out his arms, as Janie stepped into them. "I missed you," she whispered into his ear as she hugged him.

Pulling back, Paul said, "I missed you, too. It has been a long spring and summer. I am glad it is already the first of August. It will only be three more weeks until you are my wife, and you will not have to leave again." He kissed her gently.

Taking her hand, Paul led her out the door, "Come on, I'll give you the fifty-cent tour."

After walking around and going through nearly every building, Janie was amazed. "It is wonderful! Everything is wonderful! It's like my dream came alive!" she exclaimed. "I can't believe everything is almost ready for us to move into. It seemed like there was so much to build, so much to do. I didn't believe it could be finished so soon."

"Ye of little faith," Paul teased. "We had a lot of help. All of the regulars, plus some of our church friends, who plan to move with us, came up on weekends. Even Pastor Phil and some of his buddies came nearly every Saturday to help. They will all have a home here, should they need it, when the time comes. But most of them plan to stay where they are and help Pastor Phil."

"Everything has gone so smoothly. I was talking with your parents yesterday. It sounded like things have gone together with no hitches. I can't believe everyone is on the same page about all of this. They even said the inspectors have been great."

"Yes, that is so true. God even provided us with godly inspectors." Paul laughed. "Remember at lunch, after the planning meeting when we were talking about how we felt when they told us about the Sanctuary?" Janie nodded, "Well, I hate to admit three years, no four years ago, when they first told us about the Sanctuary, I wasn't joking when I told you I thought they were nuts! Jack and Mary were joking about having them committed; I almost agreed with them. There were other members of the family—aunts, uncles, and cousins, that could not accept the idea of war or struggle of any kind. It caused fear and upset. I have a cousin who still will not even consider the idea of a war or even hard times ahead, much less the need for a sanctuary. My parents had a nice home and worked hard, but to come up with the kind of money needed to build a place like this, well . . . to us it seemed impossible. But as you know, Dad kept saying 'Where God guides, God provides.' It wasn't until later he told us he believed that he would win the lottery because that was what God had indicated to him. At that point, I really was ready to have him committed to the loony bin." He chuckled.

Janie was thoughtful for a minute, and they walked in silence. A deer darted across the path in front of them. "I love seeing all the wildlife," Janie observed, and then returned to the topic at hand. "I can see why you would think your parents were crazy. I thought I was crazy after my dream, and outside of writing down everything I could remember, I didn't do anything with it. But your parents . . . they took the vision and ran with it. They probably knew you would think they were crazy. I know your Mom said they had their doubts, yet they stayed the course."

"You bet they had their doubts. Dad and I talked about them. He said they were constantly second-guessing themselves. He said it was like something got a hold of both of them and wouldn't let go. I think the Holy Spirit was keeping it in the forefront of their minds. They began making plans, long before they said anything to us. Dad said they would talk about little things, like how the chicken coop should be built, or how many greenhouses they should have. They told Aunt Sherry and Uncle Martin first; they would talk about it from time to time, long before they won the lottery. Then they started stockpiling food and giving it to Christians who needed help. They had a huge food pantry. When they announced they had won the lottery, they made it clear that it was God's money, and they would not be spending any more than necessary on themselves or us; we were really surprised, no *shocked* would be more like it. We couldn't believe it." They continued to wander around the Ranch as they talked.

"Anyway, they paid off their house, Mary's house, all of our student loans, and credit cards. They made us pay the credit card money back, but they didn't charge us interest. Next, they set up Hope Foundation; shortly after that, they began their search for the property for the Sanctuary Ranch. They never thought about taking trips, or buying much for themselves. Mom replaced some of their furniture, but none of it was fancy, just serviceable. It was amazing to watch them. I was . . . no, I *am* very proud of them; we all are. Anyway, they thought they had more time to build the Sanctuary, and then you came along and with you the plans for this ranch. All of a sudden, there seemed a great urgency to get started. Of course the state of the country helped with the decision."

"It is really amazing! I have a dream, write it down, print it out, you pick it up after a breath-taking meeting, and now we are getting ready to move here," she said, with a sparkle of laughter in her eyes.

"I take your breath away, do I?"

"Well, you certainly did then. I remember sitting on the floor, fighting to catch my breath, and meeting you for the first time." She gave him a saucy smile, "And since you are 'fishing,' I admit you are quite an attractive man, and you do take my breath away at times."

"Why thank you, my lady, and just so you know, I think you are the most beautiful lady I have ever known. I am looking forward to spending my life with you. I only wish the wedding was tomorrow," he said with a wolfish grin.

She stepped in front of him and blocked his way; reaching up on tip toes, she kissed him. "Thank you, and I am getting impatient too, so no more of that, or we will get in trouble." She gave him another quick kiss and, taking his hand, started back down the path. "What time do you have to go back to work? We have been walking around for over two hours."

"I told everyone my sweetheart was coming today, and I would not be back to work until Monday. We have been working six days a week since May first. We only take off Sunday and go down to Pastor Phil's church. When we get back, we take the rest of the day to swim, or play a ball game or something. You know how few times I came to town to see you. The others worked just as hard."

"Changing the subject, did you know Pastor Phil used to be the pastor of a very large church in Texas? He and his wife moved here ten years ago and started this church. He is a great minister and a wonderful speaker. He told Dad his old church had over two thousand members. I can see why. Yet, he humbly serves his small flock of a hundred, or so, with the same devotion and gusto he had for the much larger church. Did you know he is fifty-five, the same age as my parents?"

"He doesn't look that old. I would have guessed mid-forties."

"Well, he has lots of energy, that's for sure. On most Saturdays, he and several church members come to help. He can work rings around some of us. He is an excellent hand at carpentry. Dad has already talked to him about coming to anoint and bless the Ranch. He asked him to consider coming here, when the need arises. But he says he will do the work God has placed before him, until he can no longer do it. That means he will be on the front lines, helping others reach safety here . . . or elsewhere."

"I know there will be a need, but I am glad I will not be on the front lines. Does Mabel plan to stay with him?"

"Yes, until it gets too dangerous. Then she will have a place here. I think their daughter and her family will be coming here, but their son and his wife will be staying to help at the church."

"By the way, did you ask him to perform our wedding service?"

"No, I didn't know if you wanted Franklin or someone else to do it. What would you prefer?"

"Let me think and pray about that. You pray, too, and I am sure God will let us know. It really doesn't matter to me that much. I just want it soon," Janie smiled.

"Let's pray about it and decide before you leave. We should have already asked someone to do it." Janie nodded.

"I feel bad we didn't discuss it earlier. We talked about everything else concerning the wedding. I guess we both have had a lot on our plates."

"It will work out. Besides, we still have three weeks, so whoever we decide on will have time to let us know, so we can make different plans if needed."

They continued to walk the property, as Paul pointed out where future buildings were planned, explaining the size and what they would be used for. Janie realized they had followed her vision closely.

It was peaceful and quiet on this mid-summer day. They talked about this and that, as they wandered around the grounds. "The gardens are going to be right here," Paul gestured around a small meadow. The creek ran down the hill behind the chapel and main lodge, then across the south side of the meadow, and the concrete pads for the greenhouses could be seen on the far side. The area was nearly twenty acres. Janie knew the fruit trees alone would take a good chunk of the area.

"We have plans for irrigation from the creek. It would be difficult to water everything without an irrigation system. We will have a small hydro system to run the pumps," Paul said, as they continued away from the meadow.

Janie noticed several small cabins, here and there, that she had not foreseen. "I was surprised to see the small cabins here, and there. I remember seeing the plans, but I never saw them in my dreams."

"Most of them are for small families, especially those with younger children. Most do not mind sharing quarters, but, being realistic, we knew some need more privacy than others. We wanted to provide that if we could. There are rooms on the second floor of the meeting hall. I think that will be for married couples, or single people. The rooms all vary in size to accommodate whatever we need." Janie nodded, and they moved on. She enjoyed hearing Paul talk about the process of building such a large complex. She was even more amazed that they had made so much progress in such a short time.

The next two days flew by, and Janie and Paul stood, saying good-bye next to her car. "Mom and Dad plan to move in three weeks. When do you plan to move?"

"I think I am on the schedule to be moved in three weeks, also. That will give me a week before the wedding, and I can see to the final plans from here. Of course, that is always subject to change. I am flexible. I have given my notice at my apartment, so I can actually move any time before the end of the month."

"Okay, so three weeks from now." Thinking, Paul calculated his building schedule, considering when he would have time to make a trip back to Spokane for a visit. "I don't want to wait that long to see you, so I will come in two weeks, then I will be back to help with the move the next week."

"Alright, but it will be a long two weeks. Work safely, and I will talk with you tonight, when I get home." They exchanged a meaningful kiss, full of promise and hope for their future. Janie climbed into her car, reluctantly, and drove slowly away. Each time she left, it was more difficult. This was the home of her future. She wished she did not have to leave; however, she knew the time would pass quickly. Many details for the wedding and the future welfare of the Sanctuary still needed to be completed. Hope Foundation was moving its base of operation to a smaller office in the basement of Pastor Phil's church, until a new building could be built in his small town. The Hope Foundation would operate, until it could no longer operate safely.

Yes, time would pass quickly, she thought. In fact, she wondered if she would have the time and energy to finish everything required before the big day. She began going over list after list of things she needed to do, and, before long, she realized she was nearly home. Wow, time does fly, when you have more to think about and not enough time to accomplish everything.

Moving day arrived at last. Janie was tired. Twelve to sixteen hour days were the norm for the past three weeks. Paul was supposed to arrive any time, and she was still boxing up her things. It had been decided that she would move with George and Elizabeth, and she would stay in one of the upstairs rooms at the main lodge, until the wedding. She did not have much furniture to transport, only the few things she purchased when she first moved to Spokane. Those would be moved to Paul's quarters; that way, she would have only her clothes to move after the wedding. She stood looking around the room at all the boxes scattered around. It was surprising how much she had accumulated in the last year and a half. Many things were things she felt would help them in their new home. She had an old-fashioned butter churn, an apple peeler, several gadgets for the kitchen, several gas lamps, as well as hair combs, brushes, pins, hair ties, makeup, moisturizer, sun screen and many other female doodads. She had purchased extra jeans, shirts, shoes, underwear, and the like. She even had a sun hat and gloves to wear, while she gardened.

She smiled, as she thought of her conversation with her Dad last night. "Are you all packed, Sweetie?"

"Mostly, Dad." She had stopped packing to answer the phone.

"Do you have all the female doodads? Your mother is still adding things to her list of "must have" items she wants to bring. In fact, she is out shopping as we speak."

"I am so glad you and Mom decided to come to the Ranch. I know it was a difficult decision for you both." As fairly new believers, it was hard for them to accept the reality of a need for a sanctuary, much less deciding to move there. But they could see, as well as anyone looking, that the tone of the country was changing.

"We both prayed about it and did a lot of talking. We figure, better safe than sorry. Besides, retirement is boring. We both needed something to keep us busy. We figure there will be lots of things we can do up there to help. It was hard on your Mom to sell the house, though. It took a great step of faith to do that. But when it sold the second day for full price, we took it as a sign from the Lord that we were doing the right thing. At any rate, you and Paul will be there, and we would like to get to know the man, who won our daughter's heart, better. I just wish your brother . . . Oh, well, no sense going there."

Janie's brother thought they were all nuts. They had told him about the Ranch, though they had not told him where it was. All he could say was the government would take care of them, if things got bad, and there was no reason to worry. Until then, he could take care of his family; besides, he had accepted Jesus as Savior, and wasn't that enough? Everyone had tried to talk with him, to help him understand what they thought was coming, but he just would not listen.

"Well, I thank the Lord you and Mom are coming." She jolted out of her thoughts at the sharp knock on the door. "Coming," she called out. Looking out the peephole, she quickly opened the door and threw herself into Paul's arms. "Hello! You are late." He pulled her close and hugged her.

"I got tied up in traffic. There was an accident; several people were hurt, and the traffic was stopped for a while. I'm here now." He pulled back, looking her up and down. "You look tired but beautiful just the same. Boy, I missed you."

"I am tired, but happy. No more separation!" Janie hugged him again and whispered in his ear, "I am looking forward to next weekend." Before he could kiss her, loud voices came from behind him.

"Okay, you two. You have all the time you want together after next weekend. Until then, we have work to do." Jill came in, carrying the baby, as Janie backed away from the door. She took one look at Janie and pushed the baby into her arms. "Here, take Sari. You look tired, and I for once got a full night's sleep. So, you sit, and I will help the guys." Within seconds the room was filled with several guys, some Janie knew and others she only recognized. It took less than thirty minutes, and the apartment she had called home for the past fifteen months was empty.

"Please leave the vacuum. I need to do a once-over before I leave," Janie called out, as Paul started to grab it. Paul by-passed it and took the last box.

"Wow, that didn't take long," Janie said incredibly.

"Well, we have it all planned. The next place on the list is June and Trevor's; they live not far from here. But that will take longer; they have a three-bedroom house and two children, then we head to our house. We are hoping to get all three homes into this moving van," Jill said, taking the baby back. "Go ahead and finish vacuuming and head over to my house. I am headed that way now. I have everything packed, but I need to nurse Sari."

"Okay." Jill left as Paul came back in. "Are you staying with the moving workers?"

"Yes," Paul said, "Where are you going?"

"I need to finish here, and then the apartment manager is coming. He needs to do the final walk-through. After that, I am headed to Jill's. So, I will see you there, when you get there."

"I only just got here, and now I have to leave. See how you are?" Paul said, smiling wistfully.

"I know, but it's only for a little while. I have a special evening planned, so don't make any plans, okay?"

"That's fine. I already put out the word that I was spending the evening with you. Jill and Curt are leaving, as soon as their house is empty and the final cleanup is done. Mary said you were staying with her tonight. I already made arrangements to stay with Mom and Dad. We are going to clear out both houses tomorrow, so we won't tear the beds apart until morning."

"Oh, I didn't know Mary's things were going on the same truck as your folks'?"

"Well, I doubt it will all fit, but we are going to do the best we can. Anything they can't get in the truck will go on the next truck. But Mary's has to be finished because the new owners are moving in the first of the week. We have four more families moving out to Hope Ranch this weekend and two next weekend, then we will be done for now. I am sure God will bring others, but we will cross that bridge when we come to it. Two families refused to sign the covenant, so Dad would not let them join us. He said we must all be equally yoked together in a covenant bond and those who would not agree to sign the covenant agreement would be more willing to cause problems. There will be a lot of work, and everyone will have to pull their weight to make this work."

Janie nodded; she knew the families that refused to sign the covenant agreement. There had been long discussions concerning the covenant. They all agreed they had to have a set of rules and agreements that would govern the Ranch. Their survival depended on everyone living in harmony and working together in love. God had given them the vision for the Sanctuary Ranch, and their covenant to live in harmony and submit to the governing council was with God and each other.

They had made some very hard decisions concerning the covenant. First, everyone who would be at the Ranch must be a born-again believer in Jesus Christ, or the spouse, or children under eighteen must be in the care of their parents. If the spouse was an unbeliever, they still had to agree to the same requirements as everyone else.

Second, everyone would be required to work on the Ranch. The men were responsible for the basic outdoor work, which included field work, firewood, animal care, repairs to the buildings or expanding them, as needed, and general repairs to generators, equipment, and fences. During the hunting season and harvest season, everyone—men and women alike, would do what was needed for the good of the Ranch. The women and children were responsible for gardening, canning, cleaning, cooking, child care, and other household needs. Everyone, except children, would do patrol duty, as needed, though the men would do the bulk of the night duty.

Third, the only exceptions to the work schedule involved those who had specialized skills, like Martin, Jack and Sherry, who had medical backgrounds. They would not have to help with the other chores, unless they did not have any patients.

Fourth, all would attend regular Bible study and worship services.

Fifth, any unresolved problems would be decided by the Community Council of twelve people, six men and six women. The council members needed to be mature believers and willing to submit to each other in love.

Sixth, there would be no drugs or alcohol allowed—period. Only prescription drugs were allowed, and even over-the-counter drugs were to be dispensed by the medical personnel of the community.

Seventh, if anyone caused any major problems, they could be expelled, but only after everything was done to try to resolve the issue. It was hoped that expulsion would not be needed.

Eighth, everyone outside the Community Council and those who did not need to know the location of the Ranch would be brought in blindfolded. They had worked hard to keep the location, size, and scope of the Ranch quiet, even secret. They did not want to have to defend themselves from marauders, but they would, if the need arose. This was a sanctuary from the evils of the world, a haven, yet they were willing to defend themselves. There had been some who felt killing was wrong. There had been much discussion about personal reservations in that area. However, they went back to the Ten Commandments where it says, "Thou shall not murder." Through the years, many had changed the original text to read, "Thou shall not kill," but that was incorrect. "It has to do with the intent of the heart," George said. "We are simply going to protect ourselves and our families. There is nothing wrong with that." In the end, everyone agreed that they would have to defend themselves, if the need arose.

Stepping forward, Janie laid her head on Paul's chest and held him briefly. Pulling back, she looked up and smiled, "I will see you at Jill's. I plan to shower and change clothes, then we can leave, okay?"

"Fine, I'll bring my clothes and shower downstairs, while you are upstairs. That will save time." He kissed her lightly, and then he turned toward the door. He heard the vacuum as he headed out.

CHAPTER 20

THE RESTAURANT WAS A new, softly lit place, with a very comfortable atmosphere, situated on the shore of Lake Coeur d'Alene. A young woman led them to a table on the outside deck, next to a railing. The evening had cooled down from the ninety-degree day, to a comfortable seventy-two. A light breeze floated off the water, and the boats, docked along the edge of the lake, bobbed gently. They could smell the light floral scent of roses drifting up from the plants on the other side of the railing. They sat quietly, looking at the menus, until the waiter arrived and took their orders for prime rib and baked potato, salad, French rolls and iced tea with lemon. After the waiter left, Paul reached across the table to take Janie's hand.

"All day I wanted to hold you, but I restrained myself. I knew I would not want to let you go," Paul said, while looking seriously into her eyes. "One week from tonight you will be mine. I want you to know I promise to love, protect and cherish you. After Jesus, you are the most important thing in my life. Nothing will come before you but Him. Dad expects things to get very difficult. You have heard him; if these are not the end times, they will certainly be hard times. I just want you to know I will do everything in my power to keep you safe. But none of us knows what will actually happen. We are preparing for the worst, as you know, but . . . " he broke off.

"Paul, I know," she said, gently, in almost a whisper. "Jesus never promised us it would be an easy life; He only promised He would be with us. I don't expect you to change what you cannot change. You have already promised the things that are most important to me, and I promise to be at your side, supporting, loving, and cherishing you in return. That is all we can do. Whatever happens, we are in this together. That is all that matters."

"It's just that all this is finally becoming reality. All the time I was working at the Ranch, I knew why we were building it, yet it somehow didn't sink in."

"We cannot have a spirit of worry, anxiety, or fear; you know that. We need to be careful, but Jesus is our shield, remember? I know you love me, but what is the worst that can happen? I die and go to be with Jesus, or you go to be with Jesus. Don't get me wrong; that would be horrible. It would break my heart. But Jesus gave us hope, the expectation of seeing each other in heaven."

"My head knows all that you are saying, and it believes it to be true, but my heart has never had this kind of love before."

"To be honest, I have been having the same feelings." She smiled. "You just expressed it before I had a chance. I am telling you what I have been telling myself for several days now."

Paul smiled and then spoke, "Well, we are in this together with Jesus, and we know He wins in the end. So, let's turn the conversation to lighter subjects. Tell me what you haven't told me on the phone for the last week."

The conversation turned to the practical matters of the move and the last minute details concerning orders of supplies, animals, fruit trees, and additional vegetable seeds.

"We finally were able to get the fruit trees confirmed. Usually, the grower doesn't ship them in the fall, but I persuaded them we would plant them immediately, so they relented. We need to get them in the ground, as soon as they arrive. We need to have the holes dug and labeled ahead of time. The trees will be dormant, and they will wake up in the spring in their new home. We should have fruit in three to five years."

"Jill said something about the pollinators being wrong on the apple trees. What was that all about?"

"As you know, the trees must flower at the same time, in order to pollinate; I wasn't careful, and I started to order the wrong ones at first. Luckily, the owner of the nursery called and pointed out my mistake. So, after changing the order, we went over everything else, to make sure I ordered the right ones for our growing season and climate. It wouldn't be good to have any die, simply because it's too cold for the ones I ordered. I didn't make any zone mistakes, but he did have a couple of suggestions, so I did change things because a couple of the apples I ordered didn't store as well as others. We also changed the cherries a little. All in all, we will have four kinds of apples, one variety of pear, one plum, two cherry, and two varieties of walnut trees . . . oh, and two kinds of peach trees. In all, we will have over one hundred trees. I think we will have a good variety of fruits. Too bad we couldn't have planted them last spring, but I guess one growing season won't make that much difference. Buying them directly from the grower saved us money, per tree, and since we wanted at least five of each kind, it worked out great."

"I like fruit. I'm glad we will have a good variety of trees, and, by having so many of each, it will not be a problem if we lose one or two, here and there."

Janie gave a thoughtful nod. "That's what I thought. The vegetable seeds are another story. Everyone has favorites. Jill likes Roma tomatoes, your Mom likes cherry tomatoes, my Mom and several others like Early Girl tomatoes, and so I got some of all those and several more. Then we have several squash, four kinds of peppers, six or seven herbs, beets, and three kinds of lettuce, celery, turnips, cabbage, and carrots. Then there are red and yellow seed potatoes, red and yellow onion sets, as well as Walla Walla onions. Blackberries, strawberries, and rhubarb complete the list. Last but not least, I ordered flower seeds. Your Mom told me of some of her favorite annuals. We have petunia, marigolds, pansies, and asters, to name a few."

"I knew Mom would not be able to live without her flowers. I knew she added shrubs to the nursery order. She said it would not be spring without the scent of lilacs floating on the breeze."

"I agree wholeheartedly," Janie said enthusiastically. "I love lilacs."

As they talked, their meal was served, and they ate slowly, enjoying the evening and the privacy. When they once got settled at the Sanctuary Ranch, they would not have much private time over a meal, since all the meals would be served cafeteria style in the fellowship hall. They knew their private time would be limited, so they took their time now.

"So, is everything ready for the families?" Janie asked, as their plates were cleared away.

"Yes, for the most part; in fact, some have already moved in. There are some fences we still need to put up, and the garden still needs some work before the fruit trees arrive, but the buildings are ready. The last of the supply shipments will arrive this week, and we will be ready for winter. Of course, we will still need to bring in more firewood, but that's going to be a full- time job for several people spring, summer and fall. We won't finish the recreation area till next spring, but we won't need it during the winter, anyway."

"Well, now there will be a lot more hands to help with the work, so it should go pretty fast, don't you think?"

"True, but the first week everyone will be settling in and getting used to the newness of everything."

"Well, it won't take me long, since I don't have much to organize. How organized are the supplies that have already been received?"

Paul smiled, "Hand it to you to wonder about that. Well, as you know, Bonnie and Nathan arrived last week, so they were there when the last two trucks arrived. Bonnie took charge and saw to it they got put away in the right places. But the three we got before that are in the store room, but there is no organization. I heard Bonnie mumbling about disorganized males. By the way, Nathan is a wonderful mechanic, besides helping us put together a fire prevention program. He even put us in touch with someone we can get a used fire tanker truck from."

"He is a wonderful man. He fixed my car a while back. They are both wonderful friends. I am so glad they decided to come to the ranch with us. Anyway, Bonnie and I can get things in order pretty quickly." The waiter came and asked if they would like dessert. Janie's eyes sparkled. "Of course, it might be the last time I enjoy pecan pie for a long while, though I did slip in an order of nuts, so maybe I can try my hand at making one."

"Would you like it heated, with ice cream?" The waiter asked, writing it down.

"Please," she replied.

Turning to Paul, he asked, "You sir?"

"I think I will have a banana split."

"Yes, sir. Would either of you like coffee?"

"No, thank you," Paul answered for them both. "But we would like refills on our iced tea, please."

"Certainly, sir." The waiter left to put in their orders.

"So, you like pecan pie?" Paul asked, interested.

"Yes, there are not many pies I don't like."

"Does it bother you that there are a lot of things you may never be able to do?" he inquired.

"Not really. Well, it did for a while. I mean, I had plans for my life. I wanted to travel, to see Europe. I wanted to do some short missionary trips, both in the states and abroad. But somewhere along the way, God gave me a contentment with staying right here. Besides, I am finally getting a handle on those verses that talk about Christ living in me, and it is not me but Christ that lives. That seemed so foreign to me, but it is making more sense to me now. To me, it means doing what needs to be done today, walking quietly and humbly with God, and doing the will of the Father—wherever He leads. It means I may not want to do something, but I will anyway. It means I may not like where God is leading, but I will go. In other words, it is not about me anymore; it's about Jesus. More importantly, I am finding that God gives me the desire to do what He wants me to do. So, there really isn't a struggle there. I want to do what He asks of me. What about you?"

"Yes and no. I had just graduated from Bible college, when Dad and Mom won the lottery. As soon as that happened, I knew my life was forever changed. Not in a bad way and, back then, not in a good way, either; it was just different. I wasn't sure I liked the responsibility that fell to me, but God has a way of working everything for our good. I really enjoyed working for the foundation. The Sanctuary Ranch wasn't mentioned that much, at first, so, I really didn't give it much thought. But I had an idea things were going to change, and they did.

"God was already stretching me and confronting me about some of the ideas I picked up from some of my Christian buddies. Some of them were allowing the world to pull them from their faith in Jesus. They were compromising, settling just short of sin. They were drinking, and their talk about women was . . . well, let's just say it was disrespectful. There were some who believed they could do anything they wanted because Jesus would forgive them anyway. I knew that was wrong, but it wasn't until one of my best friends moved in with his girlfriend that I realized I was skating on the line."

"What did you do?"

"The hardest thing I have ever done; I severed my friendship with him. I didn't want to be one of those holier-than-thou Christians, but he didn't see what he was doing as wrong, that he was sinning against God and his girlfriend. He said she wanted to live with him, so it didn't matter. You know the whole line about 'it's just a piece of paper' argument. When I asked him about fornication, he said God would forgive him, so it was alright. I knew it didn't work that way. We can't just do whatever we want and then later ask forgiveness; it was a preplanned sin. I mean, you can ask at any time for forgiveness, but there has to be true repentance. Anyway, that was a turning point for me. I knew I had to make a choice . . . the world and its ways or Jesus and His ways. Jesus won, hands down. I had stopped reading my Bible and studying, so I joined a Bible study and asked Curt to be my accountability partner."

"I would have never guessed that you drifted away like that," Janie observed.

"Yes, drifted, backslid, whatever you want to call it; I drifted more than I would ever like to admit. It's surprising how fast it can happen. When you take your eyes off of Jesus, it only takes moments, and Satan can bring sinful thoughts to mind— or actions. Jesus is the armor that shields us from much of that stuff; when we drop that armor, we are open to all kinds of junk. You know the verses in Ephesians 6, where it talks about putting on the whole armor of God, and I have found it is very important to my daily walk with the Lord. It helps to protect me from all kinds of attacks.

"Pornography is a real threat to men. Movies, books, and women, in general, and the way many of them dress can bring sin into the lives of a lot of men. Unless they learn how to avoid looking at women in a sexual way, it can become a real addiction for men. Sex is important to men, but it is meant for marriage only. Unfortunately, the world doesn't see it that way, and the church has not taken a strong stand against all kinds of sexual sin. I mean, they focus on adultery or homosexuality and gloss over fornication, which includes any sex between unmarried people. But in God's eyes, it is all the same; all sex outside of marriage is all sin."

Janie blushed. She couldn't help it. "I am sorry; I didn't mean to embarrass you," Paul said in honest contrition.

"No, it's alright. We are going to be married, and I want to be a wife in every way, but I know very little about what men think about. I mean, I used to go to the movies a lot, and I saw more than my share of sex scenes, when I was younger, but having no personal experience limits my knowledge. And I certainly do not understand what men think," she smiled.

Paul reached to take her hand. "We will learn about sex together, and as for what I think, you will learn soon enough." Paul gave her a convincing smile, and Janie blushed as she nodded. Nothing else was said, and Paul wisely changed the subject. Looking around, he noticed that the deck was nearly empty of customers. "As much as I do not want this evening to end, I think they are close to closing. Oh, before I forget, the beehives and equipment arrived."

"That's good. I have a sweet tooth, and even though we have a large supply of sugar and sugar substitute, honey is better." Janie looked around and saw the place was empty, except for the employees who were doing the final cleanup. "This has been a wonderful night."

"It has been a great evening; thank you for thinking of it." Paul signaled for the check. When it arrived, Janie snatched it away.

"I invited you. I am not a women's libber, but please, let me do this, just this time, okay?" Janie asked.

Paul smiled, "Whatever you'd like; after Saturday, what's yours is mine, and what's mine is yours."

Janie paid, as Paul left a large tip on the table for their waiter. They walked leisurely, as they made their way to their car. The stars shone brightly in a cloudless sky. The temperature had dropped some, but it was still comfortable. Janie held Paul's hand and leaned against him, as they walked. Here and there, other couples walked down the street, enjoying the lingering smells of late summer. Fall would soon make its way to the northwest, bringing brisk winds, cold temperatures and snow. But tonight, summer still lingered, with the gentle sway of the leaves in the trees.

Janie woke with a stretch and a wide smile. Today was her wedding day. All her life she had looked forward to this day, even more so since becoming a believer. She knew marriage was a reflection of the relationship between Jesus and His bride, the church. There were mysteries in marriage that she did not understand because she was not married, but today, some of those mysteries would be revealed. She already understood a little because of her love for Paul, but she knew there was much more. She wanted the intimacies with both Jesus and Paul. She understood it was different with Jesus but similar, just the same. Each new understanding brought her closer to understanding her Lord.

"I am getting married today, Lord Jesus. I am so happy. Paul is a wonderful man, and I love him dearly. He is a man after Your heart—and mine, as well. Thank You so much for bringing him into my life. Help me to be an understanding and loving helpmate to him. Help us to serve You in all things. Be with us today and always!"

The service was simple, yet beautiful in its simplicity. The small chapel was filled with flowers, their aroma filling the air with their sweet perfume. People filled every bench, and others stood on the sides, watching the first wedding performed at the Ranch. There were two more scheduled, one next week and another at Christmas.

Janie walked down the center aisle, adorned in a gown of white satin, escorted by her father. She carried a large bouquet of white and red roses. When Paul saw her, he stood taller and buttoned his jacket, as a wide smile spread across his face. All he could think was how blessed he was to have her as his wife and how much he loved her. Janie smiled brightly and kept her eyes on Paul, until her father kissed her on the cheek. She looked at him briefly, as she returned his kiss, and then she turned her eyes back to her future.

Pastor Phil read the simple marriage ceremony, and then Janie and Paul exchanged the time-honored marriage vows, followed by the reading of 1Corinthians 13, the love chapter, before they were pronounced husband and wife. The married couple was greeted with a roaring applause, and the celebration began. They were celebrating not only this wedding but the beginning of a new life at the Sanctuary Ranch.

Janie looked around the garden that surrounded the small chapel. It was not exactly the same as her picture, but it was beautiful, just the same. Young lilac bushes had been planted to create a fence around the yard; as time passed, they would be wonderful in the springtime. A border of flowers lined the front of the building. Shrubs were planted along the sides of the building, with several kinds of ground covers that would fill in under them. There was a small rose garden made up of winter-hardy varieties on the south side, where several trees had been removed to provide enough sun. On the north and east side of the yard, hosta, lilies, astillbe, and ferns, mixed with annuals for color, filled the flower beds. It was very nice now and would be even more beautiful, as the years ticked by and the plants grew. All in all, it was a wonderful setting for her wedding reception.

Paul slipped his arm around her, "A penny for your thoughts."

"I was just admiring the gardens. They are lovely. I would like to plant more around the lodge. It would make it homier. Besides, I know your Mom would like them, too. I think she has just been too busy to do it herself."

He smiled a mischievous smile. He knew she thought they would be living in the main lodge; however, he had built a cabin just for her. He had not shown it to her in his tour because he wanted to surprise her with their new home today. He knew she would be delighted. He also knew that by this time next year their home would be surrounded with all the color her flowers could provide. "And here I thought all your thoughts would be of me, Mrs. Hamilton."

"So, you are greedy for my every thought?" She smiled suggestively.

"Well, not every thought. I will allow your thoughts about God, Jesus, and the like, but all others should center on me, don't you think?"

"Allow?" she asked in mock horror.

"Well, you did promise to love, honor, and obey."

"Yes, I did. Well, what has that got to do with what I think about?"

"I really don't know, but it sounded good."

Janie laughed, "Well, we will just see as time goes on, shall we?" Paul kissed her, before leading her back to visit with their guests.

The afternoon was filled with a wonderful meal, traditional wedding cake, and a toast. The sun was on the western horizon when they said their goodbyes, and Paul led Janie down the road away from the chapel. "Where are we going?" Janie asked, looking back toward the direction of the main lodge.

"It is a wonderful time for a walk, don't you think?" Paul asked, avoiding her question. Janie gave him a questioning look, as she took his hand. They walked past three cabins and turned up a small road that was leading up a slight hill. The birds sang love songs to one another, as other small forest animals scampered here and there. Before scurrying up a tree, a chipmunk scolded them, as they walked past his home. After rounding a bend in the road, a cabin came into view.

Janie drew her breath, "It's ours, isn't it?"

"Yes. I wanted to surprise you."

After standing in awe and surprise for several moments, Janie pulled his hand, propelling him forward with excitement in every step. Two barrels, filled with flowers, stood on either side of the front steps. "Oh, how wonderful," she breathed, before climbing the steps to a porch that wrapped around three sides of the cabin. She spied the porch swing that hung from the rafters on one end. Stepping to the front door, she opened it gingerly, preparing to enter her new home.

"Wait." Lifting her, Paul carried Janie over the threshold of their new home. Putting her down, he kissed her and then hugged her close, whispering in her ear, "Welcome to your new home."

Janie stepped back and looked around her. The front door opened into a great room with the living room containing a wood stove straight ahead on the left, and a dining room and small kitchen situated at the end of the room. They had decided to put small kitchens in the cabins, even though most meals would be prepared at the main lodge or dining hall. It allowed a certain amount of privacy for families. In addition, there were so many changes in their lives that they wanted to preserve some sense of normalcy. "The hall leads to three bedrooms and two bathrooms." Paul indicated to the right. "There is a laundry room and mud room through the hall over there," as he pointed to the left.

Janie wandered here and there, touching the back of a sofa and two matching chairs, then she proceeded through the dining room, admiring the oak table with six chairs. She found her pots and pans, as well as her other kitchen things, in the cupboards, along with what she assumed belonged to Paul. She checked out the laundry and bath, then turned to the hall. One room was empty, its hardwood floor gleaming as the last rays of sunlight came through the windows. The second room held her bed and dresser, with two small carpet strips on each side of the bed. A small bathroom was next. Paul propped himself against the door jamb, as Janie walked around their bedroom. A king-size bed, with nightstands and lamps on each side, took up most of the floor space of the room. A large dresser with a mirror stood on one side of the room, and windows looked out over the yard on the other. A master bathroom and closet completed her tour. Her paintings and other wall hangings were stacked in the corner, waiting for her to place them on the walls.

Janie sat down on the bed and looked at her husband of a few hours. "You did all this for me, didn't you?"

"Of course. I wanted a nice place for my wife, a place she could call her own. I knew you would be happy in the main lodge, but I wanted this for you."

With a serious expression, Janie rose and walked to Paul, "Thank you. You didn't have to do this, but it is absolutely wonderful. Have I told you today that I love you?"

"I think a time or two, but I will never get tired of hearing it."

As she hugged him tightly, she whispered, "I plan to tell you every day for the rest of my life. I love you, Paul Hamilton."

"And I love you, Janie Hamilton."

Life at the Ranch

CHAPTER 21

JILL SAT, STARING OUT the window, watching the birds fluttering from tree to tree, as the bumble bees bounced from flower to flower, gathering the last bits of nectar, before fall withered the last of the flowers and turned the leaves to a riot of color. She was surprised at the contentment she felt. Having always been a city girl, she thought she would miss the fast pace of city life, including the constant noise of a city that never really slept. Yet, here she was enjoying the quiet of the early morning. Curt had left at dawn to hunt with some of the other hunters, men and women who like the sport. The children were still sleeping, giving her a few precious minutes to herself. Her Bible and devotional books lay on the table, as she pondered her feelings and emotions.

The move to the Ranch was complete. All who planned to come now were here. Though Jill missed a few friends, everyone closest to her was here. There was peacefulness to the valley that had calmed her from the start. She understood the work to come would not be easy, but now was a calm, peaceful time, and she meant to enjoy every minute.

The last months had passed in a blur of long days and sleepless nights. Jill decided that planning, moving, and having babies should never happen close together. It was easier now that Sari was sleeping through the night, but during that first few months, she was more like a sleep-walker. There had been more chores to do than hours in the day to do them. The needs of an infant and a toddler, along with all the preparations for the move, had nearly worn her out. Thank the Lord for a wonderful husband and extended family and friends who stepped up to help. She knew her thoughts were jumping from topic to topic at a rapid pace, and she smiled, realizing that it was nice to simply sit and think. She did not have to go anywhere right away. She did not have to work on a report that was past due. She did not have any foundation work to attend to. And, for right this minute, she did not have children to care for.

Her thoughts jumped back to all those living on the Ranch. Most she had known for years. Bonnie was a new friend; she was turning out to be a wonderful friend. Peter and Harold had become best buddies. It was nice to have the boys close in age. Harold was a wonderful, little boy. He was friendly, polite, and well behaved. She enjoyed having him around, probably as much as Peter did.

Curt was impressed with Nathan. The fire prevention program Nathan put together gave everyone a sense of comfort. He had called for and led everyone through emergency drills, with meeting places for women with children, as well as firefighting drills for everyone else. So far, they had had three drills; the first had been a disaster. But by the second one, they were better, and the third was better still. They were confident now that everyone knew what to do, where to go, and who their buddies were, so they were sure everyone would get to where they were supposed to be. Every family had a neighboring family that would be their buddy family. Singles, or couples, were paired up with another couple, or single, so this way, if someone did not arrive at their designated place after the drill, their buddy would notify someone right away.

They had worked out a plan to conduct surprise drills every three months. It would give everyone practice in all kinds of weather. It would also give everyone the skills to fight a fire, should this become necessary. At Nathan's suggestion, George had purchased an old fire engine, complete with a water tank. They had built a small fire station next to the barn to house the tanker engine, as well as the other necessary fire equipment. Everyone understood the importance of fire prevention, but it was nice to know what to do in case they faced a real fire.

In addition to his firefighting skills, Nathan was an accomplished mechanic. He was becoming a great asset, repairing the tractor when it gave out after a very short time. Since it was used and acquired as is, they were responsible for the repairs. As it turned out, Nathan found it had a few other problems that could have resulted in engine problems, and so he made the necessary repairs, before the tractor was damaged beyond repair. He was now working on producing ethanol to replace gasoline for all their engines. They knew it was only a matter of time before they had trouble getting fuel of any kind. They wanted to have several alternatives ready when the need arose. Next, they would work on producing hydrogen and then methane gas.

Bonnie was an organizer. She and Janie had worked long hours, arranging the warehouse and cataloging everything. When they were finished, anyone could go to the warehouse, and after consulting the location diagram, could find anything they wanted, easily. Everyone was quite impressed with their work. They would keep the warehouse full, until they could no longer order from outside sources. It was during the time Bonnie and Janie were working together that Jill babysat Harold, and the boys played. She smiled, as she saw in her mind's eye the boys playing for hours in the little sandbox Curt had made for them in the small back yard. Bonnie and Nathan's cabin was out of sight, but just down the road. It would be easy for the boys to get together nearly every day; she smiled at the thought.

Jill knew George was a little unhappy that the houses were so far apart. He felt it would be harder to defend themselves this way. He had decided that all new buildings would be much closer to the main lodge. But Jill was happy about her home being somewhat secluded. It gave her a sense of normalcy. She loved everyone, but she liked her privacy.

Megan Lopez was another great addition to the Ranch. A longtime friend of the family, Megan had come to work at the foundation after her husband died. She was a great resource for the Ranch. Her cooking and canning skills were a wonderful asset. Having come from a very large family, she adapted the recipes to a larger group. Her warm, funny nature made everyone feel comfortable around her. She made working with her a joy. Jill could not remember a time when Megan was depressed or down. Even when talking about her deceased husband, Megan spoke with love and confidence that she would see him again someday.

Megan had two teenagers, Mario and Susan. They were great kids and enjoyed helping around the Ranch. Education was very important to everyone at the Ranch, so they had established a homeschool program for all the children. Being the oldest children at the Ranch for now, Mario and Susan helped with the younger children, when the adults were busy. They helped with their lessons, read to them, and enjoyed playing games with them. The children, in exchange, adored Mario and Susan.

Valerie and Albert Weber were Janie's parents. Jill did not know them well, but they seemed like very nice people. They were friendly, hardworking folks that were quick to help out wherever they could. When the greenhouse frames arrived, they jumped right in. With the help of several of the men, they had the greenhouses standing and ready to go within a month. She was sure you would be able to find them in the greenhouses throughout the winter making tables, arranging supplies, and preparing anything else needed for the spring planting. Valerie was putting together a seed rack and storage unit, as well as making up planting schedules, plant amounts, and mapping locations in the greenhouse for each kind of plant and its particular variety. They wanted all the tomatoes together, all the squash and so forth together to make it easy to locate later.

Manny was a black man in his late forties. He had worked with George for years and then later at the foundation. Jill liked Manny very much. Manny had lost his family in a house fire some ten years before, while he had been at work. It had been a very difficult time for Manny, and George had gone out of his way to support his friend.

Gordon was another single man who had been touched by heartache. His young son had been killed in an auto accident, followed by the death of his wife to cancer two years later. It seemed many had been through life-changing experiences that had solidified their faith in God. Where many others would blame God, these clearly understood that God was not the author of these events. He was blamed by the people in the world for everything they deemed bad in the world. Yet, Jill knew God only wanted good for people. It was not in His character to purposely bring pain—only healing and restoration.

Jill's thoughts jumped ahead to the first week of October. The fruit trees would be delivered and would be planted. They could have waited until spring, however, they felt there was so much to be done come spring that it would be one thing they could do now. The holes for the trees were nearly all finished and ready for planting. Though she knew it would take several years before the trees would produce much more than a handful of fruit, just the thought of a fresh, ripe peach made her mouth water.

Realizing her alone time today was rapidly diminishing, she turned back to her Bible reading and devotions. Everyone was working on a lesson they would present, and she still didn't have any idea what God wanted her to do. She knew He would let her know, but reading and studying would give her some idea. Maybe He already had inspired her with something, as 'The Goodness of God,' became a thought. Yes, that would be a wonderful idea. After only twenty minutes of studying, the sounds of Peter stirring from his sleep reached her ears.

"Well, Father, another day is in full swing. I thank You for this time alone. Be with me throughout the day and give me patience, understanding, and love to share with my family and friends. I love You and thank You for all your many blessings and our wonderful new home. I know it isn't as grand as heaven will be, but it's peaceful and comfortable."

Bonnie was finishing her morning devotions, when she felt the strong desire to thank God for all His blessings. The greatest part of living at the Ranch was being a part of this wonderful new family. Both she and Nathan were only children of only children; neither of them had brothers nor sisters, aunts, uncles, or cousins. It had always been a desire of her heart to have a large family, something she missed as she grew up. Now, God had provided one. Jill, Mary, and Janie were wonderful sisters. They had taken her in and embraced her, like they had known her all her life. They teased, played jokes on her, and argued with her, just like sisters did. And she loved them, even when they had short sheeted the bed, and she had had to remake it after a very long day. She smiled at the memory, though she had not smiled much at the time. She knew Nathan felt the same way about the guys on the Ranch. He had commented that he never knew what he was missing until now. "It's nice to have brothers in the Lord. They hold you accountable and help to expand your knowledge and understanding of the Lord and His ways."

She understood the reason they banded together on the Ranch, and she had an inner assurance they could survive anything, as long as they worked together as a unit . . . as the body of Christ. She thought about everything she was learning: gardening, canning, and farming, in general. More importantly, she was learning about Jesus.

Their Bible studies and discussions were wonderful. The give and take of ideas, opinions, and beliefs helped her establish her own personal beliefs. Though their core beliefs were the same, there were gray areas, and in those areas there were a variety of opinions. But even in their differences of opinions, there was the unity of the Lord . . . They simply agreed to disagree. The important thing was that they all believed Jesus is the Son of God; He lived a righteous, holy life; He suffered a horrible death on the cross, as He bore the sins of the world; He died and descended to hell, following His death, and there broke the bonds of sin and death; He then rose again and is now seated beside God in Heaven. These truths tied them together as one body. This was the foundation of the Ranch and all the people living here. This is what made them family. Bonnie could see Jesus in each one and hoped they could see Jesus in her, also.

Bonnie knelt and prayed, grateful, thankful and overwhelmed with the love she felt for all the blessings God had provided. *"Father, You are so wonderful. You have provided the family I have longed for. Nathan and Peter are wonderful, but I needed an extended family, and You have provided one. You are so good. Thank You. I praise You for all Your many, many blessings. Guide and direct me this day to do Your will in all things. My heart overflows with thankfulness for all You do. In Jesus name I pray. Amen."*

After her devotion time, Bonnie rose to start her day. While humming, "This is the day the Lord hath made," she dressed in warm work clothes. Nathan and Harold would be up any minute, and as soon as they had had breakfast, they would start their day. Nathan was still working with several others at the barn, and she and Harold would make their way to Jill's. She was watching Harold today, while Bonnie worked with Janie, organizing the last of the supplies in the warehouse. She smiled; it didn't seem like work, when you enjoyed what you were doing and the people you worked with.

When Sunday arrived, the day of rest, Paul sighed, while cradling his wife of three weeks. After the wedding, Paul and Janie spent their honeymoon time at their small cabin. There were several small cabins around the complex. Paul appreciated the privacy it afforded them. They had set aside a week alone in their new home, before they ventured back to the main complex. There was still much to do before winter arrived. The past two weeks had been filled with building new fences, cutting firewood, finishing the irrigation system, and preparing everything for the winter ahead.

The wind generators were working perfectly. They even had more power than they needed. Curt had spent many hours working on the electrical system for the Ranch. He was now working on a hydro generator, using the creek and lake to power it. They wanted a complete electrical system that would keep them off grid, yet keep them fully powered, even as the Ranch grew—and they believed it would grow. They had decided to turn off all outside lights at night and use only flashlights with rechargeable batteries, to cut down the ability of being seen from above, not that satellites had not already taken pictures of everything they had done. They simply wanted to get in the habit of not broadcasting their size and location. They had deliberately left trees around the buildings, to hide them as much as possible. Anything they could do to keep their location secret was being done.

The men and some of the more sporting women went hunting several times. They had several deer and two elk hanging, waiting for butchering and packaging. Soon, the two walk-in freezers would be full and ready for the coming year. But with a group as large as theirs, they knew it would take more than what they had to feed everyone for the long winter. There were already frozen vegetables, fruits, and juices, in addition to the four cows and two pigs, already butchered, and packaged, and in the freezer. This included sausage, bacon, ham, chicken, steaks, roasts, and lots of hamburger. Since there were no gardens to harvest this year, the women purchased fruits and vegetables for their canning. They wanted to learn together how to can, with room for errors and mishaps, before they actually harvested their first garden. The ladies had filled the rest of the indoor pantry with jars of green beans, peas, tomatoes, sauces, peaches, pears and whatever other fruits and vegetables they wanted to have on hand. They still had the late fruits yet to can or dry, while the men used the tiller to prepare the ground for the spring planting and built fences. Janie and Bonnie re-organized the warehouse and pantry of the main lodge and meeting hall.

There was serenity and unity at the Ranch, a peaceful harmony that allowed all reservations, fears, and feelings of separation to dissipate. There were five families with children, all of whom were now comfortably situated in the cabins, and eleven couples, either in the main lodge, cabins, or in the rooms above the meeting hall. In addition, there were nine single people, either in the bunkhouse or above the meeting hall, for a total of sixty-two souls at the Ranch. The singleness of spirit allowed them to work with joy and agreement.

Regular prayer and Bible studies were held daily. Everyone made an effort to attend one or another, or both, each day. Everyone realized that God was their strength, and in the days ahead, they would need that strength. No one knew what they would encounter, but all wanted to be as prepared as possible.

Janie stirred, interrupting Paul's musings. "Good morning," she said, opening sleepy eyes to look into her husband's eyes.

"Good morning, sleepy head," Paul replied, kissing her nose.

"What time is it?"

"Nearly time to get up. I knew you would be a slug getting up this morning, if we stayed and played games with Jill and Curt."

"What happened to the idea of never saying 'I told you so'?" They had wandered back to Jill and Curt's cabin after dinner and then had spent a very enjoyable evening playing board games, talking, and laughing.

"I never actually said the words," he smiled, kissing her nose again.

"Yes, well, I had a great time, so I am not sorry—at least not right now. Maybe this evening I will be, but not right now." She snuggled against him. "Hmmm . . . I like waking up next to you. Most mornings you are up and gone before I wake up."

He kissed her gently, "Well, the early bird catches the worm."

"I will never know how you can have so much energy and sleep so little." They always retired together, but Paul usually slept only six or seven hours. Janie knew she would be grumpy, if she didn't get at least eight hours of sleep each night.

"What's on your schedule this week?"

"Today," she stretched, thinking, "after church we are having lunch at the meeting hall. This afternoon I thought we could go for a walk down by the lake and spend some time alone." She snuggled closer, "Seems like we don't get much of that these days." He held her close and kissed the top of her head. "We plan to plant the fruit trees tomorrow. They were delivered to Pastor Phil Friday, and he is bringing them with him this afternoon. It will probably take a couple of days to plant them all. The rest of the week, I am not sure."

"I can help with the planting, if you like. I don't have anything pressing, until I leave on Thursday. I was helping Nathan and Mike work on the ethanol still, but I think I get in their way more than I help." He propped his head on his arm so he could look at her. "Are you sure you won't go with me?" One of the missions needed some work done after a bad storm blew off part of the roof. Paul and two of the other men were leaving to help make the necessary repairs; the time was fast approaching when they would no longer make trips of this kind. For that reason, Paul knew they needed to make the necessary repairs now.

"I would like to, but we are receiving the last of our supply shipments sometime this week. I know Bonnie could handle it, but it is a lot of work for one person. The rest of the ladies are finishing the canning and will need every hand with that and watching the young ones. Mario and Susan are doing a great job supervising the older kids, but we have more little toddlers than one person can handle by themselves. If I'm gone, that would be one less set of hands."

"Okay." He stuck out his lower lip in a pout.

Janie laughed, as she kissed him. "Poor baby; I promise I will go next time, okay?"

"If there is a next time, I'm going to hold you to it." After a last kiss and hug, they rose and dressed for a Sunday at the Ranch. "You know, the time will come when no one will leave the Ranch much, unless we are needed to help someone," he added thoughtfully.

"Yes, I know. But I really have no desire to leave. I like it here. This is home. There were times last summer that I would be sad for days after I went back to Spokane after visiting here. I am not sure what it is about this place, but it is home, like no other place I have ever lived before. Besides, there is so much to do; I don't want others to have to finish projects I began."

"Well, I can understand that, but that doesn't change the fact that I will miss you. In the meantime, I plan to make the most of our time together." Janie laughed and hugged him close.

CHAPTER 22

THE PLANTING WENT VERY well. The fruit trees were all in the ground, and the twelve-foot fence surrounding the garden protected the young trees from rabbits, deer, or any other animal that could do damage to the trees or vegetables that would grow there next summer. Janie looked around in satisfaction. The clear, cool October day was perfect for planting. She was glad to have the young trees in the fertile soil.

She looked around the garden. The trees were planted, surrounding the large garden just inside the fence. All the land had been tilled and fertilizer mixed into the fertile dirt. All was in readiness for spring planting. Now, it would rest until spring, when the baby plants they would grow in the greenhouses would be planted, as soon as the weather allowed. They needed to wait until the soil temperature would allow the plants to grow and thrive. They could not afford to jump the gun and lose their crops to a late frost.

"Looks good, doesn't it?" Bonnie asked, as she stood next to Janie, looking over their hard work of the past few weeks.

"Yes, I can't wait to get out here next spring."

"Me, too; I have never done any gardening before. I am really excited about it. I won't have a lot of time, but I want to help when I can." She gently rubbed the small child growing inside her.

"I love it," Janie confided. "My parents always had a large garden while I was young. They purchased the greenhouse business when I was in junior high, and I worked there, until I graduated from high school. I really liked working with the plants and watching them grow. I enjoyed trying to plan so that everything would bloom during the selling season. That was the challenge. People would rather buy something they can see blooming than something that only has the potential of blooming."

"I guess you're right; I never thought of it like that. I always bought plants that had flowers or buds already on them," Bonnie said and then changed the subject. "I am not looking forward to winter. It is not my favorite season, and I am afraid it will be a long winter. I don't really like the cold."

"I think it will go by rapidly. We have lots of books, board games, and several people are giving classes. Mom is going to give a sewing class for anyone who doesn't know how to sew. Sherry is giving a first aid class. There are going to be classes on cooking for large groups, canning, preserving, furniture building, and animal care. Megan is even teaching a Spanish class. I think there are a few others being offered, but I can't think of what they are right now. Time will pass quickly, and we will be starting the seeds in the greenhouse around March first."

"Oh, all those things sound wonderful. I knew they were going to be having several different Bible studies, but I need something to do with my hands, too. I will have to think about what I would like to study."

"I think I am going to go to the furniture class."

Bonnie looked at her, surprised. "You want to take a furniture building class?"

Janie laughed, "Yes, I would like to make a cradle."

"Any reason in particular?" Bonnie gave her a questioning look.

"Not yet, but I am hopeful. I know the timing isn't the best, but you understand. Anyway, I think building furniture sounds like fun. It is something I really think I would like to do."

Bonnie patted her slightly rounded belly; she was three months pregnant and would deliver in late March, or early April. "I do understand what you are feeling about bringing a child into a world that promises chaos, but life goes on, and we cannot live our lives directed by the 'what ifs.' You will be a wonderful mother. Harold is one of the best things that ever happened to me. You need to hurry up, so this little one will have another playmate," she said with a wink.

"That would be nice, wouldn't it? But it's up to God, not me. I am ready anytime. I keep trying not to be impatient about getting pregnant; we agreed to wait for a year, or so before we began trying, but we aren't trying *not* to get pregnant either. That sounds silly, doesn't it?"

"Not really, but it wouldn't hurt to have some time to get to know each other better. We were together for three years before Harold came along. It's a big change in your life, just being married. Then to add a child means even more changes, besides getting used to a new way of life here at the Ranch."

"I know you are right. But it's hard, with so many babies around. It should be easier because I get to spend time with Jill's, Mary's, and your little ones, as much as I want, but it's not the same. Having children has been a desire of my heart for a very long time. As far as getting used to the Ranch, well . . . that hasn't been so hard. Getting back to basics, doing for ourselves, instead of relying on stores, isn't so bad. Besides, we have it much easier than the pioneers. We have all the modern machinery, tools, and gadgets. Anyway, I like it here. I am surrounded with those I love. I am happy, and I love being married, too," she said, with a twinkle in her eye, as they shared a knowing smile.

"I like it here, too. I have an extended family for the first time in my life. Both Nathan and I are only children of only children, so there are no brothers, sisters, aunts or uncles; here, I have all of them. It is truly wonderful."

"I feel the same way. I have a brother, but we haven't been close for a really long time. Here, I have sisters and brothers. I agree; it is wonderful. You are a wonderful sister." Janie gave Bonnie a sideway hug, and Bonnie smiled back, as she returned the hug.

They turned and began the short walk back to their cabins. They needed to clean up and get ready for their Bible study. They were joined at the gate to the garden by one of the camp dogs, a frisky German shepherd named Sunny. The young six-month-old female was full of energy and begged for attention.

Janie reached down and gave the dog a pat. "She sure is full of energy. I sometimes wish I had that much stamina. I like having the dogs around. I never had a dog before." They had six camp dogs—three females and one male German shepherd and a male and a female Golden Retriever. They used the shepherds during the night patrols and the retrievers while they were hunting. Sunny was Janie's favorite, and she slipped little treats to her, here and there. In addition, there were four small dogs and two cats that were family members of some of the people at the Ranch.

"We always had dogs as we were growing up; since I left home there have been no pets allowed in the apartments we lived in. It's nice having them around again. I like Sunny, too. She is really good with Harold; all the dogs are, but Puddles is Harold's favorite. He is such a big softy." Puddles was a large, two-year-old, male retriever. He got his name when he was a pup and made a mess on the floor in his excitement to greet newcomers. There were no strangers around Puddles; everyone was his friend.

They parted at the branch in the road that led to each of their cabins, making plans to meet later for Bible studies. As much as Bonnie enjoyed having a new family, she enjoyed some time to be alone. Now that she lived at the Ranch, there were activities for the children every day. It allowed her time to help with the daily chores and gave Harold time to play with other children. Each day she looked forward to the quiet time for her personal Bible studies and prayer; at least she could anticipate having this personal respite for a while longer. Once the baby was born, Bonnie knew she would have little free time. She yawned. Maybe a nap would be in order after a short time with the Lord, and then she would head over to pick up Harold.

Life was good here at the Ranch, she thought. It would be a very nice place to raise children. She only hoped things in the world would not spiral out of control. She believed in divine protection, but God's ways are not man's ways, so you never knew what could happen. Oh well, she thought. No need to worry or become anxious; she was confident that God was in control.

Christmas at the Ranch was a wonderful time for everyone. Just after Thanksgiving, several men cut evergreen boughs of balsam, cedar, pine, and fir for the ladies to make wreaths, garlands, and table decorations of every kind. Pastor Phil had purchased twenty wreath rings and a roll of velvet ribbon to add color to the wonderfully fragrant greens. They planned to hang decorations everywhere. Joy filled the air, as people sang Christmas carols while they worked. The children practiced for a Christmas pageant, directed by Jill and Bonnie, and several adults worked on special Christmas music. Megan and a couple of other ladies were busy in the kitchen, making Christmas cookies and planning their Christmas dinner.

Snow was already several inches deep across the landscape. The newfallen snow reminded Mary of a song she had heard years ago; the snow covered everything, just like Jesus covers all our sin, and in the spring there is new birth, just like we have new birth in Jesus. Mary sang "Somewhere It's Snowing" as she made her fifth wreath. She couldn't wait to hang one on her front door; in fact, if she had her way, every front door would have one. She knew Pastor Phil would pick up a few more rings, if she asked. They could save them and reuse them in the future. She loved Christmas and everything about it. She loved the reminders of Jesus' birth, the sharing of memories, and the exchanging of gifts, though there would be very little of that this year. It was decided that they would limit the gifts to those for children only, and those gifts would be handmade. From the corner of her eye, Mary watched the nine-month-old, little girl, who was sleeping in the play pen. Love filled her heart. This little gift from God was all the gift she needed for a long time, at least until God blessed them with another little one. She did not realize how much joy a child could bring, until now. What a great blessing from God!

Christmas Eve was filled with laughter and song. In some way, everyone took a part in making their first Christmas something really special. Decorations were everywhere. A large evergreen tree, covered with homemade popcorn balls, popcorn chains, and handmade cutouts—which had been crafted and colored by even the smallest of children, stood in the corner of the dining hall.

The pageant of the Christmas Story was the highlight of the evening. Mary and Joseph were played by Mary and Jake, with their little Joanna as Jesus. The wise men were played by George, Jacob, and Martin; the shepherds were played by Nathan, Paul, and Curt, and the angel was Susan. The ladies sang Christmas carols, as the performers took their places, and then Pastor Phil read the Christmas story. After their Christmas service, they ate Christmas cookies of every kind, until they could eat no more. Everyone was filled with love and joy, and outside the bright northern star shimmered in the darkness. It was hard to imagine the current deterioration of their country, when they were filled with so much joy.

The community's acknowledgment of the birth of Jesus Christ, the Son of God, was the first of many celebrations for believers everywhere. Each Christmas became a reminder that the rebirth of each believer is just as miraculous as the birth of Jesus, and it reminded them, also, that the way Jesus lived His life was the way they were supposed to live. He carried the sins of the entire world and took the punishment for those sins; His burial broke the chains of bondage and death, and finally, His resurrection guarantees all a new life in Christ. *"Thank You, Jesus . . . Thank You so very much!"* certainly became the ongoing prayer of each resident at the Ranch, as they daily considered this ultimate Gift.

The New Year came in quietly. Long, cold days kept everyone inside, with the exception of those caring for the livestock. The classes were a great hit. The sewing class made curtains for every window that needed covering and cushions for the furniture built in the furniture class. The furniture class made twenty-five bed frames, three sofas, four tables and sixteen chairs, six shelving units, and one cradle. The cooking class worked on adapting favorite recipes on a larger scale, to be used for future meals. They had a reading group, who read and discussed the books they decided to read. They had an extensive library in the main lodge that was enjoyed by all the readers who now were living at the Ranch.

Four different Bible studies were being conducted; one was for the young children, one for the older children, and two adult classes were held—one on the New Testament and one on the Old Testament. There were lively debates and friendly discussions on the finer details of the Bible. There was something for everyone, and everyone joined in.

March had arrived in a muddy mess. Though the main roads were paved and the smaller ones graveled, off the main pathways it was only mud. June and Bonnie didn't let this fact deter them, however, as they sloshed through the mud toward the greenhouses.

"I think I will ask if we have enough gravel to lay on this walkway—when it dries out enough," Janie remarked.

They were cranking up the heaters today and beginning the spring planting. They would start with the seeding of all the vegetables, herbs, and flowers. These would be put into a germination chamber to promote faster germination. After the young plants sprouted, they then would be transplanted into larger containers, where they would stay, until they were transplanted into the gardens in late May, or early June.

Several other people already were gathered around, when they arrived. "Good morning. Everyone is here, so let's get to it. First off, let's pray," Albert said in greeting.

"Father in Heaven, we come before You a grateful people. We give You praise for all You do each and every day. We thank You that winter is almost over, and the signs of spring are coming. Today we begin the first seeding for our summer garden. We ask Your blessing on the germination. Bless the hands working here and everywhere around this Ranch. Be with us now and always. In Jesus' name we pray. Amen."

"Okay, grab a seed tray and fill it with starter soil, then wet down the soil, and let the water soak in, before you grab a seed packet. Make sure you check the list on the wall, so you will know how many rows in the seed tray you are supposed to seed. Some vegetables will have only one row, and others will have several. If you have a vegetable that only needs one or two rows seeded, please use the small seed trays that only have three rows. We cut them down already, so it would make it easier for you, and so we would not waste the starter soil. As you seed, make sure the seeds are spread evenly. Some of the seeds like a light top layer of soil, others do not, so make sure you read the back of each packet. It will tell you what to do; if the packets do not have any directions, check with Valerie, or me. There are labels with the seed packets. Make sure everything matches: the seed, the quantity of rows you need to plant, and the labels. After you are finished seeding the tray, put one label in the front of the tray and the other in the middle. Bring the finished tray to the end table, next to the seed chambers, and we will take them from there. There are three chambers set at different temperatures, so we will make sure each tray gets put in the proper chamber. There are also several heat mats; those are set at seventy degrees. We will be using them also. After the seeds are planted, return the extra seeds to the seed box and file them alphabetically, and then make sure you put a check in the seed column of the planting journal, along with your initials. If you have any questions, feel free to ask." Janie's Dad, Albert Weber, explained. Then, they all eagerly went to work.

It took several hours before all the vegetables and flowers were seeded. The work space was cleaned up, and everyone made their way back to their quarters. They would all return in two or three weeks and begin the transplanting. In the meantime, the daily watering and checking would be handled by Albert and Valerie.

The weeks flew by, and transplanting began in earnest. Most vegetables were put into two different-sized pots. The larger containers would be left in the greenhouse until late spring, allowing them to grow rapidly in the warmer soil, which the heat of the greenhouse provided. This would give them ripe fruit, long before those plants which were planted in the garden. The smaller plants would remain in their pots inside the greenhouse, until any possibility of frost was past. They could not afford to lose their crops because they got impatient to get the garden planted and growing; besides, the real work of gardening began once the plants were in the ground. Weeding and watering would become a full-time job for several workers, once all the plants were in the ground. The guys were working on an irrigation system that would be completed in the next few weeks, and that would help greatly.

After the transplanting was completed, it was time to plant the fruiting vines and other perennial vegetables. Blackberries, boysenberries, rhubarb, and strawberries were all ready to go into the ground. These crops would grow year after year, becoming larger and larger and more fruitful each year. By late April, they would plant the cool crops that could tolerate cooler soil temperatures: carrots, potatoes, turnips, cabbage, and radishes; these were those vegetables that would not be started in the greenhouse, but directly placed into the ground. They would not be using pesticides, so they would have to watch the gardening carefully for any pests that could damage their crops.

Bonnie and Janie worked, side by side, every day in the garden. They enjoyed working together and had formed a very close friendship. Since neither had a sister, each of them felt God had provided a sister of their hearts. As Bonnie's time for delivery came closer, Janie began taking Harold with her in the afternoons, to allow Bonnie time to rest. Harold was a joy, and Janie loved every minute she had with him. Janie looked forward to the day she would hold her own little blessing from God.

As the days grew longer, the work days grew longer. Several men were putting up fences, others were cutting firewood, and a few were helping with the irrigation of the garden. The buffalo and the cows and their calves were moved to the outer pasture. The horses were left in the closer pasture, as they would be needed on a regular basis. Several men had cleared a twenty- acre area to plant sweet grass, which would be used to make ethanol. Two other areas were cleared, one for alfalfa and the other for wheat and corn. Several more began work on another dormitory, intended for future use. The women were working in the gardens, cleaning, cooking and taking care of the children. Everyone was busy in one way or another. The work day ended at five thirty in the evening, with the ringing of the dinner bell. Everyone knew they had thirty minutes to clean up and head to the meeting hall, where dinner would be served at six o'clock. Evenings were free for everyone to do as each one desired, but a variety of activities were provided as options, though many were so tired that just going to bed seemed the best option.

They worked six days a week, most putting in eight to ten hours a day, with Sunday the only day of worship and rest. Every few weeks, they would have a play and rest day in the middle of the week. The basketball court was completed and was a big hit with the guys. The playground was half done, but the sand box and swings gave the children something to enjoy. Soon, the weather would be nice enough to swim in the lake.

Isabel Marie Morgan was born early in the morning on the first day of April. She was a healthy baby, with a great set of lungs. She made her displeasure of leaving her warm cocoon publicly known with a loud wail. Tired, yet happy, Bonnie cuddled her new daughter, as her adoring husband, son and best friend, Janie, looked on.

Sherry stood to the side, pleased and happy with the birth. She had been the mid-wife, who had delivered the baby. Nothing was as wonderful as seeing the birth of a new baby; nothing brought her more joy. *"Father, thank You so much for this tiny, new life. May You bless her with a long and blessed life. May she grow up to know You and to serve You every day of her life. Thank You for the privilege of helping bring this beautiful child into the world, for guiding me through the delivery, and for helping Bonnie control the pain. We praise You and thank You for all Your many blessings today."*

Janie made her way to the greenhouse to help with the watering. She was tired, but also overjoyed, at the birth of little "Belle." Janie had arrived to watch Harold, as soon as word came that Bonnie was in labor. She sat with Bonnie to give Nathan a short break at Harold's bedtime, giving the two friends a few minutes alone. Janie smiled at the memory. "This is such a short, painful time, compared to the years of love ahead," Bonnie said, seeing that her pain was difficult for Janie to observe. Janie was amazed that

Bonnie was concerned for *her,* while *she* was the one in pain. Yet, that was one of the many things that Janie loved about Bonnie; she placed others before herself. Now that Isabel had arrived, safely, she could not be more precious. Yes, Janie understood more clearly than ever—*all life is precious.*

CHAPTER 23

JACK AND ROSE ARRIVED the first week of May. George had sent the semi-truck and trailer the previous week, to bring back their things, along with new medical supplies, computers and communications equipment. The computers and communications equipment would fill a much-needed gap, so they could keep up with the world outside the Ranch. They planned to set a perimeter monitoring system that would help with the security of the compound. Rose was a computer whiz, and with the help of Curt and several others, they would have the system up and running in no time.

"They are here," Mary shouted toward the garden, where several were working. Everyone stopped working and headed for the dining hall, where the semi and car had come to a stop. Smiles and hugs greeted the newcomers. Lively chatter filled the air, as everyone gathered around and made Jack and Rose welcome.

Elizabeth took charge, "Okay, everyone, Jack and Rose have had a long trip. Let's get them settled in, and we can catch them up at dinner on the entire goings on around here."

That got everyone grabbing luggage and hauling it over to a pick-up truck that Curt drove up in. They could not get the semi to the cabin Jack and Rose would be living in, so everything would have to be moved out of the trailer and into the truck. Being old pros at moving people in, it only took a short time before all the furniture, boxes and luggage were in their new home. The computers and communication equipment were placed in the proper room in the main lodge basement.

The dinner bell rang, just as they were heading back to work, so everyone detoured to the dining hall.

Over dinner, people were clamoring for information on what was happening outside the compound.

"Not much has changed," Jack said. "The value of our money is dropping in other countries, which makes everything more expensive here. But you already knew that. Those who are preparing for problems ahead are in full swing, just like us. Right before we left, I talked with another friend at church, who was doing a similar thing, only on a smaller scale there. Another friend said they had had a neighborhood meeting to develop a defense plan—should it be needed. They also had a twenty-acre community garden they were planting. They planned to post guards to ensure no one came in at night and wiped them out. I heard of another group, who was securing one of the gated communities with patrolling guards. So, people are preparing all over the nation. Of course, there are those who are totally oblivious to anything on the horizon."

"I am glad others are preparing, too," Mary commented.

"Oh, yes," Rose said. "Many churches are holding preparation meetings. Others are making plans to move to their church camps in the mountains for safety. Most are well-thought-out plans. I think most people understand there is safety in numbers. They cannot survive alone and are banding together in large groups. I find it interesting that it is mostly believers that are preparing, though."

"It is obvious that God has been speaking to His people, and many are listening," George observed. "Were you able to get everything for the communications room that we talked about on the phone?"

"Yes, everything you asked for and more. Rose had a few extra things she thought we might need, so we have them also. I am surprised you forgot such an important thing for monitoring the outside activities," Jack commented to his father.

"We have several computers, but I agree we did overlook some of the advantages to using them more efficiently. Curt had mentioned a security system, but for some reason, we did not follow through. Rose and Curt will take care of that," he said, looking fondly at his daughter-in-law. "Curt said he could run whatever electrical you need to make the system run."

"Great! I plan to have a complete communications room, where we can monitor the compound for security and local, national, and worldwide news. We need to be forewarned, if there are major events happening around the world," Rose said, from her seat next to Jack. "I even picked up a short-wave radio. My uncle used to talk on one with people all over the world. It was a lot of fun. But I can see that it would be a great help, if the internet goes down. It might be the only way to find out what is going on in the rest of the country. I already have my ham license, so we are good to go. I just have to hook it all up and get the antenna put up."

"See what an intelligent wife I have," Jack said, smiling fondly at Rose.

"Yes, Rose will be a great asset to the community," Elizabeth said smiling at Rose. "So, what are your plans, son?"

"To begin with, I want to see what Martin and Sherry have set up and work with them. I will see where the Lord leads; I may venture out and help folks in the surrounding area, much like the doctors of old did, when they conducted house calls."

"We can arrange protection for you, but you will have to be extra careful not to lead anyone back here," George cautioned.

"I know, Dad, but I need to use my medical skills where I can."

"I know, and I respect you for your desire to help," George said.

The hours that followed were spent informing the newcomers of all the happenings at the Ranch during the past months. A wonderful meal was prepared in their honor, just as they always did for each newcomer to the Ranch. They wanted each person to feel welcome and part of the family, so it had become a regular celebration. They were put in a place of honor, and each person made a point of speaking with each one, welcoming them to the family.

After many had started to return to their quarters, Janie found a quiet corner to visit with Rose. "I like the idea of having winter classes," Rose said. "Do you think anyone would be interested in a computer class?"

"Oh, yes, at least I would," Janie answered. "I know quite a bit, but I am interested in helping in the communications room. Can you teach us about that?"

"Yes, that would be a great idea. That way, we can monitor twenty-four seven, it is not so important now, but if things continue to deteriorate, we will need to watch the outside world more and more. I would be happy to teach anyone who wants to learn."

"Great! I am so glad you are finally here. I have enjoyed our e-mails, but it's not the same as having you here," Janie said, smiling warmly at her sister-in-law.

Sadness crossed Rose's face and then cleared. "I am glad to be here, also, but leaving was difficult. No one in my family is a believer. The idea that I will not see them again is hard." Tears came to her eyes, and she quickly wiped them away. "If they were believers, at least I would know I would see them in heaven, but as it is, unless God can get through to them, they are lost. I did my best to witness to them, but they would not listen. They thought I was crazy for leaving—and even crazier for accepting Jesus. They can't see anything wrong with our country, much less the world. They said our country survived the depression, so we can survive this period of hard times, also."

Janie reached over and took her hand, "A lot of people here are in that same position. We must remember that prayer is the greatest weapon we have against the enemy. We shall agree together to pray them into the kingdom. I was taught once that we can bind Satan from blinding those we pray for and we can pray that God would loose His Word to pierce their stony hearts. In addition, we will pray that God will send harvesters that will minister to them. God is full of mercy and grace. It is not over until they are dead, or until Jesus comes back, so we will simply pray that God and His love will prevail over their stubborn hearts. Besides, when extremely difficult things start happening, it might shake them up enough that they will remember what you said to them. Also, there are still many believers who have decided to stay in the cities to minister to the lost. They will stay, until it gets too dangerous, or until God tells them to find refuge at a place like ours. These believers understand the cost, but God has given them that calling, just as He has called us to live here and to provide shelter to those needing refuge. We will pray that God will use one of His other servants to win their hearts for Him."

Rose was cheered greatly by Janie's word. "Thank you. I needed to hear those words." She rose and came around to hug Janie, glad she would have a sister-in-law and friend like this; pulling back, she added, "I have a friend who is working on a video game that will present the gospel. He said it would be a great tool in reaching people for Christ, especially after most of the believers have gone underground. The more games he can get into circulation, the better. My brothers are really into video games, so I asked Pete to send one to them, when it's done. That is the most I can do."

"Come on, let me give you the grand tour, before it gets too dark," Janie said, linking her arm through Rose's.

"That would be wonderful. Lead the way." The girls walked off in long steps, like the scarecrow and Dorothy in the Wizard of Oz.

"As you can tell, this is the working part of the Ranch. Most of the farm animals are out in the pastures, but we keep the horses in that pasture over there, so we can get them when we want to. Paul has taken me riding several times; it is nice to get away on the horses every once in a while. The barns, paddocks and chicken coop are close together, so it is easier to take care of the animals during the winter." They walked in a leisurely manner, so Rose could take in the beauty of her new home.

"It is lovely here and seems very functional. A lot of thought must have gone into the planning of the placement of the buildings."

"No, actually God gave us the placement. It came in a dream of the Ranch, and I just put it down on paper."

"You are kidding, right?"

"No, that is what happened. Right after I moved to Spokane and got the job at Hope, I had a dream. It was this Ranch. Somehow, I knew it was important and wrote it all down in my computer. My printer was broken, so I made a disk, and took it to work, and printed it out. It happened to be the same day that I was giving a presentation, and the printout got mixed in with my handouts. That was the day Paul and I collided, and, when we did, papers went flying. He helped me clean up the mess. He found the printout and took it. He thought it was the plans that his family had come up with, while he was out of town. But when he called his Dad, he found out that that was not the case. So, they got together, and went over the plans, and now, here we are."

"That is amazing."

"Yes, actually it is."

"What are all the containers for that are over by the barn?" Rose asked.

"Those are the shipping containers that we used to bring food and supplies to the Ranch, when we moved here last summer. George decided to purchase them. The guys cut firewood, then they stack it in the containers, and then move the containers with a forklift; George bought a really big one that would be able to lift the loaded containers. This way, they can take one container to each cabin or living area. We used three containers for the kitchen and three for the greenhouses, so I think they plan to stage three containers at *each* location this next fall, so they do not have to fight the snow, like they did this year. When a container is empty, it is moved back, and another one replaces it. It is really much easier to stock all the buildings with firewood this way, and it also is easier for those who are doing the chopping, splitting and stacking."

"That is a great idea." Rose said, marveling at the idea.

"Using the containers worked really well this winter. Every building has a wood stove, so it makes it much easier for everyone. You just go out and get the wood from your container and put a stack by the wood stove. It saves the time of moving, stacking and storing at each building. All the work of preparing the wood is done in one location."

"That is really ingenious. So, you heat the greenhouses with wood, too?"

"Yes, but there we use a boiler system. Dad did a lot of research on that last summer and came up with the system we use. We heat the water, and then we pump it through pipes in the floor, and then it recirculates, and is heated again. It worked really well this spring. Dad is going to try keeping one greenhouse heated all winter this coming year, so we can grow veggies year round."

"It is really surprising how enterprising everyone is. I have heard of others who have gone back to nature, so to speak, but not on this scale."

"Oh, you haven't seen anything yet. You should see the septic system that they put together that makes methane gas, and then they capture the gas and store it for later use."

"We have some really smart people here, don't we?"

"Yes, we sure do, but, more importantly we have a God who is a genius, and He gave you a great talent. Your communication setup is going to be fantastic."

Rose blushed with pleasure. "Thank you, but it helps when you can spend what you need to and not cut corners."

They continued their walk around the Ranch and ended their stroll down by the lake, under the willow tree, where a bench and table had been placed. "This place is even more incredible than I had thought. You guys have thought of everything: off grid, more than enough electricity—which can be expanded in time if needed, by using hydro, methane, and wind. The gardens and greenhouse, along with the chickens, cows, and buffalo, will provide enough food for everyone . . . and then some. The main lodge is fantastic. The dining hall, classrooms . . . And that kitchen . . . Who wouldn't want to cook in that? It is a wonderful kitchen. The cabins and living quarters are really nice, too. I thought we would be living in very rustic accommodations, but everything is very modern and comfortable."

"I love our cabin. Elizabeth told the men they had to make the housing comfortable. I had housing plans, but she went over them and changed a few things. She added storage and closet space. When they planned to make really small cabins, she asked that they add one or two bedrooms. It is a good thing, too, because nearly everyone has used them, at one time or another, when new people have arrived. Who knows whether we may need them again, permanently."

"Yes, the Ranch is really a small town, with everything anyone would need. If we do not have it, we can make it or build it. I love being here, and this is the best part: almost everyone I love is here, too."

The cool days of spring held on, even as the trees bloomed and leaves appeared. The young lilac plants provided an aromatic display that would increase as the years passed. Memorial Day came, and planting outside in the rich earth began in earnest. The gardens had been tilled once again. Several extra workers came to help transplant the young seedlings into the garden. It was a great day—clear and one of the first really warm days they had had.

The workers made steady headway, as they worked, row by row, planting. It was pleasant work, digging in the cool dirt. In spite of the stiff backs, arms and legs, sore from unused muscles, everyone smiled and laughed, as they made their way to the meeting hall for dinner. It had taken two days to plant everything, yet now it was complete. The satisfaction of a job well done filled the hearts of everyone. Now, the watering, weeding and general tending would begin, and, hopefully, they would be blessed with a bountiful harvest.

With constant endurance and diligence, they battled the pests that invaded the garden. At least the fence was keeping the deer and other animals out of the garden. Many of the young plants that were surrounding the other buildings had been nibbled on more than once by pesky vermin. In fact, several of the lilacs had been munched to the nubbins. It was a wonder some of them were still alive!

Elizabeth and Janie tried planting lots of marigolds around the buildings in among the flowering shrubs, in an effort to save those plants that had not already been nibbled on. This maneuver seemed to slow them down, but it did not stop the devastation to the already munched plants.

Several days later, Janie and Paul were walking to the main lodge, when a small, orange flower caught her eye. "Would you look at this? One of those pesky deer chewed the top off a marigold and then spit it out! Those rotten deer! I can't wait until hunting season. I think I will learn to shoot, just so I can eliminate one of those pesky critters," Janie said hotly. Paul just chuckled, as she continued to lament the perils of living in a forest full of deer. Everyone had been given lessons in shooting the weapons, so it was possible for Janie to join the hunters.

"Just remember, though, some of those very deer will feed us next winter," Paul said, only to then receive a foul look from Janie.

"Yes, well-fed deer . . . and I am going to enjoy eating them, too." Paul just laughed out loud at Janie's curt response.

Spring passed into summer, with a peaceful transition from warm to hot, and though everyone was busy, most found time to spend time swimming in the lake, or picnicking under the aspen trees, at least once or twice a week. The children enjoyed the playground, which had been put together for them, and the mothers enjoyed visiting, as they sat nearby.

They began harvesting from the gardens in late June and were thrilled at the fresh vegetables they enjoyed eating each day. Each week, something new was far enough along to harvest.

"These have got to be some of the best tasting vegetables I have ever eaten. I always loved cooking with fresh vegetables and fruits, but, somehow, these are even better than the ones I used to get," Megan said one afternoon, when Bonnie and Janie brought her a couple of baskets full of tomatoes, lettuce and squash.

"Well, I don't know about that," Bonnie replied. "But I do know that it's a lot more work than filling the grocery cart."

"Yes, but this is more fun," Janie chimed in.

"Well, I suppose, but it is really hot and sweaty work. I saw Jill at the lake with the kids. Let's go change and join them. A nice swim sounds wonderful right about now."

"Sounds good to me; let's go," Janie answered. When she reached the door, she turned back to Megan and the other ladies who were helping her. "Well, aren't you all coming?" She posed there with her hand on her hip, tapping her foot. "There is a water fight just beginning in my imagination. I would like to make it a reality."

"Oh, okay," Megan replied, as she put down the basket she had just picked up to move to the sink. "Come on, everyone; if dinner is late, we will blame it on Janie." Everyone in the kitchen hurried off to change. The lake and a water fight were calling each and every one.

Bradley watched, as everyone was splashing and laughing, engaged in a huge water fight. Part of him wanted to join them, but another part held him back. He did not want to be here in this isolated place. His mother had brought him here against his will. She said it was for the best, that it would be safe here. What did he need protection from? He could take care of himself. Besides, all they did here was work, work, work, he thought, unkindly.

"They are not working right now. You could join them if you wanted." Bradley ignored the voice in his head that had just interrupted his self-indulged thoughts.

Who wants to play in the water with a bunch of old ladies and their brats? Brad turned and walked away toward the garden. He had pulled his share of weeds in that garden in the last few weeks. Boy, did he hate doing that. He noticed several deer grazing on some grass at the edge of the meadow. It was then the plan formed in his head. I know how I can put a wrench in the works. I will come back at night and unlatch the gate to the garden. Then the deer can get into the garden. Brad smiled; he liked that idea.

For several evenings, Brad got up around midnight and unlatched the gate to the garden, however, the stupid deer never found the gate opening. He really did not know how he could get them inside. Every time he tried to get close to them, they ran away in the opposite direction. Oh, well, he thought, sooner or later they would find the entrance to a great meal. Until then, he would get up early and re-latch the gate, so no one would become the wiser.

"Janie, wake up! You need to go to the garden!"
Janie woke with a start, the words still ringing in her mind. Looking around, she realized it was very early morning. Glancing at the clock, she read 4:45 a. m. Now wide awake and hearing Paul's steady breathing, she rose and quickly dressed. She hurried to the door and started to leave, when she heard, *"Take the rifle."*

"Take the rifle? I am not a very good shot, yet—but if You say so," Janie thought. Quietly, she left the house and quickly made her way to the garden. It was just light enough to see the path. When she arrived at the garden, she saw a huge buck elk, munching in her garden. At first, she could not believe her eyes. She had never even seen an elk in the valley, much less eating her vegetables. "Oh, no you don't," she said. She cocked the rifle, just like she had been taught, and then she took careful aim. She took a deep breath and let it out slowly, then another, steadying herself. Just then, the elk looked up, giving her the best shot, and she took it. The crack of the rifle echoed across the valley, as the elk went down.

The sound of the rifle woke those who were not already awake and caused those who were awake to jump out of bed and hurry to get dressed. Those who were up and dressed immediately dropped everything and rushed outside. Within minutes, Janie was surrounded by most of the men and some of the women. "Janie, are you alright?" George asked, scared to his core.

"Yes, yes . . . I am fine. I didn't know it would feel this way to kill it," she said quietly.

"Kill what?" Paul asked surprised.

Janie pointed into the garden. "That elk over there; it was munching our vegetables, so I shot him." The men cautiously filed through the garden gate and over to the large animal they saw lying on some of the tomatoes and lettuce.

"Boy, is he a beaut!" Curt said admiringly. "Do you see that rack?"

"How did it get in here?" George asked.

"I just pushed the gate wider; it was already unlatched," Nathan said. "Janie, did you come inside the garden, before you shot him?"

"No, I just took aim from outside and shot him. I knew, if I just winged him, I didn't want to be inside with him. I've never seen an elk in the valley before," Janie remarked absently.

"How did you come to see him, anyway?" Curt asked.

"I woke up with a start and just knew I was supposed to come. As I started out the door, I knew I was supposed to take a rifle."

Paul knelt down to examine the elk. "Well, it was a clean shot, right through the heart. Great shooting, hon! I'm proud of you," Paul said, smiling up at her.

"I didn't know I would feel this way about killing it. I think I will let you hunters do this in the future."

"Well, let's get it gutted and hung. We might as well make use of it," George said, practically.

"I'll go get the tractor. This thing must weigh a ton," Curt offered.

The next several hours passed quickly, as the men moved the elk and prepared it for hanging. After breakfast, the ladies went to the garden to see the damage and clean things up. Over lunch, everyone was talking about the elk and speculating about how he had gotten into the garden.

After lunch Rose and Jack approached George privately. "I think we might be able to tell by looking at the camera outside the main lodge how that elk got into the garden," Rose said. "I believe the line of sight of the camera will show the garden gate. It is some distance, but we might be able to tell if the gate was left open deliberately—or not."

"Well, it's worth looking at. Let's go look," George said, while quickly heading to the new communications room.

"There he is."

"Who is it?" Rose asked.

"It is Bradley Harris, Franny's son," George said sadly.

"He has been getting up late to unlatch the gate and returning early in the morning to relatch it for a couple of weeks. This was very deliberate."

"What are you going to do?" Jack asked.

"I will start by talking with Franny. I think I will go get your mother, and we will go to see her now," George said thoughtfully.

George found Elizabeth in the kitchen, cleaning the vegetables they were able to salvage from the smashed and damaged area of the garden.

"Elizabeth, I need your help. Can you get away now?" George asked from the doorway.

Elizabeth caught the tone, as only a wife can, and she excused herself, promising to come back, as soon as possible. No one noticed anything out of the ordinary, as George often found Elizabeth and asked for her help with something.

After the door closed behind them and they had walked a few yards, Elizabeth asked, "So, what's up? You have that look."

"Bradley Harris opened the gate to the garden on purpose. In fact, he has been doing it, off and on, for a couple of weeks."

"Oh, George, why would he do such a thing?"

"I do not know, but I plan to find out. Franny is working, helping with the little ones today, so we are going to speak with her first." Elizabeth knew George was angry, and he was holding it in check. She knew George would listen to the boy and would be fair in handling the consequences for Bradley's actions. But she also knew Bradley would know he had crossed the line in his rebellion.

Franny listened, thoughtfully, as George laid out what they had seen on the camera tapes and what he planned to do. She knew Bradley had hated coming here, but she knew they could not stay in Spokane, where Bradley was falling in with the wrong crowd. Maybe she should have confided in George and Elizabeth, before moving, but she really thought Bradley would come to accept their new life on the Ranch.

"I am so sorry, George, Elizabeth. I knew Bradley did not want to come, and the winter was hard on him. But I thought he had made friends with Mario and Susan." She had seen them together often, through the long winter. Now she knew whatever bonds they had made were not strong or enduring. "I thought he was adjusting; I guess I was wrong." Tears gathered in her eyes as she spoke.

Elizabeth gently took Franny's hands, "We are not blaming you. We could all see Bradley was not doing well here. He has been disrespectful at times and rarely joined in for any of the fun activities. We had hoped, like you, that he would come to find his place here."

Franny was openly weeping now. "We will pack, and you can take us back to Spokane, as soon as possible."

"No, Franny; that would not be good for you or the boy," George said solemnly. "I am one of the spiritual leaders here at the Ranch. I am asking you to let me work with the boy for a while. No one knows about what Bradley did, except Elizabeth, Rose, Jack and me. We will not be sharing this with anyone. Others might suspect what happened, but they do not know who is responsible, and we will not tell anyone. So, I would like to propose that you and Bradley move into two of the empty rooms in our house. I would like Bradley to spend the rest of the summer shadowing me. He will work with me, eat with me, and go where I go. You get the drill. Is that alright with you?"

Franny had brightened considerably, while George talked. "Yes, yes of course it is. I know he has been mad at God, ever since his dad died two years ago. Maybe you can get through to him, where I failed . . . that God did not kill his dad. A drunk driver killed his dad. It was a terrible, awful accident."

"Well, we will see what we can do. I am sure Bradley is not going to like the arrangement, so prepare yourself for some harsh words."

Franny's face hardened, "This is the first time in Bradley's life that I can truly say I am ashamed of him. He will have to take whatever punishment he gets. I trust you to do what is best. He will be a man soon, and a man cannot act like he has been acting. Since I am not a man, that is something I cannot teach him, but you can. I am hopeful that he will come around."

"I do not consider this punishment. Time will tell, but God is bigger than Bradley. We will all be praying for him, and I will be working him hard enough that he will not have the energy to get up at night and open—and then close—the garden gate," George said with a slight smile.

CHAPTER 24

Bradley came back to the main lodge three hours later and found his room empty. Fear struck his heart for the first time since he came up with the idea to open the garden gate. He had heard about the elk that had ventured into the garden, and, at first, he was secretly pleased. Now, he had a sour feeling deep in his gut.

"Oh, Bradley, there you are." Bradley caught sight of his mother coming out of her room with a box. "Come here and help me with the last of our things." Her voice was hard and stern, something Bradley rarely heard from her since his dad had died.

Bradley obediently did as she asked, afraid to ask any questions. He followed her down the stairs and out the door. They walked to George and Elizabeth's house, and she entered without knocking. They went upstairs, and she pushed open the last door on the end. "That is your new room," she indicated, with a nod to the right. "Start getting it organized, but when you hear me call in a few minutes, come downstairs to the living room."

Bradley looked around the room that was scattered with boxes. Bradley knew that his mom knew what he had done. How she had found out, he did not know, but he knew he was in for it now.

The next half hour was hell for Bradley. He did not know what was up, but he knew that whatever it was, he would not like it. He ignored the boxes and lay down on the bed. The late nights and early mornings he had been keeping and the work during the day were catching up with him; he fell asleep. He woke with a start, nearly an hour later, when he heard his mother calling for him to come down. Well, this is it, he thought. Slowly, he rose, shoved a hand through his hair, and went down to face the music.

"Bradley, please take a seat," George said sternly. He was sitting in a recliner, looking relaxed, tilted back with his feet up. Maybe this wasn't going to be so bad, after all, Bradley thought.

He sat on the sofa, across from his mother and Elizabeth. "Would you be so kind as to tell us why you have been getting up in the middle of the night and unlatching the garden gate, then returning in the morning to latch it again?" George said quietly.

Bradley said nothing, at first, then belligerence rose up, and he replied hotly, "I figured, if the deer came in and ruined the garden, there would not be enough food for everyone. So, Mom and I would have to move back to Spokane, where we could buy it at the store. I hate all this gardening and cutting firewood, much less all the other things I have to do around here. Besides, why do we even have to be here? We were just fine in Spokane. We didn't have to come here. We were doing just fine there. I had my friends and school. I had a life." He looked at his mom, and, instead of seeing understanding, he saw anger. He stopped short.

"So, you were doing well there? I see, so those kids you were running around with, the ones who were arrested for shoplifting, were your friends . . . those so-called friends, who tried to frame you?" George asked.

Mom must have told them about that. He knew it had just been an accident that they had left the shopping bag containing stolen merchandise in his room, when they had visited that afternoon. The only thing that kept him out of jail too was the fact that he had been at the dentist when the theft took place. "They didn't do that," Bradley defended.

"Okay, so we will give them the benefit of the doubt. What about the money, stolen from the youth group car wash? It was there before your friends arrived and gone when they left. Kind of a coincidence, wasn't it?

Shall I go on? Your mom has shared several other incidents in question, incidents involving your so-called friends."

Bradley knew, full well, that his friends had done all those things—and more. He had always made an excuse not to be around when 'things went down,' but he knew they had done them. So, Bradley remained silent.

"Bradley, do you understand what you did, that you put all of us in danger? Many of the stores are closed. Without food for the coming winter, everyone would have to do with less, and we would not be able to help others, who are struggling to survive. There is another family who we just found out about. The father abandoned his wife and his four children, all under six. He took all their cash and everything else of value and just left. How are we supposed to help her, if we do not have the food to give her? Bad things are happening out there. This is a place of safety; we want to keep it that way."

"Yeah, right. I don't believe it. Nothing bad was happening when we left last fall."

"Okay, son, come with me." George led him outside and to the main lodge. He went into a small closet at the end of the hall and opened the door. Then he pushed a button on the back wall, and it slid to the side, revealing stairs going down. Bradley followed George downstairs to a large room, filled with monitors and computers. Even more equipment was still in boxes on the floor. Bradley realized how they found out he had been opening the gate, when he saw a bank of monitors. They had cameras all over the compound. They could monitor everything, in and around the Ranch. He immediately felt stupid and guilty.

"Hi, Rose," George said to the pretty young lady Bradley had only seen a few times.

"Hi, Dad," she replied.

"Would you show Bradley what is going on in Spokane, as we speak?" Rose nodded, rolled her chair over to another console, and changed the receiver to the local Spokane channel.

Bradley could not believe what he was seeing. There was rioting in the streets; people were throwing chairs through windows and stealing whatever they wanted. The view changed, and a burning church came into view. Smoke billowed everywhere, as a fire consumed the building. At first, it was hard to tell where it was, but the camera went to the front, and Bradley recognized his church, the one he had gone to for as long as he could remember, the same church he had been baptized in, and the very church where they had held the funeral service when his dad died.

"Why?" Bradley asked in a small shaky voice.

"This has been going on since the weather turned nice in the spring. These people want something for nothing. They want everything given to them. Many do not believe they should have to work for anything. This is their idea of getting their point across that they want changes, changes we do not believe in, by the way. The Bible teaches that if you do not work, you do not eat. But these people do not believe in the Bible. Government has become their god. They want the government to take care of them," George answered.

"You knew this was going to happen? How?"

"Yes, we knew. God gave us a vision of the coming times. This is just the beginning, Bradley; it is going to get worse. He directed us to this valley. We have been preparing for years."

Bradley did not know what to believe. He could see the devastation on the television. Just then, a face flashed on the monitor. He knew that guy. It was one of those who had tried to pin the theft on him; his name was Trent. He was laughing and jumping up and down, as the church burned. Remorse and shame filled Bradley. He felt stupid, guilty, and convicted. "That is my church," Bradley said softly.

"I know," George said kindly. "Now do you understand, even a little?"

"Yes, I guess so. I am sorry," Bradley said, meaning it. "So, what is going to happen now?"

"Well, I think you really are sorry, but there are consequences for your actions. Those consequences are not a punishment; I want you to understand that. Jesus took your punishment for your sin already, at least, He will, if you ask his forgiveness. So, I cannot and will not punish you. However, that being said, you will be doing a lot of chores for the foreseeable future. You will be working with me. You will get up, when I get up, and you will go to bed, when I go to bed. You will go where I go, unless it is away from the Ranch, and you will attend every Bible study I attend. You will have additional Bible reading that you will be asked to complete. I believe Proverbs would be a good place to start."

For just a moment, Bradley wanted to rebel against all that would be required of him, but in the end, he knew he was getting off easy. He looked at the monitor again and was secretly glad he was here and not facing *that* in Spokane.

"Come on, Bradley; we have one more thing we need to do."

George led Bradley to the small chapel. "I cannot make you ask God for forgiveness, but that is what you need to do. So, we are going to sit here for a bit and give you some time with God. I cannot and will not make you pray. That is between you and God alone. But I am going to spend the next few minutes praying for you." George sat down and bowed his head. He did just what he said: he lifted Bradley to Jesus.

Bradley had not prayed at all since his dad died. He didn't know what to say. There was some lingering anger, though it had dulled over the last year. He moved away from George and sat on the other side of the chapel. Suddenly, he was overwhelmed with remorse and guilt. He knew he had been wrapped up in his anger, and his rebellion had been directed at God, at his mom, and at anyone else he came in contact with. He knew Mario had tried to befriend him, but he had rebuffed him at every turn. He knew his old friends had not really been friends at all. He knew that then, and he could see it even more clearly now.

Tears began to roll down his face. Why did Dad have to die? How could things have gotten so messed up? Why did he even come up with that stupid idea to let the animals into the garden?

George looked up from his prayers to see Bradley crying, silently. He rose, walked over and sat down next to Bradley. He remembered how confused he was as a teenager. Fifteen was a difficult age, and losing a father at this young age made things even more difficult.

"I don't know what to say. I haven't talked to Him in so long. Maybe He won't forgive me,"

Bradley said brokenly.

"We have all messed up, from time to time, in our lives, son. Jesus loves you. You are not beyond His forgiveness. Just say what is in your heart."

"Jesus," Bradley hesitated. *"Jesus, I have been mad at You for a long time because Dad was not supposed to die. But I guess I know You did not do that. That drunken guy did it, but I cannot even be mad at him because he died too. I have just been mad about everything. I didn't want to come here, but I really didn't like those guys back home, either— not much, anyway. I just wanted to belong, to be part of a group. I guess I could not see them for what they really are because I do not want to be like them. I am sorry I have been the way I have been since I have been here. I know everyone has tried to be*

nice to me, even though I have not always been nice to them. Mario tried to be my friend, but I guess I pushed him away. And Susan, well . . . she is just too pretty to notice someone like me." That made George smile.

"Anyway, I am sorry about letting the elk get into the garden. Thank You that only one got in and more damage was not done. Forgive me; I know it was wrong. Please help everyone else forgive me, too. Help me to change my attitude. I do not want to be mad all the time anymore." Bradley looked over at George, "I guess that's all."

"Amen," said George.

"Oh, yeah. Amen." Bradley felt better. He was not sure why, but he didn't feel angry anymore.

George was relieved. He knew it could have gone the other way. Bradley could have felt justified in what he did and been unrepentant. Bradley was going to be okay. George and the other men would help him become the man God meant for him to be. He knew there would be other times of trial in Bradley's life, but he also knew he would do everything he could to help Bradley grow in his Christian walk, and that would make all the difference.

"You know, there are others you will have to apologize to, but that can come later, when you are ready. Come on; daylight is burning, and there is work to be done." George ruffled Bradley's hair, as he rose and led the way outside and into the sunlight.

Yes, Bradley was beginning to understand what he had done. He would have to apologize to his Mom and the other ladies. But maybe he wouldn't have to do it today. His emotions were still raw, and he just wasn't ready. It felt better to go work with George right now than face his Mom.

She had always supported and encouraged him. He knew he had disappointed and embarrassed her. Yes, he would have to apologize to her, but not right now. He knew she would forgive him, but he was not looking forward to the lecture she would give him first.

September brought cooler nights and crisp mornings. The final harvesting was upon them, before anyone was ready for the warm weather to end. They began canning and preserving in early August and continued for weeks, as the cooler days of autumn brought the crisp, clear days and the change of color. They harvested the small amount of fruit from their trees and supplemented with fruit purchased at a fruit stand nearly a hundred miles away. By the end of September all the shelves were filled, and they looked with satisfaction at the literal fruits of their labors. They would have more than enough for the coming year, and for that, they were truly grateful.

"Boy, am I glad this season is over. I am ready for the quieter times of the winter months," Jill said, as they looked around the storage room.

"I am with you there," Megan said in agreement. "I thought cooking for so many was work. It is a walk in the park, compared to canning and drying fruits and vegetables. I am ready to go back to my regular duties."

"Megan, Terri . . . you have been absolutely wonderful teaching us and putting up with our mistakes. We could not have done this without you both. So, in thanks, Jill is going to watch the kids and Bonnie, Rose, Mary and several others are going to cook tonight. You two need to go put your feet up and take the rest of the day off. We will take care of everything."

Terri and Megan exchanged a look and smiled brightly. They had taken over the kitchen since arriving at the Ranch, and they had had very little time off. They both enjoyed cooking, and they had formed a rhythm to working together that worked well. In addition, they had formed a bond of sisterhood and a great friendship. "Okay, ladies, we certainly will not argue. We are out of here." Terri said, smiling as she turned and headed for the door.

"Bye, bye," Megan echoed, as she quickly followed Terri out the door, as though she was afraid they would change their minds.

"Well," said Janie, "that went well. I thought for sure they would put up a fight. This is their domain, after all."

"They have put in some really long hours in the past months; we all have. I am sure they are tired. Their domain, or not, it is our domain for the day. Where is that menu we put together last night?" Bonnie asked.

Janie took the list out of her pocket and waved it. "Right here; okay, ladies, let's get started on lunch. The guys said they would be back with another load of firewood around 11:30. We need to have lunch ready by then."

They had everything planned, and each person got to work on their part of the noon meal. By the end of the evening meal, all were very happy that Terri and Meagan loved this kitchen because they were more than happy to leave them to do the thing they loved most . . . cooking. They would help, when needed, and each rotated with the clean-up, but they were glad it was not their normal responsibility, because none of them were looking forward to making dinner as well.

Rose looked around the communications room and smiled with pleasure. She had spent many hours setting up the communications room in the basement of the main lodge. It had taken some time and more equipment, but she now had three televisions with satellite connections, four computers with all the inventory lists of supplies catalogued, and the outside perimeter monitoring systems up and working. It was as modern as possible, with all the bells and whistles money could buy. She sat back, admiring the room. It looked like any big, corporate communications room she had ever seen, and it was hers. She was pleased that George had given her carte blanche to do what needed to be done. She even had a short-wave radio, in case the internet or satellites went down in the future.

She watched the east monitor, as a deer ambled by the camera, and she smiled. She liked living here in the northwest; wildlife was everywhere. She had never lived in the country and enjoyed the quiet, peaceful serenity of the forest.

"Hey, it's a beautiful day. Are you going to stay down here in the tombs all day?" Janie asked, entering the room. "Oh my, this is great. I haven't been down here since you got the last of the boxes we brought down opened and everything installed. I've been so busy in the garden and kitchen. I can't wait to have you show me everything."

"It is wonderful; everything is working perfectly."

"Well, as much as I would like to spend time with you, showing me around, you and I have a date with some very important people."

Rose gave her a surprised look. "A date? I didn't miss a meeting, did I?"

"No, silly. We are going on a picnic; Jack and Paul should be waiting outside for us any minute."

Rose smiled, as she turned off the televisions and unnecessary computers and rose to join Janie. "Where are we going?" They would not monitor the security system all the time, until it was necessary.

"I'm not sure. Paul showed up at the garden with Jack and a picnic basket. They went to get a jeep and sent me after you. I guess we will find out, when we get there."

"It's not Sunday. What's with the time off?"

"Paul said we have been working too hard and needed to get away this morning. I guess he meant it. He said he and Jack were talking about it yesterday, and Jack said something about putting your money where your mouth is. You know, I never really understood that saying."

Rose laughed, "Me either; anyway, Jack said something like, 'all work and no play makes a grumpy wife,' last night. I guess I have been putting in a lot of hours. I seem to remember snapping at him last night. So, the guys must have gotten together and planned the outing."

"Well, I am all for it, and you have been working down here in the tombs all summer. You do not have a tan at all. I could not stand not having windows where I work." She reached in her pocket, and pulled at a tube, and waved it at Rose. "I have sunscreen; I would not want you to sunburn on your first real outing since you've been here."

"Thanks, I guess I will need it," she said, looking down at her very white arms and legs. "Sometimes, I wish I had lovely brown skin, like Megan. Anyway, it's not so bad down here. I had Curt put up some better lights. Besides, I have been busy and have not really noticed it."

Janie understood that when she was busy with her work; things around her tended to blend into the background. She heard the quick toot of a horn. "Well, there they are; let's go have some fun, sister of my heart," Janie said, smiling broadly.

It was a wonderful autumn day. It was nice to be unhurried, to take their time enjoying the countryside. All the harvesting, canning, dehydrating, firewood collecting, hunting and butchering were finished. Now, everyone could take some time for themselves and enjoy the outdoors, without feeling the pressure of work that needed to be done.

The jeep bumped along on an old fire road, as it climbed steadily up the mountain. Here and there, a deer would crash out of the brush and run from the approaching vehicle. At the top they parked the jeep, and everyone climbed out. "This way," Jack said, leading the way.

They walked up a rise at a leisurely rate, taking the shortest way to the top of the mountain. The view was magnificent. They looked out over their valley. They could see the children playing in the playground far below them. The cows, horses and buffalo were grazing in their respective pastures. The stream flowed slowly to the lake and out again, winding this way and that, until it was out of sight. It was interesting that the cabins and buildings were not as visible as one might have thought. They could see parts of some of them, but many were completely obstructed by trees.

"It is beautiful," Rose said in awe. "It doesn't seem so big from down there. But from here, you can tell the valley covers a large area."

"I found this place a few weeks ago, when Nathan and I went to scout for lookouts for fire and other threats. I thought you all would enjoy seeing it."

"I am glad that the buildings are so obscure. Someone looking down from here wouldn't realize the scope of our settlement," Paul observed.

"This is a wonderful view. Let's get the blanket and picnic basket and eat right here," Janie suggested.

"Sounds good to me," Rose added.

They spent a wonderful afternoon exploring the mountain top. It was late afternoon when Jack finally called to Janie and Paul, "We need to head back. We want to be down before it gets dark. The road is hard enough to follow in the daylight."

Reluctantly, they gathered their things and made their way back to the jeep. "Thank you so much for thinking of this Jack," Janie said, as they climbed into the vehicle.

"How come he gets all the credit?" Paul asked, pouting.

"I was going to thank you more privately when we got home, Mister Pouty. So, this is all you get." Janie kissed him on the cheek.

"How about this for pouting and a promise of things to come," Paul said, as he pulled her to him and kissed her properly, as Jack and Rose laughed at their antics.

Winter came in with a bang, before the end of October, bringing nearly a foot of snow. Everyone had settled in for the cold months. George kept Bradley busy with memorizing Proverbs and the book of John. Several other children were memorizing Scripture for a program they were planning in the spring. The adults attended Bible studies and classes, while the children attended school classes.

The greenhouse they were heating was working out very well. The boiler system worked so well it burned throughout the night, without having to be restocked. They were still harvesting tomatoes, lettuce, and some of the hardier, cool crops, which pleased Terri and Megan greatly.

George had Pastor Phil bring ten of the foundation computers to the Ranch for the children to do their schoolwork on. They were set up in the main lodge, next to the library and classrooms, situated on the second floor. The kids were allowed to play video games, but only after they were done with their studies and chores. This was a great hit with the children, and the older children helped the younger ones so that they could play sooner. Surprisingly, they each limited themselves to one hour per day, or less, depending on how many wished to play.

On the night of the children's program, Bradley had done a great job reciting Proverbs. After he was finished, he gave a short talk on what the verses meant to him. Though George and Bradley had talked many times about the verses throughout the winter, discussing what they meant, George was impressed at the deep understanding Bradley had for what he had studied. Bradley had blossomed. He now was engaging and insightful. George had come to love him, like one of his own.

George was proud of all the children. He knew their lives had changed greatly since coming to the Ranch. Yet, they had all settled in very well. They were well-behaved and respectful. Yes, he was very proud of them all.

CHAPTER 25

THE FOURTH OF JULY brought with it the anticipation of a great celebration and a touch of sadness that our once great nation was changing. The bell rang at the meeting hall. It had been installed to help with the fire drills and now was used to call everyone to chapel, to dinner, and to meetings, as well. It was also used for announcements. It could be heard throughout the Ranch, except when someone had music playing too loudly and all the windows and doors in the cabin were closed. In those cases, someone would call, using the phone system Curt had put in place between the buildings, or they would take a horse and ride over to inform the missing person. They had begun using the horses more and more, and the vehicles less and less, to conserve fuel.

Janie heard the bell and put aside the mending she was doing, pulled on a sweater, and headed out the door. Walking down the road, she saw Jill, Bonnie and the kids, walking toward the meeting hall. She hurried to catch up. "Any idea what's up?" she called out.

Jill and Bonnie turned and stopped, allowing her to catch up. "Not really; it's not time for the fire drill, and we don't have any scheduled meetings, so we don't know."

"Well, I guess we will find out," Janie observed, as she reached them, and they all continued the walk.

It was a pleasant afternoon in mid-summer. They had been at the Ranch for nearly two years. The winter months had been spent much like the winter before, with classes and activities for everyone. During that time, they had worked out the bugs of planting, and canning, and the hunting and packaging of the meat. They had learned, by trial and error, many things about all aspects of their new life on the Ranch. They had found a better way of rotating stock, making sure everything was used before opening any new cans, or jars, or meats in the freezer.

Last weekend they had the program for the school children. Several of the ladies had made special gifts for the children for memorizing their Bible verses. Everyone had enjoyed the simple pleasure the children had in doing a job well.

Several new families had joined them. Pastor Phil had brought them, blindfolded, to the Sanctuary in the back of a windowless, panel van. They continued to believe it was important to take every precaution, in case someone should be asked to leave, or later decided they did not want to stay. They needed to preserve the safety of all who were living at the Ranch.

"Please sit down; as soon as everyone is here, I will let you know what's going on," George called out, as they entered. After ten minutes, everyone had arrived, and George signaled for quiet.

"Rose has been monitoring the news channels, and Pastor Phil has just arrived with some bad news. I am sad to inform you that it has begun. There were twenty-three successful strikes on American soil this morning; four were at train or subway stations, two at airports, eleven at malls, two at government buildings, one at a police station, and five at restaurants. There were also two unsuccessful attempts, where the terrorists were killed. There is little known about casualties, but they are estimating that there are several thousand dead and several thousand more injured. The country is in turmoil.

"There are already stories of truckers going home to be with their families, leaving their loads undelivered. Shortages will begin shortly, I'm sure. The media, and some government officials, and the liberal media are blaming the conservative Christians. They believe it is our fault we were attacked. They believe we are intolerant and will not accept other religions or beliefs. They say we are inflexible and unwilling to compromise. There is no reasoning with them, though some have tried. I believe they just want someone to blame, and, for some reason, they do not want to blame those who are really at fault . . . the terrorists. The persecution will probably escalate very soon. We will begin round-the-clock prayers for the next three days. We will use the schedule we had last month, when Sari was ill. Several of us plan to fast, also. If you plan to join in the fast, please let someone in the kitchen know, so they can plan accordingly. If you have any questions, let me know. Otherwise, it is life as usual; Pastor Phil, would you lead us in prayer?"

"*Father in Heaven, You know our hearts. Give us Your peace. We knew this was coming. You gave us a vision, asked us to prepare, and You led us here. Now, the real work will begin. Each of us has a task You have given us, whether it is staying here and keeping the Ranch operating and well stocked, or going and doing Your will by ministering out in the world. The fields are ripening for Your harvest. We are ready and willing to do Your will. Jesus, we await Your coming. Come quickly, Lord Jesus, come quickly. In Jesus' name. Amen.*"

The reality hit everyone hard. It was one thing to prepare for bad times; it was another for those hard times to be at hand. The riots of last fall had been isolated to some of the larger cities. It had been easy to explain them away as just rabble-rousers creating chaos. Now, looking back, they could see each step along the way had brought them to the place they found themselves today. The winning of the lottery brought the reality that the time to get started was here, and Janie's plans brought about urgency to begin building. The completion of the buildings brought the move to the Ranch and the beginning of a new lifestyle. All the planning and preparing would now go into action. They had food stores to last several seasons. They had learned to gather the vegetables' seeds that would be needed for the succeeding year. The farm animals had bred and now had babies grazing in the pastures. They had enough firewood cut and stacked in containers for two or more winters. Long hours, sweat, and hard work had all paid off. More importantly, hours of Bible study, conversation, and prayer and fasting had prepared them spiritually for what was to come. They would continue to walk with God. They were ready for anything God set before them.

The residents decided to go forward with the Fourth of July celebrations for the sake of the children, yet their hearts were not really in them.

Days and weeks passed after the terrorists' attacks, and, little by little, God brought believers to the Sanctuary. All were brought by Pastor Phil, or one of the other members of his church. They knew the day would come when he, or other members of his church, would move to the Sanctuary because conditions would become dangerous beyond the confines of the Sanctuary. However, until that time came, Pastor Phil would remain in the small house next to his church and would minister to those who God sent to him. If they were believers and God directed him, Pastor Phil would make arrangements to get them to a ranch. It took a great deal of discernment to know who to send. There were so many in need of help. There were some who, after hearing about the ranches, wanted to establish their own ranches, and Pastor Phil helped them, as much as possible, in their endeavors.

Pastor Phil knew the day would come when he would begin traveling to seek out believers. He knew the danger would be great, yet this was the vision God had given him years before. When the time came, he would see his wife safely settled at the Ranch, and then he would go where God led him. However, until that day arrived, he would keep the church open seven days a week and minister to all who came seeking God's help.

Pastor Phil brought Carson Smith and his family early one morning. They seemed like a personable family, eager to help wherever they were needed. They were given three rooms in the meeting hall, as there were nine of them: Carson; his wife, Judy; their son, Jacob; his wife, June; their two children, Patty and Perry; another son, Carl; his wife, Marie and their daughter, Lena and son, Jonah. They had been at the Ranch for three weeks and seemed to be settling into the routine of things when July called a family meeting.

"I don't see why we have to live in the meeting hall; they have three empty cabins. They could have given us one of those," Judy complained loudly one morning.

"I do not believe they are finished yet. Besides, we are already settled here. It is fine," Marie replied quietly.

"We are all supposed to be equal in God's Kingdom; why do the others get special quarters? Carson had the same vision, but he didn't have the money. He should have been the one to win the lottery. We could have done a much better job of putting things together. Just last night he was telling me about several things he thought could be done better. I'm sure if we were in charge, things would run more smoothly. Why, did you see how slow dinner was in being put on the tables last night? Such inefficiency! Someone should say something to the kitchen staff!"

"Now, Mother, they are not staff you can hire or fire. And I said I would have done things differently, but that doesn't mean I thought they would be better. I shared a couple of ideas with George; he liked them, and I think they will change a few things," Carson said.

"I surely hope so," added Jacob. "I do not like having to do guard duty. They have cameras after all; I don't know why that is not enough. I simply cannot sleep during the day, and June needs to watch the kids. She can't be working in the garden all day." Even as Jacob said the words, he knew he was being whiny. He really did not mind the guard duty that much.

"Honey, it wasn't all day. It was only for four hours, and the kids had a wonderful time, playing with the other kids," June said softly, knowing her words would fall on deaf ears, yet feeling she needed to say something, nonetheless.

Sighing deeply, June knew things were not going to improve. It was always the same. They had changed churches several times in the seven years she and Jacob had lived near his family. First, they would become involved, Judy would complain, and begin to demand changes. She would try to have Carson placed in a position of authority. Usually, the pastors and elders would try to be gracious, but eventually they would have enough, and either they would be asked to leave, or angry words would be exchanged, and they would leave on their own. Either way, the Smith family would move on. Judy simply did not understand that God promotes the called; man does not. In addition, who was to say Carson's ideas were better? They were just different.

June could not believe the wonderful man she married was so different when he was around his family. He seemed like Doctor Jekyll and Mister Hyde. They had met at Good Shepherd University, a conservative Christian college. She was in her freshman year; he was a sophomore. They spent long hours talking, and June loved him dearly, long before he asked her to marry him. It seemed like a marriage made in heaven, those early days with Jacob. He was attentive, kind, and loving. When their twins, Patty and Perry, were born, their little family seemed complete. They visited Jacob's family twice a year, and, though she enjoyed the visit, there was always an undercurrent. Back then, she was not sure what it was, or why she felt the way she did . . . uneasy, so she made a point to shrug it off and never made an issue of little criticisms that Judy would make. Now, all Judy could do is complain, and, unfortunately, Jacob complained along with her.

June wanted to retreat to their room and cry. She loved being here. Never before had she felt so accepted and loved by people. Since the family rift with her mother, while she was in college, Jacob and the kids were all she had. She saw her father every few months, but now she did not know when she would see him again—or if she would see him again. What she did know was that, if things continued the way they were going, they would be told to leave. It was only a matter of time.

"Father, what am I supposed to do? All Judy does is murmur and complain. She always believes they have a better idea, a better way of doing things, and she does not see she is the problem. She will work and work hard, but only if they are in charge. I know Carson doesn't always think the same way, but he will not stand up to Judy. Why does this keep happening? I am afraid they will alienate everyone. I have never had friends and sisters in the Lord, like I have here. I love Janie, Jill, Mary, Bonnie, and so many others. Please tell me what to do." Tears began to gather in her eyes as she tried to hold them back.

"Tell them."

June looked around; knowing in her heart the voice had not been audible, yet it was so distinctive.

"But Father, they never listen to me. What do I say to make them hear?"

"Speak from your heart, Daughter."

June looked at her extended family and took a deep breath. She listened, briefly, as they continued to voice their displeasure. "Enough!" she said in a firm, yet quiet voice. All conversation ceased and eyes turned to her. "You all know I love you dearly, but I have watched for the past several years, as you have gone from church to church, doing just as you are now. You get involved and then pick every ministry apart, piece by piece. You love the Lord Jesus, I know you do. But none of you has ever learned to allow Him to guide you, and you have never learned to submit to the authority God has placed over you. Jesus does not like all this murmuring and complaining, yet you can never accept things as they are. Nothing is ever up to your expectations; this cannot go on," She took a deep breath and continued.

"If God wanted you to win the lottery, you would have. If He wanted you to be in charge, you would be. The reason you are not is because you cannot accept a servant's role. Look at George and Elizabeth; they are the most generous and loving people I have ever met. They work wherever they are needed, doing anything that needs to be done. George is out in the fields, hunting, and chopping wood with everyone else. Elizabeth works in the kitchen, or gardens, or watches the children. In the winter, she teaches school and helps with the tutoring. Did you know they kept less than two percent of the lottery money for themselves? They paid off their bills, their mortgage and those of their family; that's all. They didn't take any vacations, or spend money on a fancy new mansion, or extravagant autos. The lottery money was considered God's money, and they refused to spend any more than necessary on themselves. Could you say the same, if you had won?

"Everyone here is hard working. I never hear any words of complaint from anyone but you. They have spent months working, building, planting, canning, and everything else . . . working in the harmony of the Lord. Remember the verses in the Bible about everyone being part of the body, and each part having a function, and each member being important for the success of the whole? You are important; you each have something to give, yet you are not the head. Jesus is the head, and He has not chosen to put any of you in charge." June stopped, looking at each person in the room. "How much time do you spend praying for this Sanctuary Ranch?" She stopped waiting for a response; when no one replied, she continued. "Did you know that every morning George, Elizabeth, the rest of their family, and more than half of residents here meet in the chapel for prayer? If any of them do not make it to the morning meeting, you will probably find them there in the afternoon. Yet, to my knowledge you have never gone to any of the prayer meetings." She saw Jacob begin to answer and held up her hand to stop him. "What about the Bible studies? There are several that meet throughout the day, yet I would venture to say none of you have ever attended. You only attend the required studies in the evenings." She met the gaze of each person and saw discomfort in each one.

Tears gathered in her eyes and rolled down her cheeks, "I would like to stay here. I have never felt the love of Jesus in so many people before. They all love Jesus, and they love us. You can see it in everything they do. They are constantly seeking God's will before every decision. I believe they are being directed by God. I believe they are doing His will. Are you? Are you doing His will? Are you being directed by Him? Is your complaining honoring God? Your complaining is telling God that He did things wrong. Who are you to tell God that He did things wrong?"

Flee to the Mountains

June signaled Patty and Perry then left the room with them in tow. The room remained in silence for a long time, each convicted by her words. They all knew she was right. Yes, they loved the Lord but . . . Carson moved toward the door, his daughter-in-law's words ringing in his ears. He needed time away to sort all this out. When had he allowed his wife to convince him he would be a better leader than all the others? Looking back, he could see the pattern that had formed behind him: new church, new excitement, finding a ministry to help in, and . . . He placed a hand over his face in sadness and regret; yes, June was right.

"Carson, I do not know what got into that girl. You" Judy began, only to be cut off by Carson.

"No, Judy!" He turned to face his wife. "June is right; I have allowed you to place me on a pedestal. You had me believing I had better ideas than anyone else, but that is not true. You had me believing I should be the one Jesus chose, but that is not true. I love you dear, but I have sinned. I have allowed my pride to swell my head and muddle my thinking. Everyone must answer to someone, and I should have submitted to George and those God placed in authority in the churches we have attended in the past, but I haven't—we haven't. Now, I am going to spend some time with Jesus and ask His forgiveness, then I am going to find George and ask his. I really think everyone in this room should consider doing the same." Carson left, as a stunned Judy stared at the closed door.

One by one, the Smith family left the room, leaving Judy alone. Anger filled her heart. "All this is June's fault," she said to the empty room. "She never was right for our son. We have every right to let people know when they are doing things wrong. I cannot believe Carson listened to her." Bitterness surged in her heart, blocking every effort the Holy Spirit made to reach Judy's heart.

Jacob knew his wife was right about him, also. He realized that he had changed since returning home. The first years of their marriage had been wonderful; laughter and love filled their home. But since moving to Seattle, in his mind he could see the look of sadness that crossed June's face every time he complained or muttered his disapproval. He knew he had allowed his mother's negative attitude to enter his heart, and he had not realized it. He knew he needed to make things right with June, but Jesus came first. He walked to the far side of the lake, before dropping to his knees in prayer. Regret and remorse filled his heart. He was supposed to be the spiritual leader of his home, yet he had done a very poor job of things. *"Lord Jesus, please forgive me."*

Jacob found June in the garden two hours later. Love swelled in his heart for this beautiful lady God had given him. She was overweight, something she fussed about often, yet she was the love of his life. Her cheerful disposition had drawn him seven years earlier, and every day since then, she brought color into his gray life. She brought Jesus alive in his life, through her firm faith and love for her Lord. Looking at her now, he knew her wealthy family would be appalled. Yet, June was happy and content in her new life with him. How had he ever gotten so blessed, without even realizing it?

"June," Jacob said, quietly, from two feet away. June looked up into the tear-stained face of her beloved husband. June rose and walked into Jacob's arms. He didn't need to tell her; she knew he had spent the last hours seeking Jesus and His forgiveness. "Please, forgive me. The Holy Spirit spoke to me, time and time again, yet, I ignored Him. I am so sorry."

June had gone to the garden because working there eased her spirit. There she had shared with Janie the horrible scene with her family. After praying together, they worked side by side in prayerful contemplation. Now, looking over her shoulder, she asked, "Would you please watch Patty and Perry?" They were playing in a small play area set up for the children, next to the garden.

"Of course, go on. I will finish weeding this row, and then I will head to the play area. I can watch them better there, and I need a break." She glanced down at her watch. "We will head to the main lodge for dinner in forty-five minutes. Take your time. I will be praying for you." Janie gave her a brief hug.

June and Jacob made their way to the small area next to the lake. It was a picnic area with tables and benches. Off to the side, under an old weeping willow, set several chairs and a double swing, hanging from the tree. Seeing no one, they made their way to the swing, and Jacob took June's hand, as they sat quietly for a time.

Peaceful serenity surrounded them. Birds sang overhead, chipmunks barked at each another, and fish jumped in the lake. A gentle breeze sang through the trees the music of love sent from their Father above. June could feel the harmony between them, flowing back and forth, just as the trees swayed back and forth overhead. She loved this man and waited quietly for him to speak.

"June, I need to ask you for forgiveness for my behavior, since we moved from Seattle. As I said before, I knew I was out of line on several occasions, and the Holy Spirit was trying to get my attention, but I just didn't want to listen. I don't know why I behaved like I did. But I love you; please forgive me."

"You are forgiven, but then I forgave you each time along the way, even without your asking" she said with a smile. "I knew it was an adjustment, going back to your home town. You always behaved differently around your family, when we went to visit; that is why I didn't really want to move near them. But God had a plan. We would never have come to be here, if we had stayed in Seattle. This place is . . . " June hesitated, not knowing the words to describe her feelings. "is like no place I have ever been before. I can feel the presence of Jesus. When I walk around talking with Him, it's like He is right beside me. While I am working, I find joy in whatever I do because I know it helps everyone. I have sisters for the first time in my life, and it is wonderful. I never knew what I was missing by never having any sisters. I had lots of girlfriends but none that were like sisters. There is harmony here, everyone working for the good of all. There is no greed, envy, or desire to be better than everyone else. We are all equal and are equally loved by all."

"I know what you mean, and I have felt it, too. I don't know why I allowed Mom to . . . " Jacob stopped, "No, that is wrong, Mom didn't do anything. She was just being who she has always been. No, I am responsible for the way I acted and the things I have said. I do not understand why I did what I did, but, rest assured, I will try not to act that way again. I would like you to hold me accountable." June nodded but remained quiet. She knew Jacob needed to talk this out in his own way.

"You were right about so many things. I'm not sure why my heart began to harden, and I began to ignore the Holy Spirit, when He tried to tell me I was out of line; but I can almost put my finger on when, but that's not important right now. I know I have allowed my pride and envy to get in the way of a lot of things. I know I have sinned. Now, I just want to be the person God wants me to be. I want to serve Him in everything I do. And I want to be the husband and father you and the kids deserve." Jacob had been talking as he looked out over the lake. Now, he turned to look at June. "I would like to begin praying together each morning, before we head over to pray with everyone else. We are one in God's sight, so we need to be more unified. I would also like to study together and have devotions with the kids. I want the kids to be committed believers, and we need to be their example."

June leaned over and laid her head on his shoulder. They talked about the past and dreamed about the future. They prayed together and asked God to establish new habits. They prayed for Jacob's family, especially his mom and dad. They sat enjoying a renewed spirit of unity between them, knowing that they were looking at a new beginning in their relationship. It was not until they heard the dinner bell that they rose and walked hand in hand back toward the fellowship hall.

"Thank You, Jesus! Father! And especially You, Holy Spirit; thank You for answering my prayers," was June's silent prayer.

CHAPTER 26

ONE OF GREATEST DAYS for Janie, since moving to the Ranch, was the day her brother, Bill, and his wife, Holly, and their two children, Charlotte and Stan, arrived. Albert had told them to contact Pastor Phil, if they wanted to join them at the Ranch. After Bill lost his job and there were food shortages in the coastal areas, they had decided to make their way to the Sanctuary. They had been skeptical about the warnings of persecution and food shortages. They were young and had a very difficult time accepting that their long-term plans would need to change. They simply could not believe the prosperity of their youth would not continue throughout their lives.

With Bill and Holly came the news of widespread fear and hunger. The government had declared Martial Law, and food was being rationed. Several in the media and government were blaming the Christians of hording and saying the end times were beginning. Some ministers were saying that all this was happening because America, as a whole, had turned their back on God, removing Him from our schools, courts, and government. And now God was removing His blessing. They pointed to the fact that a nation could not have the innocent blood of millions of aborted babies on its hands, without repercussions and consequences. Others pointed to the breakdown of the family and acceptance of sexual sin, as additional reasons for God's displeasure of America. Yet, most felt people had simply turned to the government to meet their needs, instead of looking to God to care for them. Many unsaved and a few saved people believed the government should take care of them, provide them with a living, and guarantee their happiness, instead of working hard and providing for themselves in their pursuit of their own happiness. Of course, there were enough reasons for the difficulties, yet the non-Christians were blinded to the truth of their words, and hate swelled in their hearts.

Every day churches were being burned or vandalized, and members were being threatened. Each day more citizens accepted the lie that the problems were caused by radical Christians. Each day someone new called to have all believers rounded up and put in camps, so they could not cause any more problems. The people, at large, paid no attention to the fact that nearly every food kitchen or food pantry was run by a local church; in fact, many churches had banded together and joined resources to help the poor families with shelter, food and clothing. Widows, or abandoned wives, and their children were being cared for in church-run houses. The media and some government officials needed a scapegoat to blame for the mess they created, and Christians fit the bill. The lost believed all the lies, never realizing the government did very little to help anyone. It was the very people the media and government were blaming who did the most to help those in need.

Janie, Paul and Janie's parents helped Bill's family settle into the last two empty rooms in the fellowship hall. "I know it is a bit cramped here, but they are working on plans for more living quarters," Paul said.

"No worries," Bill said. "We are just glad to be here in one piece. We were getting worried for the children."

"Well you are safe now. Get settled and come downstairs to the dining room. Dinner will be served in forty-five minutes. We can catch up then," Janie said, turning to leave. "We are so glad you are here."

The Sanctuary Ranch was now home to over two hundred people. Construction had begun on an additional housing complex, which would have room for fifty more people; Janie, Elizabeth, Nathan, Bradley, and Mike, all being forewarned in dreams of the need for more housing, told Paul and George. They, in turn, had decided to begin construction. Now, even though construction was nearly complete, they were considering another building, as thirty people were already waiting in tents for its completion.

Janie marveled at the harmony and unity that remained at the Sanctuary, even with the influx of new people. Some of that was due to the fact they had begun housing potential residents at a smaller sanctuary fifty miles away. God had led them to the creation of a smaller ranch, a place they called Haven Ranch. After several months of being at the Sanctuary Ranch, it became obvious they would need to screen people. George had been challenged by a man who came to the smaller sanctuary, saying God had told him he was to be in charge. The man began ordering others around, demanding changes. Everyone worked hard to be cordial, yet continued doing things the way they found worked. The sanctuary family was gracious, and, not wanting to miss God in the event that God had sent this man and his family, they gave him the benefit of the doubt. Yet, after several weeks and many difficulties, the elder board had voted to expel him and his family. Luckily, he and his family had come to Haven Ranch blindfolded and were removed from the ranch blindfolded. They were unhappy about being expelled. They were dropped hundreds of miles away from where they had met Pastor Phil, which caused the man to strike the driver of the van who dropped them off. The safety of the ranches was more important than the upset of troublemakers. The fact was, they were warned several times before the unfortunate events of their expulsion. The entire family had caused so much trouble that the entire community had sighed a sigh of relief, when they left.

Janie's thoughts moved back to June's family, grateful they had not been as bad as this family. She remembered the day June had come to the garden in tears. After some prodding, June had shared with her what had happened. They had prayed together and gone back to work. The next day, June had told her everyone, with the exception of Judy, had repented. Since that time, they had worked in harmony with the rest of the Ranch family. As for Judy, she had withdrawn. Everyone was concerned for her, yet, she made it clear she wanted no friendship, no prayer, and especially no conversation. Janie was saddened that someone could see the wonder of great unity of spirit and not want to be part of that spirit.

Janie was headed to the fellowship hall to help with dinner. She rarely helped with the meal preparation because they had a group of ladies who really loved cooking, and it was not a chore she really enjoyed. Today, she was helping because several of the regular crew had gone raspberry hunting and would not be back in time to help. She did not mind the occasional venture into the kitchen, as long as it remained occasional.

It was now the practice to have people stay at the smaller sanctuary several weeks or months until the elder board gave permission for them to come to this ranch. At that point, they were blindfolded and transported here. They had found, early on, troublemakers could be avoided at the main ranch, by following this procedure. Those who complained, or caused problems, were left at the smaller ranch indefinitely—or expelled.

Early August brought the completion of the new housing complex, and people were moving into it as soon as the last of the painting was completed. Now, they had begun work on a dormitory that would be completed before the first snow of the season. There were more and more single people, whose families had disowned them because they refused to denounce Jesus. They came in all ages, from teens to an elderly man, who was nearly eighty. The Ranch now housed nearly four hundred souls.

By mid-August, Rose had come across a news report of hundreds of abandoned children, roaming the streets of many of the large cities across America. Many parents could not feed themselves, much less their children. Some had just packed up and left town, leaving their children to fend for themselves. This horrified nearly everyone at the Ranch, but especially Elizabeth and George. They had immediately made plans to gather as many as they could. If they came across the parents, they would get them to sign over custody, but, if they could not, they would take the children to the Ranch anyway. Every adult at the Ranch was being encouraged to take on the care of at least one child.

Ten-year-old Hector Gonzales watched as the three vans parked along 5th Street. Six men got out and came together to talk on the street corner. Hector moved closer so that he could hear what the men were saying. He had good reasons for being careful. The bad men had nearly taken him and his sister two weeks earlier. The bad men had taken Bill and Trent, who then had escaped four days later, bringing horrible stories of punishment for anyone who dared disagree with them. Finally, he was close enough to hear, so he crouched down and listened.

"We must be careful not to scare any of the kids," George said. "Pastor Phil got word yesterday that some official vehicles went around this area and gathered up as many children as they could carry in their vehicles. He has an acquaintance who was a guard at the children's dormitory. He reported that a young girl was comforting the others with Bible stories about Jesus. She told the other children to be brave, and Jesus would be with them. During the night, two women came and took her away. They gave her an overdose of sleeping medicine and killed her. They said they could not have her telling the other children lies and fairy tales. The guard said that was it for him. He was one of those people who always said nothing like this could happen in our country. I guess they proved him wrong."

"So, murder is better than fairy tales?" Gordon said sarcastically.

Hector held back a sob. He was sure that that was Becky. She was always telling the street kids about Jesus. She was kind and loving to everyone. Her father had been a pastor or elder of some large church, until he was killed by a drive-by shooter two months ago. Several days later, the dark vans pulled up, and they had taken Becky's mother and her two brothers. Becky had seen the van pull up and had hidden in the bushes in her special place, like her mother had told her to do, if any strangers came to their house. They had loaded her family into the van and driven off. That was the last time Becky had seen them. Becky did not stay at her house and she never used the lights when she checked to see if anyone came. She had fed many with the food in her pantry. Hector was sure many of them would have starved to death, if Becky had not helped them. Hector really liked Becky. Hector forced himself to go back to listening to the men, even though all he really wanted to do was go back to his hideout and cry.

"These kids have been traumatized enough. We will try to get them to come with us, but we will not force anyone. They come only if they want to."

"Can we tell them about the Ranch and what we do there?" Manny Hollister asked.

"I think it would be best to tell them as little as possible, until we are on our way. We do not want many to know about the Ranch, in case the officials come back again, and they get taken. Let's pray before we get started." The men bowed their heads and asked for guidance from above.

"Father in Heaven, we are on a rescue mission here. We know there are many children who are out here on the streets, fending for themselves. We know some of these children have been abandoned, others physically and mentally abused, and some have run away from bad circumstances. Father, we bind Satan from lying to these children, telling them we mean them harm. We loose your spirit of love, kindness and compassion to flow through us and draw as many children as possible to us. We are Your servants. Guide and direct us, as only You can. Amen."

"Okay, let's go. Stay in teams of two, and let's meet back here in two hours." They had checked carefully for the past two days for any official vehicles in the area, while they had contacted the local pastors they could find. They brought food and blankets for those who might need them. They did not want to explain their real reason for being there.

Gordon Jensen and George were teamed together. They started by checking out the alleys and empty buildings. Hector followed at a comfortable distance. The big man who prayed seemed to be the one in charge. The prayer had sealed it for Hector, these men were here to help, but, being cautious by nature, he followed for a while. His Mamma had been a Christian. She had taught Hector and Suzanna about Jesus since they were tiny. Now, he would watch and see if these men could be trusted.

"Jesus, if these men are Christians, and if they really mean to help us, please let me know," Hector prayed silently.

"They are Mine. You can trust them. Go with them." Hector smiled brightly and walked a little faster to catch up.

As the men were walking down the street, Gordon heard the sound of crying from an alley. He went to investigate and found Chong huddled under a makeshift covering of cardboard boxes. Gordon and George spoke softly and kindly to the crying child, but they could not coax him out of his hiding place. Finally, Hector knew it was time to reveal himself, and he walked up to the older men.

"Chong is his name; mine's Hector," Hector said. "I think he is about five years old, but he seems really small to be five. My sister is four, and she is almost as big as he is."

George and Gordon turned toward the voice behind them. "Hello. Do you think you can help us to get him out of there? We do not want to scare him any more than he already is."

"I guess I can try." Hector went into the box and talked to Chong for several minutes. "Chong, I have been following these men for over an hour. I believe we can trust them. They are Christians, like Mrs. Madison. I prayed, and God said we are supposed to go with them. He said they belong to Him, so they must be good people—not bad people, like those others who came here. I think you should come with me. I am going with them." Hector and Chong came out of the box shelter holding hands.

Gordon knelt down in front of the small boy. "We came to get you and take you home with us. We will care for you and give you a place to live. Would you like to come with us? You do not have to, if you do not want to." The boy nodded 'yes,' and Gordon picked up the boy as he said, "We would like you to come, too, Hector."

"The bad men never gave anyone a choice. They forced many, kicking and screaming, into their vans," Hector observed. "You give us a choice, so I will come, and my sister Marianna will, too."

George nodded, his face grim. "We had better be getting back. We can check the next street over on the way back."

Chong had clung to Gordon, not allowing anyone else to carry him, until they got to the vans. Gordon was already lost. He had not felt the unconditional love of another since his own boy had died in an accident years before. This little child needed him, and for the first time in a long time, he knew he needed the little boy.

"Hector, are there more children out here that need a home, a family?" George asked.

"Yes, but many will not trust outsiders, not after the bad men came through. My sister stays with Mrs. Madison; she takes in any children who want to stay with her."

"Will you show us where she lives?" Hector nodded 'yes.'

They made their way back to the vans, where the others already waited with three other children: Sara, a ten-year-old, black girl; Tommy, a fourteen-year-old, white boy; and Frances, a four-year-old, Japanese girl. The children had banded together to care for each other. It would take time to remove the fear from their faces, but all the men were determined to turn their somber expressions to laughter and smiles.

Hector climbed into the van and directed them to a large, run-down house, ten blocks from where they found Chong and eight other children. Mrs. Madison was a middle-aged woman, who had a tired, worn look. In fact, from the looks of her, she had missed many meals, in order to feed her charges.

"Mrs. Madison, I am George," deliberately avoiding giving his last name. "We are here to take as many children as possible to safety," George said. "We have a ranch with lots of room. We grow our own food and can provide for these children. I cannot tell you where, but I can guarantee they will be loved and cared for."

"I believe you. I have been praying for many days for help. God told me help was coming. You may talk with the children, but I am warning you that some will not go with you. Some firmly believe their parents will come looking for them. I promised them I would stay with them until then. Most have been here for months; I really doubt anyone will come, but I encourage their hope. Everyone has to have hope."

"Yes, hope is important in these times," George said kindly.

George spoke with the children and invited them to the Ranch. Then Hector put in his two cents, also. "These guys are on the level. God told me to go. You should, too."

"If you would like to come, we are leaving as soon as you are ready. Please go gather your things," George said to the thirty-plus children present.

George turned to talk with Mrs. Madison again, when Hector asked, "Can we go and get the food Becky had at her house, before they took her? It would help Mrs. Madison."

George turned back at the question, "Is it close by?"

"Not far, about ten blocks or so. The area is pretty deserted. Riots chased out most people last fall. Looters went through everything, but Becky's dad was really smart. He had a hidden room. Becky showed it to me a while back. She wanted me to know because she said, if anything happened to her, I could help others with the food." He turned slightly, as tears filled his eyes at the thought of Becky.

"How much is there?" George asked, curious. He prayed quickly, asking if it was worth the time and exposure, but he did not get an answer one way or the other.

"Lots and lots; I have been going there every few days. It would last a very long time."

"Okay, I think we need to check it out." George turned to Mrs. Madison. "Please, get the children ready, so we can leave as soon as we return."

The trip to Becky's house took nearly ten minutes. It was late afternoon, and George wanted to be gone, before the night prowlers came out for the evening. Hector led them around to the back of the garage and through a door hanging by one hinge. "It's through here." Hector moved a long table that sat next to the wall. There was a trap door in the floor. George pulled up the door, and they headed down. Lights came on automatically, as they descended the stairs.

The room was a full basement under the garage. It was filled with shelves and shelves of food. It was a goldmine for Mrs. Madison. George knew it would take several hours to move everything.

"Wow, this guy was ready for the long haul," Curt observed. "It will take hours to move all this."

"Yes, I know," George said, thinking. He felt an urgency to remove the children, as soon as possible. "I think we need to take as much as we can now and make plans to return for more children next week. We can move the rest of the food then." They all agreed, as they began carrying out the cases of vegetables, canned meat, and fruit. In the corner, they found a freezer. Expecting to be overwhelmed with rotting meat, Manny lifted the lip quickly, ready to close it just as quickly. Inside, the freezer was filled with meat, still frozen.

"Jackpot!" Manny called out. "I don't know how it is still working, but I guess we should not be surprised, since the lights came on. Everything is in great shape." There were no lights in the neighborhood, so where the electricity came from they did not know.

"Well, fill that box over there. We will take the rest next week," George responded.

Curt, still curious about the freezer, took a few minutes to check it out. "He had it on a battery backup system. This is an old transformer he modified to run just the freezer and lights, with just a trickle charge coming from a solar panel on the roof. This baby could keep running for a long time. I think we should try to move the whole thing, when we come back. It would go a long way towards helping Mrs. Madison."

"I am really hoping we can convince her and the rest of the children to come back to the Ranch," George said, hopefully.

It took nearly a half hour to carry up and load what they could into the vans. Hector kept watch, to make sure no one was around who would get curious later and check things out. The men marveled at the wide variety and the amount food. "This guy sure did the best he could to prepare and provide for his family. Too bad things ended the way they did for them," Manny said, thoughtfully.

They unloaded the vans and reloaded them with the children and their possessions in just under an hour. George turned to Mrs. Madison, "Please consider coming back with us next week. It is not safe here for you or the children."

"I will pray about it, George. Thank you so much for the food. I think you know what it means to us. I will be praying for your safety on your way, also." She said good-bye to each of the children and watched until the vans were out of sight. Maybe she should go next week. She and the children always hid in the evenings, when the gunfire and drunkards came out. It really was getting more and more dangerous every day. But it was the government officials that scared her the most. They knew she was here. When they came around the last time, they had left all the children under five in her care. Would they come back and take them next time? Because she was sure there would be a next time.

The men stopped after a hundred miles, to give the twenty-seven children time to run around and relieve themselves. They were a subdued group of children of all ages, sizes and colors. Many had been abused, prior to being either left at the children's home or abandoned to the streets. The men knew that Jake and a loving family would help.

They arrived at the Ranch at five in the morning. The children all slept through the night, as the vehicles rolled along the highways. Several whimpered in their sleep but never really woke. They were safe now. The men all hoped it would not take long before these somber, unsmiling children were running and playing with all the other Ranch children.

The next morning found Hector venturing boldly into the dining hall, holding Susanna's hand. His excitement was evident in his expression, though he did not smile. Whatever this place was, he knew they would all be safe here, or at least as safe as they could me in a world gone crazy. George spotted Hector and waved him over.

"Hector, Susanna, I would like you to meet Paul and Janie," George said, when Hector arrived.

"Good morning," Janie and Paul said at the same time.

"Good morning," the children both returned.

"Hector, Susanna, you will be staying with Janie and Paul in their cabin, if that is alright with you," George said kindly.

"You mean we have a choice?" Hector asked surprised.

"You always have a choice." George said, matter of factly.

Hector looked at Susanna, who smiled timidly at Janie, as she held her arms out for Susanna. For months Susanna had been reserved and fearful of everyone, speaking only to him and Mrs. Madison. Therefore, he was surprised when she went to Janie and allowed Janie to lift her into her lap. "Would you like to live with these people, Susanna?" Hector asked.

"Yes, Hector, I would like that." She smiled at Hector, then at Janie. Hector nodded to George, and it was settled.

"Great!" Paul said, speaking for the first time. "We are so glad you will be joining us. Right after breakfast, we will show you your new home."

Over the next hour, George, Elizabeth and Sherry introduced and placed each of the children in families. Most work was suspended for the day, to give everyone time to settle the children and make them feel welcome. They would have their normal welcome celebration, with cake and homemade ice cream, after the evening meal. Tomorrow, they would get to work and finish the dormitory. They were hopeful they would have need of it next week. It would mean long days of work to complete it in the time allotted, but it was doable.

Janie and Paul settled into a routine with the children. Hector and Susanna were very polite and considerate. Susanna would not venture out without Janie and wanted to have her in sight at all times.

"She is afraid you will leave her, like Mamma, Dad, and so many others have," Hector said.

"We never know what the future will bring, but I will promise you that I will never leave, if I can help it. You and Susanna are our children now. We take care of what God has given us. Besides, how could we give up such a good looking young man like you and a beautiful girl like Susanna?"

Hector gave a slight smile. "How come you do not have a problem with colors?"

"What do you mean?"

"Well, my Dad, he hated white people and most black people. He said they all were bad. My Mamma said that only some white and black people were bad, not everyone. We are brown; does that bother you?"

Janie laughed, "No! God is color blind and so am I. All true believers are color blind. When I look at you, all I see is a wonderful young man who God has blessed me with. I do not care what color you are."

"God is color blind? Are you sure? I have heard others say he made colors because some are better than others."

"Oh, Hector, that is not true. God likes variety, so He made people different. What is your favorite color?"

"Blue," Hector replied.

"I like yellow," Susanna chimed in.

"My favorite color is lavender. See, we all like different colors. God is like that too. He tells us in the Bible that He has no favorite color; He likes them all equally. He meant for people to love each other and work together for the good of all people, regardless of their color. He wanted people to enjoy the differences in each other. But some men and women have evil in their hearts. They want division and turmoil between people, so they cause trouble, and they enjoy saying bad things and stirring up trouble."

"At my old church, they did not like whites or blacks to come. They were not friendly to them, if they did."

"I do not want to say anything bad about your church, but that is not what the Bible taught us. The Word says when visitors come treat them well and treat everyone equally. It was talking about those with money and those who did not have any money, but I believe it is okay to expand it to include the color of one's skin. Everyone is to be treated equally."

"I noticed that there are all different colors here at the Ranch. Does everyone get along here?

"Yes, because we are bound together in love through Jesus."

"What about slavery? They taught us in school that the blacks were slaves to the white people? And my Dad said Mexicans are used as slave labor today, too, doing all the work the whites do not want to do and not getting paid very good for it."

"Such a political conversation for such a young man, but here goes. Slavery is bad. God never wanted people to do that to other people. See, God gave men and women free will. He has always allowed them to make decisions for themselves. He gave them a set of rules, what He called laws, but we have to choose to use them. The people with evil hearts do not care what God says, and they sin. Slavery is one of the sins. They sin against God, and they sin against their fellow man. There is no way to make it right at this point. We can only keep our own hearts pure and treat everyone with love and respect. In fact, I remember a verse in Galatians that says, 'There is no Jew or Greek, no free or slave, no male or female, for you are all one in Christ Jesus.' I think that included that there is no color that is better than another; all are one in Christ Jesus."

"That's just it. My church talked about love all the time, but they were not very nice to some people."

"You cannot do anything about that. You can only do something about yourself. In 1Corinthians 13 God explains to us what real love is. Love is patient and kind, not jealous or boastful, it endures all kinds of bad things, like someone calling you names; it is not envious, it is not arrogant or prideful, it is not self-seeking, and that means that you do not do things that only help yourself. Love is never rude or does things that are hurtful or things that embarrass others. When others are rude to us or embarrass us, we do not hold it against them. Love does not insist on having everything the way we want it. Many times we will do things we do not want to do, simply because we want to do something to please another. Love is never happy when bad things happen, but it rejoices when good things happen. Love is happy when good things happen to anyone, not just when something good happens to us. Love never gives up on people. Love never dies."

"That is a lot more than I ever thought love was. I just thought it was feeling good and being happy, when you are with someone you care about. "

"Yes, but that is not all. The most important thing you need to remember about love is that other people must always come first. You must think about how they will feel or how they will react to what you do. You must think about whether what you do or say will bring harm or bring pain to them. All of this is more important than what you want or feel. Love always puts others before myself or yourself. Love is treating others as you want them to treat you. Love is the way Jesus treats us. He is always kind, nice, considerate, caring, respectful, compassionate, and filled with mercy and forgiveness. When we apply all that to how we are with other people, you can see that color never should make a difference. Here at the Ranch, we love everyone, and so this is how we treat each other."

"I love you, Janie," Susanna said in a small voice.

Janie reached over to pull Susanna onto her lap. "I love you, and I love Hector, too. You are mine, and I will always love you both. When you are ready, Paul and I would like you to call us Mom and Dad," Janie said smiling. Hector smiled the first real smile Janie had seen from him. She reached out and pulled Hector to her, also, and hugged them both.

The next week found George back at Mrs. Madison's house. Mrs. Madison was at the door immediately, hurrying them in. "You cannot stay; the officials are across town, and if they follow the same pattern, they will be here by the afternoon. I have decided we will all go with you. We were hoping you would come today. We are all packed."

Relief flooded George, as he looked closely at Mrs. Madison. She had a large bruise on her cheek and was walking like her ankle hurt. "Are you okay? How did you bruise yourself?"

"Oh, nothing nefarious. I tripped over one of the children's toys in the dark, when I got up to check on them. I never use a light, and I didn't see it. I hit the door frame as I went down."

"I am sorry you hurt yourself. I am relieved you are coming; let's get loaded and get out of here." He hated leaving all the food, but they did not really need it. He would give Pastor Phil detailed directions to Becky's home and the hidden room. He would get word about the food being left here, also. Phil told him in a recent conversation that he knew of a minister who was still in this area that could use it. They had an underground communications system and would get word to those who could use it.

In less than thirty minutes, they were on the road. They had thirty-three more souls. Mrs. Madison had put out the word that children who wanted to leave could come with her. Over the past week their numbers had grown from five, after the others left for the Ranch the week before. She did not look back at the home that she had lived in for the last twenty-six years. All the good memories were a haze of tears, as she thought of the loss of her beloved husband last year. They had never been able to have children, much to their regret. Well, now she had all the children she could handle—and more. "Well, Harold, I am leaving our home. You said it might come to this. Tell Jesus I love the children He has given me."

Everyone breathed easier, once they were out of the city. Since it was early in the day, they made several turns and twists in their travels, to throw off anyone who might be watching. They added four hours to their trip, to allow them to arrive after midnight.

Elizabeth and several other ladies were waiting in the main lodge when they arrived. They quickly took the sleeping children to the area prepared upstairs. They would get them to their permanent homes in the morning.

"You must be the famous Mrs. Madison. I am Elizabeth, George's wife," Elizabeth said back downstairs, after they got all the children settled in sleeping bags on the floor.

"I am pleased to meet you. Your husband has been wonderful to us. Please, call me Theresa." Janie gave the tired woman a cup of hot chocolate.

"I'm Janie. I know hot chocolate in the summer seems silly, but it is cool outside, and this always calms me."

"Thank you, thank you all," Theresa said, tears coming to her eyes.

"Just for tonight, you will be sleeping on the sofa bed upstairs with the children," Elizabeth said softly. "Tomorrow everyone will be placed in their new homes; most will go to families. We do have a couple of guys and gals who have volunteered to sleep in a dormitory setting, if we need it. We have a couple of options for you. You can take a few of the children and create your own little family in one of our housing units, or you can take the room in the girl's dormitory. We just finished it. We did not know how many more souls the guys would bring, so we all pitched in and got it done earlier than planned. You look ready to drop. There is a bathroom at the top of the stairs. There is a shower, if you would like one. The towels are already laid out for you. I am headed home, but Megan and several other ladies will be downstairs at five, to start breakfast."

Theresa just nodded her thanks again and headed upstairs. She was bone tired. She could not remember being this tired. Maybe it was just that she was not alone anymore and could finally rest. She really wanted a shower but was so tired that she just lay down, instead. She was asleep, as soon as her head hit the pillow.

Downstairs, the rest were making their way back to their homes. George and Elizabeth walked, hand in hand. "She seems like a very nice lady," Elizabeth observed.

"Yes, she is. She lost her husband last year in the riots. He got caught at the wrong place and at the wrong time. It has been a big struggle for her ever since. She said she started helping the children about six months ago. She said she was heading home from a Bible study when she heard crying. Normally, she would ignore it, but she said it was so pitiful that she went to investigate. She found three children, who were trying to wake up their dead mother. There are so many dying from starvation, she was not surprised. They didn't look like they had eaten in weeks, she said. She made arrangements for their mother and took them home. All social services have ceased, so she did not feel she had a choice."

"She was very tender, as she checked each one as we put them down. How did she get that bruise?"

"She said she tripped over a toy, checking on the children in the dark. I think she was telling the truth. But I think other bad things have happened in the past year."

"Well, thank God she and the children are here now."

"Yes, thank God."

The next day was busy, matching up children and families, along with getting everyone settled. Hector welcomed all of them with a bright smile and great stories of the past week. "This is a great place. You are going to love it! Of course, we have to do chores, but even that can be fun." Most of the new children had never seen Hector smile, so that went a long way toward making them feel at ease.

In the morning, Theresa decided to take a room as a house Mother in the newly-completed dormitory, keeping all of her girls. "This is so nice," she said, walking around her bedroom. She liked everything about it, from the log bed to the patchwork quilt that covered the bed and the matching curtains. Across from her room was the bathroom and a storage closet; from there the hall opened up into a large room with ten bunk beds for the girls. "Everything is wonderful."

"We are glad you like it," Elizabeth said sincerely. "Our ladies wanted the girls to enjoy their room. They are the ones who painted the trees, flowers, and butterflies on the walls."

"They are very talented. It is beautiful."

"Well, get settled and then come back to the dining hall, and we will give you the run down on the Ranch. We have schedules and chores for everyone, even the smallest child. School will start when the weather changes and the harvesting is done. It helps them to learn that they are part of a community that works together. Besides, it helps to occupy them and get them thinking about other things, rather than all the changes in their lives."

Theresa reached out and took Elizabeth's hands. "I do not know how to thank everyone. We are so glad to be here."

"Give your thanks to God. He led all of us here," Elizabeth said sincerely.

CHAPTER 27

JUDY PACED THEIR ROOM after Carson left to go hunting with the others. She hated it here. She hated this ranch. June should have kept her mouth shut. Carson never talked to her like he did this morning. All of this was June's fault.

She went around the room, straightening everything she came across. Coming to the night stand, she accidently bumped Carson's Bible, and it fell to the floor. It landed open to 1 Corinthians. Picking up the Bible, she sat heavily on the chair in the corner of the room. How long had it been since she had read her Bible? She really could not remember. She did remember how peaceful she felt when she first came to Jesus as a young girl. She remembered walking down the dirt road next to her house and pouring out her heart to the Lord. She remembered the feeling of unconditional love she received that night. Where was that feeling now? Why could she not feel His presence now?

Niggling doubt filled her heart, not doubting Jesus but doubting herself. Could June and Carson be right? Could she be the one who was not seeing things rightly?

Judy began reading in chapter one of 1 Corinthians. When she finished, tears filled her eyes and flowed down her face, as remorse filled her heart. She had not been loving toward others for years. She was not kind; she was jealous, envious, covetous, and boastful. She was everything she did not want to be. Though she had been active in church for many years, she realized she had not been listening. Horror filled her heart, as she realized how selfish and self-centered she had become. She dropped to her knees in front of her chair and cried out to her Lord and Savior.

"Lord Jesus, I am so sorry. I do not know when I began to drift so far from You and Your love. I wanted to serve You, but I admit I really thought my ideas were better than others' ideas. I wanted credit for those ideas. I realize I was trying to earn my way into Your good graces, when Your grace has always been a free gift. I did not need to earn what I already had . . . Your love and acceptance. Now, I see I was not being loving, when I was not willing to accept the ideas of others. I realize I do not have a corner on You. You speak to each of us as You will. I realize I have not heard Your voice in a really long time. Please, please forgive me. I thought in pushing Carson I was promoting You, but I was just trying to promote myself. I promise to try hard to change, but I ask You to change my heart. I cannot do this on my own. I need You to help me. I know You promised to never leave or forsake me, so I am standing on that promise. I do love You."

Judy had stayed on her knees for long moments when she heard in her spirit, **"You are loved my child. Welcome back."** New tears poured from her eyes, as she felt the restoring spirit of love filling her heart.

Rising, Judy felt new and clean. Joy filled her heart, and she could not wait to tell Carson. She knew he had joined the hunters that morning, but she did not want to wait to share her news. Hurrying outside, she went down to the barn and took one of the farm trucks. The keys were already in it, so she did not have to hunt them down. Though she was not sure where the hunters went, she drove up the mountain road. After several miles, she found several parked vehicles at the side of the road, and she knew she had found the hunters.

Excitement filled her heart. It would be different now. She could become a useful member of this community. She could learn to be a part of a group, giving and suggesting—but not insisting. She smiled, as she crashed through the forest, following the small trail.

Pain, sudden and sharp, hit her chest. Never had anything hurt so much. She fell, as she heard people coming toward her. Her hand went to her chest, and, looking down, she saw her hand had blood on it . . . her blood.

"Oh, my Lord God!" Manning said in horror. "Get Martin and Sherry, immediately," as he bend down and put pressure on Judy's chest. There was so much blood. "Get Carson, too!"

Judy was fading in and out. She heard the hysterical crying and voices all around her, when Carson appeared before her. "Judy, Judy, I am here; honey, I am with you. Hold on, Judy."

"Carson, forgive me," she croaked out. "I was wrong. I love you."

"Oh, Judy, I love you, too. Stay with me," Carson said, holding her hand. He moved aside, as Martin, followed by Sherry, arrived to help.

"We have to move her. We cannot get the bleeding controlled here," Martin said solemnly. "It does not look good. Pray, everyone, pray!"

Late September of the third year brought the final day of the harvest; now the canning, preserving, hunting, butchering, and packaging was completed. Firewood had been cut and stacked in the containers by each building, in preparation for a long winter. The warehouse, freezers, and storage closets were filled to the brim. The Ranch residents were preparing for a celebration. The days of preparation for winter had been long and sometimes grueling. Everyone was tired and ready for the down time winter would bring.

"I think I will read a book," Janie said, as she rinsed out the last cooking pot.

"I'm going to lie in bed, until I can't stand it anymore," Bonnie said, as she took the pot and dried it, before putting it away.

"I'm going to take Patty and Perry for a walk to the playground. I want to simply watch them enjoy themselves," June added, wiping down the countertops.

"I think I will join you; I think my kids would like that, too," Jill said, as she put the last of the apple sauce onto the roll-away cart, then pushed it toward the inside storage closet. They had already filled the warehouse storage with the peaches, and the rest would be stored here for immediate use.

"I think I would like a movie night, cuddling on the sofa with my husband. We have not had time or energy for weeks," Mary said.

"You know, a walk does sound good. Hector and Susanna would probably like that." Janie thought about the new additions to their family. She already loved them deeply. "You know, Hector asked me something that really hit me the other day. Hector asked how we could all get along with so many colors. At first, I did not understand what he was talking about. But he clarified his remarks, when he said he was brown and I am white, and then there are black. He said his father hated all whites, though his mom said only some whites were bad. It led to an interesting conversation about God. I told him God was color blind. He chose the color for each person, so people should be color blind, too. I told him real believers are color blind. They do not care about color; they love everyone equally. Then I told him that he and Susanna were ours now, and I loved them very much. It was the first time he hugged me. I thought my heart would overflow and burst with love." She smiled, remembering.

"Color blind. I like that. You know that Hector is a smart one," Meagan said. "Mario loves that kid already. Says he learns really quick too."

"I like color blind, too. I wasn't always color blind. I learned prejudice from my family and friends. But when I really got a hold of the idea that God created each person, I realized He chose their color, too. I realized that I had to love people, no matter what color they are, just like Jesus loves them. So, I have to say, people can unlearn their prejudice and become color blind because I did," Shirley, a beautiful, black sister said. "The new children have really brought a lot of joy to the Ranch, and I do not think anyone has ever considered their color. They are great kids. I do not think there is even one troublemaker among them," Shirley remarked. "Peter and Tom are wonderful. Sometimes we have trouble understanding them, when they speak Korean, but we just remind them to speak English, and we are fine. Trent loves being a dad."

"My parents were as far from color blind as two people could be. But it was not only color that was a problem for them, it was economic snobbery, also. If you were not in the right wage bracket or social status, you did not deserve notice of any kind. The only thing that saved me was the lady who was my tutor during my high school years. She was a wonderful Christian lady who taught me to look beyond color, status, or gender. She introduced me to Jesus. He makes all the difference, when you allow Him to change your heart and thinking," June added.

The talk continued, as the ladies finished up the last of the cleanup and began putting everything away for the season. They were pleased with the harvest and the results of their canning season. The pantries were full, the freezers were full, and the sense of accomplishment was high. Yet, they were all tired from the long days of work and were all looking forward to a much-needed time of rest and relaxation.

"The great hunters should be getting back soon," Mary said. "I do not think we really needed the meat to get through the winter, but our hunters really wanted one last hunt."

"Marie was more excited than Carl. She really enjoys hunting, and she is a better shot than Carl too. She said she used to go with her family all the time, while she was growing up. I think there were several other ladies who joined this hunt. Joan said she wanted to go before but felt the harvesting and canning was more important. I'm glad she was able to go this time. I like eating meat, but I don't think I could shoot another animal. One elk was enough for me," Janie stated firmly.

"I'm with you. I do not think I would want to kill one, but I am glad others do not mind. I do not mind packaging it or cooking it, but I would not want to gut or dress them out," Jill said.

"I do not mind gutting the chickens and plucking them, but I refuse to cut their heads off. I draw the line there," Janie confided. "It grosses me out, when they run around without a head."

"I agree with you there," Jill stopped to listen. "I think I hear the hunters now." She went to the window and looked out. She watched one of the pickup trucks pull up to the clinic, and Carson and Jacob jumped out and ran to the back of the truck. "Something is wrong."

The other ladies went to the window and peaked out, before heading out the door. They arrived at the truck just as Judy was being carefully carried inside, Carson at her shoulders and Martin at her feet. "What happened?" June asked in a worried voice. "Is she going to be okay?"

"It's bad," Jacob replied in a strained voice. Two other vehicles arrived in a spray of gravel, and Sherry jumped out and ran into the clinic. "I'll be back with word, as soon as I can. Please pray, it's not good," she called out, as she ran inside.

Several tense minutes passed, as those outside joined in prayer. Jacob returned two hours later, tears flowing freely down his face. "She's gone," he said, simply, as he walked into June's embrace, and they shared their sorrow together.

Later, the story, as best they could piece it together, came to light. Judy and Carson had an exchange of words that morning. She wanted to leave the Ranch. She hated it here and wanted Carson to take her away. When he refused, she went into a rage. Carson had calmed her down and thought everything was alright before he left with the hunting party, but she had taken the cattle truck and followed the hunters. She had parked next to the other parked cars and went looking for the hunters. She was dressed all in brown, and one of the youngsters had accidently shot her, thinking she was a deer. Martin had been there almost immediately, but the bullet was too close to her heart and had nicked a major artery. The youngster, Joel, was hysterical. He thought they would make him leave the Ranch. He was so upset that they had to sedate him. No one knew why Judy had gone into the forest, but she had told Carson she was sorry and that she loved him, before she passed out. Now, they would have the first funeral at the Ranch.

Judy had not made many friends at the Ranch because of her critical and negative attitude; however, the next day nearly every resident of the Ranch walked to the spot chosen for the Ranch cemetery. It was located on the hill behind the chapel. There were several big aspen trees in a cluster on the edge of a small clearing where Judy Smith was laid to rest. Pastor Phil read the Twenty-third Psalm, and they all sang "Amazing Grace," before returning to their daily chores. Carson remained, saying a tearful good-bye to his wife of nearly forty years.

A week had passed since the hunting accident that killed Judy. Jake made his way from the main lodge where Joel was staying with his new parents. He had seen the pain, fear, and horror on the young man's face, when they found he had not shot a deer but Judy. He had turned his attention to Joel, as the others worked on Judy. He was glad he had been there to help. He had tried to calm Joel, yet nothing he said got through to him. When they returned to the Ranch, he had Martin sedate him.

Joel was one of their recued children. He had settled into his new family very well. He knew Joel would have to deal with the accident and knew it would take some time. Today was the second visit of the several Jake knew the boy would need. Joel was better today. His adopted parents were wonderful Christian parents and had given Joel a great deal of support and love. Carson had come in the evening, after the funeral, and spent time with Joel. His loving and forgiving attitude had gone a long way toward helping Joel. He gently told Joel that it was a tragic accident, but that was all it was . . . an accident. Judy was now in heaven, and they would see her again, someday.

The next morning, the rest of the family had come to see Joel. He was grateful that Carson and his family had gone to see the boy; their visits had made a world of difference. Jesus was showing Joel His love through the love of this grieving family.

Jake slowed his steps, as he made his way back to his own cabin. He looked around as he walked. Work was winding down after a very busy harvest season. He found he enjoyed the hard work of the Sanctuary. Having never done the physical work of a working ranch, like gardening, etc., he was unaware of the work involved. Yet, now he found the fresh air and warm camaraderie fulfilling. He knew Mary was very happy in their new environment. She and the baby were doing very well. She also liked the simple life. They had joked about going Amish, yet now they had a great admiration for them. They had not foregone the electricity, modern appliances, tractors, and the like, yet their life was similar. They were self-sufficient and totally off the grid. They did not rely on outside electricity, food, or help of any kind.

Jake was happy and content. He knew others outside the Ranch were suffering. There was widespread chaos across the country. Christians were being rounded up and placed in camps, where the survival rate was very low. They had found there was little food in The cities in August, when they went after the children. They heard there was nearly none in the camps. Mostly, the Christians who had been placed there were left to starve to death, out of sight and out of mind. Many officials believed it was just punishment for not renouncing Jesus. Jake thought to himself, if this was not the end times, he did not think anyone could survive them at all because this was really bad.

Jake took time to speak with each person as they arrived at the Sanctuary. Some had suffered greatly, enduring the loss of homes, jobs, friends, and loved ones. The Lord was the great Healer, yet talking with Jake helped some, through his counseling and prayer. He knew they were blessed because of the foresight of those willing to take the step of faith to create this sanctuary.

He and Mary had asked not to take on any children, until Sari was another year older. It would be difficult for her to manage any new children that would need extra care and love. Fortunately, they had more offers for taking the children than they had children.

"Father, I humbly thank You for Your grace and care; it could have easily been my family searching for safety, instead of those who arrive here or at Haven Ranch each day. Without Your help, I know we would all be dying in camps, instead of living here in relative comfort and safety. Help us to prepare for all those You send to us. Help us to do Your will in all things. Be with all the havens and sanctuaries around the world. Give them the resources they need to help others. Help Joel and Judy's family in this difficult time. Surround them with Your love and comfort. I love You and praise You for all Your many blessings. In Jesus' name I pray."

He continued walking toward the cabin he shared with his family, thinking about how his life had changed. He had everything mapped out before the visions, the lottery money, and the move to the Ranch. Much had changed from his intended path, yet he was content. He was helping where he could with the day-to-day activities on a working ranch, but, more importantly, he was helping those who were having a difficult time adjusting to the sudden changes in their world, particularly those who had left believing family members behind who refused to forsake the world and take a step of faith, as well as unbelieving family members who looked to the government to save them, instead of Jesus Christ. Jake knew these were the ones who had the most difficulty. The world was now clearly divided between two communities—those who believed in Jesus and those who did not. Those who did not follow Christ were easily deceived into thinking all believers were evil. Even family ties were not enough to bridge the gap. There were many believers who had been turned in to government officials by unbelieving family members, their misplaced loyalty creating an open wound for many believers.

Jake realized that God had prepared him for his work here at the Ranch. Many who came here, or to the Haven Ranch, needed his help . . . his training in psychology, as well as his spiritual understanding. He was coming to understand that, even with all his book learning, it was God who was the greatest Teacher. He knew God was expanding his understanding and insight in ways he never expected. He was grateful because he had been able to help so many in ways he would not have thought he could.

Looking back he could see God's hand in bringing nearly everyone who came at the beginning, from the carpenters, electricians, cooks, ranch workers, gardeners, to the mechanics, medical people and many more. Everyone had a skill that was needed here, and all worked together to make the Ranch run smoothly. Now, he could clearly see God's hand each step of the way and was amazed, standing in awe.

"Father, I am amazed! I see Your hand in everything that has happened to prepare us for our life here on the Ranch. I see the people You brought to join us, to help us survive. I can even see my calling to counsel others as preparation for this time. You have provided for all our needs. I am awed by Your love and care for every detail; thank You for preserving my family and providing shelter for all of us. I praise You and thank You so very much!"

CHAPTER 28

WHEN CONDUCTING OFFICIAL BUSINESS, the community council met in the main lodge. They had created the council shortly after moving to the Ranch. It was the governing body of the ranch residents. They made the major decisions, worked out problems between residents, and made the plans for the future, all looking to God to guide and direct them. The council was made up of six men and six women. Many times the men were gone, and they felt it was important for leadership to continue in their absence. In the beginning there had been a few raised eyebrows at the thought of including the women. However, George reminded them that Jesus taught that in His kingdom there was neither male nor female; all were equal. That seemed to satisfy the residents' doubt that God would approve of the decision to include the women. In addition, most of the squabbles were between the women, and, therefore, it was easier to allow the women on the council to take care of those situations. Blessedly, there was very little need for the council to meet.

On this occasion, the council was holding an open meeting; everyone living at the Ranch was invited to attend. Many chose not to attend, though. They had faith in the council and only attended when asked, or if they had a request to make.

They were going over day-to-day events, when John Perkins arrived. He brought news that Pastor Phil had taken in a group of believers that had come down from Canada. "Some are in need of medical attention. Pastor Phil asked that Jack or Martin come and check them out."

"Do we know how many people?" George asked.

"We are not sure, but we know there are at least thirty; some are in poor shape." John Perkins looked solemnly at Martin. "We plan to take everyone to Haven Ranch. Pastor Phil wanted to know if you can set up a permanent medical center at Haven Ranch, like you have here. We do not want to bring anyone here, if they are troublemakers."

"Of course." He looked over at Jack, who gave a quick nod of his head. "Jack, Sherry, and I will gather what we need and head out this afternoon. We should be ready to see the worst of the sick in the morning."

"How many do we have room for at Haven Ranch? I have not been there in over two weeks," John asked.

George looked to Jake, "You were there last week; what kind of room do we have?"

"We have room for twenty to thirty, even more if we put them in RV's or trailers. They have room for nearly sixty RVs in that trailer park, so if we can get our hands on more we can set them up too. It could be a problem heating the trailers in the winter, but for now, it would be okay. You know Uncle George; we need to move someone from here to take charge at Haven Ranch. They have been doing alright, with the help of Pastor Phil making regular visits, but he plans to do more traveling. We cannot take the chance that someone will take over and force those we are trying to help to leave in our absence."

"Good thought." The room was quiet, each person looking over the paperwork on the table, thinking, or praying about the days ahead. After a long silence, George continued, "Carson, I would like you to consider going to Haven Ranch and form a leadership council, like we have here."

Carson was stunned. It was only a few weeks since he had come to George in repentance, asking for forgiveness. Now, George was placing him in a position of importance. It had only been three weeks since Judy's accident; how ironic. This was what Judy had wanted. His next thoughts were of humble and thankful acceptance. "I am honored that you have that kind of faith in me."

"Not only me; as I prayed, God brought you clearly to mind. You are His choice," George replied firmly. "You have become a great help to all of us here. The testing period God brought you here to go through has passed, and you have gone to the next level. You learned some very difficult lessons and have suffered a great loss, yet you have stood strong in your faith. I believe I speak for all of us, when I say that the love of Jesus shines brightly through you."

Carson could not speak, as he looked around the room and caught the smiles and nods. He was overwhelmed by their support. He had never cried in public, not even as he buried his beloved Judy, yet he was close to tears now; never had so many had so much faith in him. He reminded himself that it was Jesus within him that they had faith in, not Carson himself.

Clearing his throat he said in a humbled voice, "I will do my best."

"Good. If your family wants to join you, we will make arrangements for all of you to go, say in three days? Will that give you enough time to pack?" George asked.

"That will be fine. I will talk with my family and let you know who will be joining me. We will let you know, as soon as possible."

"You can take over the cabin that Pastor Phil stays in, when he is there. It is the old ranch house they use as overflow. It is pretty big. I believe it has four bedrooms, if my memory serves me well. If that is not enough room, we will make plans to build something next summer."

"Again, I am overwhelmed by your faith in me."

"You have earned it."

Carson left the meeting in a mild shock. He never in a million years expected this to happen, after all the years of arrogance and pride and only a few short weeks since he humbled himself before his God. He simply had trouble taking it all in.

"Father, I am humbled by Your faith in me. I will do the very best I can. Help me to rely on You in all things. Help me to seek Your wisdom and guidance, but most importantly, help me to continue to love You and to love people."

Carson went directly to his family, when the meeting was over. He found Marie and Carl working with their children, they were taking the wood from the container by their building and stacking it in the wood box connected to the building. "Grandpa, I missed you; where have you been?" Lena threw her small arms around his knees.

Carson bent down and lifted his small granddaughter into his arms, hugging her closely. "I was asked to attend a meeting his morning." He turned his attention to his son and daughter-in-law. "I need to speak with you for a few minutes. I am sure you wouldn't mind a break."

They were sweating with the effort to get their share of the firewood stacked quickly. They wanted to take the children to the lake and needed to get this done first. "Sure Dad, let's get some water, and we'll sit at the picnic tables." He indicated the tables under the trees to the south end of the building.

Several minutes later, they were seated at the table with water and cookies. They made small talk with the children, as they were getting settled. After they were munching on cookies, Carson told them about the move and asked if they would like to go with him. "I know you are settled here, but I believe this is what God wants me to do," he said, looking at his son. "I would like you to consider coming with me."

Carl and Marie exchanged looks, and Marie gave him a slight nod and a shrug. She didn't really care where they were, as long as they were together. "Sure Dad, we can go with you; when do you plan to move?"

"They want us there in three days, but I was thinking it would be best if we moved tomorrow. There are going to be thirty new people moving to the Ranch, and I would like to be at Haven Ranch to help as soon as possible, to welcome them and get them settled. Some of them will need extra care, so you could help with that, Marie." Marie had some nursing training but had never graduated. She nodded her agreement.

"That's quick, but we don't have much, so we can start getting things ready this afternoon and be ready to leave tomorrow morning. Do you know where it is?"

"No, and we will be taken blindfolded. I know it seems melodramatic, just like it did when we came here. But I think it best we do not know where this ranch is—or the next; we are safer not knowing."

Carl and Marie nodded. "Are June and Jacob coming, too?" Marie asked.

"I haven't talked with them, yet, but I really don't think they will. I'm really not sure why I think that, but I do." They all knew both Jacob and June had made very close friendships here. They were also very involved in the Bible studies. Jacob had begun teaching a study every other day, teaching what he learned at Bible college.

"I will miss them, if they decide to stay, but they do seem happier than I have ever seen them. So, I won't be surprised, either, just a little sad," Marie said. They made plans to meet for dinner, and Carson left to find Jacob and June.

Carson found Jacob, teaching his Bible class in the chapel. He slipped into the seat next to June, and she smiled brightly at him in welcome. He sat, half listening and half praying. He was proud of this son of his . . . He was proud of both his sons. His mind moved back to their decision to leave their homes. His sons and their families had joined him and Judy, with little or no prodding, after Carl's house was ransacked and then burned. They were fortunate that everyone was gone that day. They had heard of marauders who were looking for food and burning homes, but they had been fifty miles away. They knew it was only a matter of time before the marauders came back, and anyone caught in their path would be lucky if they got away with their lives. That very day the family had banded together and left to find safety. It had been by God's grace that they had stumbled on Pastor Phil. They had missed their turn and taken a small country road trying to get back on track. Instead, they had found what they were looking for . . . a small church with a loving and gentle Pastor who offered them safety and sanctuary.

They had been driving for several hours, when they had come upon the lights of the church, where the congregants were having an evening service and a dinner. They were surprised to see it open, as most churches had closed their doors because they had become targets. Marauders, Christian haters, and government agents, who were all looking for "Christian terrorists," had caused many to flee. However, the reality was that there were not any Christian terrorists. True believers . . . true Christians did not cross the line into terrorizing others, but that did not matter. They were guilty because the people in power needed them to be and for no other reason. Those who stood fast, claiming they were law-abiding citizens, were taken to camps and detained there indefinitely. There was no rhyme or reason for these incarcerations, no court order or crime for their detainment, just the whim of a nervous and angry public. They needed to blame someone, and Christians were taking the blame.

Carson and his family had joined the service and had been warmly welcomed. After the service, they had been invited to join them for supper.

During the meal Pastor Phil had joined the group, introducing himself. After explaining their circumstances, Pastor Phil had introduced them to the owner of a small motel on the edge of town. They stayed at the motel for nearly two weeks, before Pastor Phil asked if they would like to go to a small community of believers. They were told they would be blindfolded, but they would be safe at the Sanctuary Ranch. He explained that they would all be required to work, to carry their weight at the Ranch. The family had all agreed that they would like to find a permanent home, and the idea of staying in a community of believers appealed to them all. That was what brought them to the Ranch and led up to today. Carson was saddened by the loss of Judy, but he was overjoyed by his renewed faith and commitment to Jesus.

Carson turned his attention back to his son. He had missed the entire study, lost in his own thoughts and memories. He was sorry he had not pulled his attention away from the past. He knew Jacob and his family would not be joining him at Haven Ranch. He had prayed, and in his spirit, God had given him a negative answer, just as he had received a positive answer concerning Carl and Marie. Yet, he would ask them anyway.

The study was over, and clusters of people were chatting, here and there. Carson stayed in his seat waiting for Jacob to finish answering questions and visiting. Jacob had flashed his give-me-a-few-minutes signal, before turning his attention to those around him. They had used the signal many times through the years. Carson could not remember how, or why, they had started using it, but it had proven helpful on many occasions.

June was the first to turn her attention to her father-in-law. "Hi, Dad. I didn't expect to see you here today; I thought you were attending the council meeting."

"I did. I came to talk with you and Jacob about it, when he is done with his admiring students," Carson said with a chuckle.

"They can go on for hours, debating and discussing Scriptures," June said with a smile, "and you know he loves it."

"Yes, he surely does, and so do you."

June flushed, "Yes, you are right. I find it so interesting that each person can read a Scripture and get something different out of it. I just love it. I never stop learning something new. It helps me expand my knowledge and understanding."

"It is wonderful to hear the exchange of ideas and understanding of the Bible. More importantly, we can agree to disagree on certain minor points, as long as we agree that Jesus is the Son of God and the Savior of the world."

"Here, here to that. Some people believe tongues are used today, others do not; some believe in the spiritual gifts, others do not. Some believe in a pre-tribulation rapture, others mid and others post, and all have their reasons for believing as they do, and there are many more areas of different interpretations. Yet, we can all live, work, and study together in harmony."

Carson smiled at his daughter-in-law. He loved June, as much as he could love anyone. She was perfect for his son in every way. He felt so blessed to have her in his life. "What?" June caught the look on Carson's face.

"I was just thinking how much I love you. You are a wonderful wife for my son. I was just thinking how blessed I am to have you in my life," he answered honestly.

June didn't know what to say, so she just put her arms around his neck, kissed his cheek, and hugged him close. "Thank you; that's the nicest thing you have ever said to me. I love you, too."

"Hey, that's my girl" Jacob said, coming up to his Dad and his wife. He was smiling, as he watched them pull apart and smile back.

"Yes, and you could not have made a better choice." He looked around and saw the last person leave the chapel. "Have a seat; I need to talk with you both. Are the kids okay where they are for a bit?"

June looked questioningly at Carson before answering. "Yes, they are playing with Jill's kids." Jacob took a seat in the row in front of his dad and wife and turned the chair to face them. "So, what's up?"

"I met with the council today. There is a group of believers that arrived from Canada, and they are taking them to Haven Ranch. Until now, Pastor Phil has been checking on that ranch, but he is planning to do more and more traveling. There are small underground churches that need a shepherd, people, who for whatever reason, do not want to seek safety in one of the ranches, havens, or sanctuaries. So, he is going to act as a traveling pastor for them. George wants me to go and form a community council, like we have here. Carl and Marie are coming with me. I wanted to let you know and give you the opportunity to join us, if you want."

"Mom was right; you will make a wonderful leader. Too bad she didn't live to see it," Jacob said, skirting the issue at hand.

"Yes, but I had lessons to learn first, things I needed to correct in my life. I can see that now." There was silence in the chapel, as Jacob and June thought about moving. "I do want to say, I believe you are needed here, both of you. When I think and pray about your coming along I get the feeling you are supposed to stay here. But you both need to think about it and pray, before you give me an answer."

"When are you leaving?" Jacob asked.

"Tomorrow, if you aren't going with us; Carl and Marie are packing right now, and I am heading out to do the same. I am leaving your Mom's clothing. Her things can be used by whoever may need them."

"You may need them for some of those who are coming from the camps," June replied, thinking. "They probably do not have as much as we have. You might want to consider taking them with you."

"You are right. Then I will plan on taking them with me then." It was quiet again for several minutes. "Well, I need to begin my packing. I will leave you two to talk things over." Carson gave them both a smile and left.

"What do you think we should do?" June asked in a small voice.

"I really like it here. But I think we need to pray about it and then talk about it after dinner, okay?" Jacob knew June would not want to leave. She would go, if he asked it of her, but he knew it would leave a hole in her heart.

"Let's pray together before we leave," Jacob said, taking her hand.

"Father God, as You know, we have been presented with a move. To be truthful, neither of us really wants to go. But we want to do whatever You want us to do. If they need teachers of the Word there, we will go. Please guide and direct us in the path You would have us go. Amen."

With heavy hearts, they made their way out of the chapel. Each lost in their own thoughts and prayers. For Jacob, he felt fulfilled in ways he never had before. He loved teaching and working on the Ranch. He had made some very close friendships, as well. Still, he knew it would be even harder for June. She had what he considered sisters for the first time in her life. It would be hard for her to leave them.

"Okay Lord, please tell me what to do," Jacob prayed, silently.

CHAPTER 29

JUNE WENT THROUGH THE motions that evening. She was on KP duty, so she made her way to the meeting hall kitchen. She did whatever she was asked, but her mind was a million miles away. No one made any comments, as they had all heard Carson, Carl, Marie and the kids were moving to Haven Ranch. They knew June and Jacob had not made a decision yet. They gave her space to pray about it. Everyone liked June and would hate to see her leave, yet they knew it was up to them, so they prayed for God's guidance for the couple and their family.

June's mind wandered here and there. She thought about her coming to the Lord and what a miracle that was. She was the only daughter of a very wealthy family. She had two much older brothers. She was born when her parents were in their early forties. She was unexpected, as her parents had been told they could not have any more children. Neither of them really wanted June, but had her anyway. The moment she came home from the hospital, she had been turned over to a nanny.

Her parents were movers and shakers in the political world of Washington, DC. They were strong atheists. They did not believe in God. They did not believe God had any place in their personal lives, the lives of their children, or the government. June realized that the government was their god. They looked to it for everything, instead of the God of the universe, the Great I Am. They successfully raised their boys to believe in nothing but success. They were both well connected lawyers at the highest level, in fact, Donald was a judge and had his eye on the Supreme Court.

June had everything she ever wanted, or needed, except parents who spent time with her and loved her. When she turned fourteen, she was diagnosed with mononucleosis. Her nanny was afraid of contracting the illness and had quit; as silly as that seemed to June at the time, it had not been much of a loss. Jewel had been strict and unloving. The new nanny was hired quickly, with little interviewing, as her parents were out of town at the time. The nanny service had sent Lydia Simpson with glowing references. After a quick phone conversation, June's parents had hired her, sight unseen.

Lydia was a small compact woman in her mid-fifties. Her husband, Thomas, of nearly forty years had died suddenly the previous year, leaving her at loose ends. Thomas had been a minister their entire married life, and she was the perfect minister's wife, playing piano for the church choir and leading the women's ministries. They had been unable to have children, which had become the source of Lydia's greatest pain and much prayer. After Thomas's death, Lydia had determined to help where she could. God had led her to June, who had become the child of her heart. A friend at the nanny agency had called out of the blue, and Lydia felt strongly that God was calling her to help this young girl.

A strong believer, Lydia lived her faith quietly. She did not talk about her faith, as much as she lived her faith. People who met her could immediately see a difference in her, in comparison to others, yet most could not tell what that difference was. It was Jesus. In everything she did, she lived her life for Him. When she did talk of Jesus, it was like listening to her talk about her best friend in the entire world . . . because to her, He was.

Lydia loved June from the start; though she could have been a very spoiled and difficult child, having been born in a family of wealth and privilege, June was, instead, friendly, kind, and thoughtful. Unable to attend school, Lydia tutored June. She gave her studies and required the youngster to complete the work on time. They had long talks about history, government, and religion. Slowly, Lydia shared her faith. June knew from the beginning that her parents would not approve. Yet, she was drawn to this wonderful lady, and she was hungry for her words of truth and life. Within a short time June accepted Jesus as her Savior, and, though they did not want to deceive June's parents, they kept her salvation to themselves.

When June was well enough to return to school, she convinced her parents that she was learning more having Lydia tutor her than she was learning at school. After some trepidation, they allowed the tutoring to continue. June was required to test frequently, and after scoring high on every test, her parents agreed to allow Lydia to continue June's education, until she was ready for college, providing her high scores continued.

Lydia taught June carefully. She knew God had something special for this young, impressionable girl. She was a joy, truly the child of Lydia's heart. They had a special bond, one they both treasured. When June left for college, Lydia moved to Georgia to live with her sister and her family. They stayed in touch until the move to the Sanctuary. June knew Lydia and her family had moved to a similar community somewhere in Kansas. She missed her adopted mother . . . the mother of her heart, but she knew God would look after her, and she would see her again, even if she had to wait until they met in heaven.

June had gone to the college of her parents' choice. However, she also took classes at a small Christian college nearby. It was at the Christian college that June met Jacob. They began dating soon afterward. They spent their extra time together and began making plans to marry after they graduated. Problems arose when June's parents arrived for an unexpected visit during June's final term. They found her Bible open on the coffee table. Her mother demanded that she renounce Jesus and follow the plans she had made for her.

"You do not need this crutch, this dead religion. There is no God; there is no Jesus. How could we have raised a daughter who believes this dribble?" June's Mother said hotly. "You have had the best of everything we could give you. Haven't we proved people do not need God to get ahead in the world? Your father and I, as well as your brothers, never fell into that trap, why you?"

June knew her mother did not really want an answer, but she had to try. "Mom, Jesus is not a crutch; He is the Savior of the world." She knew the minute the words came out of her mouth she had said the wrong thing.

"We do not need saving, June Cherie! We are doing just fine on our own, thank you very much. Now, I want you to put all this God stuff aside. We have plans for you. You graduate in two months, and your father and I have several young men in mind that would make a perfect addition to our family. The ties between our families would solidify relationships, both financially and politically."

June knew the time of reckoning was upon her. *"Father, help me,"* she prayed silently. "Mom, Dad, I love you, but I love Jesus more. He comes first in my life. Second is Jacob Smith, he and I have been talking about marriage."

"Let's get this straight; I want no misunderstanding. Are you saying you will not do as we say? That you plan to marry some nobody?" Her mother grew suddenly still and calm, with an underlying hostility.

"Yes, I will not denounce my Lord. Jesus is my Savior and Redeemer. And, yes, I plan to marry Jacob," June answered, letting her answer be still and calm, though she was quivering inside.

When June refused to comply, they disowned her; well, her mother did anyway. June did not know what her father thought, until later because he never said a word. Cut off completely, June was grateful the tuition, room, and board were already paid and that she was in her last term. She was sure if her parents could have, they would have demanded a refund. However, frugal with her finances, she had saved a good amount of her allowance, and this covered all her expenses until graduation.

Harland Quinn III, June's father, sat in the audience and watched her graduate. He was proud of his daughter. He was ashamed that he had not stood up to his wife that awful day three months ago. He watched as his daughter hugged a tall young man after the ceremony, as she laughed out loud her delight at finally being done with school. He assumed this was Jacob Smith. He had used his connections to check out the young man and his family. They were a middle class family, who owned their own home and a small business. They were not wealthy, but they were on solid financial footing. They did not owe money, either, on credit cards or their cars, and they had only a small mortgage.

Jacob was a studious man, graduating at the top of his class with a degree in business and religious studies. He did not have any student loans to repay because he had worked two jobs to pay for his education. He drove an old car, which he had paid for while he was in high school with money he earned himself. Most importantly, he loved June. Harland remembered that he too had loved his wife when they married years before, but that love had died a slow and painful death, as he became aware that his wife married him only for his money, his connections, and the children they had. He remembered the harsh words they had exchanged when Martha realized she was pregnant with June. "I do not want this child. If you do, I will carry it, but it is yours after it is born."

Harland stood, watching his beautiful daughter, trying to decide if he should approach her or not. He knew he and Martha had hurt their daughter greatly. He did not know if she would want to see him or not. The decision was taken away moments later, when she spotted him. Surprised, she said something to her young man, and taking his hand, started toward Harland.

June was shocked to see her father standing across the field, watching her. "Jacob, my father is here." Jacob looked in the direction she indicated and noted a distinguished man in a three-piece suit. He was tall, with graying hair, and he wore a solemn and reserved expression. June took his hand, and they started toward the man.

"Hello, Father," June was hesitant. She hugged him lightly, kissed his cheek, and quickly stepped back.

"Hello, June; I hope you don't mind my coming."

"No, no of course not; I'm glad you did. I just didn't expect you to."

"I know you didn't, but I wanted to be here for your graduation."

"Oh, Jacob, this is my father, Harland Quinn. Father, this is my fiancé, Jacob Smith."

Harland reached out his hand and shook Jacob's hand. "I am very pleased to meet you, sir," Jacob said.

"The pleasure is mine," Harland hesitated, looking around at the thinning crowd. "I know you probably have plans, but could we meet later, for dinner maybe?"

June looked to Jacob. They had plans to meet with friends, but Jacob knew this was more important. "Actually, we don't have any firm plans. We could meet at MJ's Diner on the corner of Third and Center in thirty minutes, or so. Would that work?" Jacob asked.

"Yes, I will see you there." Harland turned to leave and then turned back to his daughter. "I was really proud to see you up there today."

"Thank you, Dad," June replied, smiling.

June and Jacob said little on the way to the restaurant. Jacob had held June as she cried out her hurt and pain weeks before. He knew she felt she would never see her family again, now here was her father. Jacob felt a need to protect June from further pain, yet he knew he could not protect her from it, if Mr. Quinn decided to dish it out. However, he had a feeling it would be alright.

They were seated in a corner booth in the nearly-empty restaurant. They made small talk, as the waitress came and went, getting their drink orders of tea and coffee, bringing the drinks, and taking their food orders.

Clearing his throat, Harland began, "June, I want you to know I do not share your mother's feelings about religion and faith; I never have. I allowed her to think what she wanted because it was better than arguing about it. I was not raised to believe in God, but I always have. Actually, you could call me a closet Christian. Several years ago I met a man, who talked with me about Jesus, while I was on a business trip. We met many times over the next year, before I finally accepted Christ. But I never told your mother, and you can understand why. Even before I became a Christian, I did not believe in divorce, but I knew if I told her, she would be making an appointment with a lawyer before the day was out. So I kept quiet." He looked uncomfortable and a bit sad.

"I began to realize I had done you and your brothers a great injustice. I know now the law and my work was my god. I was not a good father at all. But God has been working on my heart, asking me how I would feel, if I never said a word to you about my faith, just to keep peace in my marriage, and you died in your sins. I had planned to come to see you myself that day, but your Mother decided to join me, and everything went very differently than I had planned. However, since then, I have spent hours praying and seeking God, trying to find a way to make things right. Finally, I decided I couldn't live this way any longer. I talked with your brothers first because we had a business meeting to attend together, then three days ago, I told your Mother. She did just as I thought; she moved out that evening and served me with divorce papers yesterday morning."

He paused and cleared his throat, as tears threatened to choke him. "I know I have not been a very good father, but I want you to know I have always loved you. I am so glad that, in spite of me, you have found the Lord Jesus. Please forgive me for not standing up for my faith and sharing my faith with you."

Tears were flowing down June's face, as she rose from her seat and moved to hug her father. "Daddy, you are forgiven. I am so glad you know Jesus, too; I am so relieved. Praise the Lord Jesus!" They clung to each other for several moments, all the hurts washing away in their tears of joy and forgiveness.

"So, tell me, how did Hank and Trevor take the news of your salvation?" June asked, after she resumed her seat.

"Actually, quite well; Hank's new girlfriend is a believer, and she told him she could not continue to see him, if he didn't at least go to church with her on Sundays."

"Good for her," June stated.

"Harland, Jr. was a little more closed. I guess his wife has been going to church for some time and has been asking him to join her. He is reluctant; I think it has a lot to do with your mother. Junior was always her favorite, and you know how she is."

"Well, we'll just make it a matter of prayer," Jacob added.

"Yes, that is all we can do; now, tell me about your upcoming wedding."

They spent the next hour talking about their plans. "Dad, I know we haven't talked about it, but could you walk me down the aisle?"

A wide smile spread across his face, as joy filled his heart. "Nothing would please me more," Harland answered. He wanted more than anything to share her special day with his daughter; he had missed a great deal in her life, and this one time he meant to make her first instead of last.

Jacob and June were married the next weekend, before God, family, and friends, their love and happiness evident for all to see. To June's surprise, her brothers attended the wedding, along with Hank's girlfriend and Trevor's family. The only one not in attendance was June's mother, and though it grieved her, June was not surprised. Jacob had called the airlines and delayed their flight two days, in order for June to have time to visit with her family. She loved him all the more for his consideration.

After their marriage, June made Jacob's family her own. She loved her in-laws, but there was something missing in their relationship. Here at the Sanctuary Ranch, she had a closeness she had missed growing up; here, she had brothers, sisters, aunts, and uncles. This was the family she had always dreamed of, and she loved each and every one of them.

"This is my family . . . Your family, Father God. You adopted me, when I accepted Your Son Jesus as my Savior, and now all these wonderful people are

my family. So, how can I leave them? Oh Father, if You ask me to, I will go, but I would really like to stay. Please guide us in the direction we should go."

Jacob was wrestling with the same dilemma. He loved his family and knew his Dad would like him to join them at the other ranch. He knew there would be those he could minister to there, as well as here, yet . . . As he mulled it over, his Dad's words came back to him: "When I think and pray about your coming along, I get the feeling you're supposed to stay here." Jacob knew his Dad was right. He and June needed to remain here; June needed to stay here. He knew these people had become the family of her heart. They had become his family, also. They would stay. Certainty filled his heart and mind, as he went in search of June.

June was overjoyed when Jacob told her he felt they should stay. "Oh, Jacob, thank you."

Jacob and June, along with nearly thirty others, came to say their goodbyes to Carson, Carl, Marie and the kids. They gathered around them to lay hands on them, praying for God's protection, help, and guidance. They watched, as they were blindfolded, and the van drove away. Jacob and June watched until the van was out of sight.

"I am going to miss them," June said softly.

"I will too, but we will see them again soon," Jacob replied, as he lifted five-year-old Penny and took June's hand, as she carried Penny's twin, Perry. They went to the daycare to leave the children, before joining the others for the daily chores.

CHAPTER 30

PASTOR PHIL HID BEHIND the trees, as he waited for the refugees. He thought back to early spring when his life took a new turn...He rose from his prayers and made his way to the meeting hall. He had been praying and fasting for several days. He knew Father God was directing him on a new mission. He understood the danger. He understood the importance. He knew there were already many believers in safe havens around the country, yet many more were hiding in plain sight, and others were being detained in camps. God was directing him to find and help as many believers as he could. Most churches had moved underground, having been threatened, burned, or closed by the government. Believers had scattered, parents afraid for their children and grandchildren. Others stood firmly, speaking out in faith and truth, only to be herded together and forced to the camps.

Since late spring, he had been traveling to underground churches and Bible study groups for the last few months. Every day he heard of more and more believers who were being rounded up and sent off. His heart was heavy for his fellow believers.

The camps were little more than prisoner work camps. Though there were no trials, hundreds were sent to the camps each week. The conditions were sparse, and food was limited to two meals a day of bread and whatever they could grow in the garden. Heaven only knew what would happen come winter.

Little was being said on public television about the camps, yet everyone knew they existed, however, most turned a blind eye to what the government officials were doing. Those who had said this could never happen in this country were strangely silent.

In June, Pastor Phil had been approached by another pastor in a large city nearby and told of the plight of those in a camp by Boise, Idaho. It was nearing fall, and he feared those in the camp would be left to starve or freeze to death, if left through the winter. God had directed him to help these brothers and sister make it to a sanctuary, and that was what he planned to do. In the meantime, he would take supplies to help them, if the guards would allow it.

Phil thought back to his conversation two months ago when he first approached George with the idea of helping those in the camp.

"George, can I have a word with you and the elder council today?" Pastor Phil asked, as soon as he spotted him at a table eating breakfast and chatting with those around him.

George looked up, surprised. He knew Pastor Phil had been fasting for several days. He had joined him the first day, however; the work of the Sanctuary Ranch was difficult, and each day he needed his strength to do the work required of him. "Of course, I will call a meeting for this afternoon, say four o'clock?"

"Yes, thank you," Pastor Phil nodded. "May I join you?"

"Of course; pull up a chair."

Janie was sitting next to George and began to rise as she said, "I am finished and need to be on my way. Please take my seat." She kissed Paul on the cheek and left saying, "See you all later."

Pastor Phil filled his plate with fruit and toast, preparing to break his fast, and then he took his seat. He said a silent prayer and began to slowly eat.

George gave Pastor Phil several minutes to eat, before asking what the Lord shared with him. "I know you have been seeking the Lord; what have you been shown?"

"I believe I must go to the camp near Boise and do what I can to help them," he said simply.

"I thought it would be something like that. What do you have planned?" George asked, curious.

"I will take what food I can and go from there."

"Do you think they will let you in?"

"That is not the question; the question is, will they let me leave?"

"That is the million dollar question."

"God is with me, so I can do all things through Christ who strengthens me."

"Amen, brother."

Later that afternoon Pastor Phil met with the Sanctuary Ranch council and others who happened to attend the open meeting, explaining his plan and asking for prayer support. He didn't need to ask, of course, but acknowledging his need for God's help was important for all concerned. It was also important for others to agree together to pray and support Pastor Phil's calling. Each had their area of concern, and each understood the need for group support; ranch life was not a "do it my way" society, an each one for himself mentality. Now, it was an "all for one and one for all" society, where each person needed one another; they were a family, and family helps one another. They might not be a natural family, but they were a family through the blood of Jesus Christ . . . adopted into the family of Father God.

Pastor Phil and two others left three days later. Their plan was simple. They would take a truck filled with supplies to the camp and request permission to give the supplies to the residents. They had no other plan, just a simple in-and-out approach to help those in need. If all went well, they would provide supplies through the winter, and as much as possible, keep the believers alive and healthy. The rest they would leave in God's hands and pray for His help with whatever came their way.

Everything went as planned. Pastor Phil was able to deliver the goods and was allowed to leave. Though he was unable to speak with any of the detainees, they seemed to be in fairly good condition from a distance. The guards were not mean spirited and treated the people well. They had a good garden and flour to bake bread. The problem would arise in the winter because they did not have canning supplies. Pastor Phil decided he would try to bring canning jars and lids on the next trip.

The rest of the summer, Pastor Phil made bi-weekly trips with supplies to the camp. He also took canning jars, lids, and large cooking pots. As long as the captain allowed it, he would bring everything he could to help them prepare for winter. He was hopeful there would be enough to provide the necessary quantity of provisions before winter came.

Each time Pastor Phil went to the camp, he spoke briefly with Captain Ferguson. He was a pleasant man, who appeared to hate the job he was required to do. He compensated by treating his captives well and requiring his men to do, also. Pastor Phil knew the captain was giving him special favor, and though he wondered about it, they never spoke of it to each other. He had his suspicions that the captain was a believer, and, therefore, he frequently asked God to protect the kindly captain.

Late summer brought word of another small group of believers who were coming down from Canada, looking for a safe haven. Persecution of believers was becoming widespread throughout the region; people were threatened, food stolen, and homes burned to the ground, while the believers were forced to look on in horror. Pastor Phil decided to help once they crossed into the United States. They planned the route methodically, working carefully to keep the plans secret. All went well on the first three runs; problems arose the fourth time out.

Now months later, Pastor Phil and Dennis waited, hidden in the trees, watching the trail that the refugees would take to reach them. Darrell was waiting more than a mile away, with the van they used to transport people. He had pulled off the road and was nearly hidden by the trees. As an extra precaution, he lifted the hood up and spent his time fiddling with the engine. He saw several government trucks pass by and knew it meant trouble. He began to fervently pray for Pastor Phil and the others.

The refugees had just met up with Pastor Phil, when the government trucks arrived and surrounded them. A short man separated himself from the rest and showed his ID to the man in charge. "I am Reggie O'Hare, and I work for Henderson." Phillip Henderson was the area enforcement officer for the government, the one in charge of camp detentions. "I learned of this group coming down from Canada and joined them, in hopes of catching those who were helping them on this end. I see we have been successful." He smiled an evil grin, showing his delight.

Neither Pastor Phil, nor any of the others, said anything, as they were herded into the trucks. Darrell watched in horrified silence from his hiding place, as he remained unnoticed, as he caught a clear view of Dennis as the trucks went by. He waited nearly thirty minutes before he closed the hood of the van. He didn't think they saw him, but he made numerous stops and turns, in case he was followed, but it seemed they had their quota for the day because he never saw another car or truck at all.

Pastor Phil was questioned for hours. "Who are you working with? Where is your base of operations? How many are you hiding? What are you plotting to bring down the government?" Questions came at him, over and over, until he simply shut down from fatigue. He knew God gave him supernatural strength to endure their questioning and to avoid telling anything of importance. When the interrogation was done, those questioning him decided he was simply a gopher and not worth pursuing.

"What do we do with him?" a local officer asked.

"Send him and the other one along with those that came from Canada to the Boise camp. We won't hear from him again," Reggie said snidely. "They won't make it through the winter, so we won't have to worry about him anyway."

Pastor Phil and the others were loaded into trucks and hauled down to Boise, like a truck full of sheep led to slaughter. The trip was cramped and uncomfortable, lasting many hours, with no food and only one bathroom stop.

It was nearly midnight when Darrell arrived at Haven Ranch. He had stopped at a local motel and checked in, as was previously planned. After dark, he left the hotel and walked to the small house on the edge of town. He made a quick phone call, learning that Pastor Phil and the others had been questioned and were being transported to the camp in Boise. After grabbing a sandwich, he drove toward the Ranch in a different vehicle.

Word reached the Sanctuary that Pastor Phil, his three associates, and seven refugees were being detained and would be transported to the camp outside Boise. It seemed ironic that they were being sent to the very camp Pastor Phil had gone to help on numerous occasions.

"What should we do? Anything?" Paul asked his Dad. "Should we try to release Pastor Phil and the others?"

"I really do not know," George replied honestly. "I think we need to gather everyone together for prayer and ask those who can to fast. We need to know what God would have us do." They made a point of never making any feel they had to fast, when asking God's help. Their work was very physical and many simply became too weak to do the chores required for running the Ranch when fasting. They wanted and needed God's help, but they needed to be practical. There were those who could fast and seemed to receive supernatural strength. But many more could not handle the rigorous work during a fast.

"I'll go ring the bell," Janie said, as she rose and headed to the door. She prayed as she walked to the gathering bell. *"Father, be with Pastor Phil and the others. Give them Your strength and courage. Help us to know Your will. Thank You for Your safety here at the Sanctuary; we know You give us Your protection and covering here. Help us to continue to provide a safe haven for others. Bless all the sanctuaries around the country and world, as we await either these hard times to be completed or Jesus' coming,"* she continued praying as the bell began to ring.

Everyone rapidly finished what they were doing and made their way to the meeting hall. As time went on, people began to dread the ringing of the bell; it rarely brought good news. They had begun to ring the bell two beats and pause, then two more to announce a birth; on the rare occasion there was a death, it would ring three times and a pause, then three more. They had phone lines between the buildings, but they rarely used them. They had radios for those working in the fields, and for those cutting firewood, and for those who were away from the main buildings. It was important that they have communication with all their people at all times. Several security teams had seen marauders in the area; though they did not come close to the compound, it was important to keep a close eye out for them. They did not want to rely only on the cameras they had set up on the perimeter of the Ranch. They sent people out to check on things firsthand.

It was a quiet group that hurried in and took their seats in the meeting hall. Though no one knew the reason for the gathering, silent prayers began throughout the hall. Expectant eyes went to George as he rose and drew their attention.

Not one to waste words, George came right to the point. "Pastor Phil and Dennis, as well as seven refugees, were taken into custody yesterday morning. Darrell was waiting by the hidden vehicles. He saw the trucks carry everyone away. He believes they were betrayed; the patrol was watching for them. He called a friend in the local police department and was told they were being transported to the Boise camp."

There was silence in the room. Everyone loved Pastor Phil; he brought laughter, hope, and encouragement to everyone he came in contact with. His teaching was solid meat, something they all craved these days; the bread of life, the Word of God that they fed on, gave them the strength they needed to get through each day.

"We will begin prayer and fasting, immediately. We need to seek God and His guidance. Do we go to the camp and release Pastor Phil and the others? Or is it too risky?" he trailed off. "Pastor Phil and the others knew this could happen. They knew the risks and chose to take them. If we are led to release them, we must be extremely careful. God has given us a great responsibility here. This is our first priority. Let us all pray for the next twenty-four hours; for those who can, we ask to fast, also. We will meet here tomorrow morning at nine."

Everyone left with very little conversation. They heard Boise was one of the better camps. Thanks to Pastor Phil, they had much better conditions than others. The camp commander was a kind man, who did not like the orders he received about detaining Christians, but orders were orders. Everyone was aware this kind treatment could change at any time. They knew their best window of opportunity to intervene would be now, before they got any closer to winter.

Pastor Phil entered the captain's office and sat in the chair he was directed to. "You are dismissed," Captain Charles Ferguson said, firmly. He waited until the door closed, before addressing the quiet man seated across from him. "Well, Pastor, you landed in the soup this time."

"Hello, Captain," Pastor Phil smiled sheepishly.

"I hate this." Captain Ferguson pounded his fist on the desk. "What in the world is our country coming to?"

"You already know the answer to that question," Pastor Phil answered softly. Phil believed Charles was a closet Christian. He did what he could from his position, as the commander of the camp, to make things easier for those detained here.

Charles wiped a weary hand over his face and nodded. "Yes, but I do not have to like it."

"No, none of us do, but we know Who wins in the end."

Charles looked up and smiled for the first time. "Yes, I do." He was careful not to say anything out loud that could be used against him later;

one never knew when the walls were listening. Clearing his throat, he got down to business. "Well, Pastor Phil, you know the drill. I run a fair camp here, you know that. Keep your people in line, and all will be well."

"Yes, sir," Pastor Phil smiled and winked, as he rose to leave.

"Phil," Charles said softly. Pastor Phil turned to look at the captain. "I am sorry it came to this. I do not like what our government is doing. I never, in my wildest imagination, believed it would come to this."

"I know, and so does God. It will be alright; I am praying." Pastor Phil left, and Captain Ferguson whispered under his breath, "I am, too."

There were a wide variety of people housed at the camp. There was a Native American Indian family, a Chinese family, three Hispanic families, four black families, and three white families—all sisters and brothers in the Lord Jesus. They did not look at color or ethnic backgrounds, any more than God does; they looked at the heart. They worked in harmony and in love to survive. Throughout the weeks and months, they had become a close-knit family; they lived, worked, and suffered together. Now, they had a spiritual leader to lean on. Yet Pastor Phil wanted nothing to do with that. They had learned to lean on Jesus, and he gently reminded them Jesus was the One who could and would help; after all Pastor Phil was just a servant of Jesus, just like they were.

Pastor Phil spent the next three days encouraging the believers at the camp. The previous times he came to the detention camp, he was allowed to leave his supplies at the gate and speak with the captain, before he had to leave. However, he had been unable to speak with anyone held at the camp. Now, he made the effort to speak with each person, offering comfort, words of hope, and encouragement.

On the second day Pastor Phil came to a woman and her son, Dave, who were two of the hardest working in the camp. They worked tirelessly in the gardens to help provide food for the detainees. He held out his hand as he introduced himself. "Hello, I am Pastor Phil."

Doris turned her tired but hopeful eyes on him. "Hello, Pastor; you wouldn't be the pastor who has a friend named George, would you?"

Surprised, Pastor Phil said, "Yes, I am. Why do you ask?"

"I was hoping you would have word of my son, Sam, and my daughter, Becky. They were in a group of people coming from the Seattle area three months ago. There were nearly fifty souls that were heading east to find you and safety with a man named George and his group."

"I have not met anyone named Sam or Becky, though a group from Seattle did arrive in early July."

"Was there a young man named Harland and his wife, Charlene?" Doris asked anxiously.

"Yes, he brought a large group. They were split between the two ranches we have."

"Praise God they got there," Doris said, though her eyes dimmed a bit.

"Did Harland say anything about Sam and Becky?" Dave asked, speaking for the first time.

"I am sorry son, not that I recall." Phil saw the sadness fill the eyes of the two in front of him, and he wanted to say something that would encourage them. "Don't lose faith. God is a mighty God. He will work all things together for good."

"Thank you, Pastor; we know that. It's just that we have already lost my husband and several close friends. We were hopeful that you would have word of Sam and Becky."

Phil moved on, though his heart was somewhat heavier, as he thought of all the loss so many had suffered and would suffer as time went on.

"Pastor Phil, why is all this happening? Doesn't God love us?" fourteen-year-old Penny asked in a small voice.

"Oh, Penny, God loves us very much. You see when He created the world, along with Adam and Eve, He created them perfect. Everything was righteous and holy, just like God designed. God gave them charge over the earth. The only thing He told them they could not do was to eat from a special tree."

"I remember that story. Adam and Eve ate the fruit, when God told them not to," Penny said excitedly. Eager to hear the pastor speak, the others had come to sit nearby and listen as Pastor Phil was talking.

"Yes! The problem came when Adam and Eve disobeyed; Eve was walking around, and an evil snake, possessed by Satan, told her it would not hurt, if she ate from the special tree, in fact she would become like God if she did. So, instead of listening to God and obeying what He said, she ate from the tree and gave some to Adam, and he ate also. They both knew they were not supposed to, but they did it anyway. Their disobedience brought sin into the world and it was the sin that caused everything to change. The instant they ate that special fruit, their spirit changed. It was no longer righteous and holy; it became fallen and corrupt. Nothing stayed the way it was supposed to be. Before sin came into the world there were no weeds, no bad weather, no pain, no suffering, no illness, or disease; those things came when sin entered God's perfect world. Evil took over in the world, and Satan and his demons have been deceiving, corrupting, and manipulating men and women ever since. God is still here, but He and his angels are in constant battle with evil. There is a battle going on for the hearts and minds of all the people in the world."

"That's why Jesus came to save us, right?" ten-year-old Pete asked.

"Yes, Pete you are right. You see, sin created a separation between God and man. God is holy and is always good; He loved us, but He had to create a way to bring us back to Him because the only punishment for sin is death. So, He implemented the plan He had had from eternity past, knowing that humans would sin. He would send His Son Jesus to earth as a man. While He was here, Jesus taught the people how God wants them to live. But His teaching made a lot of religious leaders really mad, and they plotted to kill Him. When it was God's appointed time, they captured Him and beat Him so badly that no one could tell what He really looked like. Then they nailed Him to a cross. He was on that cross for a long time, suffering greatly before He died. And even after He died, the soldiers stabbed Him in the side to make sure He was dead. After that, a man named Joseph of Arimathea, who loved Jesus, asked if he could take Jesus down and bury Him. After receiving permission, Joseph took Jesus and put Him in a tomb. Then a huge stone was placed at the entrance. But do you remember what happened then?"

"Some ladies went to the tomb and found the stone was rolled away. When they looked inside, Jesus was gone because He rose from the dead," Penny said triumphantly.

"Yes, He did! He was gone three days, and then He rose again. After that, Jesus spent a few more weeks on earth, and then He went back to heaven, where He is right now, sitting with Father God."

"So, how does that help us?" fifteen-year-old Julia asked, shyly.

"Well, you see, when Jesus died, He took all the sins of every person and died in their place. He offered Himself as the blood sacrifice for us. In other words, He gave His life in place of ours. Do you understand what that means?"

"It means He died for my sins, and your sins, and everyone else's sins," Julia responded.

"That is right. Because He did that, when we accept the truth that Jesus is God's Son and that He died to save us from our sins, we can ask Jesus to forgive us and come into our hearts. Then our old broken, fallen spirit dies, and God gives us a new spirit. This new spirit is a born-again spirit, alive in Jesus. Whatever we decide will determine where we spend eternity—in heaven or in hell."

"Can anyone get a new spirit?" Pete asked.

"Yes, anyone who asks Jesus to forgive them can get a new spirit."

"Why doesn't everyone do it? And why do so many people hate us? What did we do to cause them to put us here?" Julia asked.

"Ah, Julia those are some very important questions. The reason many people do not ask Jesus to forgive them is because they do not see their need. They do not believe they are sinners. They think they are good people. They don't understand they are very easily deceived because they do not have the Holy Spirit that Jesus sends to us when we become believers to help us discern truth from lies. So, some people believe the lies others tell them, and that causes them to be afraid of us."

"But we never did anything wrong," Pete protested.

"You and I know that Pete, but when you are deceived, you believe lies. There are some people who have deliberately caused the problems in the world because they love power and money, and they believe they can get even more power if they are in charge of everything. They tell lies about us and others, and people believe these lies that say we are bad people and that we are planning to do bad things. You know and I know that we would never hurt others, except to defend ourselves, but some people need to blame others, when they do not understand why things are getting so bad in the world; those people have decided that we are the cause for all the bad stuff. God will try to speak to their heart, to help them understand, but many times their hearts are hard, and they will not listen. They want to do things their own way, not God's way. That is the problem with most of the people who do not believe in Jesus, they have hard and disobedient hearts, or they look to governments or people to take care of them. So that becomes the god they look to for help. What I really want you to understand is that God did not do this. He is not the author of any kind of evil. The sins of people are the reason we are here."

"Pastor," small nine-year-old Francis spoke from beside her mother.

"Yes, dear?"

"I have never asked Jesus into my heart. Can I ask Him right now?"

Pastor Phil was overcome with emotion. Here, in this desolate camp, a new believer was being born. "Oh, yes, Francis, you surely can, and anyone else who would like to ask Jesus into their heart can, too."

In the next hour, six children and three adults gave their lives to Jesus; in addition, four rededicated themselves to the Lord. It was the most wonderful evening Pastor Phil had had in a very long time. Unknown to those inside the small room, the guard listening at the door gave his life to Jesus, also. He understood the danger; he could end up in a camp like this, but these people had witnessed to him for weeks. They had shared God's love and God's plan of salvation. Now, he was ready to join their ranks.

Pastor Phil awoke with a start. He had been dreaming, yet it seemed so real. In his dream, the guards were sleeping, and the entire group of Christians simply walked out of the camp. Rising, he went to the door of the men's dormitory and peeked out. The normal guard was gone and a young man soundly slept, slumped next to the neighboring building. Slipping past the guard, Pastor Phil crept toward the main gate. Surprised, he found no other guards anywhere. Hurrying back to the dormitory, he quickly woke all the men, telling them what he found. He then rushed to the women's quarters and woke them. "Let the smallest children continue to sleep; it will be easier to carry them, if they are asleep, and get everyone else ready. We are leaving in five minutes. Hurry, Hurry!" The urgency in his voice got everyone moving.

Within minutes the group was slipping quietly through the camp, toward the main gate. Captain Ferguson moved the curtain slightly and watched them go. When they were all safely outside the gate, he took one of the sleeping pills he had slipped into the employee coffee pot at dinner and went to bed. He had received orders to move the entire group to a larger detention camp outside Portland the following week. He knew it would lead to the death of most of the believers here, and he was determined to provide a way of escape. He knew he could not get word to Pastor Phil, without drawing attention to himself, so he simply prayed; he knew God would take it from there. *"I did what I could, Father. Please guide their steps from here."*

Pastor Phil led the way and had six of the men watch their back trail for anyone who might follow. He had seen the curtain at the captain's window fall, as he walked by, and knew the sleeping guards were somehow his doing.

"Father, please protect Charles. If they suspect him, it will not be easy for him. Be with us and protect us as we travel; it's going to be a long walk." He had heard the mocking of the guards and knew they were supposed to be moved next week. He understood that moving would mean death to many of them. Many times before he had heard the horror stories of the detention camps outside Chicago, Los Angeles, and Atlanta. Guards were allowed to beat and rape at will. This was no longer the land of the free and the home of the brave. Now, America had become the land of the oppressors and the oppressed.

Paul and Janie sat holding hands, swinging on the front porch swing outside their cabin. Each lost in their own thoughts. Hector and Susanna were asleep in their beds, giving them some time alone. They had been married three wonderful years. They both enjoyed the Ranch life. When they were not building, Paul had found he liked working with the cattle and horses. It was not something he would have ever thought, but it was true.

Janie broke the silence, "I spoke with Sherry today. She gave me a pregnancy test. We are having a baby in the spring."

Paul sat, stunned for a brief moment, then hugged her close, "That is wonderful. We had been trying for so long I was afraid . . . "

"I know, I was too, but God is good. We just had to be patient. I saw you with Peter and Harold today at the chicken coop. I thought, what a wonderful uncle you are to both of them, and what a wonderful father you are to Hector and Susanna. I admit that I had been impatient about starting a family, until Hector and Susanna came. "

Paul laughed, "The boys wanted to help collect the eggs, but they couldn't get them without getting pecked. I was trying to show them how, but I think I got pecked as much as they did." He sobered and took Janie's hand in his. "You are a wonderful mother too. I have watched you with the little ones for the past three years. You are patient and kind, and they all like playing games with you. You are great with them and they all love you."

Janie leaned her head on Paul's shoulder and smiled, as they continued to swing on the porch swing, enjoying the evening cool. "It's been a good three years hasn't it? As hard as it's been at times, I am happy. I think country life is good for all of us. We are healthier, we have everything we need, and we are surrounded by family and friends who love us. We can have spirited debates and discussions about Scripture, and everyone accepts the other's position without pushing theirs. I think we have all grown in the Lord, learning about His life, His love, and what it truly means to be in the family of God. What more could anyone want?" Paul observed.

"I agree. I enjoy those discussions. I have learned a lot from them. It has helped me to firm up my beliefs, and they have given me greater understanding of the Word. I know I will never know and understand everything, but it is fun learning something new each day. The Word is truly alive, and it gives me new insights into myself and those around me. It gives me the ability to understand and help those around me, and they help me too. I have been truly blessed by each person here. God is so good."

"Yes, God is truly an awesome God!"

"Are you going to join the rescue party?" Janie asked.

"No, Dad asked me not to. But I will, if need be."

"Why did he ask you not to?"

"He did not want all the men on the council to be away on this mission. Besides, Manny and Drew are ex-marines and have the training for this. I do not. They will be leading the mission."

"I am relieved. When Hector heard about the mission, he was worried. I had to tell him to pray about it. He has been doing so well. He seems a different boy than the somber one who came to us last month."

Paul chuckled, "He is a delight. He asks so many questions about everything. Some are easy but many others make me scramble for answers."

"Susanna is a sweetheart, too. I have started calling her my little shadow. I love it . . . I love them both."

"Come on, let's turn in for the night. I want to see the guys off in the morning."

Final plans for the rescue were made, and the men now readied themselves, both physically and spiritually. They knew any number of things could go wrong. They knew there was always the possibility they would not all make it back. Prayer support had begun at daybreak and would continue around the clock, until the mission was complete.

Flee to the Mountains

Everything was in readiness. Men and women gathered around the vehicles, as those going on the mission did a last-minute check. Janie watched, praying silently for all the men, as Paul readied himself to leave with seven others. Nathan had been injured last evening, while chopping wood. George and Martin had come to their cabin early this morning to ask Paul to join the mission. Several times fear had tried to steal into her heart, since Paul had agreed to take Nathan's place. Every time fear began to rear its ugly head, she would cast it out, commanding it to leave. She knew they needed Paul, just as she knew there was the possibility he might not return. What they were doing was dangerous. Yet, it needed to be done. The overwhelming direction they received from God was the need to go to Boise.

All was ready and the men said their final goodbyes, as Paul turned to Janie. "Please do not worry. Trust God; He will look after us," Paul whispered into her ear, as he held her tightly.

"I do trust God, and I will be praying for you every minute, until you return safely to us," Janie whispered back. She held him tightly, also. She really did not want him to go. They had just found out they were expecting their first child and had not shared the joyful news with anyone yet; now, that sharing would have to wait until his return.

"We will have a party when we return and then share our news with everyone. Until then, take care of yourself and our children."

"I'll be fine. You just take care of yourself; I will be praying for all of you." After one last kiss, Paul hugged Hector and Susanna and then joined the others, and they loaded up to leave. They were gone just as the first light of day was spreading across the eastern sky.

Bonnie came over and put an arm around Janie. "Nathan feels terrible that he got hurt, and Paul had to take his place."

"How is he doing?" Janie asked, trying to take her mind off Paul's leaving.

"Very sore; Martin put twenty-eight stitches in his leg, but there is no sign of infection, so that is good." The axe had slipped, and the rebound had jumped back and landed on Nathan's leg, cutting a clean slice in his flesh.

"Accidents happen; at least we have skilled people to stitch us up when we have mishaps." There had been several mishaps, while chopping wood, cutting vegetables in the kitchen, and gardening, that had required the handy stitching of Jack, Martin or Sherry.

"What are your plans for the rest of the day?" Bonnie understood Janie's feeling. If not for the accident, it would be Janie trying to distract Bonnie, while Nathan was gone. Now, it was up to her to help Janie.

"First, I am going to get the children up, and dressed, and then fed and off to school. Then, I am going to the chapel for a while. Later this morning, I am helping at the reading room. There are several kids who are having trouble reading; I am going to help tutor them. Then down to the communication room for a while before my two-hour prayer time at the chapel. I will meet up with the children at the main hall for dinner. By the time we get back from dinner and get them ready for bed, hopefully, I will be able to sleep."

"Well, if you need anything, let me know. Theresa asked the kids to come for a play day. She and Gordon are doing a great job with the children in the dormitory. Most are too young for school, so they have started a preschool program for them. All the little children love it."

"Yes, I heard all about it from Susanna. She attended the preschool a couple of times, before they said she was more than ready for the kindergarten program, over in the main lodge school. I will let you know if I need anything. But I cannot see what that would be. I'll be fine, as long as I stay in prayer and stay busy," Janie said confidently. "Jesus is with the guys, and I know He will send His angels to watch over them, also."

Bonnie still marveled at Janie's faith. She knew her faith had grown in leaps and bounds over the last few years; however, Bonnie wondered if she would be as trusting, if it was Nathan that had just left. She hoped that she would be, and she knew that it was just a matter of time before it would be her. *"Father, give me the same strength of faith and assurance when my time comes. Be with all the men and bring them back safely. In Jesus' name I pray. Amen."*

A couple of hours later, Janie entered the chapel and found several others already praying. She sat on a bench next to the window, overlooking the gardens. The summer flowers still bloomed, yet Janie barely noticed, while a deep feeling of concern and heaviness covered her. She shifted positions, kneeling in front of the bench and bending over the top; supporting her upper body and arms on the bench, she began to pray.

"Help me, Father; I am afraid for Paul and the others. I know this fear is sent from the evil one to shake my faith. So, I command that fear to leave me in the name of Jesus. Replace the fear with Your calm peace and assurance.

Send Your angels before the men and give them safety. Be with Pastor Phil and all who are with them.

I praise You and thank You for all Your care. You alone are the Great I Am. You are my Creator and the Creator of this wonderful blessing growing within me. There is no one like You in the entire universe. Praises I give to You Father, Jesus, and Holy Spirit.

Your love is like a blanket that shelters me from the cold. Your love is like a mighty oak, never wavering in the storm. Your love is like the mighty eagle, soaring up above, always watchful, always near, ready to pick me up and carry me should any danger come near. My love for You is great, my love for You sincere. My love for You is endless and will last throughout the years. With You I want to be throughout eternity, where we will live together and praises will I sing. Each morning, noon and night, my song of love will ring and others will join in to sing for You are worthy."

Janie began to sing "Victory in Jesus," softly. The others in the chapel joined her, and their voices drifted to others working nearby. The workers stopped what they were doing and joined in the singing, as they walked to the chapel. Soon, the chapel was filled, everyone singing and praising God, and the spirit of heaviness that tried to settle on the community lifted, as joy filled the chapel. Mabel rose from her place of prayer and led the worship, singing one song after another, as they turned all their worry, concerns, and depression over to Jesus. They stayed in the chapel for over an hour, before the chores of the day called them back to work. However, the spirit of comfort, peace, and joy stayed with each one, throughout the time the men were away.

Everyone knew that God was with them. They were grateful for this home, this safe haven. They would stand firm on their Foundation, their Rock, their Lord Jesus Christ.

Janie caught Mabel as she was leaving. "Mabel, thank you. My heart was so heavy with the burden of Pastor Phil being held and Paul leaving to rescue all those at the camp. This helped me more than you know."

The men from the Ranch drove at normal speeds to the meeting location. Each of the eight vehicles had taken different routes, or waited thirty minutes before taking the same route. They would meet three miles from the camp and wait until two a.m., before making their way to the camp. At six in the evening, the last vehicle arrived and was hidden in the brush, near an abandoned logging camp. The men stretched out and rested, then ate a cold dinner of sandwiches, before resting again.

Harland, his wife and a group from the Seattle area had come to the ranch mid-summer. The day they left his closest friend and his family had been taken by the enforcers. He volunteered to join this mission. He was hopeful that Sam and his family would be among those in the camp. He had been very busy at the Ranch since they arrived, but he constantly prayed for Sam and those left behind in Seattle. He had heard things were getting worse, and he was concerned for them.

The men waited, watching a full moon that lit the sky, as the stars shone brightly in the heavens, twinkling their encouragement during the last few minutes before their departure time. Suddenly, a shooting star fell from the heavens, and Paul quickly said "Jesus, Jesus, Jesus." Just as many said, "money, money, money," when wishing on the star, as it fell to earth, wishing only for money. Paul was wishing, hoping, and praying that Jesus was coming very soon.

It was nearly time to go, when they heard movement in the bushes, coming from the direction of the camp. Everyone froze in place as several people came into view. As they watched, the clearing filled with people, some helping others to walk, others carrying small children, and some staggering from exhaustion. Paul was the first to recognize Pastor Phil, who was carrying a young girl of about four at the head of the group.

"Pastor Phil, it's Paul," Paul said with excitement and awe.

"Lord, I do not know why I am amazed after seeing all You have done, but I am!"

Pastor Phil looked into the bushes, as Paul made his way into the clearing. *"Thank you, Jesus! Praise the Lord!"* Pastor Phil called out, "We are rescued."

Immediately, the others with Paul made their way out of the bushes. The people with Pastor Phil sat, clearly worn out, but there was instant jubilation from the entire group.

"How many of you are there?" asked Paul.

"Forty-nine total; do you have room to take all of us?"

"Yes, we have eight vehicles hidden. How did you get away?"

"Remember the story of Peter, when he got out of jail right under his jailers noses?"

Paul nodded, then remembered it was dark, and answered, "Yes."

"Well, it was pretty much like that. I was asleep, when I dreamed we were walking out the main gate. I woke, and looked out, and saw the guard sound asleep. We simply walked out, while the guards were sleeping. It was truly a miracle we got everyone out without a shot fired. I wasn't sure which way to go, but we found a game trail that led this way, and we followed it right to you. What are you doing here anyway?"

Paul chuckled, "We came to rescue you. Well, let's get you out of here, before they wake up, discover you are gone, and come looking." Hurriedly, they began loading every man, woman, and child into the waiting vehicles and drove away. Even though it was dark, each person was blindfolded. It was better safe than sorry.

Harland spotted Doris and Dave right away, and a quick scan of the group revealed that Sam was not with them. He hurried over to wrap a blanket around Doris and hug her close.

"I am so glad to find you." Harland said, pulling away and turning to hug Dave. He immediately noticed their loss of weight but made no comment. "Sam . . . what of Sam and Becky?" he asked anxiously.

"We just don't know," Dave said. "Sam escaped almost right away. He was determined to find Becky. All we know is that he was able to get away."

"Well, that is something anyway," Harland said. "Come on, the vehicles are waiting. The Ranch is several hours away, but it is a wonderful place." He smiled, wrapping an arm around each of them and guiding them to the vans. "You might want to talk with Paul about Sam and Becky. He and his dad have contact with other ranches. I ask every week, or so, if they have heard anything, but no one has so far."

Doris nodded and smiled for the first time in a long time, as she sat beside Harland. He was not Sam, but he was still someone she cared for deeply, and she was glad he and Charlene had made it to safety.

Carson had everything ready and waiting, when they arrived at Haven Ranch. Jack, Martin, and Sherry had arrived the day before and examined everyone quickly. If they appeared to be in good shape, they were sent with Carson and set up in a bed for the night. They would do a more thorough check tomorrow; then everyone would be moved to permanent housing. After getting everyone settled, the men from the Sanctuary Ranch took spare beds and slept the rest of the night. They planned on leaving for home after lunch.

There were eight people who were in such poor shape that Jack kept them in the clinic hospital that had been set up. Most were suffering from untreated illness, such as diabetes, cancer, or other diseases. They lost an elderly man, who died early the next morning. He simply went to sleep and woke up in heaven. He had held on, knowing that God would free them. He grasped that promise close to his heart and encouraged everyone with his upbeat faith. He had kept their spirits up, when it would have been easier to despair. Once they were free and in safety, he let his spirit fly to his Lord.

The men from Sanctuary Ranch did not leave until after the funeral for Joseph Ferris. It was a great celebration of his life in Jesus. There was no sadness, only joy and thanksgiving for the great love Joseph had shown everyone at the camp. His life, especially the past seven months, became a testament to God's great love for His children. His knowledge of gardening and survival had helped all of them greatly. The miraculous escape from the camp was the icing on the cake; anyone who had had doubts about God's care for His children were completely convinced in light of their safe passage to Haven Ranch. Now, they would live in relative safety with other believers. There was enough food and safety in numbers. That did not mean things could not change, but, for now, they could rest in the Lord.

Paul met with Carson, before he left, to tell him how impressed he was with the Haven Ranch. "You have done a great job here, Carson. Several of the men have come to tell me how much they appreciate all you have done."

"I have not done much," Carson said humbly. "I simply established the governing board, like your Dad requested, and created a central storage place. I guess everyone was storing at their own lodging, instead of working together and joining forces. They were a unit, yet not a unit, if you know what I mean."

"Yes, I do understand. I think Pastor Phil just did not have the time to spend getting things organized right. I know he tried, but it really takes someone who is there, consistently keeping things on track."

"Do you know if there are any extra containers at the Sanctuary Ranch?"

"I believe so. We only filled about twenty of them with firewood, so I think there are fifteen or twenty more. I take it you need them here."

"Yes, we do. Mitchell Ryan said it took them all summer to put up what we put up in six weeks. I know it has to do with having the containers and the forklift. I just hope we can find a forklift."

"Well, if not, we are not so far that we cannot bring one over and then move it back. That is not the ideal solution, but it will work, if that is what we have to do. Margaret Harris said she loves the new Bible studies you have started. She says you are a great teacher."

Carson blushed, and Paul chuckled. "Marie said she was sweet on you. I could not help but tease you a little."

"She is a nice lady, but it is too soon for the kind of attention she wants," Carson said carefully.

"I understand, and Marie told me she is trying to run interference. If she becomes a problem, we can move her somewhere else."

"I do not believe it will come to that, but thanks for your concern."

"Well, I guess we are about ready to leave. Let us know if you need anything. I know these people are in good hands. God's blessings on you Carson," Paul said sincerely.

"God's blessings on you, too," came the reply.

Harland did not want to leave Doris and Dave at the Haven Ranch, but there was no more room at the Sanctuary Ranch right now. "We are finishing up several cabins and another dormitory in a couple of weeks. I have already asked Paul if you and Dave can come to our ranch then, and he said 'yes.'" Harland looked around and saw the others climbing into the vans. "I really hate leaving you."

Doris lifted up on tip toes and kissed his cheek. "It's okay. We will be fine here. We will see you in a few weeks. Give Charlene a hug for me. I think I will try to catch Paul," Doris said, before walking toward a group of men several vehicles away.

"She is worried, though she really tries not to show it," Dave said, watching his mom.

"I know, but God has brought us this far. We have to have faith," Harland replied.

"I know. God has become more real to me now than ever before. He has given me a great peace about Sam and Becky. I just know in my heart they are okay, and we will see them again soon."

Harland gave Dave an appraising look. Dave had never been a very strong believer, yet now there was a new assurance about him.

"I have a peace, also." The men embraced, before Harland climbed into the van, and Dave walked over to where his mom was speaking with Paul.

Doris approached Paul, as he was turning toward the vehicles. "Mr. Hamilton, may I speak to you for a few minutes?"

Paul turned toward the middle-aged woman, who had been in the camp with Pastor Phil. She was very thin. "Certainly, Mrs.?"

"Holton, Doris Holton. Harland told me you hear things from the cities from time to time. Have you heard anything about Sam or Becky?" Doris asked anxiously.

"I am sorry, Mrs. Holton, we have not heard anything."

Doris's lips trembled, as she tried to hold back the tears. "My daughter, Becky was not at home when the officials came and took us away. Later, we learned she hid, and the enforcement officers didn't find her. Sam was worried about her, even though Harland was still there. He is Sam's best friend." Paul nodded his understanding, and she continued. "Anyway, Sam wanted to make sure she was safe, so he escaped from the detention center, before they moved us to the camp. Several days before the officials came, we had talked about trying to find your ranch. In fact, we were ready to leave, when the officers came, so I was hoping they would already be here."

"I know Harland told us about all of you. I am sorry we have not heard anything about Sam and Becky. But do not lose hope, Mrs. Holton. God has done some really miraculous things lately. We just need to pray and hope they will arrive soon. We have several weeks before the winter weather makes travel difficult, so keep hoping. If we hear anything, we will make sure we let you know, as soon as possible."

"Thank you so much; I never lost hope while we were in that horrible camp. I am not about to lose hope now."

"Please know that we have been praying for them, since Harland shared what happened with us," Paul said kindly.

"I appreciate that very much," Doris said. She watched as the men climbed into the vehicles and drove away.

"Mom, did he have anything to say about Sam or Becky?" Dave asked hopefully.

"No, but I am not surprised. He would have told Harland if he heard anything. But I am not giving up hope. They had plans to come, and I know only death will keep them from making it." Dave put his arm around his mother's shoulders, as they walked back to their quarters.

There was a great celebration when the men returned and shared their story. They decided they were past due for a harvest celebration, and they quickly put together a feast. As they sat down together, George gave the blessing.

"*Father God, we are humbled at Your greatness. You led many throughout the Bible, and we marveled at Your love for them, stories close to our hearts and manna for our souls. Yet to see You work, time after time in our own time, is amazing. You gave us a vision, You provided the funds to build, You gave us Your favor time and time again, in bountiful harvests, successful hunting, in safety and security. You have blessed us with the new lives of several children, new sisters and brothers in the Lord, and very little illness. We cannot do anything but praise You for all You have done. You are a mighty and glorious God. Jesus, we thank You for Your grace and mercy at the cross; we would not be here if not for You. Holy Spirit, thank You for Your inspiration, Your guidance, and love. You have given us knowledge and understanding when we had none of our own. We are truly a grateful and thankful people. We praise You and adore You. We celebrate Your love this evening! In Jesus' name we pray. Amen!*" Choruses of "Amen!," "Hallelujah!," "Praise the Lord!," and other words of praise and thanksgiving filled the room.

The winter months would bring a time of calm and restoration. The long days of spring, summer, and early fall were at an end. Pastor Phil was safe, and forty-plus souls had been delivered to Haven Ranch safely. The announcement of Paul and Janie's expected child added to the excitement. The days ahead would bring the snow, and though it was cold and barren, in their isolation, there would be peace and safety in the winter months. More classes and activities were added to accommodate the newcomers to the Ranch. The increase in children meant the addition of more school classes and activities. Several adults helped with plays and puppet shows for the children. Musical sing-a-longs were a great hit for everyone. The furniture class was kept busy with the need for more beds and dressers.

The Ranch now had two deaf children, and a class was started to teach signing to any who would like to learn. They had nearly sixty at the first class, and though some dropped out through the winter, due to time restraints, they had nearly fifty who completed the class and were able to at least communicate some with their special-needs children.

They were monitoring the communications twenty-four hours a day now. They found the winter months brought more nationwide unrest; food shortages caused widespread panic in the large cities. Grocery stores could not keep food on their shelves; gangs began killing for food, and more people were dying from starvation. People froze in their homes due to the lack of heat. Rural communities had it better; large community gardens fed most of their people, but they had to have guards twenty-four-seven, and many had wood stoves, or fireplaces, that they used for heat. Gated community residents banded together to provide security for their homes and gardens. Many times staying connected to a close-knit supportive and well-equipped community was the difference between survival and destruction, as there was safety in numbers. Those who read the signs and prepared in advance had the greatest opportunity for survival, quite unlike those who were caught totally unprepared.

Economic collapse caused the government to fall into disarray. The government that remained was corrupt beyond imaginings. Regular folk were unable to retrieve their funds from the banks, just like it had been during the years of the depression in the 1930s. Many people who depended on the government to care for them were now without help, as there was no longer a government who cared, or even was able or willing to provide help. Most of the churches who helped with food kitchens and food pantries have gone underground, and, therefore, were difficult to find, due to the persecution of believers. Some areas had state governments that were able to maintain some control, and in some places, city governments were able to continue with basic services, but that was mostly in the rural areas. The big cities and towns had roving gangs and marauders that plagued the local population. Police tried to keep order, but corruption was rampant there, also. The peace and prosperity of a once-blessed nation was a thing of the past. Lawlessness reigned supreme. Good people stole, cheated, and murdered to survive. Without the Lord, evil ate like cancer at the very foundation of the society.

Police, city officials, and state officials were scrambling to secure their own power base. Even those who the public looked to for help now needed help themselves. The twisted and perverted volunteered for jobs at the camps. Their perverse pleasure, at the expense of others, evident in everything they did.

More and more believers were arrested or detained each day. Those Christians who were not grounded in the faith and did not have a personal relationship with Jesus fell away, looking to the government to save them, only to find the government made promises it could not keep. Many more caved into pressure from family, or friends, who blamed Christians for every problem they had, whether there was foundation for the blame or not. They believed the lies because the media and government said so; they were "sheeple," blindly following those they desperately wanted to believe. They did not understand this was no longer "The home of the free and the brave." They did not understand that this great country, once founded on God's principles, was now founded on the whims of ungodly people.

Each day, more and more Bible prophecy came true. Secret groups of believers formed to support each other, only to be betrayed and sent to holding camps around the country. There was persecution in homes, where one was a believer and another was not, as well as in the private workplace, and in all government jobs. Turning someone over to the officials became the norm, instead of the exception. Some even turned others in to secure their position, even when the accused person was not a believer. Fear reigned throughout the land.

Terrorism became a daily event around the world; all was in chaos . . . It was ripe for the coming of the antichrist . . . someone to save an unbelieving world . . . the world who refused to believe in Jesus, to accept His atonement for sin, His saving grace, and His love.

The winter provided a time for planning at the ranches. The two ranch councils met together and made plans for several more ranches. The slow months of winter would give them extra time to study and learn more about Jesus and His ways; as true believers were convinced that there was always something more to learn. There was safety in the sparsely populated area of the country, and they knew they would have safety a while longer. The time could come when it would no longer be safe anywhere, but, until then, they would go on living, day to day, safe in God's care.

In the spring everyone would go back to work. The gardens would be planted, animals cared for, firewood cut, and all the other day-to-day chores performed. Pastor Phil and several would go back to work. They would travel where God led and minister to believers who decided to remain where they were or lead believers to a haven. Every person they could save and bring to safety was one more soul won for Christ Jesus. Everyone would do their part, as they waited for Jesus to return to a world gone crazy, or they would rebuild their lives, after the craziness was over, if the time for His return was at a later date. Either way, they would remain faithful to the Author and Finisher of their faith, Jesus Christ.

Believers, This Is a Call to Prepare

THIS STORY CAME FROM the vision of preparation God gave us in 2007. We wanted a way to share the vision in a way that would be informative, yet not alarming. We have already begun our own preparations, storing food, collecting seeds, and studying different ways of generating electricity. Times are coming that will test our faith and perseverance.

Many will ask why there is any difference between now and the 1920s-1940s. Our answer is back then most people acknowledged God and Jesus in this country. In addition, our government still recognized The Ten Commandments as a foundational cornerstone of our country, and, finally, we had little or no governmental or personal debt, at large. People relied upon God and themselves for support. They understood they could pursue happiness, but it was up to them to receive it.

Today, America is much different. God has been removed from the schools, government, and the public square. The government owes a huge debt that we will have difficulty paying back in the years ahead, and individuals have a great deal of debt, also. In addition, we have an entitlement segment of society that believes the government owes them a living, so they no longer need to pursue their own happiness because they believe the government is supposed to supply it. Finally, many have fallen away from the church, any church. People look to themselves, or the government, rather than to God for their daily needs in life. We have churches that preach what people want to hear, instead of teaching the Word of God.

We are calling people back to the Word. There are several verses in the Bible that tell us to prepare ourselves. Noah was preaching repentance for many years, while he built the ark. He was warning others, as he was preparing for the flood. Noah and his family were saved because they listened to God and prepared.

Matthew 25 tells of ten bridesmaids. Five were wise and had prepared ahead. They had enough oil for their lamps; five were not prepared and were left behind, when the groom came.

We truly feel we must prepare a place of safety for our loved ones, ourselves, and whoever God brings to join us. We are currently making plans for our sanctuary ranch. The ranch may not be as big as this story talks about, or have as many people living there, but we are making our plans, so that we can grow if needed. We have not won the lottery, but we have faith that God is guiding, and He will provide whatever we need.

God promises He will save His people, His remnant. He will provide sanctuary. We who believe must have ears to listen.

The vision we had is of the decline of our country. We did not receive the "how" of the decline, only that it would come. We understand that when it begins, conservatives will be blamed for the problems of the country, and as the decline continues, Christians will be singled out, and persecution will become horrific.

The fact is, the persecution has already started. Right now the persecution is minor. We are called intolerant and hate mongers. But as the persecution gets stronger, many weak Christians will denounce the faith and point their finger at stronger Christians. Throughout the book, we use the word "believer" in place of Christian because there are many people who claim to be Christians who do not have a personal relationship with Jesus. They attend church, warm the pews, and go through the motions, but they have no personal relationship with the Lord Jesus. They talk real good and may even know a great deal about the Bible, but these people do not walk the walk of the believer, that of *faith*. In addition, they have no fruit in their lives. The Bible talks over and over of people who hear the Word, yet it makes no real difference in their lives. It is our hope you are not in that category.

**God has given us His Word to make us wise.
Note well the following Scriptures:**

Matthew 13:25-30 (NIV)

25 But while everyone was sleeping, his enemy came and sowed weeds among the wheat, and went away.
26 When the wheat sprouted and formed heads, then the weeds also appeared.
27 "The owner's servants came to him and said, 'Sir, didn't you sow good seed in your field? Where then did the weeds come from?'
28 "'An enemy did this,' he replied. The servants asked him, 'Do you want us to go and pull them up?'
29 "'No,' he answered, 'because while you are pulling the weeds, you may root up the wheat with them.
30 Let both grow together until the harvest. At that time I will tell the harvesters: First collect the weeds and tie them in bundles to be burned; then gather the wheat and bring it into my barn.'"

Matthew 25:32-46 (NIV)

32 All the nations will be gathered before him, and he will separate the people one from another as a shepherd separates the sheep from the goats.
33 He will put the sheep on his right and the goats on his left.
34 "Then the King will say to those on his right, 'Come, you who are blessed by my Father; take your inheritance, the kingdom prepared for you since the creation of the world.
35 For I was hungry and you gave me something to eat, I was thirsty and you gave me something to drink, I was a stranger and you invited me in,
36 I needed clothes and you clothed me, I was sick and you looked after me, I was in prison and you came to visit me.'

³⁷ "Then the righteous will answer him, 'Lord, when did we see you
hungry and feed you, or thirsty and give you something to drink?
³⁸ When did we see you a stranger and invite you
in, or needing clothes and clothe you?
³⁹ When did we see you sick or in prison and go to visit you?'
⁴⁰ "The King will reply, 'I tell you the truth, whatever you did for
one of the least of these brothers of mine, you did for me.'
⁴¹ "Then he will say to those on his left, 'Depart from me, you who are
cursed, into the eternal fire prepared for the devil and his angels.
⁴² For I was hungry and you gave me nothing to eat, I
was thirsty and you gave me nothing to drink,
⁴³ I was a stranger and you did not invite me in, I needed
clothes and you did not clothe me, I was sick and
in prison and you did not look after me.'
⁴⁴ "They also will answer, 'Lord, when did we see you
hungry or thirsty or a stranger or needing clothes
or sick or in prison, and did not help you?'
⁴⁵ "He will reply, 'I tell you the truth, whatever you did not do
for one of the least of these, you did not do for me.'
⁴⁶ "Then they will go away to eternal punishment,
but the righteous to eternal life."

Mark 4:4-9 (NIV)
⁴ As he was scattering the seed, some fell along the
path, and the birds came and ate it up.
⁵ Some fell on rocky places, where it did not have much soil.
It sprang up quickly, because the soil was shallow.
⁶ But when the sun came up, the plants were scorched,
and they withered because they had no root.
⁷ Other seed fell among thorns, which grew up and choked
the plants, so that they did not bear grain.
⁸ Still other seed fell on good soil. It came up, grew and produced
a crop, multiplying thirty, sixty, or even a hundred times."
⁹ Then Jesus said, "He who has ears to hear, let him hear."

All of the above verses speak of two kinds of people. Those who hear the Word of God but do not walk the walk or have true faith; again they have no fruit in their lives; they do not have the light of Jesus burning brightly in their lives. The second kind of people are those who are believers in the Lord Jesus Christ, and walk in faith, and seek to live their lives in service to God and people.

True believers are the branches; Jesus is the Vine, and those who bear no fruit will be pruned. Only you and God know the true condition of your heart. We urge you to examine yourself and ask God to give you insight into the condition of your heart. It is our hope, through the writing of this book, that many will see their need to take the step of faith and seek Jesus. He is the only Way to God. He is the only Way to have a spirit-filled life, a life full of love, hope, peace and joy.

Difficult times are coming; without the Lord Jesus in your life, the hard times ahead will become nearly impossible. We are promised that God will never leave or forsake His children. We have strength, through Jesus, to do all things. We will prevail, but that does not mean everything will be sunshine and roses.

You can choose to embrace the world and all it has to offer. Unfortunately, life in this world leads only to death . . . spiritual death and eternal death. Or, you can choose Jesus and life in Him. He has already won the victory over death. He has already won the battle against Satan and his demons. Therefore, we, as born again believers, walking in life with Jesus, experience perpetual love, hope, and life.

We urge whoever reads this to take a step of faith and begin your own preparation to protect and provide for your families in the difficult times ahead. Whether there will be a war, or some national difficulty, or whether we are actually in the last days, we do not know. But we believe there will be nationwide fear and national hunger. Be forewarned: God is telling His people to get ready and prepare, both physically and spiritually, for difficult times ahead.

With all that has been said, some might become fearful. Just remember, God does not give us a spirit of fear. We do not need to fear the unknown future. We simply need to prepare for it. If nothing happens, wonderful! You will have food and supplies ahead. However, if things do turn for the worse, you and your family will be ready.

Let those with ears to hear listen and take heed.

Things you can do to prepare for hard times:

1. Study and memorize Bible verses that will provide guidance and encouragement in days of struggle and hardship.
2. Learn who lives in your community that is like-minded and equally yoked with Jesus, so that if—or when, times get bad you already know who you can trust.
3. Start practicing gardening, canning and food storage now.
4. Store food. We are putting away 1-2 years worth of food for ourselves and our family.
5. Canning
    a. Purchase jars, lids (make sure they are reusable lids)
    b. Pots for canning and preserving your own food.
    c. Pressure cooker
6. Dry your foods
    a. Get a dehydrator and practice, so you can dry your own food. Shelf life is longer.

      b. Get airtight containers to help with shelf life.
      c. Purchase long-term storage food stocks (if desired)
7. Purchase Heirloom Seeds only. Place in an air tight storage in a cool dry place. You want to make sure they stay dry. They will store for several years though the germination may be lower as years go by. (These can be bartered later, if needed.)
8. Learn how to harvest your own seeds and store them.
9. Do not forget toilet papers, feminine hygiene supplies, diapers, cleaning products, candles, matches, rags, etc.
10. Clothesline and clothes pins
11. Lye, laundry soap, bleach
12. Get a good medical kit and supplement it with extra:
      Aspirin Antibiotic ointment/colloidal silver/ colloidal silver home processor
      Bandages Tape Sterile scissors
      Butterflies Gauze Cold/hot compresses
      Ace bandages Alcohol Cold and cough medicines/allergy medicines
      Splints
13. If you take medications, try to get some ahead.
14. Lip gloss, sunscreen, hand lotions, shampoo, conditioner, razors/blades toothbrushes/toothpaste, eyeglasses, contacts & necessary solutions, vitamins
15. Make sure you have drinking water and a good kit to sterilize and filter additional water.
16. Make sure you have the tools you will need to garden.
      Rakes Shovels Water hose
17. Set up a greenhouse, if possible/if wanted.
      Remember heating system, if necessary.
18. Get a good set of knives for butchering.
19. Purchase a good propane stove and extra propane (optional), or wood burning stove.
20. Freezer bags and freezer paper
21. Get as many 'How to' books you think you might need.
22. You may need to defend yourself, or hunt for your own meat, so prepare, as you feel comfortable. Guns, Ammo, Bow, Arrows

23. Get extra pillows, blankets
24. Clothing, sweaters, coats, extra shoes in larger sizes for growing children.
25. Survival gear is helpful.
    Tents Sleeping bags Canteens
    Lanterns Batteries {rechargeable and a charger}
    Oil/lanterns Camp stove/fuel Tarps
26. Repair parts for autos/trucks
27. Local terrain/topical maps
28. Set of 2-way radios and short wave (Ham) radio if possible. This requires licensing.
29. Sewing machine and supplies
    Needles Cloth
    Cloth Thread
    Pins Misc.
30. Learn as much as you can about solar, hydro, wind sources, etc., for generating electricity.
31. Make your own power unit and prepare to go off grid.
32. Start gathering family games, puzzles, card games, etc.
33. Expand your library, written and video (DVDs)
    Old Encyclopedias are good to have.
34. Purchase extra Bibles

For additional ideas on things you can do to prepare for emergency situations, check out the internet and visit websites that support independent lifestyles, i.e., living off the land and living off-grid. You can contact us at: TheSanctuaryRanch.com Or FleetotheMountain.com

We will be posting ideas and information you can check out. We would love to hear your ideas and plans you are making.

Notes

CPSIA information can be obtained at www.ICGtesting.com
Printed in the USA
BVOW010843231112

306246BV00001B/6/P